Rumours
in the
Regency
BALLROOM

Diane Gaston

Mills & Boon, an imprint of Harlequin (UK) Limited,
Eton House, 18-24 Paradise Road, Richmond, Surrey TW9 1SR

RUMOURS IN THE REGENCY BALLROOM
© Harlequin Enterprises II B.V./S.à.r.l 2013

Scandalising the Ton © Diane Perkins 2008
Gallant Officer, Forbidden Lady © Diane Perkins 2009

ISBN: 978 0 263 90676 9

052-1013

Harlequin (UK) policy is to use papers that are natural, renewable and recyclable products and made from wood grown in sustainable forests. The logging and manufacturing processes conform to the legal environmental regulations of the country of origin.

Printed and bound
by CPI Group (UK) Ltd, Croydon, CR0 4YY

As a psychiatric social worker, **Diane Gaston** spent years helping others create real-life happy endings. Now Diane crafts fictional ones, writing the kind of historical romance she's always loved to read. The youngest of three daughters of a US Army colonel, Diane moved frequently during her childhood, even living for a year in Japan. It continues to amaze her that her own son and daughter grew up in one house in Northern Virginia. Diane still lives in that house, with her husband and three very ordinary housecats. *Scandalising the Ton* features characters you will have met in *The Vanishing Viscountess*.

Visit Diane's website at http://dianegaston.com

In The Regency Ballroom Collection

Scandal in the Regency Ballroom – Louise Allen
April 2013

Innocent in the Regency Ballroom – Christine Merrill
May 2013

Wicked in the Regency Ballroom – Margaret McPhee
June 2013

Cinderella in the Regency Ballroom – Deb Marlowe
July 2013

Rogue in the Regency Ballroom – Helen Dickson
August 2013

Debutante in the Regency Ballroom – Anne Herries
September 2013

Rumours in the Regency Ballroom – Diane Gaston
October 2013

Rake in the Regency Ballroom – Bronwyn Scott
November 2013

Mistress in the Regency Ballroom – Juliet Landon
December 2013

Courtship in the Regency Ballroom – Annie Burrows
January 2014

Scoundrel in the Regency Ballroom – Marguerite Kaye
February 2014

Secrets in the Regency Ballroom – Joanna Fulford
March 2014

Scandalising the Ton

To my sister Judy,
my first and forever friend

Chapter One

Once the finest ornament of the *beau monde*, a beauty so astounding and sublime a man would kill to possess her hand in marriage, the notorious Lady W— mourns her murderous husband in secret. How much knowledge did she possess of her husband's villainous acts?— *The New Observer*, November 12, 1818

"Leave me this instant!"

A woman's voice.

Adrian Pomroy, the new Viscount Cavanley, barely heard her as he rounded the corner into John Street. Not even halfway down the road he saw the woman stride away from a man. The man hurried after her. They were mere silhouettes in the waning light of this November evening and they took no heed of him.

Adrian paused to make sense of this little drama. It was most likely a lovers' quarrel, and, if so, he'd backtrack to avoid landing in the middle of it.

"One moment." The man kept his voice down, as if fearing to be overheard. "Please!" He seized her arm.

"Release me!" The woman struggled frantically to pull away.

Lovers' quarrel or not, Adrian could not allow a woman to be treated so roughly. He sprinted forwards. "Unhand her! What is this?"

The man released the woman so quickly she tripped on her long hooded cloak. Adrian clasped her arm before she fell, holding her until she regained her balance. From the mews nearby a horse whinnied, but otherwise it was quiet.

The man backed away. "This is not as it appears, sir. I intend no harm to the lady." He raised his hands as if to prove his words.

The lady? Adrian assumed he'd rescued some maid from a stableman's unwanted advances, but the woman's cloak was made of fine cloth, and the man was dressed more like a tradesman than a stableman.

Adrian turned to the lady. "Did he harm you, ma'am?"

"No." The hood of her cloak shrouded her face. "But I do not wish to speak to him."

The man stepped forwards again. "I merely asked the lady a few questions—"

"I will not answer them," she cried from beneath her hood.

Adrian had the advantage of size on the man. He straightened his spine to make certain the man knew it. "If the lady does not wish to speak to you, that is the end of it."

"Let me explain, sir." The man stuck a hand in his pocket and pulled out a card. He handed it to Adrian. "I am Samuel Reed from *The New Observer*."

Adrian glanced at the card. "You are a newspaper reporter?" He had read the new London paper, quite recently, in fact.

The man nodded. "All England wishes to know Lady Wexin's reaction to the events surrounding her villainous husband. I am merely requesting the information from her."

"Lady Wexin?"

Adrian regarded the cloaked figure with new interest. Adrian had just called upon his friend, the Marquess of Tannerton. Tanner had shoved *The New Observer* article about Lady Wexin under Adrian's nose not more than half an hour ago.

His friend, Tanner, had recently returned from Scotland with a new wife and news about Lord Wexin that had consumed the newspapers ever since. Truth to tell, Tanner's marriage had shocked Adrian more than the tale of murder, betrayal and death that involved the Earl of Wexin.

Lady Wexin interrupted Adrian's thoughts. "Do I take it by your silence that you agree with this man, sir?" She stood with one hand braced against a garden wall. "Do perfect strangers have a right to know my private matters?"

Adrian still could not see her face, but he recalled the *ton* beauty very well. What gentleman would not? Adrian had never been formally presented to Lady Wexin, but they had occasionally attended the same society gatherings. Years ago Tanner and Adrian had briefly included Wexin among their set, but that had been before Wexin's marriage.

"You owe this man nothing, my lady." Adrian gave her a reassuring smile. "He will trouble you no further."

According to Tanner, Lady Wexin was an innocent party in the perfidy that had so titillated the gossip-lovers. The newspapers had indulged the public's seemingly insatiable appetite for the scandal by speculating about Lady Wexin's part in it. Wexin might be dead, but his wife was not.

Lady Wexin let go of the garden wall. "I shall be on my way, then." She turned, her cloak swirling around her. She took one step, paused, then resumed walking.

Adrian frowned. She was limping.

Mr Reed's gaze followed her as well. He appeared to be considering whether to pursue her with more questions.

Adrian clapped him on the shoulder. "Best you leave, Mr Reed."

Mr Reed's eyes flashed. "This is a public street, sir."

Adrian smiled, but without friendliness. "Nonetheless, you do not wish to be in my bad graces." He glanced at Lady Wexin, now fumbling with a key in the lock of a garden gate. "The lady looks as if she's had enough to deal with today. Leave, sir."

Reed hesitated, but eventually his gaze slid back to Adrian.

"Leave, Mr Reed." Adrian repeated, quietly but firmly.

Reed bowed his head and nodded. He cast another look at Lady Wexin before strolling to the corner and disappearing from sight.

Adrian walked quickly over to where Lady Wexin still worked the lock. "Let me assist you."

She waved him away. "I can manage."

He gestured to her legs. "You are standing on one foot."

She averted her face. "My—my ankle pains me a little. I believe I twisted it, but I assure you I can manage." The lock turned and she opened the gate. When she stepped into the garden she nearly toppled to the ground.

Adrian hurried through the gate and wrapped an arm around her. "You cannot walk."

The hood of her cloak fell away, fully revealing her face, only inches from his own.

Her skin was as smooth and flawless as the Roman sculpture of Clytie that had once captivated him in the British Museum. Unlike cold white stone, however, Lady Wexin's cheeks were warm with colour. Her lips, shaped like a perfect bow, were as pink as a dew-kissed rose. Adrian had often appreciated her beauty from across a ballroom, or from a box away at Covent Garden, but, this close, she robbed him of breath.

"Is this your house?" he finally managed.

She edged out of his embrace, but continued to clutch his arm. "Of course it is."

He smiled. "Forgive me. Yes, it must be."

She looked over her shoulder. "I must close the gate. Before they see."

"Before they see?" He followed her glance.

"More newspaper people. They loiter around the house, looking for me."

Ah, now it made sense why the lady entered her house through the garden gate. It did not explain why she had been out alone. Ladies did not venture out unless accompanied by a companion or a servant.

Adrian closed the gate with his free hand.

"I need to lock it." She let go of him and tried to step away, again nearly falling.

Adrian reached for her again and helped her to the gate. "I'll walk you to your door as well."

"I am so sorry to trouble you." She turned the key and left it in the lock.

Adrian kept his arm around her as they started for the house. When she put the slightest weight on her ankle, he felt her tense with pain.

"This will not do." Adrian scooped her up into his arms.

"No, put me down," she begged. "You must not carry me."

"Nonsense. Of course I must." Her face was even closer now and her scent, like spring lilacs, filled his nostrils. She draped her arms around his neck, and he inhaled deeply.

"See? I am too heavy," she protested.

Too heavy? She felt as if she belonged in his arms.

He smiled at her. "Do not insult my strength, Lady Wexin. You will wound my male vanity." He made the mistake of staring into her deep blue eyes, now glittering with unspent tears, and his heart wrenched for her. "You must be in great pain," he murmured.

She held his gaze. "It hurts not at all now."

He could not look away.

Somewhere on the street a door slammed and Lady Wexin blinked.

Adrian regained his senses and carried her the short distance to the rear door of the townhouse. Voices sounded nearby, riding on the evening breeze.

"The door will be unlocked," she murmured, her hair brushing his cheek.

He opened the door and brought her inside. To the left he glimpsed the kitchen, though there were no sounds of a cook at work there. He carried her down the passageway and brought her above stairs to the main hall of the house.

It was elegantly appointed with a gilded hall table upon which sat a pair of Chinese vases, devoid of flowers. Matching gilded chairs were upholstered in bright turquoise. The floor was a chequerboard of black-and-white marble, but no footman stood in attendance. In fact, the house was very quiet and a bit chilly.

"Shall I summon one of your servants?" he asked.

"They—they are all out at the moment, but you may put me down. I shall manage from here."

He looked at her in surprise. "All out?" It was odd for a house to be completely empty of servants.

She averted her gaze. "They have the day off." She squirmed in his arms. "You may put me down."

He shook his head. "Your ankle needs tending." He started up the marble staircase, smiling at her again to ease her discomfort. "By the way, I ought to present myself. I am—"

She interrupted him. "I know who you are."

Adrian's smile deepened, flattered that she'd noticed him.

He reached the second floor where he guessed the bedchambers would be. "Direct me to your room."

"The second door," she replied. "But, really, you mustn't—"

It was his turn to interrupt. "Someone must."

Her bedchamber was adorned with hand-painted wallpaper, bright exotic birds frolicking amidst colourful flowers. A dressing table with a large mirror held sparkling glass bottles, porcelain pots and a brush and comb with polished silver handles. Her bed was neatly made, its white coverlet gleaming and its many pillows plumped with what he guessed was the finest down. The room was chilly, though, as if someone had allowed the fire in the fireplace to go out.

He set her down on the bed, very aware of her hands slipping away from his neck. "I'll tend the fire."

"Really, sir. You need not trouble yourself." Her voice reached a high, nervous pitch.

"It is no trouble."

He removed his hat, gloves and topcoat and crossed the room to the small fireplace, its mantel of carved marble holding another empty vase. To his surprise, the fire had not died out at all. It was all set to be lit. He found the tinderbox and soon had a flame licking across the lumps of coal.

He returned to her. She had removed her cloak and clutched it in front of her. Adrian took it from her hands and draped it over a nearby chair. It contained something in its pocket. Adrian felt a purse, heavy with coin.

He turned back to her and their eyes met, hers still shimmering with tears.

He touched her arm. "Are you certain you are not in pain? You look near to weeping."

She averted her gaze. "I'm not in pain."

He knelt in front of her. "Then let me have a look at that ankle. If it is broken, we will need to summon a surgeon."

She drew up her leg. "A surgeon!"

"A surgeon would merely set the bone," he said, puzzled at her alarm.

Her hand fluttered. "I was thinking of the cost."

"The cost?" Concern over the cost was even more puzzling. Adrian gave her a reassuring smile. "Let us not fret over what is not yet a problem. Let me examine it first."

She extended her leg again and Adrian untied her half-boot. He slipped off the shoe, made of buttery soft white kid, and held her foot in his hand, enjoying too much its graceful shape.

She flinched.

He glanced up at her. "Am I hurting you?"

"No," she rasped. "Not hurting."

He grinned. "Tickling, then. I'll be more careful." He forced himself to his task, feeling her ankle, now swollen. His hand slipped up to her calf, but he quickly moved it down to her ankle again, gently moving her foot in all directions.

She gasped.

"Does that hurt?" he asked her.

"A little," she whispered. "I—I should not be allowing you to do this."

Indeed. He was enjoying it far too much, and desiring far more.

He cleared his throat. "I believe your ankle is sprained, not broken. I predict you will do nicely in a day or two." He did not release it. "I should wrap it, though, to give you some support. Do you have bandages, or a strip of cloth?"

Her eyes were half-closed. She blinked and pointed to a chest of drawers. "Look in the bottom drawer."

Adrian reluctantly let go of her leg and walked over to the chest. The bottom drawer contained neatly folded under-clothing made of soft muslin and satiny silk as soft and smooth as her skin.

His thoughts, as if having a will of their own, turned carnal, and he imagined crossing the room and taking her in his arms, tasting her lips, peeling off her clothing, sliding his hands over her skin.

He gave himself an inwards shake. He would not take advantage of this lady. Her peace was disturbed by reporters hounding her for a story, and her whole world had been turned head over ears with news of her husband's crimes. And his death.

He frowned as he groped through her underclothing, finally coming up with a long thin piece of muslin.

He returned to her and knelt again. "I must remove your stocking."

She extended her leg.

He slipped his hands up her calf, past her knee, until he found the top of her stocking and the ribbon that held it in place. He untied the ribbon and rolled the stocking down and off her foot. Her skin was smooth and warm and pliant beneath his fingers.

Adrian quickly took the strip of cloth and began to wind it around her ankle.

"Did you study surgery?" she asked, her voice cracking.

He looked up and grinned at her. "I fear it is horses I know, not surgery."

She laughed, and the sound, like the joyful tinkling of a pianoforte, echoed in his mind.

He tried to force his attention back to the bandage, but she leaned forwards and gave him a good glimpse of her décolletage. "Are you so gentle with horses?"

He glanced back to the bandage and continued wrapping, smoothing the fabric with his other hand.

"What is your name?" Her tone turned low and soft.

He glanced up. "I thought you said you knew me."

"I do not know your given name," she said.

"Adrian." He tied off her bandage and reluctantly released her.

"Adrian." She extended her hand. "I am Lydia."

He grasped her hand. "Lydia."

Lydia's heart raced at the feel of his large masculine hand enveloping hers. His grip was strong, the sort of grip that assured he was a man who could handle any trial. She now knew better than to make judgements based on such trivialities as a touch, but she could not deny he had been gentle with her. And kind.

It seemed so long since she'd felt kindness from anyone but her servants.

And even longer since she'd felt a man's touch, since her husband left for Scotland, in fact. It shocked her how affected she was by Adrian Pomroy's hand on hers. He warmed her all over, making her body pine for what only should exist between a husband and wife.

She took a breath. She'd always loved that part of marriage, the physical part, the part that was supposed to lead to babies…but she could not think of that. It was too painful.

It was almost easier to think of her husband. The Earl of Wexin.

The newspapers wrote that her husband had killed Lord Corland so that Wexin could marry her. Lord Corland's death had been her fault.

She gripped Adrian's hand even more tightly, sick that Wexin's hands had ever touched her, hands that had cut a man's throat.

She thought she'd loved Wexin. She'd trusted him with everything—the finances, the decisions, everything. But she had not known him at all. He'd betrayed her and left her with nothing but shame and guilt.

Her happiness had been an illusion, something that could not last, like the baby that had been growing inside her the day Wexin left.

The cramping had started the very next day after he'd gone, more than a month ago now, and she'd lost that baby like the two others before.

She swallowed a sob. Now she had nothing.

"Lydia?"

She glanced up into Adrian's eyes, warm amber, perpetually mirthful, as if his life had been nothing but one long lark.

He smiled, and the corners of his eyes crinkled. "You are squeezing my hand."

She released him. "I am sorry."

He stood and took her hand in his again. "It was not a complaint. You look troubled." He lifted her hand to his lips, warm soft lips. "You have been through a great deal, I suspect. I will act as your friend, if you will allow me."

Her senses flared again and her breathing accelerated. "If you knew how I need a friend."

He smelled wonderful. Like a man. And she felt his strength in his hands, in his steady gaze. She took a deep breath and reached up to touch his hair, thick and brown with a wayward cowlick at the crown that gave him a boyish appeal.

His eyes darkened and the grin disappeared, though his lips formed a natural smile even at rest.

This man pleased women, it was said. He was a rake whose name was always attached to some actress or opera dancer or widow. Well, she was a widow now and her whole body yearned to be touched, to be pleased, to be loved.

She spoke, but it was as if her voice belonged to someone else. "You can do something for me, Adrian. As a friend."

He smiled again. "You have but to ask."

She wrapped her arms around his neck, and with her heart thundering inside her chest, she brought her lips near to his oh-so-tempting ones. "Make love to me."

She felt his intake of air and watched his lips move. "Are you certain you want that?" he whispered.

"Very certain," that voice that only sounded like hers said. Before she could think, she closed the distance between them, tasting his lips gently at first, then more boldly.

He tasted lovely, but this kiss was not enough, not nearly enough. She opened her mouth and allowed his tongue to enter, delicious and decadent. She slid as close to the edge of the bed as she could, as close to him. She pressed herself against him, loving the feel of his firm chest against her softer one.

While his tongue played with hers, she worked the buttons of his coat and waistcoat. He parted from her long enough to shrug out of them. She pulled his shirt over his head and ran her hands over his muscular chest. She'd not known a man's muscles could really be as sculpted as the statues of antiquity, nor as broad. No wonder women wanted to be his lover.

"Turn around," he murmured.

She twisted around so he could reach the hooks at the back of her dress. He made short work of them.

She pulled her dress over her head, and he untied the laces of her corset with the practised ease of a lady's maid. Lydia felt a *frisson* of excitement at the prospect of coupling with a skilled lover. She had never even kissed a man besides her husband.

Her corset joined the growing pile of clothing on the floor, and Lydia made quick work of removing her shift. She wanted—needed—to feel her skin against his, but he held her at arm's length and caressed her with his gaze.

Her breathing accelerated. She reached for the buttons of his trousers.

He smiled and his hand rose to stroke her cheek. "I was merely savouring you for a moment."

He stepped back and pulled off his boots and trousers. Lydia removed her remaining shoe and stocking, taking in his naked body through half-closed eyelids.

He was indeed a magnificent man.

And an aroused one. Her eyes widened. Here must be another reason he pleased women so well.

Lydia extended her hand to him and pulled him towards her, making room for him on her bed, pulling the blankets away as she did so. He joined her and covered her with his body, warming her—she had not realised she'd been so very cold. His hands stroked her with exquisite gentleness, relaxing her in places she'd not known she'd been tense. She stretched, arching her back like a cat. He closed his palms over her breasts and need consumed her.

She grasped his neck and pulled him down to her lips again, wanting him to breathe his strength into her. She longed for him to join himself to her. She longed not to feel so alone. So betrayed. So abandoned.

He broke the kiss and, as if reading her mind, took charge, moving his lips down her neck, tasting her nipples. Then he slid his hand to her feminine place and slipped his fingers inside her.

She had never experienced such a thing. Wexin had never done anything like this with his fingers. The intensity of the pleasure stunned her. Adrian seemed to know precisely where to touch, how to touch, until she was writhing beneath him, moaning in a voice that sounded more primal than her own.

Her climax burst forth inside her, so intense she cried out and clung to him as the waves of pleasure washed over her, and washed over her again.

When it ebbed, confusion came in its wake.

"But what of you, Adrian?"

Her husband always saw to his own pleasure first. She did not know her pleasure could come in such a different way.

He held her face in his hands. "We are not finished, Lydia."

She took in a ragged breath.

He lay beside her, his head resting on one hand, the fingers of the other hand barely touching her skin, but stroking slowly and gently until she forgot her confusion and became boneless and as pliant as putty. To her surprise, her desire grew again, but less urgent than before.

His lips traced where his hands had been, his tongue sending shafts of need wherever he tasted her. He touched her feminine place again, with such gentleness she thought she might weep out of sheer bliss. It still seemed it was her pleasure, not his, that guided his hand. He made her feel cherished, revered.

"Adrian," she murmured, awash in this new sensation.

Slowly, very slowly, her desire escalated, until again she writhed with need.

"Now, Lydia," he whispered into her ear.

He climbed atop her again and stared into her eyes as he slowly slipped his entire length into her, each second driving her mad with wanting. Lydia gasped as he began to move, still slow and rhythmic, like the intricate moves of a dance. She moved with him, but the pace he set kept the ultimate pleasure just out of her reach. He moved with such confidence, she gave herself over to him, trusting he would bring her to where she so very much wanted to go.

His pace quickened and her need grew even greater. The sound of their breathing filled the room, melding together like voices singing a duet.

Her release burst forth and she saw stars brighter than at Brighton. She thrilled when his seed spilled into her. They pressed against each other, moaning with a pleasure that burned away her desolation.

Gradually the pleasure waned, but left in its wake a delicious feeling of satiation.

He slid off of her and lay next to her, breathing hard. "Lydia," he whispered.

"Mmm," she murmured, snuggling against him.

She must have fallen asleep, but the knocker sounding on the townhouse door woke her with a start. She heard voices outside.

The newspaper people. Would they never stop hounding her? She sat up, covering herself with the bed linens and realising what she had just done.

She'd begged the dashing Adrian Pomroy, who conquered women more easily than Napoleon had conquered countries, to make love to her. And he had obliged.

"There is no one here to answer your door," he said.

She groped around for her shift. "I do not want my door answered." Covering her mouth with her hand, she squeezed her eyes shut. "They must not see you here." Finally her fingers flexed around the muslin of her shift. She pulled it on over her head and climbed off the bed. "You must get dressed." Hopping on one foot, she tried to gather his clothes. "Leave here by the rear door." She twisted his shirt in her hands. "The gate. You cannot lock the gate." She shook her head and reached for his waistcoat. "Never mind the gate. The servants will be here soon and they will lock it behind them."

He seized her arm. "Lydia, calm yourself. They will not see me."

It was not only the reporters or creditors fuelling her alarm. Her own wanton behaviour had shocked her much, much more.

She shoved the shirt and waistcoat into his hands.

He dressed as quickly and efficiently as he had undressed. Buttoning his waistcoat, he said, "I will call upon you tomorrow."

"No!" she cried. She forced herself to sound rational. "You cannot come here again, Adrian. If you are seen here, there will be more scandal." She hopped over to the chest of drawers and pulled out a robe of Chinese silk. She wrapped the robe around her. "Please, just go."

He strode over and enfolded her in his arms, pressing her

ear against his beating heart. "Be calm," he murmured. "Your troubles will vanish soon."

She wanted to laugh hysterically. Once she had believed that troubles were what other people experienced, but she knew differently now. Now it seemed trouble would follow her to the end of her days.

"I'll lock your gate and throw the key back into the garden." He released her, but placed one light kiss on her forehead. "And I will return."

"You must not return," she pleaded.

He flashed a smile before walking out of the bedchamber.

She hobbled to a room at the back and peered into the garden, telling herself she just wanted to be certain he left by the rear of the house. She could never allow him to call upon her, but she could gain one last glimpse.

He, no more than a shadow now, appeared in the garden and crossed to the back gate with a long-legged stride. When he reached it he turned back towards the house and lifted his face to the upper windows. With a gasp, Lydia jumped back, although she doubted he could have seen her. Slowly he turned back to the gate, opened it a crack, and peeked out before walking through, out of her sight.

Out of her life.

Chapter Two

What magic allure does the Lady possess, to turn a man
to such desperate acts? Who will her next victim be, this
Siren, this daughter of Achelous, who sings men to their
deaths?—*The New Observer*, November 12, 1818

Adrian entered White's gentlemen's club, his senses still
humming, the lovemaking with Lydia still vibrating through
him so powerfully he wondered if others could sense it.

He felt strong and masculine and completely devoid of the
amorphous discontent with which he'd been lately plagued.
It had vanished when he had walked into Lady Wexin's life.
Adrian fought the impulse to turn around and retrace his steps
to John Street, to scale the walls of her garden if necessary,
to enter her house, and repeat the lovemaking that had stirred
his senses to such heights.

The footman stationed at the door of White's greeted
Adrian with undisputed normality, chatting about the weather
while assisting Adrian out of his coat. Adrian glanced over to

the bow window, but no one sat there. He made his way through the club to the coffee room.

Several men nodded a greeting, and Adrian had to suppress a smile. They had no idea that he'd just left the bed of one of London's most beautiful, and now most notorious, women. And they would never know of it.

A voice called from across the room, "Cavanley! Over here. Join us."

Adrian glanced around, expecting to see someone summoning his father, but it was his father who was waving to him from a table in the corner of the room. Adrian rubbed his face in dismay. He, not his father, was Cavanley now.

Since Adrian's father had inherited the title Earl of Varcourt from a distant and elderly cousin who had very recently passed away, Adrian now had the use, by courtesy, of his father's lesser title of Viscount Cavanley. Inheriting his father's titles with all their rights, responsibility, and property would only occur upon his father's death. At present, he merely gained the privilege of being called Viscount Cavanley. Adjusting to the new appellation was more difficult than he'd anticipated.

The new Earl of Varcourt waved with more vigour, signalling Adrian to join him. His father sat with the Marquess of Heronvale and Heronvale's brother-in-law, Lord Levenhorne.

Adrian crossed the room and greeted them. "Good evening to you." He bowed to each in turn. "Lord Heronvale. Lord Levenhorne. Father."

His father gestured for him to sit. "What are you drinking, son?"

"Port will do," Adrian responded.

His father clicked his fingers to a nearby footman. "Port for Lord Cavanley," he cried in a loud voice.

At least his father had no difficulty using his son's new title.

The new Lord Varcourt turned back to Adrian. "Are you bound for the card room?"

Adrian's father relished his son's success at cards, boasting that Adrian's winnings would eclipse the family fortune one of these days. An exaggeration, of course, although Adrian did often win.

"Not today," he replied.

His father beamed and turned to Heronvale and Levenhorne. "It is said my son won a bundle off Sedford the other night."

Adrian drummed his fingers against the white linen tablecloth. "The cards were good to me."

The loss must have hurt Sedford, Adrian thought with some guilt, but he guessed Sedford would be in the card room again tonight, drinking just as heavily, losing just as swiftly. Sedford would be better off if he spent more time at his wife's musicales, even if they were deadly affairs.

"They say Sedford played foolishly." Levenhorne drained his glass and signalled the footman for another drink. "I'm sick to death of reckless card players and the problems they cause others."

"I'd heard the man enjoyed cards a great deal more than his skill at them ought to have permitted," Heronvale said.

Adrian glanced from one to the other. "You have lost me. Do you speak of Sedford?"

"Of Wexin," his father explained. "We were speaking of Wexin before you arrived. Levenhorne stands to inherit his title, you know."

Levenhorne rolled his eyes. "Of course, I must wait the blasted ten months to see if Wexin's widow produces an heir.

Ten months during which I could be solving problems that are likely to be mine and will only become worse for the wait."

Adrian straightened in his chair.

The law gave a peer's widow ten months to give birth to an heir. As next in line to inherit, Levenhorne had no choice but to wait.

Levenhorne gave a dry laugh. "It is fortunate Wexin died, is it not? Things would be in even more of a mess if he'd been hanged for treason."

Seizure of the title, forfeiture of the property—all would have been possible had Wexin been convicted and hanged. It was complicated, indeed, but Levenhorne could not know how truly complicated. Tanner had confided to Adrian that Wexin shot himself, but Tanner had convinced the Scottish officials to declare Wexin's death accidental. "To minimise the scandal and ease Lady Wexin's suffering," Tanner had explained. It also vastly simplified the settling of Wexin's estate.

"Ah, the drinks have arrived." Levenhorne looked towards the footman who approached the table carrying a tray. He grabbed his glass, shaking his head. "Wexin's debts are staggering. The man owes money all over town." He took a fortifying drink. "Or I should say, owed money. He was damned reckless in his spending. Or perhaps it was Lady Wexin who spent like an empress. The trustee has clamped down on her, I tell you."

"Indeed?" Adrian's interest increased.

Levenhorne shrugged. "Her father will pay her debts, I suspect, although he will be none too pleased when he discovers the townhouse he purchased as a wedding gift is now mortgaged to the hilt."

Adrian's father spoke up. "I heard Strathfield was on a tour. His son as well. Headed to Egypt and India."

Strathfield was Lydia's father and as wealthy as any man could wish.

"True." Levenhorne waved a dismissive hand. "Let her depend on her sister, then." Lydia's sister had married quite well. "I'll be damned if I'll use my own funds."

Adrian frowned.

Heronvale broke in. "Her sister's husband has refused any contact, my wife tells me." He sipped his drink. "In my opinion Lady Wexin deserves our pity, not our castigation. The newspapers are brutal to her."

Adrian's father grinned. "Did you see the caricature in the window at Ackermann's? It shows her and Wexin standing with a clergyman while Wexin hides a long, bloody knife. One had to laugh at it."

Adrian failed to see the humour. He tapped on his glass. "Tanner told me Lady Wexin knew nothing about Wexin killing Corland. In fact, Tanner told me that Wexin's motive was to have been kept confidential."

Tanner had been on the run with the woman fugitive whom Wexin had framed for Viscount Corland's murder. The newspapers called her the Vanishing Viscountess and, at the time, her name filled the papers like Lydia's did now. Tanner had married her in Scotland, and she and Tanner were the ones who had exposed Wexin.

"Who divulged that he'd killed Corland before the man could ruin his chance to marry her, I wonder?" Heronvale frowned. "Someone present at the inquest, I suppose."

Adrian's father laughed. "Come now. Who could resist? Tanner is a fool to think such delicious gossip can be silenced."

Heronvale looked at Adrian. "Tanner is certain of her innocence?"

Adrian bristled at the question. "He assures me she had nothing to do with her husband's crimes."

Levenhorne lifted his glass to his lips. "I am not so certain. The papers speculate she knew what Wexin was about."

Adrian gripped the edge of the table, angry at this man's insistence on believing the worst of Lydia. Had he not heard Adrian say that Tanner had proclaimed her innocence? Did they believe a newspaper over a marquess?

Another worry nagged at him, one that explained the unlit fire and the absence of servants, if not the purse full of coin.

"How severe was Wexin's debt?" Adrian asked Levenhorne.

Levenhorne leaned back in his chair. "He was in dun territory, both feet in the River Tick. The whole matter of his estate is a shambles. The executor is Lady Wexin's brother, who is on that bloody tour of Egypt or wherever." He shook his head in disgust. "Mr Coutts, the banker, you know, is the trustee. He had the audacity to ask me for funds, which I refused, I tell you."

Adrian glanced away. Poor Lydia! Adrian could not simply walk away from her difficulties without assisting her, could he?

Lydia sat up in the bed where only two hours before she'd made love with a man she barely knew, one of London's most profligate rakes. She wrapped her arms around herself, remembering the passion of his lovemaking, the delightful pleasures he had given her. His reputation as a lover was deserved, well deserved.

She blushed. Her life was a shambles, a mockery, a laughing stock. She was a widow who could not grieve, a lady who could not pay her debts, a daughter who could not run to her parents. Only God knew where her parents or brother might be. Greece. Egypt. India. She'd written to all the places on their itinerary. Her sister, merely a few streets away, had been forbidden to help her. Forbidden to see her. And what was Lydia doing? Tumbling into bed with the handsome Adrian Pomroy.

Her maid knocked and entered the room, carrying a tray. "Cook said tomorrow we will have soup, but tonight there is but cheese and bread. I've brought you wine. We seem to have a lot of wine."

Her husband had a great fondness for purchasing the very best wine. Perhaps she could sell it. How would one go about selling one's wine? She must discuss the idea with her butler.

She smiled at her maid. "It is good of you to bring my meal above stairs, Mary."

When the other servants had left, Mary, one of the house-maids, had begged to stay and act as Lydia's lady's maid. The girl took her new duties very seriously.

Mary set the tray upon its legs so that it formed a bed table across Lydia's lap. "I ought to have been with you, my lady." The girl frowned. "I told you not to go to the shops alone."

But Lydia needed to go to the shops. Had she not, they would have had no money at all. She'd taken several pieces of her jewellery to Mr Gray on Sackville Street and he had given her a fair price.

"Do not fret, Mary," Lydia responded. "I would have twisted my ankle had you been there or not." That odious newspaperman would not have allowed a mere maid to deter his pursuit, but events would have transpired very differently if Mary had been there when Adrian had come to the rescue.

She must not think of him.

"You deserved a visit to your mother." Lydia's voice came out louder than she intended. "Is she well?"

"Indeed, very well, my lady, thank you for asking." The girl curtsied. "My brothers and sisters are growing so big. Mum expects them to go into service soon. She is making inquiries."

"I wish I could help them." Once Lydia might have given Mary's siblings a recommendation, but now a connection to the scandalous Lady Wexin was best hidden.

"They'll find work, never you fear," said Mary, plumping the pillows.

Would Mary be able to smell Adrian upon the linens? Lydia could. She felt her cheeks burn again and turned her face away, pretending to adjust the coverlet.

"Lord knows how you got yourself home and up the stairs," Mary went on. She peered in the direction of Lydia's foot, even though it was under the covers. "You even wrapped your ankle." She looked pensive. "And managed to undress yourself."

"I wanted to get in bed." Lydia's cheeks flamed. How true those words were!

She glanced quickly at Mary, but the girl did not seem to notice any change in her complexion. Lydia would be mortified if even her loyal Mary discovered her great moral lapse.

Mary straightened the bedcovers again and stepped back. "Is there anything else I can do for you, my lady?"

Dixon, her butler, and Cook would be waiting for Mary below stairs where they would share their meal in the kitchen, the other warm room in the house. "You took the purse to Dixon, did you not? Was there enough to pay the household accounts?"

"I gave him the purse, my lady, but I do not know about the household accounts. Shall I ask Mr Dixon to come up to speak to you?"

Lydia shook her head. "I would not trouble him now. Tomorrow will do." Let her servants enjoy an evening of idleness. Goodness knows the three of them had toiled hard to keep the house in order and to take care of her, doing the work of eight. Lydia missed the footmen, housemaids and kitchen maid she'd had to dismiss. The house was so quiet without them.

Mary curtsied again. "I'll come back for the tray and to ready you for bed."

Lydia gazed at the girl, so young and pretty and eager to please. Mary would be valued in any household, yet she'd chosen to remain with Lydia. Tears filled her eyes. She did not know if she could ever pay her, let alone repay her. "Thank you, Mary."

Mary curtsied again and left the room.

Adrian's father lingered after Heronvale and Levenhorne took their leave, both hurrying home to dinner with their wives. "What diversion awaits you this evening, son?"

Adrian tilted his chin. "None, unless I accepted an invitation I no longer recall."

His father looked at him queryingly. "No visits to a gaming hell? Or, better yet, no lusty opera dancer awaiting you after her performance? A young buck like you must have something exciting planned."

Adrian finished his second glass of port. "Not a thing."

"You are welcome to dinner, then. Your mother and I dine alone this evening. I am certain she would be pleased to see you." His father stood. "Come."

Why not? thought Adrian. A glance around the room revealed no better company with whom to pass the time, and he had a particular dislike of being alone this night.

As they strolled through the streets of Mayfair where all the fashionable people lived, Adrian was mindful that he'd walked nearly this same route before. The Varcourt house, part of his father's new inheritance, was on Berkeley Square, only a few roads away from Lydia's townhouse on Hill Street.

And the garden gate he'd carried her through on John Street.

"You are quiet today," his father remarked.

Adrian glanced over at him, realising he had not uttered a word since they'd left White's. "Forgive me, Father. I suppose I was woolgathering."

His father's brow wrinkled. "It is not like you at all. Are you ill? Or have you got yourself in some scrape or another?"

"Neither." Adrian smiled. "Not likely I'd tell you if I were in a scrape, though."

His father laughed. "You have the right of it. Never knew you not to get yourself out of whatever bumble-broth you'd landed in."

It was perhaps more accurate to say Tanner always managed the disentanglement, but Adrian's father probably knew that very well.

"What is it, then, my son?" his father persisted.

Adrian certainly did not intend to tell his father about his encounter with Lady Wexin. Likely his father would see it as a conquest about which he could brag to his friends. Adrian was not in the habit of worrying over the secrecy of his affairs, but Lady Wexin's name had been bandied about so unfairly, he had no wish to add to the gossip about her.

Adrian did wish he could explain to his father the discontent he'd been feeling lately. His father would in all likelihood pooh-pooh it as nonsense, however.

His father seemed to believe there could be no better life

than the one Adrian led, spending his days and nights gambling, womanising and sporting. Adrian had lately wished for more than horse races or card games or opera dancers, however. He was tired of having no occupation, no purpose, of feeling it would take his father's death to bring some utility to his existence.

Adrian's discontent had begun about a year ago when he'd accompanied Tanner on a tour of his friend's estates. He'd marvelled at Tanner's knowledge of his properties and the people who saw to the running of them. Adrian had learned a great deal about farming, raising livestock, and managing a country estate during that trip, more than his father had ever taught him. Adrian's restlessness had increased recently after learning of Tanner's sudden marriage. He did not begrudge his friend's newfound domestic happiness; surprisingly enough, he envied it.

His father came to an abrupt halt. "Good God, this is not about some woman, is it? Do not tell me. I'll wager it is Lady Denson. The word is she is quite enamoured of you, as well any woman would be."

An image of Lydia flew into Adrian's mind, not Viola Denson, who had indeed engaged in a flirtation with Adrian, but one in which he could not sustain an interest.

"Not Lady Denson," he replied. "Nor any woman, if you must know."

And it seemed his father always wanted to know about Adrian's romantic conquests. He told his father as little as possible about them.

If his father were paying attention to more than Adrian's love life and gambling wins, he'd recall that his son had asked to take over some of the family's lesser holdings. He'd thought it proper to ease his father's new burdens of all the Varcourt properties, but the new Earl of Varcourt would have none of it. "Plenty of time for all that," his father had said. "Enjoy yourself while you can."

Adrian glanced at his father, a faithful husband, excellent manager, dutiful member of the House of Lords. His father might glorify the delights of his son's bachelorhood, but, even without those delights in his own life, his father was a contented man.

Unlike Adrian.

Adrian attempted to explain. "I am bored—"

His father laughed. "Bored? A young buck like you? Why, you can do anything you wish. Enjoy life."

He could do anything, perhaps, but nothing of value, Adrian thought. "The enjoyment is lacking at the moment."

"Lacking? Impossible." His father clapped him on the shoulder. "You sound like a man in need of a new mistress."

Again Adrian thought of Lydia.

"Find yourself a new woman," his father advised. "That's the ticket. That Denson woman, if she wants it."

Typical of his father to think in that manner. His father had inherited young, married young and lived a life of exemplary conduct, but that did not stop him from enjoying the exploits of his son.

"Do not forget," his father went on, "your friend Tanner's marriage has deprived you of some companionship, but you'll soon accustom yourself to going about without him." His father laughed. "Imagine Tanner in a Scottish marriage. With the Vanishing Viscountess, no less. Just like him to enter into some ramshackle liaison and wind up smelling of roses."

Indeed. Under the most unlikely of circumstances Tanner

had met the perfect woman for him. Why, his wife was even a baroness in her own right, a very proper wife for a marquess.

Adrian's father launched into a repeat of the whole story of Tanner's meeting the Vanishing Viscountess, of aiding her flight and of them both thwarting Wexin. Adrian only half-listened.

Adrian glanced at his father. The man was as tall, straight-backed and clear-eyed as he'd been all Adrian's life. Even his blond hair was only lately fading to white. He did not need Adrian's help managing the properties or anything else.

Adrian was nearly seven and thirty years. How long would it be before he had any responsibility at all?

"Did you know Wexin's townhouse is on Hill Street?" he suddenly heard his father say.

"Mmm," Adrian managed. Of course he knew.

"Strathfield purchased it as a wedding gift. Nice property. There's been a pack of newspaper folks hanging around the door for days now. I agree with Levenhorne. Those newspaper fellows know a thing or two about Lady Wexin that we do not."

Adrian bristled. "Tanner says—"

His father scoffed. "Yes. Yes. Tanner says she is innocent, but when you have lived as long as I have, son, you learn that where one sees smoke, there is usually fire."

There was certainly a fire within Lady Wexin, but not the sort to which his father referred.

They reached Berkeley Square. His father stopped him before the door of the Varcourt house. "When your mother gives the word, you must give up your rooms and take over the old townhouse. She is still dithering about what furniture to move, I believe, so I do not know how long it will take."

Splendid. Adrian had wanted an estate to manage. He would wind up with a house instead.

* * *

Samuel Reed stood among three other reporters near the entrance of Lady Wexin's townhouse. His feet pained him, he was hungry, chilled to the bone and tired of this useless vigil. The lady was not going to emerge.

"I say we take turns," one of the men was saying. "We agree to share any information about who enters the house or where she goes if she ventures out."

"You talk a good game," another responded. "But how do we know you would keep your word? You'd be the last fellow to tell what you know."

The man was wrong. *Reed* would be the last fellow to tell what he knew. He was determined that *The New Observer*, the newspaper he and his brother Phillip owned, would have exclusive information about Lady Wexin. He'd not said a word to the others that he'd caught the lady out and about. She'd been walking from the direction of the shops. Why had she gone off alone?

He glanced at the house, but there was nothing to see. Curtains covered the windows. "I'm done for today," he told the others.

"Don't expect us to tell you if something happens," one called to him.

Reed walked down John Street, slowing his pace as he passed the garden entrance. He peered through a crack between the planks of the wooden gate.

To his surprise, the rear door opened, though it was not Lady Wexin who emerged but her maid, shaking out table linen.

Reed's stomach growled. It appeared that Lady Wexin had enjoyed a dinner. He certainly had not. He watched the maid, a very pretty little thing with dark auburn hair peeking out from beneath her cap. Reed had seen the young woman before, had even followed her the previous day when she'd gone to the market. For the last several days, Reed had seen only this maid and the butler entering and leaving the house. He'd surmised that Lady Wexin had dismissed most of the servants.

He'd been able to locate one of Lady Wexin's former footmen, but the man refused to confirm whether or not other servants had left her employment. The man had refused to say anything newsworthy about Lady Wexin, but perhaps a maid might have knowledge a footman would not.

He watched her fold the cloth and re-enter the house. A carriage sounded at the end of the street, and he quickly darted into the shadows until the carriage continued past him.

He glanced at the moonlit sky. Time to walk back to the newspaper offices, get some dinner and write his story for the next edition, such as it was.

If only he could identify the gentleman who had come to Lady Wexin's aid. He could make something of that information. The man was familiar, but he did not know all the gentlemen of the *ton* by sight. He'd keep his eyes open, though, and hope to discover the man's identity soon enough.

Chapter Three

The scandalous Lady W— walks about Mayfair without a companion...or was it her intention to rendezvous with a certain gentleman? Beware, fine sir. Recall to what ends a man may be driven when Beauty is the prize...—*The New Observer*, November 14, 1818

Sheets of relentless rain kept indoors all but the unfortunate few whose livelihood forced them outside. Adrian was not in this category, but he willingly chose to venture forth with the rain dripping from the brim of his hat, the damp soaking its way through his topcoat and water seeping into his boots.

He turned into Hill Street, watchful for the reporters who'd lounged around Lady Wexin's door the previous day when he'd made it a point to stroll by. As he suspected and dared hope, no one was in sight.

To be certain, he continued past the house to the end of the street and then back again. Not another living creature was about.

Apparently there were some things a newspaper reporter would not do in pursuit of a story, like standing in the pouring rain in near freezing temperatures. Adrian was not so faint of heart. What was a little water dripping from the brim of his hat, soaking his collar and causing his neck to chafe? A mere annoyance when he might see Lydia again.

Still, he wished he might have brought his umbrella.

Adrian strode up to the green door of the Wexin townhouse and sounded the brass lion's-head knocker.

No one answered.

He sounded the knocker again and pressed his ear against the wooden door. He heard heels click on the hall's marble floor.

"Open," he called through the door. "It is Pomroy. Calling upon Lady Wexin."

"Who?" a man's muffled voice asked.

"Pomroy," Adrian responded. He paused. He'd forgotten again. "Lord Cavanley," he said louder.

He heard the footsteps receding, but pounded with the knocker again, huddling in the narrow doorcase so that only his back suffered the soaking rain. He planned to knock until he gained entry.

Finally, the footsteps returned and the door was opened a crack, a man's eye visible in it.

"I am Lord Cavanley, calling upon Lady Wexin." Adrian spoke through the crack.

The eye stared.

"On a matter of business." Adrian reached into his pocket and pulled out a slightly damp card. He handed it through the narrow opening. "Have pity, man. Do you think I wish to stand out in the rain?"

The eye disappeared and, after a moment, the crack widened to reveal Lady Wexin's butler. The man was of some indeterminate age, anywhere from thirty to fifty. He did not wear livery and possessed the right mix of hauteur and servitude that befitted a butler. Adrian liked the protective look in the man's eye.

"Be so good as to wait here a moment, m'lord." The butler bowed and walked away, his heels clicking on each step as he ascended the marble stairs.

Adrian remembered carrying Lydia up those flights of stairs.

His gaze followed the butler, puzzled as to why the man had not taken his coat and hat, but left him standing in the hall like a visiting merchant.

Adrian removed his hat and gloves as puddles formed at his feet on the marble floor. The gilded table still held its vases, and the vases were still empty of flowers.

Finally the butler's footsteps sounded again as he descended and made his unhurried way back to Adrian. "I will take you to Lady Wexin."

Adrian handed him his hat and gloves and removed his soaked topcoat carefully so as to lessen both the size of the puddles and the amount of rainwater pouring down the back of his neck. He waited again while the butler disappeared with the sodden items, daring to hope the man might lay them out in front of some fire to dry a bit.

When the butler returned, he led Adrian up the stairs to a first-floor drawing room. Even standing in the doorway, Adrian could feel the room's chill. There was a fire in the fireplace, but Adrian guessed it must have just been lit.

Lydia's back was to him. She stood with arms crossed in front of her, facing the window that looked out at the rain.

"Lord Cavanley," the butler announced.

She turned, and her beautiful sapphire eyes widened. "You!"

The butler stepped between her and Adrian.

She waved a dismissive hand. "It is all right, Dixon. I will see this gentleman."

Frowning, the butler bowed, tossing Adrian a suspicious glance as he walked out of the room and closed the door behind him.

Adrian was taken aback. "I announced myself to your man."

She shook her head. "But you are Mr Pomroy."

He realised the mistake. "Forgive me." He smiled at her. "You must not know me as Cavanley."

"I certainly do not!" She stepped forwards and gripped the back of a red velvet chair. Her forehead suddenly furrowed. "Did...did your father pass away? I confess, I did not know—"

He held up his hand. "Nothing like that." He caught himself staring at her and gave himself a mental shake. "Well, a cousin of his passed away, but he was quite elderly and had been ill for many years. My father inherited the title, Earl of Varcourt, so his lesser title passed to me." Good God. He was babbling. He took a breath. "How is your ankle?"

Stepping around the chair, she stared at him as if he had just sprouted horns. "It troubles me little."

"I am glad of it," he said. His voice sounded stiff.

She walked closer to him and his breath was again stolen by her beauty. Her golden hair sparkled from the fire in the hearth and lamps that he suspected had also been hastily lit. While the rest of the room faded into greyness, like the rainy day, she appeared bathed in a warm glow, as if all the light in the room was as drawn to her as he was. She wore a dress of rich blue, elegantly cut. Its sole adornment was a thick velvet ribbon tied in a bow beneath her breasts. A paisley shawl was wrapped around her shoulders, the blue in its woven print complementing her dress and her eyes.

She cast her gaze down. "Why do you call upon me, sir, when I asked that you not do so?" Her voice was steady, but no louder than a whisper.

Once Adrian might have cheekily proclaimed that he could not resist calling upon her, that her beauty beckoned him, that the memory of their lovemaking could never be erased. Once he would have presented reasons why their affair ought to continue, needed to continue, and that he was there because he could not stay away.

Those sentiments were true, but his decision to call upon her involved another matter. Still, it stung that she looked so wounded and angry. "Did you think it was my father who called upon you?"

"I did," she admitted.

He stiffened. "You would have allowed my father entry, but not me?"

"I would."

He shook his head, puzzled. "But why?"

She glanced away. "I thought perhaps your father was on an errand for Lord Levenhorne. He and Levenhorne are friends." She glanced back at him. "They are friends, are they not?"

"Indeed." All the *ton* knew they were friends.

She went on. "Levenhorne is my husband's heir, and I thought perhaps it truly was a matter of business, as you told Dixon it was."

Adrian did not miss her accusing tone. He had told the butler that one lie. Although, in a way, it *was* business.

He took a breath, releasing it slowly before speaking, "I did not mean to deceive you, Lydia. I merely wished to see you."

Her eyes flashed. "I cannot believe you thought I would welcome this visit." She snatched a newspaper from a table. "Did you not read this? That reporter connects us."

He had indeed read *The New Observer* and every other newspaper that mentioned the notorious Lady W. "The reporter did not name me. I fully comprehend that you do not wish any contact between us to be known. I would not have come but for the rain. I knew the weather would drive the reporters away from your doorstep."

She gave a mirthless laugh. "Do you think it matters to me that the man did not name you? It is *my* name that suffers! I am linked to a gentleman. There will be no end to what will be written about me now." She threw the paper back on the table.

"I merely responded to your need," he retorted. "I refuse to apologise for it."

"My need?" Her voice rose.

"Yes," Adrian shot back. "That man was attacking you. I could not walk by and do nothing."

"Oh." Her shoulders slumped. "That need. My need for rescue, you meant."

He realised that she'd thought he meant the other needs they'd indulged that day.

Their gazes connected and it seemed as if those needs flared between them again, like the hiss of red coals about to burst into flame. He wanted to cross the room, to touch her and re-ignite the passion that was burning inside him, as real as the thumping of his heart, the deep drawing of his breath, the pulsing of blood through his veins.

However, his purpose in calling upon her had not been to indulge in that pleasure again, to enjoy each other as they had done before, although Adrian could see no harm in it. Society rarely censured a widow for such conduct as long as she acted discreetly, and he could be very discreet.

Of course, she was not just any widow. She was society's latest scandal.

"Lydia." The sound of her name on his tongue felt as soft and smooth as her ivory skin. "I have no wish to see you harmed in any way. I will keep our association secret."

She laughed. "Do you think I believe in secrets, Adrian?" She stepped closer. "I have been hurt by secrets. Those kept and those divulged."

She was so close Adrian's nostrils scented lilacs. Her eyes, however, were filled with pain and accusation.

He wanted to assure her he was a good sort of man, with a good proposition for her if she would only listen to him.

"My husband kept secrets from me," she went on, lifting her gaze to his. "What makes you think I can trust anything you say?"

He had no answer.

He forced himself to look directly into her lovely face. "Please know, dear lady, that I speak truly when I say I have no wish to hurt you, no wish to ever hurt you." He gave her a wan smile. "I told you before that I would act as your friend. I came here as such."

"A friend." Her gaze softened.

She stepped forwards and touched his arm. Even through his layers of clothing, the contact seared him with need, a need he knew he must deny. When he looked in her eyes, though, he saw a yearning to match his own.

"Lydia," he whispered.

Lydia thought she must have gone completely mad. She

gazed into his eyes and was content to be caught there, like a leaf caught in a whirlpool that pulled it into its depths.

She ought to send him away now. She ought to forget what she'd done two days before, wantonly bedding him, a man well known for his conquests of women.

He had acted nothing like she'd supposed a rake would act. He had never pushed himself on her, never spoke words of seduction. She had pushed herself on him, in fact. *She* had been the one who'd spoken words of seduction. And she felt herself about to do so again.

Her hand on his arm trembled against the fabric of his coat, damp from where the rain had soaked through. She had only to move her hand away and let him go.

Instead, she raised her hand to his face and lightly grazed his cheek.

God help her, she *was* weak. And wanton.

From the moment of seeing him framed in the doorway, her body had craved the return of his touch, the passion of his lovemaking.

She traced her finger from his temple to the perpetually upturned corner of his mouth. He remained still, giving her the power to choose if she wanted more or not. She almost wished he would seize her now, take her by force. Even though his eyes darkened and his breathing accelerated, he still waited for her to choose.

What harm would it do? she thought. What harm to have his arms around her again, to have his practised touch drive away the worries that seemed to double and triple with each passing day? She was lonely. What harm to pass time with him? He knew the same people, attended the same entertainments. She missed being a part of it all more than she would have guessed.

But what she missed most was what a man could give her, what Adrian had given her. If the newspapers only knew what a wanton woman she'd turned out to be, a woman who bedded a man merely because he'd been kind. She shuddered to think what would be written of her if they knew.

She let her hand fall away.

Adrian's gaze turned puzzled. He did not say a word. He did not move. He would leave if she told him to, she knew.

Or he would stay.

Her choice.

She stepped closer to him, her aching ankle reminding her how he had so gently tended it. What had come after his gentle care now consumed her. His kiss. What his touch had aroused in her.

What harm to feel that delight one more time? What harm?

Lydia slid her hands up his chest until her arms encircled his neck. The hair at the nape tickled her fingers and his collar felt cool and damp. She rose on tiptoe and tilted her face to him, letting him know she'd made her choice.

He groaned with a man's need and bent forwards, placing his lips on hers, tentatively, as if he still would permit her to change her mind.

She did not want to change her mind. She wanted her body to sing with the pleasure he could create. She wanted to be joined to him, like one. She wanted to not be so terribly alone.

He drew away slightly, then crushed his lips against hers with a man's command. The effect was exhilarating.

His kiss, familiar but new, deepened. Her lips parted and their tongues touched, the sensation intimate and delighting.

He pressed her to him, and she could feel the evidence of his arousal beneath his clothing. That womanly part of her ached with desire to feel his length inside her again. She wanted him to sweep her away, to make her forget everything but him.

Her heart pounded wildly.

She'd once forgotten everything but Wexin. Wexin's kisses—chaste compared to Adrian's—had once made her feel secure in a future of happiness, but Wexin, while kissing her, had the stain of blood on his hands, the murder of a friend.

Lydia pushed hard against Adrian's chest and backed away. The look he gave her was wild, heated, aroused and confused.

She put a hand to her forehead. "Forgive me." She dared to glance into his eyes. "Forgive me. I cannot do this. I must not."

He breathed heavily, and it seemed to her he was fighting to keep calm.

"Lydia." His voice was so low she seemed to feel it more than hear it. "Why deny this passion between us?"

She stared at him. How could she explain that she could never again allow a man to have that sort of power over her?

"I must deny it." Her voice sounded mournful and weak. She must never again be weak. She lifted her chin. "Please leave, Adrian. Do not return." She walked behind the chair again and clutched its back.

"Lydia." His eyes pleaded.

She held up a hand. "Do not press me, Adrian." She took a deep breath. "I have enough worries."

He turned and started to walk away. Lydia did not know which feeling was the greater: relief at his departure, or sorrow.

Before he reached the door, he stopped and turned back. "Before I walk out, tell me something, Lydia."

She waited.

He looked directly into her eyes. "Do you need money?"

She inhaled sharply. "What makes you think I need money?"

His hand swept the room. "You light fires only for show. You have no flowers. And there is the matter of your servants—"

"I have servants," she retorted. Well, three servants, but he need not know the number was so small.

Would he tell the creditors and reporters? If word of her true situation escaped, all of England would know the shocking state of her finances. Even Levenhorne and the men at the bank did not know how bad it was, how close they'd come to having nothing to eat.

"I came here to offer you help," he said. "How much money do you need?"

"I don't need money." She felt her cheeks heat. "But if I did, I would not take yours."

His brows rose. "Why?"

"Why?" She gave a nervous laugh. "Would that not mean I was in your keeping? Do not mistresses accept money from their…patrons?"

His eyes creased at the corners. "I make the offer as a friend, nothing more."

She glanced away. Truth was, she still needed money for the most pressing debts. It would buy her time until her parents returned and her father could help her. At present, her only hope was that her sister could find a way to help her, to get money to her without her husband's knowledge. Lydia had sent Mary to pass on a letter through her sister's maid.

"I do not need your money, Adrian," she whispered.

"I offer it without obligation."

He said this so sincerely, she almost believed him, but she'd believed Wexin, a murderer who professed to love her, who bought her trinkets, while spending every penny of her dowry. It made no sense that a near-stranger, a known rake, would offer her money without expecting something in return.

"It is not your place to help me," she told Adrian. She blinked. "*If* I needed help, that is." She squared her shoulders and forced herself to look directly into his eyes. "Please leave now, Adrian."

For a moment he looked as if he would cross the room to her, but instead, he turned and walked to the door. She twisted away, not wishing to watch him disappear out of her life.

His voice came from behind her. "I am your friend, Lydia. Remember that."

She spun back around, but he had gone.

Chapter Four

All eyes are on Kew Palace this day where the Queen remains gravely ill, her physicians declaring the state of her health to be one of "great and imminent danger"…—*The New Observer*, November 15, 1818

Samuel Reed lounged in the wooden chair while his brother, Phillip, the manager and editor of *The New Observer*, sat behind the desk, his face blocked by the newspaper he held in front of him.

"We must find something more interesting than the Queen's illness for tomorrow's paper, else we'll be reduced to printing handbills and leaflets like Father."

Their father had been a printer with no ambition, except to see how much gin he could consume every night. It was not until the man died of a drunken fall from the second-storey window of a Cheapside brothel that Samuel and Phillip could realise their much loftier ambitions: to publish a newspaper.

They were determined to make *The New Observer* the most popular newspaper in London, and Samuel's stories about Lady Wexin had definitely set it on its way. Each London newspaper had its speciality, and the Reed brothers had deliberately carved out their own unique niche. Not for them political commentary or a commitment to social change. The Reed brothers specialised in society gossip and stories of murder and mayhem, the more outrageous the better.

"Anything interesting in the out-of-town papers?" Samuel asked.

"Not much…" Phillip's voice trailed off.

Like all the newspapers, they freely stole from others, often passing the stories off as their own. Every day Phillip perused the out-of-town papers looking for the sort of sensational and unusual stories that fitted their requirements.

The New Observer had other reporters besides Samuel to provide shocking or remarkable items from all around London, including the seediest neighbourhoods. Fascination with the most lofty and with the lowest, that was what the Reed brothers banked upon.

Samuel rose and sauntered towards the window. At least the rain had passed. The previous day had been nothing but rain, and, therefore, precious little news.

"Here's something." Phillip leaned forwards. "Fellow in Mile End set a spring gun to shoot at intruders. Except his own feet tripped the wire and he shot himself. Died from it."

"That's reasonably interesting."

"Not to the fellow who died." His brother laughed.

Phillip picked up another paper and read. "The spinners are still rioting in Manchester." He rolled up the paper and tapped it on the desk. "What news of Lady Wexin?"

Lady Wexin guaranteed profit.

"Nothing from yesterday because of the rain." Samuel

examined the grey sky. "If you send someone else to watch her house today, I will set about discovering the identity of the gentleman who came to her aid."

Phillip grinned. "The gentleman who rescued her from you, do you mean?"

Samuel returned the smile. "I mean precisely that."

Samuel had a plan to scour St James's Street where White's and Brooks's were located. Whether this fellow be Tory or Whig, he'd walk down St James's Street to reach his club.

Phillip crossed his arms over his chest. "Her Majesty the Queen is doing poorly. We need some detail about her illness that the other papers do not know."

Another priority of the paper was royal news, and the Reed brothers would not make the same mistake as Leigh and John Hunt, who went to prison for printing a mild criticism of the Prince Regent in the *Examiner*. *The New Observer* lavished praise on the royals.

"Do not send me to Kew Palace, I beg you." Samuel was eager to pursue what he considered his story. Lady Wexin.

"I would not dream of it." His brother waved his hand. "Hurry out there and find your gentleman."

Samuel soon found himself strolling back and forth on St James's Street, trying to look as if he had business there. He'd been strolling in the vicinity for at least an hour and was prepared to do so all day long, if necessary, until he laid eyes upon the gentleman who had come to Lady Wexin's assistance.

Samuel had done a great deal of thinking about why the lady would have ventured out alone that day. When he had first spied her, she'd been walking from the direction of the shops, but it was quite unlikely that a lady would visit the shops in the afternoon. That was the time young bucks lounged on street corners to watch gentlemen with their less-than-ladylike companions saunter by.

It was more likely Lady Wexin had been calling upon someone, but who? Samuel had not known her to make social calls since her husband's story became known.

Samuel's scanty exclusive—knowledge that she'd been out and about alone and knowledge that a fine-looking gentleman had come to her aid—still gave him an edge over the other reporters who wasted their time watching her front door. All he needed was the tiniest piece of new information. Samuel was skilled at taking the tiniest bits of scandal and inflating them larger than any hot-air balloon.

Samuel reached the corner of St James's and Piccadilly, sweeping Piccadilly Street with his gaze.

Carriages and riders crowded the thoroughfare, and the pavement abounded with men in tall beaver hats and caped topcoats. Curses to that Beau Brummell. Gentlemen dressed too much the same these days because of him. Samuel searched for a man taller than average, one who carried himself like a Corinthian.

Such a man appeared in the distance. Samuel shaded his eyes with his hand and watched him for several seconds. He decided to come closer. Samuel crossed Piccadilly and walked towards him, holding on to the brim of his hat so the man would not see his face.

Within a foot of the man, Samuel's excitement grew. This was the one! His instincts never failed.

Samuel walked past the gentleman and doubled back as soon as he could, quickening his step. If he could follow close behind, perhaps he would hear someone greet the man by name.

To Samuel's surprise, the gentleman turned into New Bond Street. Samuel almost lost him when several nattily attired young fellows, laughing and shoving each other, blocked his way. His view cleared in time to see the man enter the jewellers Stedman & Vardon.

Jewellers?

Already Samuel had begun spinning stories of why the gentleman should enter a jewellery shop, all of them involving Lady Wexin. He preferred learning the real story. True stories had a way of being more fantastic than anything he could conjure up.

Samuel wandered to the doorway of the shop and peeked in. The gentleman spoke to the shop assistant and suddenly turned around to head back out the door. Samuel ducked aside as the man brushed past him.

Samuel ran inside the shop. "I beg your pardon," he said. "Who was that gentleman?"

The shop assistant looked up. "The gentleman who was just here?"

"Yes. Yes." Samuel glanced towards the door. He did not want to lose track of the man.

"Lord Cavanley, do you mean?"

"Cavanley!" Samuel's voice was jubilant. "Thank you, sir." He rushed out of the shop in time to catch a disappearing glimpse of the gentleman.

Lord Cavanley. Samuel did not know of a Lord Cavanley, but it should be an easy matter to learn about him.

Samuel hurried to catch up. He followed Cavanley to Sackville Street where he entered another jewellery shop. Puzzling. Perhaps Cavanley was searching for the perfect jewel. He did not, however, even glance at the sparkling gems displayed on black velvet beneath glass cases. He merely conversed with the older man with balding pate and spectacles. The jeweller, perhaps? In any event, the man seemed somewhat reluctant to speak to this lord.

Finally the jeweller nodded in seeming resignation and said something that apparently satisfied Cavanley. The men shook hands, the jeweller bowed, and Lord Cavanley strode out the door. Samuel turned quickly and pretended to examine something in the shop window next door.

After Cavanley passed by him, Samuel entered the shop. He smiled at the jeweller. "Good day to you, sir. I saw you with Lord Cavanley a moment ago. Did he make a purchase?"

The jeweller's eyes narrowed. "Why do you ask?"

Samuel dug into his pocket and pulled out his card. "I am a reporter for *The New Observer*. I am certain my readers would relish knowing what lovely object Lord Cavanley purchased."

The man frowned and the wrinkles in his face deepened. "His lordship purchased nothing, so you may go on your way."

"He purchased nothing?" Samuel, of course, had already surmised this. "Then what was his purpose here, I wonder?"

The jeweller peered at Samuel from over his spectacles. "Wonder all you wish. I am not about to tell you the business of a patron, am I now?"

Samuel gave the man his most congenial look. "I assure you, kind sir, our readers would relish knowing where a man with such exquisite taste in jewellery would shop. I dare say one mention of your establishment in our newspaper will bring you more customers than you can imagine."

"Hmph." The jeweller crossed his arms over his chest. "I am more interested in keeping the customers I have, thank you very much. Telling the world what they buy from me will not win me their loyalty."

"Sir—"

The man held up a hand. "No. No more talking." Another customer, more finely dressed than Samuel, entered the shop. "I must attend to this gentleman. Good day now. Run along."

Dismissed like an errant schoolboy.

Samuel bit down on a scathing retort. He might have need of this jeweller at a later time and he'd best not antagonise him. Back out on the pavement, he scanned the street for Lord Cavanley, but too much time had passed and the man was gone.

Samuel pushed his hat more firmly upon his head and turned in the direction of *The New Observer* offices. He planned to learn all he could about this Lord Cavanley. He'd start with old issues of their rival newspapers saved for just such a purpose.

Adrian dashed to a line of hackney coaches. "Thomas Coutts and Company on the Strand, if you please." He climbed in and leaned back against the leather seat.

At that last shop Mr Gray had confirmed what Adrian had suspected. Lydia had sold her jewels.

A lady did not resort to selling her jewels unless she was in desperate need of money. No matter her protestations to him, she was skimping on coal and candles, he was certain of it.

It rankled Adrian that Levenhorne and Wexin's trustee, a banker of considerable wealth, would allow an earl's wife to exist in such poverty. If her parents and brother were abroad and her sister forbidden to assist her, to whom could the lady turn for help?

Adrian had no connection to her, nor any obligation. It would certainly be commented upon if he stepped forwards to assist her, but assist her he would. In secret.

He smiled as the hackney coach swayed and bounced over the cobbled streets. At least he'd found something of interest to occupy his time. Solving the puzzle that was Lydia and easing her troubles seemed a better purpose than seating himself at a card table, checking out good horseflesh or, God forbid, entangling himself with Viola Denson. It mattered not one whit to Adrian that no one would know of it, least of all Lydia.

Although a part of him would not mind having Lydia look upon him with sapphire eyes filled with gratitude.

He shook that thought away. The coach passed Charing Cross as it turned into the Strand, and Adrian had a whiff of the Thames. He mulled over his plan until the hack stopped in front of Thomas Coutts and Company, a bank favoured by aristocrats and royalty. Adrian climbed down from the hack and paid its jarvey. He entered the bank.

In the marbled and pillared hall Adrian approached an attendant and identified himself. "I wish to speak with Mr Coutts. He is expecting me, I believe."

Earlier that morning Adrian had sent a message to Mr Coutts, telling of his intention to call.

The attendant escorted him to a chair and returned shortly to lead him to Mr Coutts's office.

As Adrian entered the room, the old gentleman rose from his seat behind a polished mahogany desk. "Ah, Lord Cavanley."

Adrian extended his hand. "Mr Coutts, it is a pleasure. Thank you for seeing me."

Coutts gestured for Adrian to sit. "Your note indicated that you wished to discuss Lord Wexin's estate?" The man looked wary.

Adrian smiled. "On behalf of a friend."

Mr Coutts nodded. "It is a trying affair, but I suspect there is little I might do for you. Allow me to direct you to Wexin's solicitor, who is tending to the entire matter."

"I would be grateful."

"Delighted," said Mr Coutts. "And how is your father? And the Marquess of Tannerton?"

Adrian responded, accustomed to people asking him about Tanner. In fact, in this situation, he'd counted upon it. Mr Coutts scribbled the direction of Wexin's solicitor on a sheet of paper and handed it to Adrian.

The solicitor's office was close by and Adrian quickly found the building and entered. A moment later he had been admitted to the man's office.

The solicitor was a younger man, near Adrian's age, but obviously trusted with a great deal more responsibility. His desk was littered with papers that he hurriedly stacked into neat piles at Adrian's entrance.

"I am Mr Newton, my lord," he said.

Adrian shook his hand and explained his purpose, stressing it was at the behest of a friend that he inquired about Lady Wexin's financial affairs.

Adrian's intention was to imply to Mr Newton that Lydia's benefactor was Tanner, not Adrian. It was widely known that Tanner was a generous man, the sort of man who would assist Wexin's widow. No one would suspect the frivolous Adrian Pomroy of such a thing.

"I am certain you understand that my friend—" Adrian emphasised the word *friend* "—does not wish his name to be known. He fears the lady would refuse his assistance. My friend would say, however, that it is the right thing for him to do for her."

Because Tanner had been instrumental in exposing Wexin

as a murderer, it was not too much of a leap of the imagination to think that Tanner might feel an obligation to assist Wexin's innocent widow. In fact, Tanner would be very willing to assist Lydia, if he knew she needed help. He was that kind of man.

Mr Newton blinked rapidly. "Of course, sir."

Adrian nodded. "The mar—my friend, I mean—" he smiled "—sent me in his stead. He is anxious to discover if Lady Wexin has any financial difficulty and, if so, charges me to see it remedied."

"I do understand." Newton gestured to a chair and waited for Adrian to sit. "Would you care for tea?"

"No, thank you." Adrian lowered himself into the chair. "Tell me about Wexin's finances."

Newton rubbed his face. "Wexin's debts, you mean." He peered at Adrian. "We speak in complete confidence, I presume."

"Indeed," Adrian agreed.

"Because even Lord Levenhorne does not know how bad it is." Newton leaned over the desk. "There is nothing."

"Nothing?"

"Worse than nothing. The townhouse is mortgaged to the hilt. There is only the entailed property, but even that is mortgaged, and it provides nothing to Lady Wexin. There is no money for Lady Wexin's widow's portion. I do not know how she is getting on. I have been unable to give her any funds at all." His hand fluttered. "She assures me she is able to manage, but I do not see how."

Adrian's chest constricted. "It is as I—we—feared." He straightened in his chair. "Tell us what needs to be done."

Newton pulled out a wooden box, opened the lid, and lifted out a handful of small pieces of paper, letting them flow through his fingers like water. "Gentlemen have sent their vowels." He picked up a stack of papers. "Shopkeepers have delivered their bills—"

Adrian had no interest in Wexin's debts. His purpose here was solely for Lydia. "What was the marriage settlement supposed to provide Lady Wexin?"

Newton closed the lid of the box. "In the event of Wexin's death, she was to receive the amount of her dower and the Mayfair townhouse."

Adrian could guess the value of the townhouse. "And the value of the dowry?"

"Nine thousand pounds."

Adrian leaned back and drummed his fingers on the mahogany arms of the chair. He calculated the sums in his head and leaned forwards again. "This is what I will do..." Adrian glanced up at Newton. "On my friend's behalf, I will assume the mortgage of the townhouse." Levenhorne said the house had been a gift from Lydia's father. Adrian would give it back to her. "And I will restore the dowry, but only under the stipulation that creditors are not to seek redress from Lady Wexin. Any debt must be attached to what was Wexin's."

Newton's jaw dropped. "Your friend would pay so much?"

"He can afford the sum." Adrian smiled inwardly.

It was a staggering amount, but one Adrian was well able to afford. For years he had kept his gambling winnings, and the investments made from them, separate from his quarterly portion. It had been a game he played with himself to see how much he could win and also how much he could afford to lose. His quarterly portion from his father was more than adequate for his other needs.

He'd done quite well at the game, quite well indeed, so well that he could restore Lydia's widow's portion, keep her in her London house and still have plenty of gambling money left over.

"My friend wishes the lady to have fifty pounds immediately and to have the townhouse in her name."

Newton nodded, his eyes still wide with disbelief.

Adrian pointed to the wooden box. "How many unpaid bills pertain to the lady's belongings or to the contents of the house?"

Newton riffled through the papers again. "I would have to do a careful calculation, but it is not as bad a debt as some of the others. Perhaps as much as two hundred pounds?"

"Those will be paid as well. I want—and my friend wants, as well—that Wexin's debts do not cause her any more suffering."

"I understand completely, sir." Newton's mouth widened into a smile.

Adrian returned the expression. "Need I add that no hint, no speculation as to the identity of her benefactor must ever be divulged to her? Or my small part in this?"

Newton gave him a level gaze. "It will be kept in complete confidence. I have been successful in keeping the extent of Wexin's debts from becoming public knowledge, and I certainly can keep Lady Wexin's affairs private."

Affairs.

The word sparked the memory of Adrian's very brief affair with Lydia, an affair she was loath to continue.

He supposed he was mad for bestowing a small fortune on a woman who wanted nothing to do with him. It was not like him to invest time or money in a lady who had no regard for him, but what would happen to Lydia if he did not assist her? He was investing in her happiness, a divergence from indulging in his own.

What's more, it was his money to do with as he wished. And he wished to do *good* with it, to feel a scant bit useful in this world. Besides, it gave him a new game to play, to see how long it would take to recoup the amount of money he had invested in Lydia. How many card games and horse races and other wagering would he have to engage in before he earned back the total amount? It was a game.

Nothing more.

Adrian and Newton completed all the arrangements and shook hands. When Adrian walked back to the Strand, the sun was peeking through the clouds. He headed in the direction of waiting hackney coaches, feeling both exhilarated and deflated.

The next morning from the drawing-room window, Lydia watched Mr Newton leave her townhouse. As soon as he stepped onto the pavement, he was accosted by a throng of newspaper men. Mr Newton pushed his way through them, waving a hand and shaking his head.

She breathed a sigh of relief. Mr Newton had not stopped to talk to the newspaper men. She ought to have known. Mr Newton had not breathed a word of how distressed Wexin's finances had been, and still were. It appeared Mr Newton would also not discuss this reversal of her misfortune, this restoring of her finances.

It was too remarkable to be true. Her widow's portion was restored and the house was securely hers. She had income and a place to live.

Lydia hugged herself and twirled around for joy. The news was too good to keep to herself a moment longer. She dashed out of the room and hurried down the stairs.

"Dixon!" she cried. "Mary! Oh, get Cook! I have something to tell you!"

Mary leaned over the second-floor banister above her. "What is it? What has happened?"

Lydia called up to her. "Come! I will tell you all." She flew down the stairs to the hall.

Dixon appeared from the back staircase, trailed by Cook wiping her hands on her apron and looking frightened.

Lydia ran up to the woman and gave her a squeeze. "Do not worry. It is good news."

"Good news from Mr Newton, my lady?" Dixon looked sceptical. There had, after all, been so much bad news from him.

Lydia clasped her hands together. "Oh, it is so unbelievable. It must have been my sister—"

Who else but her sister? Lydia had no indication that her letters had reached her parents. No one else knew of her distressed finances. No one but—

Adrian.

It was unthinkable that he would pay such sums. Ridiculous, even. Her sister's husband was extremely wealthy. Her sister must have convinced him to do this in secret.

"Tell us, m'lady," Mary cried.

Lydia took a breath. "Mr Newton informed me that someone—it must have been my sister—has restored my widow's portion and has signed the house and its contents over to me! Mr Newton assures me the interest on the six-percents will give us income enough!"

"Oh, my lady!" Mary exclaimed.

"May God be praised." Cook fell to her knees. "We can buy food!"

Lydia grabbed her hands and pulled her to her feet. "Food

and coal and whatever we need!" She turned to the butler. "Will you find our servants, Dixon? Hire those who wish to return and pay the others what we owe them?"

Dixon beamed. "It will be my pleasure."

Still holding Cook's hands, Lydia swung her around in a circle. "Everything shall be as it was!"

Not precisely as it was, but so much better than she thought her future ever could be when she'd risen from her bed that morning.

Lydia gave Cook another hug. "We must celebrate today! I even have money to spend! Fifty pounds! We must fill the larder and celebrate!"

"I shall make a dinner fit for King George!" Cook cried.

Lydia swept her arm to include all of them. "We must eat together, though. I insist upon it. Just this once."

"May I suggest, my lady, that I bring up a bottle of champagne from the cellar?" Dixon asked.

"That would be splendid!" Lydia clapped her hands. "Champagne for dinner."

Dixon lifted a finger. "I meant immediately, my lady."

"Yes," cried Lydia. "Mary, find four glasses, and all join me in the morning room."

Lydia walked into the morning room, the small parlour off the hall, a room where callers were often asked to wait until they could be announced.

A sound sent her spinning towards the windows.

Outside the reporters, all abuzz, were all facing the house, craning their necks over the railings to try to see into the room.

With a cry, Lydia drew the curtains.

Her celebration did not include them.

Chapter Five

The certain gentleman, whom we have now identified as Lord C—, and with whom Lady W— was so recently linked, has lately visited several jewellery shops. Will the notorious beauty soon receive some adornment for her widow's attire?—*The New Observer*, November 17, 1818

"Oh!" Lydia threw down the paper and pounded her fist on the table. She picked up the paper again and reread the lines.

Lord C, *The New Observer* said, Lord C, with whom Lady W was so recently linked...

Lord Cavanley. The reporter had discovered it had been Cavanley who had rescued her.

"Ohhhhh." She squeezed her fist tighter. What else had the man discovered?

She read the account again. No hint of Lord Cavanley calling upon her in the rain and definitely no hint of the earlier time she'd spent with him. Adrian would not have betrayed her. Or so she hoped.

She looked through the other papers that Dixon had purchased for her earlier that morning. There was no news of her in either *The Morning Post* or *The Morning Chronicle*, only the silly mention of *Lord C* entering jewellery shops. Likely he was shopping for one of the other women with whom his name was for ever linked.

At least the newspapers said nothing of Mr Newton's visit.

"What is it, m'lady?" Mary bustled into the bedchamber, carrying one of Lydia's day dresses. "I heard you cry out. Is it your ankle?"

"No, not my ankle." Lydia spread her fingers and forced her voice to sound calm.

Mary had brought the newspapers and breakfast to Lydia in her bedchamber. In front of her on the small table were a plate of toast, a cooked egg and a pot of chocolate, the most sumptuous breakfast she'd had in weeks.

Lydia picked up a piece of toast. "I am mentioned in the newspaper again."

"About the money coming to you?" Mary's eyes grew wide.

"No, thank goodness." She bit into her toast.

Mary clucked her tongue. "Mr Dixon told you the doors and the walls were too thick. Those newspaper men could not hear us cheering, I am certain of it, m'lady."

Lydia swallowed. "So far, it appears you are right."

Mary pursed her lips. "What did they write about you?"

Lydia cast her eyes down. "My name is linked to a man, who will buy me jewels."

"They said such things?" Mary cried.

"One paper, that is all."

The maid's brows knitted. "But how can they make up such a story? It isn't right, m'lady."

Lydia gave her a wan smile. "I agree." She sighed. "I sometimes think they will never leave me alone."

Mary's expression turned sympathetic. She lifted the dress. "I brought the pink."

Lydia nodded. "That will do very nicely."

Any dress would do, because Lydia did not intend to go out, nor to have callers. She could wear anything at all, anything but black. Lydia refused to wear black. She refused to mourn for Wexin, refused to even think his given name. He'd been a stranger, really, and one did not formally mourn strangers.

She took another bite of her toast. The jubilation of the previous day was dampened by reading her name in the paper once more.

And the connection to Adrian.

Lydia straightened her spine and took a fortifying sip of chocolate. She would forget all about that episode with Adrian. Soon the newspapers would find someone else with whom to attach her name.

She planned to spend the day perusing the household accounts. Now that she was in control of her money, she intended to spend wisely and never have to worry over money again. First she must learn the cost of ordinary things, such as lamp oil and beeswax and the food for their table. She must learn how to make a budget that included the servants' salaries, taxes on her menservants and the house, and whatever amounts she would be expected to pay throughout a year. It would be like assembling a puzzle, and she enjoyed assembling puzzles.

"My lady?" Mary laid the dress on the bed. "I thought I would go to the shops this morning to purchase the items you requested."

Lydia had asked for pins and also silk thread. She planned to embroider new seat covers for the dining-room chairs. She needed something to keep her fingers busy and to fill her time. To keep her from becoming lonely.

Mary turned to her. "Won't you come? You've not been out in ever so long."

Only a scant few days ago, Lydia thought, but Mary knew that outing had not been for pleasure.

Although Lydia had gained pleasure from it. She glanced at her bed and thought of Adrian.

Lord C in *The New Observer*.

"Not today, Mary." She shook her head, more to remove his image than to refuse Mary's invitation. "I fear I would be followed by the newspaper men."

Mary walked over to the window and peeked through a gap in the curtains. "They are still out there."

Lydia had already seen them loitering near her door.

"I suppose you cannot come with me, then," Mary said.

Lydia smiled at her. "You must purchase something for yourself when you are out. A length of fabric for a new dress, perhaps. Or a pretty hat. I will give you some extra coins."

Mary curtsied. "Thank you, my lady, but I could not—"

"I insist." Lydia stood. "Would you help me dress?"

Samuel stood shivering on the corner of the street where he had a clear view of Lady Wexin's side gate. He had already seen the butler hurry out. Samuel almost followed him, but made a snap decision to remain where he was. He really hoped the maid might come out next.

All the reporters knew that something had made the household jubilant two days previously, but none of them had discovered what it was. It had been noted that Mr Newton, Wexin's solicitor, had called and shortly after whoops of joy were heard. Perhaps the widow had come into more money, but coming into money when one was wealthy was not too interesting.

He needed something more.

The hinges of the gate squeaked, and, as Samuel had hoped, the trim figure of the maid appeared.

In Samuel's experience, maids knew everything that went on in a household and they could often be encouraged to talk about what they knew.

The maid headed towards Berkeley Square. If Samuel hurried, he could catch up with her, but he needed to detour so that neither she nor the other reporters saw him.

He walked to Charles Street and practically ran to Berkeley Square where he caught sight of her just as he'd hoped to do. Keeping a good distance between them, he followed her as she walked to the shops.

It was almost peaceful following her on her errands. Samuel watched her select threads and pins and pieces of lace. She did not hurry at her tasks, but instead examined all the wares at a leisurely pace, as if this excursion was merely for her own pleasure.

Instead of making him impatient, it seemed a treat to watch her. She had a trim little figure, a graceful way of walking, and a sweet way of smiling at the assistants in the shops. Her heart-shaped face was as pale as the finest lady's, fringed by auburn curls that escaped from her bonnet. Her lips were so pink they might have been tinted, but what intrigued him the most were her huge blue eyes.

She filled a large basket with her purchases, adding

bouquets of flowers from the flower vendors until she looked more like a girl who had come from a stroll in a lush garden than a servant about her errands.

When she headed back towards Berkeley Square, Samuel realised he'd not found an opportunity to speak to her, although it somehow had not seemed like time wasted.

When she entered Gunter's Tea Shop, a confectionary in Berkeley Square, he saw his chance. Samuel hurried into the shop behind her.

"A lemon ice, please," she said to the shop assistant. "And six of those." She pointed to marzipan displayed under glass, perfect miniature pears and peaches and apples, confections made from almonds, sugar and egg whites.

He stood behind her, his heart beating a little faster. He could easily see over her head. She was no taller than the level of his chin. She turned and gave him the briefest glance with those big blue eyes. He nodded to her, and she turned away again.

The shop assistant produced the lemon ice and packed the marzipan into a box, tying it with string. The maid handed the shop assistant her coins. When she walked past Samuel he had a whiff of lemon from the lemon ice, but also a hint of lavender.

He stepped up to the counter. "A lemon ice, as well." He wanted to ask the shop assistant to be quick about it, but held his tongue.

The maid took her time leaving the shop, admiring the delectable fare displayed under glass on both sides of the aisle. He'd nearly had a chance to speak to her and still might if the shop assistant hurried with his lemon ice.

His quarry walked out of the door.

"Your ice, sir." The shop assistant handed over the dish.

Samuel threw down his coin and hurried out after the maid. As he'd hoped, she was seated on a bench near a tree, her basket beside her. He sauntered over.

He nodded to her again. "I see you, like me, could not resist a lemon ice even on this chilly day."

She glanced up, a spoonful in her hand, "That is so," she said softly. She shivered prettily as she swallowed it.

Samuel dipped his spoon in the treat, taking a generous portion and swallowing it at once. Pain seized his entire chest.

"Oh, that hurt," he gasped. "Did you ever do that? Swallow something cold and have it feel as if someone had punched you in the chest?"

She glanced at him, looking uncertain as to whether to speak to him. "You should take it a little at a time," she finally said.

After dipping his spoon into the ice again, he lifted it to show her the tiny portion before letting it slide slowly down his throat. He grinned at her. "That was a great deal more pleasant."

She glanced at him again and turned her attention back to her own lemon ice.

He took another spoonful. "I am Mr Samuel…Charles," he said, taking the name of the street that had been his detour in following her. "I know it is forward of me to speak to you, but I am new to London. I do think it is so much nicer to share the eating of such a treat as an ice, than to eat it alone, do you not agree?"

She nodded ever so slightly and shifted in her seat, knocking the box of marzipan out of her basket.

Samuel picked it up and put it back in.

"Thank you, sir," she said, briefly meeting his gaze.

"Will you be eating all that marzipan alone?" he asked.

She smiled. "Oh, no, sir. It is my treat for my lady and the others."

"For your lady?"

She nodded again, but with less reserve. "I am a lady's maid, sir."

"Do you always bring your lady such delicacies?" He kept his tone soft and friendly. It was not difficult to do with such a sweet and pretty girl.

She smiled at him. "Oh, no, but it is my treat. We are celebrating today."

His brows rose and his heart accelerated. "Celebrating? And what do you have to celebrate? Something wonderful?"

Her smile widened and her eyes sparkled and, for a moment, Samuel forgot everything but how charming she looked. "We are celebrating good fortune!"

"Good fortune?" By his tone he encouraged her to go on.

She merely nodded happily and scraped the last of her lemon ice from her dish. She picked up the basket and stood.

He quickly finished his own ice. "Allow me to return your dish for you." He reached for it and his glove scraped hers.

"Thank you, sir." Her eyes caught his again.

He continued to peer into their depths. "Would…would you like to share a lemon ice again? I could meet you right here whenever you say."

Her expression turned serious, but she did not look away. Finally she answered him. "Saturday. Around one o'clock? I think my lady might not mind."

His smile was genuine. "I will be delighted. It…it pleases me to have a friend with whom to share my lemon ice."

Her lashes fluttered and her face flushed pink. Before he could say another word, she curtsied and hurried off.

Samuel watched her rush away before he returned the dishes to the tea shop. He had not wormed very much out of her, but more would come.

Saturday at one o'clock.

He was surprised at how much he looked forward to sharing another lemon ice with her.

Adrian opened his eyes to bright daylight illuminating his bedchamber. He twisted around in the bed linens to look at the clock on the mantel.

It was about to chime two o'clock.

He groaned and swung his legs over the side of the bed.

His valet appeared. "Do you rise now, m'lord?"

Adrian rubbed his face, wondering how his man always seemed to know the instant he awoke. "I suppose."

Dawn had been showing its first glimmer of light when Adrian walked home from the gambling den where he'd spent the night hours at a table of whist. His profits had not been spectacular, but, then, he had not been as keen at keeping track of cards. Too many other thoughts intruded.

Every win, every loss, was measured against the sum he had given to Lydia and, thus, he'd kept her constantly in his thoughts, distracting him, leaving him feeling unsettled.

Hammond stood next to the bed, holding his banyan so that Adrian had no choice but to stand and be assisted into the garment. He padded over to the basin, not surprised that the water in the pitcher was warm. How Hammond accomplished having warm water no matter what the hour of Adrian's rising was another unfathomable mystery.

Adrian splashed water on his face and brushed his teeth, then sat so that Hammond could shave him. Same as he had done the day before and the day before. Boredom was a dreadful thing. What did one do when that which once relieved boredom now merely added to it? Hammond left to prepare Adrian's breakfast while Adrian finished washing up.

He walked into his drawing room where Hammond had prepared a table for him with slices of cold ham, cheese, bread and jam. There was also a fresh pot of hot coffee and copies of the morning newspapers.

Adrian sipped his coffee while looking through the papers. He came to an article in *The New Observer*:

The certain gentleman, whom we have now identified as Lord C—, and with whom Lady W—was so recently linked, has lately visited several jewellery shops...

Adrian sat up. *Good God.*

This was Reed's newspaper. Reed had identified him.

Adrian turned hot with fury.

The damned man had probably followed him, as well.

If Adrian caught Reed following him again, there would be hell to pay and he'd see Reed paid it.

How much did the man know? Adrian perused the column again and blew out a relieved breath. Reed thought he'd been purchasing jewels.

It was nearly half past three before Adrian ventured out. For wont of any other place to go, he headed towards White's. The air felt damp as if rain was in the offing, and other pedestrians on the street seemed to keep their heads down. To Adrian, the cold was bracing and it felt good to walk at a fast clip.

He was almost invigorated by the time he walked into

White's, but, as soon as he stepped into the coffee room, he knew something was wrong.

The room was quiet and the gentlemen present were whispering among themselves or keeping their eyes downcast. Adrian saw Tanner sitting alone at one of the tables. He crossed the room to him.

"Who the devil died?" he asked.

Tanner looked up and gave him an ironic smile. "Actually, the Queen."

Adrian dropped into a chair. "My God. I was merely joking."

The Queen had been ailing for some time, and news of her condition was printed often in the newspapers. She'd been convalescing at Kew Palace for some time. Even lately, she'd been reported taking the sun in the garden.

"When did you hear?" Adrian asked.

"Not more than an hour ago." Tanner took a sip of coffee. "She died at one o'clock, it was said."

Adrian signalled the attendant. "Tea, please."

Tanner lifted a newspaper that had been lying on the table in front of him. "Did you see this?"

It was a copy of *The New Observer*.

"I read it."

Tanner twirled his finger. "Before news of the Queen arrived, they were all speculating about who was this Lord C *The New Observer* writes of."

Adrian kept his eyes steady. "*The New Observer* writes of a Lord C?"

Tanner tapped the paper. "It does. *Lord C—*, it said… *Lord C—, with whom Lady W— was so recently linked.*" Tanner grinned. "You don't suppose he means Lord Cavanley, now do you?"

Adrian made himself roll his eyes. "Of course, *you* would think of me. Not Lord Crawford or Carlisle or Crayden."

Tanner feigned being offended. "I would expect you would tell me before it appeared in the newspaper. I mean, we are friends and there is, of course, my recent connection to Wexin."

This was the moment that Adrian ought to tell Tanner the whole—only he could not quite bring himself to open his mouth.

"I was about to head off to Gentleman Jack's," Tanner said. "Come with me."

The moment passed. "Very well."

A good bout of fisticuffs would not hurt.

When they were outside, Adrian asked Tanner, "I know you have been concerned about Lady Wexin. What do you think this newspaper report means?"

Tanner shook his head in dismay. "I cannot know. After our return to London, Marlena and I sent Lady Wexin a note asking if we could call upon her, but she refused."

Adrian walked several steps in silence. Here was another moment for him to tell Tanner of his encounter with Lydia.

"How is Lady Tannerton?" he said instead. "I do hope she is well."

Tanner smiled, but it seemed to Adrian that the smile was meant for Tanner's wife. "She is splendid, Pom. She is splendid." He stared off into the distance for a moment before glancing back at Adrian. "Lady Heronvale has taken her under her wing. They are making calls to other ladies today."

"Good of Lady Heronvale."

Tanner turned pensive. "I suppose there will be much involved with the Queen's funeral. I wonder if Marlena will be up to all the pomp so soon."

After what Tanner's wife had been through already, Adrian

suspected a royal funeral would seem like a simple ride through Hyde Park. "She'll do splendidly."

Tanner laughed. "Pom, I am so unused to this. I feel amazingly at loose ends. I have become so accustomed to being at her side."

Adrian, at least, knew precisely how it felt to be at loose ends.

He clapped Tanner on the shoulder. "Then it is good that I am with you. Let us beat each other to a bloody pulp at Gentleman Jack's, and we will both be certain to feel better."

Chapter Six

The Ceremonial for the Internment of her late Most Excellent Majesty Queen Charlotte of blessed memory, will take place in the Royal Chapel of St George at Windsor, on this day, Wednesday of the second day of December, 1818.—*The New Observer*, December 2, 1818

Lydia stood at her window watching the carriages roll by. It looked as if the funeral procession for the Queen had begun in Mayfair, rather than Windsor. Most of the peerage, it seemed, would be in the procession for the Queen.

She felt apart from it all, separated from the life into which she had been born. It was true that wives and daughters of peers would not be greatly in attendance at the funeral, but they would have been intimately involved in conversations about its planning and would hear every detail of the ceremonial at the end of the day. She had no one with whom to converse about it.

One fine carriage after another rumbled by, the gentlemen wearing tall black beaver hats or plumed regimentals just visible through the carriage windows.

Would Adrian be among them?

Lydia groaned. She ought not to think of him, but with her empty days it seemed he came much too often into her mind. Even when she ventured to Piccadilly Street to browse in Hatchard's or to purchase jams at Fortnum and Mason, she found herself searching for him among the passers-by.

At least now she was able to walk to the shops unmolested. The reporters had vanished from her doorway when it became known that the ailing Queen had reached the end of her suffering. Lydia could not be glad the beloved Queen had died, but she was ecstatic that the reporters' attention had turned towards the King, the Prince Regent and the Royal Dukes and Princesses. The newspapers were filled with every step the royals took. Speculation was rampant about the Queen's will and the fact that she had only recently composed the document. Who would she remember in her will? And who would she leave out?

The Queen had always seemed like a formidable figure to Lydia. She had shaken in terror when she'd been presented to the Queen during the Season of her come-out. Lydia imagined all sorts of mishaps, like tripping on her skirt or losing one of the huge feathers she wore in her hair. When it had been her turn to be announced to the Queen, Lydia had been convinced she would faint, but somehow she'd made her approach and performed a graceful, if overly practised, curtsy.

The Queen had actually spoken to her. "Why, you are quite a beauty," Her Majesty had said. "Quite a beauty."

Lydia smiled at the memory of herself, so young and giddy and full of hope. It had been a time when she'd dreamed of love and marriage and children.

It had been a long time ago.

"Thank you, Your Majesty," she said aloud, curtsying again, just as she'd done that day.

Lydia had dressed in black today. She'd wear black to honour the dear Queen. She turned to leave her bedchamber and to make her way to the morning room where her breakfast would be served.

When she entered the corridor, the sweet sound of Mary humming a happy tune reached her ears. Lydia smiled.

Two weeks ago Mary had met a young man who'd put stars in her eyes and a skip in her step. Mary had seen the fellow only twice, when Lydia gave her permission to spend a little time to meet him at Gunter's, where they shared some treat together. Those two meetings had been enough to keep the girl humming through all the other days.

"You must be thinking of your young man," Lydia said when Mary came into view.

Mary blushed. "Oh, I suppose I should not hum on such a sad day. I do beg pardon, my lady."

"Do not be silly, Mary," Lydia scolded. "It is perfectly acceptable for you to be happy."

It was more than acceptable. It was the one bright spot in Lydia's life.

Mary beamed. "Well, I am very happy and that is the truth."

Lydia reached out and touched the girl's hand. "And I am happy for you."

Lydia turned to walk down the stairs. As she descended she heard Mary's cheerful tune again and almost felt like humming herself.

But a wave of queasiness came over her, so strong she almost missed a step. She grasped the banister to keep from falling.

She'd had such a feeling before, but that had been when she—

No. It could not be. It must not be.

"I'm hungry, that's all," she said aloud, although the thought of food made her stomach roil again. She pressed a hand to it and walked more slowly to the morning room.

She glanced at the food set out on a little table in a spot where the sunlight shone in from the window. The fare was simple. A pot of chocolate, a cooked egg, toast and jam, but her stomach rebelled at the sight. She took deep breaths and walked over to the window to wait for the nausea to subside.

There were still plenty of coaches rumbling by to entertain her. From this window it was easier to see the crests on the sides of the carriages. She recognised some of them. They were numerous enough to form a queue on her street, all waiting for the traffic to clear at South Audley Street, she supposed.

A fine shiny black town carriage came to a stop directly in front of her house. She examined the crest, but did not know to whom it belonged. Her gaze lifted to the window of the carriage. There staring back at her was Adrian. He nodded to her, and she quickly stepped back out of sight.

"By Jove, I believe that is Lady Wexin at the window." Adrian's father leaned over him to see better, but Lydia had already disappeared. "Did you see her?"

"I was not looking at the windows," Adrian lied.

He'd seen her. His stomach muscles had clenched when his eyes met hers, like some besotted whelp in his first infatuation, but she'd quickly stepped away when he acknowledged her.

The message was clear. She had no wish to see him, even by accident.

"I am certain it was she." His father leaned over him to get another look, but Adrian could have told him she would not show herself again, not while their carriage stood in front of her house. "Cannot mistake her. She is a beauty, that one. Can see why Wexin wanted her."

"Mmm," responded Adrian, not wishing to encourage this turn in their conversation.

It was merely his vanity that was wounded when she did not smile at him or nod in return, nothing more. Besides, not every woman he met wanted him. Why would they? He did not want every woman he met, including Lady Denson, the widow who seemed to appear at any society affair he attended.

"Did you hear?" His father chuckled. "Bets have been placed in White's book on the identity of this Lord C who was connected with Lady Wexin in the newspapers."

Adrian glanced over at him in surprise. "Indeed?" He'd hoped the story would have been forgotten in the wake of the Queen's death.

His father lifted a finger. "Odds are on Crayden, you know."

"Crayden?" Adrian should have been glad his father had not named him, but why Crayden, who was an impoverished Irish Viscount?

His father shrugged. "Word is he was a suitor of hers before Wexin. Never married. Needs the money from her dowry and a rich father-in-law as much as Wexin did."

It ought not to matter to Adrian, but this news depressed him, even though he knew he was the Lord C of *The New Observer*'s story. He also knew her financial situation was not likely to attract Crayden, if the man knew of it, that is.

Betting on her at White's didn't please Adrian either. He disliked this manner of attention on her. She did not deserve it. Wexin had been the villain, not Lydia.

Adrian had discovered that Lydia had hired back most of her servants. Or rather his valet had discovered it at Adrian's request. He had no idea how his man had accomplished it, but within a day Hammond had produced the information of how many servants had been dismissed originally and how many had returned. The number was sufficient to ensure her comfort.

He leaned back against the padded upholstery, trying to feel some satisfaction in having helped her.

The coach lurched forwards, the unexpected motion causing both father and son to grip the seats.

His father frowned. "I do hope the springs in this carriage are up to a trip of this length. I do not relish being jostled about."

This was Adrian's first ride in the elegant carriage bearing the Earl of Varcourt's crest. "It is a damned sight better than the last hack I rode in."

His father huffed. "Why you ride in those things is a mystery to me. Our old coach is at your disposal any time you require it."

"That is generous of you, sir." Adrian's father was always generous.

This carriage did have a tendency to sway to and fro in a manner as lulling as a ship in gentle waters. After leaving the busy streets of London, they lapsed into silence. His father dozed and Adrian lost himself in thoughts that seemed as unfocussed as his life. The day promised to be long and tedious, but it was their duty to be present at the Queen's funeral.

"When duty calls, a gentleman must always rise to do what

is required of him," his father always said. And always added, "So enjoy life while you can, my son."

His father would deny it, but Adrian knew he relished doing his duty in whatever form it took, and probably had enjoyed it even from his youth, when he inherited the family title. Adrian's father was a man who could be counted upon to do what must be done, but he also tended to glorify what he'd missed, the chance to be a frivolous, pleasure-seeking youth. His father could not fathom how such trivialities could grow tiresome over time.

When they reached Kew Palace there was a jumble of carriages, cavalry and foot soldiers, royal grooms and pages. Also in attendance were the royal physicians and countless other members of the royal entourage. Somehow this multitude sorted itself into a dignified and orderly procession, moving solemnly towards Windsor and St George's Chapel.

The procession kept its snail-like pace the whole distance, reaching Houslow Heath shortly after noon and the chapel at seven in the evening. By that time most of the London carriages had turned off, making their way back to town. It was appalling how few peers actually endured the day long enough to attend the Queen's funeral service.

Adrian and his father endured it, as duty demanded. By the time their coach was again pointed in the direction of London, his father's energy had flagged and his rhythmic snores joined with the sound of the horses' hooves and the creaking of the coach's springs.

Adrian stared at the darkness outside, alone again with his thoughts.

What was there to look forward to in the weeks ahead? Within days London would empty, the *ton* fleeing to country houses or the Continent, places where they might find entertainment. With the official mourning of the Queen, the London entertainments would disappear. The theatres were already dark, and no one had hosted a ball or dinner or rout since the mourning commenced.

Adrian supposed he could accept his mother's invitation to spend Christmas at the Varcourt estate. No doubt several of his parents' friends would be in attendance. There would be card playing at night and perhaps he could ride in the mornings. There would be plenty of land to give his horse a good run.

Tanner had invited him to Tannerton, as well, but Adrian had already begged off. He knew Tanner would prefer to be alone with his new wife.

Perhaps he should travel somewhere, somewhere like… Paris.

Yes. Paris would be a novelty. Things were a bit gayer there now than they had been right after the war, he'd heard. More money was pouring in to the city each day. There were plenty of casinos he might visit, as well as the various sites of interest in the city.

Yes, he made the decision. He would go to Paris.

Anywhere to battle this cursed ennui.

Chapter Seven

The notorious Lady W— has gone back into hiding, no longer venturing to visit the shops on Piccadilly or to take walks in Hyde Park. All of London wishes to know why. Could she perhaps be in an interesting condition?—*The New Observer*, April 11, 1819

Adrian sat in the dining room at the townhouse on Curzon Street. While he'd been in Paris, his father had written to him that the Pomroy house would be ready for him on his return. Adrian made arrangements for his belongings to be moved from his rooms near St James's Square, and wrote to tell the servants at the townhouse when to expect him. He'd entered the house he'd known as a child, just the day before this one. It continued to be a curious combination of familiar and strange. Adrian had slept in the room and on the bed he'd always known as his father's and was now seated at the head of the long dining-room table in what seemed like his father's chair.

His family's butler, a man hired by his father years ago,

entered the room. "The newspapers, my lord." The butler even addressed Adrian in the same tone he'd always addressed Adrian's father.

"Thank you, Bilson." Adrian tried at least to sound like himself. He returned his coffee cup to its saucer and took the papers in hand.

He supposed he ought to send an announcement to the papers telling of his return. In fact, Bilson could see that it was done—one of the benefits of having more servants. He had even less to do.

The New Observer happened to be the newspaper on top. Adrian rolled his eyes. Bilson could forgo the subscription to the scandal sheet that had so maligned Lydia.

Adrian took a deep breath and dug his fork into a slice of cold beef. It made no sense to think of Lydia. He'd done an excellent job of forgetting her in Paris. Several high stakes' card games had taken his mind away.

Until he won, that is, and remembered he was replacing funds he had given to her. He had also met a few very pretty French *mademoiselles*, but he could not sustain an interest in them. He attributed this to his general malaise, not to comparing them to Lydia.

Adrian shook his head and skimmed *The New Observer*, its columns full of gruesome murders and titillating affairs.

His gaze caught on the words *the notorious Lady W—*.

Damned paper. What were they saying of her now?

He read on.… *All of London wishes to know… Could she perhaps be in an interesting condition?*

Adrian sprang to his feet, toppling the mahogany chair onto the carpet. "What the deuce is this?"

Bilson stepped in. "Is anything amiss, my lord?"

Newspaper still in hand, Adrian strode towards him. "My hat and gloves, Bilson, and be quick. I'm going out."

Bilson lost no time in retrieving the hat and gloves, and Adrian was on the street in less than a minute. He set a quick pace in the direction of Hill Street and Lydia's house, an easy walk away.

When he reached the street he saw several men clustered around.

Newspaper reporters.

He had half a mind to send them about their business, but that would certainly not remove her name from the papers. It would merely add his. He blew out a frustrated breath. He could not call upon her while the reporters watched who was admitted to her house. He crossed the street.

He thought about calling upon Tanner, but what would he say? Lady Wexin is with child and, if the child is not Wexin's, it might be mine?

Adrian wasn't ready to burden his friend with that information, especially as Tanner had written to him that he and Lady Tannerton were expecting a baby.

Adrian walked past Lydia's house. As he passed by, a gentleman approached it—Lord Levenhorne, holding a newspaper and wearing a determined look upon his face. He was almost immediately swarmed by reporters.

Adrian watched Levenhorne beating them off with his newspaper. Adrian decided to head to White's. With luck, Levenhorne would stop by there, and, when he did, Adrian would be present to hear all about his call upon Lady Wexin.

A soft light diffused through the curtains of the morning room and illuminated the page of the newspaper.

Lydia stared at the words. *Could she perhaps be in an interesting condition?*

A wave of nausea overcame her, not morning sickness this time, but a sickness of another kind. "How could they have discovered this?"

She'd secluded herself ever since the familiar symptoms emerged several months ago—aching breasts, inability to keep food in her stomach, heavy fatigue. Mary had noticed and knew from the start that Lydia was with child. Mary also had witnessed her last miscarriage and knew this child was not Wexin's. The maid had not asked the baby's paternity, though, and Lydia had explained nothing.

Five months had passed and Lydia's figure showed the telltale changes. The other servants now also knew her condition. Lydia trusted her servants had kept this secret. They had been as loyal and caring as a family, but perhaps one of them had slipped and said something to someone and someone had said something to *The New Observer*. Or perhaps that vile reporter, Mr Reed, had decided to make this up and accidentally hit upon the truth.

She heard the murmur of voices outside. Tiptoeing to the window, she peeked through the gap in the curtains. They were out there again, the reporters. She'd been totally free of them ever since the poor Queen had died and had hoped never to see them cluster around her door again. They were back this morning, gathering around a gentleman who flailed at them with a newspaper in one hand and his walking stick in the other.

Lord Levenhorne.

Lydia pressed a hand protectively against the rounded mound of her abdomen. She had never carried a baby inside her this long.

She ought to consider it a tragedy that she'd conceived a child from that one brief moment of making love with Adrian, but she could not. It was a miracle. *A miracle.* One last chance to have a baby. She did not expect to ever have another chance. She would certainly never marry again, even if some man wanted her. She would never again put her life and her future in a man's hands. She pressed her belly again, thankful this child was not Wexin's.

Still, she mourned the loss of his babies, the three little lives she'd been unable to hold inside her long enough. Every morning now, she woke expecting to feel that cramping, that spilling of blood, but this baby still grew within her. She could feel it flutter, blessedly alive.

She wished now she had written to her sister to give her the excellent news. Instead her sister would read it as gossip in the newspapers.

After her money had been restored to her, Lydia had sent her sister a letter of thanks. She'd heard nothing in reply, and her sister's maid told Mary there should be no more correspondence. Lydia still felt she ought to have written to her with the news of her pregnancy.

She wondered if her sister would contact her if she heard from their parents or brother. Lydia had heard nothing, which distressed her greatly. Surely if they were safe, one of their letters would have reached her by now, even if her letters had not reached them.

Lydia heard footsteps approach. She took in a deep breath. Lord Levenhorne could not upset her. Even the vile reporters could not upset her. Not when her baby moved inside her.

"Thank you, Adrian," she whispered to herself. "For such a gift."

Dixon entered the room, his expression distressed.

Lydia saved him from having to inform her who had called. "I know who it is, Dixon. I saw him through the window."

Dixon cleared his throat. "I shall tell him you are not receiving callers if you wish it."

Lydia gave him a reassuring look. "I will see him." She touched her abdomen. "This is no secret, is it, Dixon? He will have to know at some time."

Dixon's features softened. "'Tis no secret, my lady, but we cannot allow his lordship to cause you distress."

She was touched by his concern. "Do not fear. I shall manage nicely."

She followed Dixon out to the hall where Levenhorne paced back and forth. The moment he saw her, he started towards her. "Lady Wexin—"

She extended her hand to him. "How kind of you to call upon me, Lord Levenhorne."

He looked taken aback by the offer of her hand. He shook it, and belatedly gave her the bow politeness required of him.

Lydia turned to Dixon. "We'll have tea, if you please."

Levenhorne blustered, "This is not a social call—"

She swivelled back to her guest. "I would still serve you refreshment, sir. Let us go to the drawing room where we might be more private."

She led him up the stairway into the more formal drawing room with windows so high no reporter could see into them. She settled herself on a sofa and gestured to her guest. "Do sit, sir."

His eyes flashed with impatience, but he lowered himself into the chair opposite her.

"How is Lady Levenhorne?" Lydia made her tone polite,

as if this were indeed a social call. "I have not seen her in an age. Is she in town yet?"

"She is well," he answered curtly. "She is in town."

Most of the *ton* would be in town. The London Season had commenced, as gay as always, since the Regent had ended official mourning for his mother after only six weeks.

"And the children?" Lydia asked.

Levenhorne waved a hand. "They are well. All of them."

"I am delighted to hear it." Lydia made herself look Levenhorne in the eye. "I confess, I had thought to see Lady Levenhorne before this. I had thought perhaps she would call on me."

It was bad manners to point out his wife's neglect—and his—but these people had hurt her. The Levenhornes were related to Wexin, after all. True, Lord Levenhorne had called after Wexin's death, but, like today, only to speak of the inheritance and to ask if she were increasing. Indeed, the only person who'd reached out to her in kindness had been Lady Tannerton, but Lydia had refused to see her. How could she face the widow of the man her husband had murdered, the woman he had framed for the deed?

Lydia felt her baby flutter inside her. She'd forgotten. One other person had called upon her and had been very kind.

Adrian.

Her butler accompanied the footman who carried the tea tray and set it on the table in front of Lydia. She knew Dixon had come out of worry for her.

"Thank you so much." She glanced at Dixon, hoping he knew she thanked him for his concern as well as the tea. "I shall let you know if I require anything else."

Dixon left the room and Lydia looked across at Lord Levenhorne. "How do you take your tea?"

He squirmed in his chair. "With milk. One lump of sugar."

Lydia busied herself with pouring his tea and then handed the cup to him so he was forced to take it from her. She watched him until he took a polite sip before pouring her own cup.

She was proud of herself. A few months ago she might have cowered in front of Lord Levenhorne. That had been when she'd had no money and no child to give her life purpose. He could not frighten her now.

She sipped her tea quietly, not making it easy for him to blast her with what the newspapers implied and her waistline verified.

He put down his tea cup and picked up the newspaper, now creased from having been folded in his hand. "Have you seen this?"

She blinked at him, pretending to be confused. "A newspaper?"

"Blast it," he swore more to himself than at her. "*The New Observer.* Have you seen it today?"

She did not answer directly. "What does it say that distresses you so?" Let him utter the words.

He glanced down at it for a moment, then he tapped it with his finger. "It says you are in an *interesting condition.*"

Lydia made herself laugh. She stood so that her skirt draped against her thickening middle. "I *am* in an interesting condition, as you can see, sir, but I have announced the happy event to no one."

"They know." He tapped the paper again. "It says Lady W."

She lowered herself back into her seat and picked up her cup of tea. "Oh, then it could not possibly be Lady Wilcox or Willingham or Warwick…"

"Come now, they must mean you." He pushed the paper towards her as if that would prove it. "What is the idea of this?"

"Of what?" She gave him her best ingenuous expression.

"Of your—your—your—delicate condition."

She placed a hand on her abdomen. "My baby, do you mean?"

"Of course I mean that!" he cried. "Why was I not told of it? Why must I learn of it from this scurrilous newspaper?"

Lydia took a sip of tea before answering him. "First of all, Lord Levenhorne, I am not at all certain you have learned of *my* condition from a newspaper. Surely your wife knows very well that I have lost other babies. If I preferred not to make any announcement until I was more certain I might carry this baby to term, I cannot see how you can fault me."

His face turned red and he bowed his head.

She went on. "I do appreciate that you have some interest in the information, sir." If she produced a son within ten months of Wexin's death, that son would inherit Wexin's title and estate instead of Lord Levenhorne. "I would have told you as soon as I believed the baby had a chance to survive."

Which was true, but it was also true that she'd wanted to keep the precious news to herself as long as possible.

Levenhorne grimaced as he lifted his head and met her eye. "You cannot tell me this—this—child is Wexin's."

She kept her gaze level, but her heart beat frantically inside her chest. "If my child is not born within the ten months, you have the right to make that statement to me, sir. Not before." She stood. "Do you have anything else you must say to me?"

He rose to his feet, still looking as if he wanted to chew her for breakfast. "You have not heard the end of this."

He might make all the accusations he wished. No matter what she knew to be true, the law stated that this child was Wexin's if born within ten months of his death.

It was not a huge risk she was taking. She'd conceived the

baby only a month after Wexin's death; surely the baby would be born within the ten months. Her prayer was that she could hold the baby inside her long enough for the baby to live. Nothing mattered more to her than birthing a healthy child.

Levenhorne marched out of the room, and Lydia collapsed onto the settee.

"Well, that is done," she murmured, touching her belly where the child that was not Wexin's kicked inside her.

The baby that was Adrian's.

Adrian chose a table in White's coffee room with a clear view of the doorway. Should Levenhorne appear, Adrian would be the first person he encountered. There were very few gentlemen present at this hour, men who had no better place to eat breakfast and no better place to spend their time.

Like him.

He had checked the betting book on his way in. The wagering about which Lord C had been linked with Lydia seemed to have ended with the Queen's death and the exodus from town. His name was still not among the suggested Lord Cs.

He finished two cups of coffee and read all of the newspapers. He read a great deal more than he wished to know about the state of herring fishing as reported to the House of Commons. He read of a terrible fire in corn mills in Chester and of the trial of a former soldier who had robbed the White Horse Inn. The only paper that printed anything about Lydia's condition had been *The New Observer*, and the reporter had been Samuel Reed.

Adrian lifted his head every two minutes to see if Levenhorne had arrived. Eventually he glanced up, and Levenhorne indeed strode in the room, looking like thunder.

Adrian was ready for him. "Good God, Levenhorne. Come tell me what has happened."

The man looked no further into the room, but sat down across from Adrian, a crumpled newspaper in his hand. "Have you read this?" He waved the paper in Adrian's face.

"I've read several papers this morning." This was obvious as they sat in a pile next to his coffee cup. "Which one is that?"

"*The New* blasted *Observer*." Levenhorne signalled the servant who quickly took his request for coffee…and brandy.

"Ah, the gossip newspaper." Adrian responded. "Was there something of you in it?"

Levenhorne shook his head and opened the newspaper, jabbing it with his finger. "Not of me. Of Lady Wexin."

The servant brought his coffee and brandy, and Levenhorne downed the brandy in one gulp. Adrian waited for him to continue.

He added cream and sugar to his coffee and lifted the cup for a sip. "The newspaper said she was increasing. I have just come from calling upon her and it is bloody well true."

"Increasing." Adrian spoke in as non-committal a voice as he could.

"Increasing," repeated Levenhorne. "And if she produces a son within the ten-month period, the title and property go to him."

"And not to you." Adrian made himself take a sip of coffee.

"Not to me."

Adrian gave him what he hoped was a puzzled look. "But I thought you lamented this inheritance, saying Wexin had riddled it with debt."

The man grimaced. "That was before Mr Coutts persuaded

me to fund some rather substantial repairs to the buildings on Wexin's estate and to finance the spring planting."

"Ah," Adrian said.

"Thing is, it is a good piece of property, worthy of the investment. Prime land. Could make an excellent profit." Levenhorne shook his head in dismay. "I had no intention of providing for Lady Wexin's brat, however. Let her father do that. I dare say he can afford it better than I."

"Has her father returned from his tour?" Adrian asked.

Levenhorne shook his head. "Not that I have heard. God knows what has happened to them. No one has heard from them, it is said." He bowed his head. "I'm afraid I was unforgivably rude to Lady Wexin. Said the baby could not be Wexin's."

Adrian took the creased newspaper in his hand and pretended to read it for the first time. "It says nothing of that here."

"I know." Levenhorne tapped his fingers on his coffee cup. "Besides, who else could have fathered the child? The lady is a recluse."

But not by her desire. Because the society whose darling she once had been had turned its back on her. And Adrian knew precisely who else could have fathered the child.

Levenhorne's eyes widened. "I say, Cavanley. You will say nothing of this, will you? I'd prefer no one knew I spent good money on that blasted estate. I probably ought not to have spoken so plainly."

Adrian waved a hand. "I'll speak of it to no one, you have my word."

Levenhorne stared into his coffee for what seemed like a long time. "The more I think of it, the more I think that baby is not Wexin's. Too much time has passed. Conception would have to have taken place in October before Wexin travelled to

Scotland. She'd be six months along and, let me tell you, at six months, my wife's belly was always bigger than this lady's."

Adrian frowned. He knew nothing of such matters, but he did know that it had been almost five months to the day that he'd lain with Lydia.

Levenhorne pounded his fist on the table. "She's pulling a fast one on me, I'd wager on it, and she has my hands tied until the ten months is over. Crafty wench. There's not a blasted thing I can do about it." He sighed. "Except hope the baby comes late or she pushes out a girl."

Adrian made himself sit very still lest he launch himself over the table and put a fist into the other man's face.

This child, girl or boy, to which Levenhorne so scathingly referred, might be Adrian's, and Lydia did not deserve to be spoken of in such a coarse manner.

Adrian stood. "Forgive me, Levenhorne. I must be on my way."

Levenhorne glanced up at him again. "I have your word you will tell no one of our conversation?"

"You have my word."

Adrian walked out, collected his hat and gloves and left White's. He headed back into Mayfair, again walking by Lydia's house.

The reporters still clustered. He did not see Samuel Reed, the man who seemed to know more and do more damage than the others.

Adrian continued past the house. He decided he must gain entry in another way besides knocking upon her door in front of the London press. He'd return when daylight was gone, and somehow, some way, he'd speak to Lydia before the dawn of a new day.

* * *

Reed stood near Lady Wexin's side gate. Night was falling and he waited with anticipation for Mary to appear.

Sweet Mary. He liked meeting her this way, in secret, at a time he might pull her into a dark corner and steal a few kisses. He liked it a bit too much, knowing he must eventually cut off the liaison. He just hoped he could do it without her discovering his true purpose for romancing her. Dear sweet Mary. He despised the idea of causing her that kind of hurt.

He heard the familiar creak of the gate and stepped out from the shadows. She ran towards him, propelling herself into his arms.

"Oh, Samuel, I am so glad to see you," she cried against his chest.

She was hatless and wore only a thin knitted shawl over her dress to ward off the evening's chill. He wrapped his arms around her tighter.

"I am glad to see you, too," he responded truthfully. She smelled so clean. Of lavender and soap.

She clung to him. "I have had the most wretched day!"

He kissed her on top of her head, his heart beating faster. "Tell me what has happened."

"Well, the reporters are back." She moved out of his embrace and rearranged her shawl. "One of them wrote something in the newspaper, and now they are all back."

"What did he write?" As if Samuel did not know.

Her hand fluttered to her forehead. "I do not know, really, but it upset m'lady."

He reached for her again. "Is that all it is? Newspaper reporters?"

She didn't fall back into his arms as he'd hoped. "And then his lordship came."

"His lordship?" Samuel felt a rush of excitement.

"Lord Levenhorne. He inherits Lord Wexin's estate." She paused. "Unless…"

"Unless what?"

She shook her head and her curls bounced around her face. "Oh, I do not understand all this. I just know m'lady is made unhappy by it."

He took her in his arms once again. "Do not fret, love. Is it about money? Wealthy people seem always to distress themselves about money."

She snuggled against him. "I suspect so. It is about the inheritance at any rate."

She felt so good next to him that he could hardly think and hardly wanted to. Mary had never actually told him Lady Wexin was going to have a child, but she'd skirted around the topic enough for him to guess.

Mary lifted her face and looked at him with her huge, trusting eyes. Samuel felt a twinge of conscience for pressing her. Enough for one night. He could concentrate on Lord Levenhorne next and just enjoy being with Mary for a while.

He dipped his head and touched his lips to hers, so soft and sweet.

Yes, he would enjoy these stolen kisses with Mary. He would enjoy them very much.

Chapter Eight

Does she hide out of shame? What would it be like, we wonder, Dear Readers, to carry the child of a murderer in one's womb? —*The New Observer*, April 11, 1819

Adrian watched the maid locked in the embrace of her lover. The two stumbled into the garden, still in each other's arms.

They had left the gate slightly open. Adrian stole over and peeked in. The lovers were headed for a far corner, away from the house.

Adrian had planned to knock at the front door, to be announced to Lydia properly even if the hour was unforgivably late, but one of the newspapers had left a young fellow watching the house, so Adrian had walked on by. He turned the corner just when the maid and her lover had wrapped their arms around each other.

It was all too easy. Adrian slipped through the gap in the gate and crept through the shadows to the back door. When he reached the door, it was unlatched.

He walked in, still intending to announce himself.

Sounds came from the kitchen, but when he peeked in, he could see no one. He continued to the stairs, climbing them as quietly as he could and opening the door a crack to see if anyone was in the hall.

Empty.

He ought to call out. Announce his presence.

Instead he climbed the marble stairs and saw a glow of light coming from the drawing room. Taking in a breath and holding it, he opened the door.

Lydia rose from a chair near the window, book in hand. An oil lamp on the table next to her gave more illumination than the waning daylight through the glass. The lamp lit her face with a soft glow, making her hair appear tinged with gold where the light touched it.

He had forgotten how lovely she was.

She gasped and dropped her book.

He stepped into the light. "Forgive me, Lydia, I know I intrude."

"Adrian!" Her voice was breathless. She took a step forwards as if glad to see him, but she quickly shrank back. "Why didn't Dixon announce you?"

"He does not know I am here." He gave a rueful smile. "I fear no one knows I am here. I truly did intrude, Lydia. I entered without anyone seeing me."

"Without anyone seeing you?" She picked up her book, closing it and placing it on the table.

"I entered through the back door." He did not wish to get the maid into trouble. "One of your servants stepped out for a moment, and I came in unseen." Saying it made him realise how outrageously he'd acted.

She looked rightfully indignant. "You *sneaked* into my house?"

"I know it sounds bad," he said with chagrin. "But there was a fellow watching the front door. From a newspaper, I expect." He paused, feeling as if he was not making sense. "Otherwise I would have knocked for admittance."

She held up a hand, stopping his explanation. "Never mind. Tell me why you are here when I asked you not to call upon me again."

"The newspaper this morning—" he began.

She swung away. "That—that—*horrid* paper."

In the low light and with her loose dress, he could not perceive any telltale changes signalling her condition. If anything, her figure appeared even more voluptuous than he remembered, as if she'd had enough food to eat.

"Is it true?" he asked.

She turned her head to him. "Is what true?"

He could think of no delicate way to say it. "Are you increasing?"

She blinked rapidly. "That is a very private matter, not one to discuss with a gentleman I hardly know."

He walked closer to her. "But it is how you know me that makes it my business. At least to ask."

Her breathing accelerated.

"Lydia?"

"You need not concern yourself, Adrian. I am well able to handle whatever my situation might be." She lifted her chin. "I am not as forlorn as when you first encountered me."

And he had been the one to take away her pitiable state, even if she would never know it. "I am glad of it."

She met his gaze steadily. "So there is no reason for you to come here."

She looked elegant and regal, even though her dress was a simple one more suited to morning. Her hair was piled in a loose knot on top of her head, tendrils escaping to caress her forehead and cheeks. He remembered how soft her curls had felt, slipping loose and luxuriously through his fingers. Even now he itched to pull the pins from her hair so that it would fall about her shoulders and he could grab a fistful in his hand.

He forced himself to his task. "Lydia, cut line. Are you going to have a child or not?"

He walked close enough to touch her. If he could place his hand on her belly he might feel for himself if a child grew within her. That would, he supposed, be even more of an intrusion than entering her house.

She raised her eyes to his, and he felt a jolt of attraction, the same attraction he'd been unable to resist when she'd asked him to make love to her. He waited for her to speak, his heart beating so hard, he thought she must be able to hear it.

She said nothing.

He tried again. "If the child is mine, Lydia, I will do my duty."

"Your duty?" Her voice rose. "What do you mean by your duty?"

His emotions were in a muddle about this, but he was enough of his father's son to know what was expected of a gentleman. "Marriage, if you should wish it."

"Marriage!" She spat out the word and quickly turned her face from him, silent for so long he had an impulse to prowl the room like a caged cat. Finally she cast her gaze upon him again. "Do you expect me to believe you would marry me?"

Why not? he wondered. "I am an honourable man, Lydia."

She gave a scoffing laugh. "You are a libertine, Adrian. Libertines do not marry."

Her words stung. "A libertine? And how is it you are so certain I am a libertine?"

"It is what people say of you. They call you a rake, at least, which is the same thing, is it not?"

He was not about to debate the differences between a rake and a libertine. His eyes narrowed. "You of all people should know not to give credit to gossip."

She glanced away, two spots of colour rising to her cheeks. "It is, nonetheless, all I know of you. I have no experience to tell me otherwise."

He waved his hand as if erasing that piece of conversation. "It matters not what you believe of me. If the child is mine, I will take responsibility, and that means marrying you, if that is what you desire."

Lydia glanced away, her muscles taut with anxiety. The *ton*'s most devil-may-care bachelor said he would marry her out of duty. She almost wished to laugh. The last thing in the world she desired was another marriage. She'd married once with stars in her eyes and look what a horror that husband had turned out to be.

But Adrian was not Wexin.

She darted a glance to him, so handsome, standing so tall and still. Masculine energy emanated from him, and, God help her, attracted her.

She'd be a fool to give in to the desire that pulsated inside her, a fool to entrust her life—and her child's—to any man.

She took in a fortifying breath. "There is no need for you to do anything, Adrian. There is no responsibility that I would hold you to."

He stepped away and bowed his head, seemingly lost in thought.

It would be so easy to simply lie and tell him the child was Wexin's, but she could not make herself say the words.

Think of what the newspapers would write about her if she married him and acknowledged the child as his. The world would know that she'd bedded a man before her husband was cold in his grave.

Her indiscretion had been the cause of this pregnancy. That made it her problem to handle, not Adrian's. If her child was born within the ten months stipulated by law, the child, son or daughter, would be considered Wexin's, but she would be in charge of her finances and her life.

She made herself look directly at Adrian again, even though looking at him made her heart leap and flutter and her body yearn for him. She could not forget how his hands had felt upon her, the softness of his lips, the firmness of his muscles. Her carnal urges flared into life and it was all she could do to keep from propositioning him again.

Dear God, she could not possibly want to couple with him again, not when she was hiding that this child was his.

"You need not have an attack of conscience or duty or whatever it is that men have," she said to him in an angry voice, although the anger was at herself for her weakness, not at him. "It is quite all right with me if you forget this matter."

He met her gaze and she thought she saw a wounded look in his eyes. "I have done nothing to deserve your bitter tone."

Her cheeks flamed at the truth of his statement, but she recovered quickly. "Nothing?" She hit him with the one dishonourable thing he had done. "I asked you not to call upon me again, and you break into my home like a thief."

"I did it to find out about the child," he shot back, taking a step towards her, coming so close she caught the clean scent of lime soap on his skin.

She held her ground with difficulty. "Is it so hard to believe that this baby is my husband's?"

His voice turned so low it vibrated inside her. "It is when I know there is a chance it is mine."

"Believe me, Adrian," she whispered, "it is not so easy for me to conceive a child that I would conceive after one time." At least it had not been that easy with Wexin. She softened her tone. "Take your leave. You have done enough by coming here. There is nothing I need from you."

To her surprise, he reached out to her and gently touched her arm. "Forgive me for not knowing. I have been abroad. They say you have been a recluse. Are you not going out at all? Is there no one who has renewed acquaintance with you?"

She was startled by his concern. Besides Lord Levenhorne calling today, and the occasional bank representative, no one but Adrian had called upon her. "No member of the *ton* wishes to see their name in the newspapers, I suspect."

He frowned. "You must not allow the newspapers to make you a prisoner in your house. Go where you please and ignore them."

He could say that with ease. He was not the one followed about, or stopped on the street and asked rude questions.

She glanced at his hand, still upon her arm, then back at him. "I am not certain I should heed advice from an intruder."

He did not take the hint and release her. "Then accept the advice as from a friend," he said. "Our connection may be brief and… unusual, but enough for me to be concerned for your welfare. I am here, if you need me. I will come, if you need me to."

She held her breath.

His words felt like a proposition, an invitation to seduction. His touch melted her like a flame melts wax. She felt she would only have to put her arms around his neck and her lips against his and in a moment they would be making love on the settee. God help her, she did need him. She needed to feel him hold her with strong arms, needed to run her hands up his firm chest, to dig her fingers into his hair. She needed to feel him fill her again, as a man fills a woman. She trembled with need.

But she backed away. "I need nothing from you."

He stared at her, a hint of pain in his angry eyes. Her guilt escalated. Obviously he had not shared her carnal thoughts.

He swung away and started walking towards the door. It felt the same as when he had left her before, loneliness engulfing her.

He reached the door and turned back to her. "I will trouble you no further."

As he disappeared into the dark hallway, she collapsed in her chair and placed her hand over where his baby grew.

Adrian went straight to Madame Bisou's, a gaming hell he knew on Bennet Street. He and Tanner had often spent a night at the tables there, and Adrian had been known to flirt with the pretty girls Madame Bisou employed.

When he walked into the gaming room looking more for a drink than a seat at a table, a voice greeted him. "Pomroy!"

A flaming red-haired young woman wearing a dress of ice blue ran over to him and grabbed his arm.

"Katy Green." He kissed her on the cheek. "But it is not Pomroy. It is Cavanley."

She laughed. "I forgot. Sir Reginald told me about you being called lord now."

She released him and examined him with her elbows akimbo and a line creasing her forehead. "I declare, you look healthy enough. I thought you must be very ill. You have not been here in an age."

He had not been to Madame Bisou's since the previous spring, and it seemed a lot had happened since then. "I've been in France." France was as good an explanation as any.

She grinned at him and winked. "Wait until Madame Bisou hears. You will make her homesick."

The closest the *madame*, born Penny Jones, had come to France had been drinking a bottle of champagne and he and Katy both knew it.

Katy took his arm again and escorted him through the room where the tables were covered with green baize. Three of the walls were lined with faro and hazard tables. Against the fourth wall one of the girls served drinks.

"What are you looking to play tonight?" Katy asked him. "Faro? Hazard?"

He rolled his eyes. "Fool's games." Luck, not skill, made winners in hazard and faro, and luck always favoured the house. "What I really want is a brandy."

"Brandy!" she cried. "Come with me."

He was soon sipping the burning liquid, but it failed to ease the hard rock of emotion inside him.

He'd done his duty by offering to marry Lydia. He ought to be glad he'd escaped marriage. The parson's mousetrap, he and Tanner used to call it, but it nagged at him that she did not think him worthy of marrying. *A libertine*, she had called him. And she wanted nothing to do with him.

It also nagged at him that she'd not actually denied that the child was his. He only knew she did not wish him to be her husband. Why had she not accepted his proposal? He was wealthy. He came from a good family.

Adrian finished the brandy, took another, and answered his own question. She had no wish to be married to a *libertine*.

He could not blame her for that opinion of him. He'd cultivated the reputation of a rake, even if it had never been entirely accurate. He did not trifle with women's hearts. His liaisons with women involved mutual desire, and their partings were mostly amicable.

He finished the second brandy in one gulp and asked for another.

Katy's eyes grew wide. "Oh, ho, you are thirsty tonight."

He extended his glass again for the girl to refill. "Very thirsty. Thirsty enough to get thoroughly drunk."

"Oooh. That must mean a problem with the ladies."

He downed the third glass and thrust his hand out once more. "Have you not heard, Katy Green? Libertines do not have problems with ladies."

At a proper morning hour, Samuel Reed waited in a small parlour off the hall of Lord Levenhorne's townhouse, a place where, undoubtedly, tradesmen and other men who toiled for a living waited for his lordship. Samuel did not resent it. He was only grateful that he had not been summarily ejected.

After at least a quarter of an hour, a footman entered. "Lord Levenhorne will see you now."

Samuel was led to the library, where Lord Levenhorne sat behind an elegant desk with thin carved legs and made of some dark wood—mahogany or oak, perhaps.

"Mr Reed, m'lord," the footman said before bowing and leaving the room.

When Levenhorne looked up, Samuel bowed as well. "Thank you for seeing me, my lord."

"What business do you have with me, Reed? Your card tells me you are from that *New Observer* paper." Lord Levenhorne sounded none too pleased.

But he had agreed to see Samuel, so that gave him courage. "If you read my paper, sir, you will know that I am following the story of Lady Wexin—"

Levenhorne coughed. "I've seen what you wrote."

Samuel nodded. "I wonder, my lord, what you can tell me about the lady. My sources inform me that she is to bear a child—"

"That, unfortunately, appears to be true—" Levenhorne seemed to catch himself. He stopped talking and peered more closely at Samuel. "These are family matters, Reed. Not the stuff for newspapers."

Samuel took the liberty of advancing one step closer. "Ah, but I have a reporter's sense, and I believe there is a story in Lady Wexin." He gave Levenhorne an intent look. "If she produces a son, he will inherit Wexin's property and title, is that not correct?"

"Such as it is," the man murmured just loud enough for Samuel to hear him.

"And you will inherit if she produces a daughter, or if the child is not born in time."

"That is so," Levenhorne said in a careful voice.

"If this child is not Wexin's, however…"

Levenhorne leaned forwards. "What do you know?"

The man was interested. Samuel had him. Levenhorne

would tell him what he wanted to know. He spoke carefully. "I am speculating that Lady Wexin's child is not Wexin's."

Levenhorne rubbed his chin. "She certainly did not appear to be a woman in her sixth month."

Samuel almost smiled. He had his verification. Lady Wexin was breeding and the baby was not her husband's.

Levenhorne waved his hand. "It is of no consequence. All she must do is give birth in time and it bloody well doesn't matter who the father is."

Samuel gave Levenhorne an earnest look. "But what if my newspaper can bring pressure on the lady to openly identify the father? Would not there be a chance she'd marry the fellow? If they both acknowledge the baby as that other man's, then the inheritance goes to you."

"Indeed," said Levenhorne in a contemplative voice.

"I will write the story. We have four months to put pressure on her." Four months of building sales of the newspaper. Everyone would want to see what next would happen with the scandalous Lady Wexin. "All I ask is that you support the idea that another man is the father."

"I do support it," said his lordship.

"I am in your debt, then, my lord." Samuel bowed again. "If you hear anything about who the man may be, please send word to me."

Levenhorne stood and extended his hand. "I will do so, indeed, sir."

Chapter Nine

The question remains—who is the father of Lady W—'s child? The time advances quickly that will tell for certain if the baby is the late Lord W—'s heir or another man's child.—The New Observer, July 21, 1819

On this warm July day, almost three and a half months after Samuel had first broken the news of Lady W's *interesting condition*, a gentleman walked into *The New Observer* office where Samuel and his brother Phillip sat at their desks. The man's white pantaloons were so tight his legs seemed made of wood. His blue coat fitted so well his forearms barely budged from his sides. With some difficulty he reached up to remove his high-crowned beaver hat. With this in one hand, he struggled to pull a white handkerchief from his pocket to mop his brow.

Samuel cast a glance at his brother, and Phillip clamped his mouth shut, a cough covering laughter.

"I wonder if I might speak to Mr Reed," the fashionable creature said in a voice as soft as the fabric of his pristine neckcloth.

"Which one?" Phillip asked him.

"Is there more than one? Oh, dear." His eyelids fluttered. "I desire to speak to the Mr Reed who writes about Lady Wexin—I beg your pardon—I mean *Lady W*."

"You want Samuel Reed," Phillip said.

"Do I?" He made a slight bow. "Then perhaps you might tell me how I might get hold of him."

Samuel stood. "I am Samuel Reed, sir, and you are?"

The man tittered. "I must beg pardon once more. I ought to have presented myself. I am Lord Chasey, at your service." He bowed again.

"Lord Chasey," Samuel repeated. "What do you wish to speak to me about?"

"About Lady Wexin—I mean, *Lady W*." He tittered again.

"What about her?" Samuel and Phillip asked in unison.

"I am certain that I might be the father of her child."

"You?" Samuel's voice rose an octave. He did not believe this for an instant.

"I do think I am certain of it." Lord Chasey repeated, all seriousness.

"Why do you come here to tell us?" Phillip asked.

From a pocket in his waistcoat Chasey pulled out a quizzing glass and peered at Phillip through it. "And who might you be?"

Phillip rose. "Phillip Reed, the editor of the newspaper."

"Oh!" exclaimed Chasey. "You have the same surname."

"Brothers usually do," responded Phillip.

Chasey's eyebrows rose. "You are brothers?"

"Yes, we are," replied Samuel. "What is it you want of me, my lord?"

"Why, to print my name in your newspaper as being the

father of the unborn child. You can call me Viscount C from Yorkshire. That should do it."

Phillip shot Samuel another amused glance. If he was not careful, the two of them would burst out laughing.

"Let me make certain I understand you." Samuel gave him a droll look. "You wish me to report that you take responsibility for Lady Wexin's unborn child?"

"Responsibility?" Lord Chasey squeaked. "Dear me, no. I merely want you to imply that I could possibly be the father."

This man wants his name in the paper. Samuel had encountered many like him before. Who knows? Perhaps Viscount C from Yorkshire thought this would raise him in the esteem of his companions, the way the latest in waistcoats might do.

Samuel rubbed his face. He might as well print the story. The more men who came forwards claiming to be the father, the more newspapers they sold. "Very well, sir."

Chasey beamed.

Samuel could not resist adding, "But you must promise to report back to me every detail of your next meeting with her—all that a gentleman can tell, that is."

"My next meeting—?" Lord Chasey glanced around in distress. He took several quick breaths and mopped his brow again. "I…uh…will certainly report every possible detail of any…uh…future meeting I have with the lady."

Phillip twisted away, covering his mouth. His shoulders shook.

Samuel extended his hand to Lord Chasey. "I shall compose a mention of you for tomorrow's paper."

Chasey stuffed his handkerchief back in his pocket and accepted Samuel's handshake, grinning like an excited schoolboy. "Excellent! That is excellent." He managed to put his hat back on his head. "I will take my leave of you, then."

One more bow and Chasey was gone, the door closing behind him. Phillip let loose, laughing so hard tears came to his eyes. "I'll wager you ten pounds that popinjay has never been within four miles of Lady Wexin."

"No bet." Samuel grinned. "I'll use his name, though. We might as well share the joke with our readers."

Samuel wanted to keep the speculation alive as to whether another man had fathered Lady Wexin's unborn child. To own the truth, Samuel had discovered nothing to suggest that the baby was any man's but Wexin's, but his gut told him there was someone else. Unfortunately, his meetings with Lady Wexin's maid, Mary, had yielded nothing.

No information, that is. Samuel's time with Mary was the best part of his week. They met whenever she could get away, sharing ices at Gunter's or strolling through Hyde Park. The best times were evenings when he waited near the gate for her. He'd stolen no more than kisses, but Mary's kisses were sweeter than another woman's favours.

Lord Levenhorne reported that August 16 was the crucial date. If Lady Wexin's baby was not born at the stroke of midnight, separating August 15 from August 16, it would prove that the father was another man. The story would remain alive at least that long, and Samuel would have reason to keep seeing Mary. She would keep thinking he was Samuel Charles who worked for a printer, but this idyll could not last for ever.

Frowning, Samuel pulled out a sheet of paper and trimmed a quill pen before dipping it into a pot of ink. He scratched out several lines about Lord C, the Irish Viscount who claimed to be the father of Lady W's child.

Ironic that Chasey possessed the same initial as the man Samuel had first suspected to have been Lady Wexin's lover. Beyond the one brief encounter of which Samuel had been a part, Samuel could not discover from Mary or anyone else that Lord Cavanley had ever set foot in Lady Wexin's house. Mary did not seem to know who Cavanley was.

Levenhorne said the betting book in White's did not give Cavanley any odds of being the father. Odds favoured Lord Crayden, who had been known to court Lady Wexin before her betrothal to her murderous husband, but Samuel could not discover that Crayden had called upon the lady either. There were other men who had boasted of being Lady W's secret lover, but none proved more than idle boasting.

The child's paternity remained a mystery. Samuel did not mind using the mystery to keep speculation alive, but the newsman in him pined to beat the other papers to the real story.

He finished the short but tantalising column and poured blotting sand on it, carefully shaking the excess sand back into its container.

Chasey would have to do for the moment, one small step in Samuel's quest to make *The New Observer* number one above *The Morning Post*, *The Morning Chronicle*, *The Times* and all the other papers vying for the position.

Adrian walked into his parents' library. His father was seated behind the desk attending to his correspondence; his mother reclined on a chaise reading.

She closed her book. "Adrian, we were so worried about you!" Her white hair made her look every inch the countess she now was. She'd always been a beautiful woman and remained so in her maturity.

Adrian crossed the room and kissed her on the cheek. "Forgive me. I did not mean to distress you."

His father looked at him over spectacles perched on his nose. "I wrote to you two days ago."

Adrian had received his father's missive, but had stuffed it in his pocket and headed off to Madame Bisou's, where he'd engaged in a marathon of card playing and drinking, something that had become a pattern for him of late. When he'd woken up this morning at Madame Bisou's, he'd had no clear memory of how he'd spent the entire previous day. His father's letter and one from Tanner were still in the pocket of the coat he had slept in.

Adrian answered his father. "I came as soon as I read it." Which was true enough. "I confess, I feared bad news, but you both look the picture of health." Better to shift the attention to their health than to dwell on his own.

"There is nothing amiss with us," his mother said. "Would you like a sherry, love?"

Adrian's stomach roiled. "Later, perhaps."

His father ceremoniously took off his spectacles and folded them, placing them on the desk. "I summoned you because of concern about *you*."

"Me?" Adrian was genuinely surprised.

"This dissipated life you are leading—" his father began.

"—is not healthy for you, dear," his mother finished.

He looked from one to the other. "Dissipated life?"

His father leaned forwards. "This drinking. Spending all your time in gaming hells. Coming home looking as if you slept in your clothes."

Obviously someone from Adrian's household had been reporting on his behaviour. Adrian's bets were on Bilson, the loyal butler. Loyal to Adrian's father, that is.

"Father, my behaviour is not much altered from what it has always been." Except perhaps for the drinking to excess and finding himself in a bed with no memory of how he had arrived there.

"You are drinking entirely too much." His father rose and walked from behind the desk.

His mother cupped her hand against his face. "You will lose your handsome good looks if you drink too much. You'll get a red nose and have blotches on your cheeks."

"Where have you heard such things about me?" Adrian gaped at them.

His father looked chagrined. "Well, people talk, you know."

Former servants obviously did.

Adrian lifted a hand to his forehead. The headache from the previous night's drinking lingered there, no longer a sledgehammer, but a dull thudding. He shook his head. "A few months ago when I asked for something to do, take over one of the estates, perhaps, you all but told me to go drink, gamble and otherwise cavort. Now you are outraged that I am doing what you said I should?"

"I would never have told you to get a red nose, dear," his mother said.

His father huffed. "You wanted to take over one of the estates? How can you expect me to trust you with such a task when you are being so reckless with drink?"

What else was he supposed to do? Adrian wanted to ask.

"I think it is high time Adrian went searching for a wife." His mother nodded decisively. "The Season is over, but he might go to Brighton. There were plenty of eligible young ladies in Brighton when we were there, were there not? It is something to consider."

"I did not mean to put the boy in shackles, Irene," his father retorted.

His mother stiffened. "Marriage is akin to being shackled?"

"I did not say that." His father hastened to his wife's side and put his arm around her. "I merely meant he ought to enjoy life while he can, without duty dictating to him."

His mother pouted. "You implied a man cannot enjoy life if he is married."

"I did not say that," his father murmured.

"You did say it," his mother persisted.

Adrian held up a hand. "Do not argue over this."

His mother pressed her mouth closed, but his father lifted her chin and gave her a light kiss on the lips.

She reluctantly smiled.

His father kissed her again and strode over to a side cupboard, removing a decanter of sherry and three glasses. "Marriage is a great responsibility," he said to Adrian. "I do not encourage you to marry now, while you are engaged in such dissipation. I urge you to show more restraint. Stop the drinking." As he spoke Adrian's father poured sherry into the glasses and handed one to his wife and one to Adrian.

Adrian almost laughed. Only his father could chastise him for drinking at the same moment as handing him a drink.

His mother took her glass. "Well, I do urge you to look about for a wife. There is no hurry for it, I agree, but you might as well discover who will be out next Season."

Adrian set his glass down on the table.

All he could think was that had Lydia accepted his proposal all those months ago, he'd have no reason to become dissipated.

But Lydia had not accepted him.

Adrian picked up the glass of sherry and drained it of its contents.

As soon as he was able, he extricated himself from the insane asylum that was his parents' townhouse and headed back home, vowing to be more discreet in his activities so the details did not get whispered in his father's ear.

Adrian winced at the brightness of the day. The sky was a milky white and hurt his aching eyes if he looked up. He tilted his head just enough to keep his eyes shaded by the brim of his hat. He neared Hill Street, depressing his spirits even more. All of London was depressing him.

Perhaps he should visit Tanner after all. Tanner had written to invite him to Scotland where he and his wife were spending the summer months and awaiting the birth of their first child.

Ha! Not likely he would be welcome there. What was this with having babies? Was every woman bearing a child this summer?

Adrian vowed he would not think of that. Nor of Lydia refusing his proposal.

But Tanner had also offered Adrian another of his estates, Nickerham Priory in Sussex. Adrian had visited Nickerham with Tanner on Tanner's tour of his properties the year before and could agree it would be an excellent place to spend a summer. High on a cliff overlooking the sea and cooled by sea breezes, there would be nothing to do but ride the South Downs or walk along the seashore.

Adrian might very possibly go insane there, left to nothing but his own company and his own thoughts.

Vowing to write Tanner a gracious return letter this very day—or tomorrow—Adrian crossed into Hill Street. He rarely walked through Mayfair without finding himself passing by Lydia's townhouse.

He spied the reporters lounging about her door and became angry on her behalf all over again. The leeches. Why did they not leave the lady in peace? Why could they not content themselves with writing about the thousands of weavers assembling in Carlisle in protest against low wages, the trade crisis in Frankfurt, or an earthquake near Rome? Why devote so much space to speculation about Lydia? He'd read in the papers that the father of her child was anyone from the Prince Regent to a passing gypsy.

Was she in good health? he wondered. Bearing children might be the most natural thing in the world, but many women died from it. Babies died, as well. His mother had borne Adrian a brother and sister, neither of whom had lived longer than a few days.

Staying on the opposite side of the street, Adrian tried not to glance at her house. Another gentleman approached in the opposite direction.

"Good day to you, Cavanley." The gentleman greeted him in clipped, but jovial tones.

"Crayden." Adrian tipped his hat.

Crayden possessed thick black hair that women fancied and a face that always held a smug expression. Adrian was not among Crayden's admirers. Crayden curried any favour that was possible to curry. He insinuated himself into investments lucrative enough to keep his debt-ridden estate from doom's door, but he was equally as likely to drop a friendship if it failed to gain him a profit.

Lord Crayden smiled his ingratiating smile and put his hand on Adrian's shoulder as if he was accustomed to sharing confidences with him. "I suppose I shall have to run the gauntlet, eh? I am calling upon Lady Wexin, you know."

No, Adrian didn't know, and he did not very much like knowing it now. What business did this ferret have with Lydia? Lydia's fortune was modest, Adrian knew for a fact, having been the one to restore it.

"Are you?" Adrian said.

"I am indeed." Crayden clapped Adrian on the shoulder and winked. He crossed the street and ploughed right into the nest of newspaper men, who clamoured after him, waving their hands and asking him questions.

Adrian watched as Lydia's butler answered the door, and Crayden said with a voice loud enough to reach Adrian's ears, "Lord Crayden to see Lady Wexin."

The reporters all pressed forwards, yelling their questions. After Crayden gained entry and the door was closed again, the newspaper men buzzed among themselves for a moment, before turning to look towards Adrian.

Adrian hurried on his way.

Lydia walked to the window of the drawing room and peeked through a gap in the curtain. She thought she'd heard a commotion outside. The newspaper men were still there, all talking about something, but it was not their vile presence that caught her attention, but the figure of a man across the street, looking towards her house.

She'd know Adrian anywhere, even from such a distance, even with his hat shading his face. Had he decided to call upon her again? Even though she'd refused him?

No one called upon her. No one except Lord Levenhorne and he did so merely to check the size of her waistline.

She ought to feel outrage that Adrian would ignore her wishes so blatantly, but instead she felt flushed with excitement. The baby kicked inside her. The baby kicked often now and would be born soon, the physician who attended her said.

She rushed over to the mirror above the fireplace and checked her appearance. Her hair hung undressed in a plait down her back. The gown she wore was an old one Mary had let out so her now larger breasts would not spill over the bodice, and her big tummy would be shrouded by a full skirt. She contemplated changing, but feared nothing else would be ready to wear except nightdresses and robes, and she did not trust herself in such attire around Adrian.

In any event, there was no time, because Dixon entered the room. "There is a Lord Crayden to see you, my lady."

"What?" She thought she had misheard him.

"Lord Crayden, my lady." He held out the gentleman's card.

She stared at it, her spirits plummeting. It was Adrian she wanted to see, wanted to be with even for a little while. She pined to see his eyes filled with concern for her, to feel less alone in his presence.

"But why would this gentleman call upon me?" She handed the card back to Dixon.

She had not even seen Lord Crayden in an age. He had once been a suitor, but never a favoured one. He had no connection to her family or to Wexin's. He certainly was not a friend. His biggest shortcoming, however, was that he was not Adrian.

"I do not want to see him," she said.

Dixon bowed. "Very well, my lady." He turned to leave.

"Wait." She stopped him. "Do you suppose he has been abroad and brings news of my parents?"

It was the only reason she could think of that the gentleman would call. One letter from her parents, dated months ago, had finally reached her from India, but, from its contents, it was apparent that none of Lydia's letters had reached them.

"He did not say so, my lady," Dixon replied.

"Well, send him up, I suppose."

A few minutes later Crayden was announced.

"Lady Wexin." He bowed.

She took a step towards him. "Lord Crayden, do you bring me news?"

"News?" He looked puzzled.

"Of my parents? My brother?" She braced herself.

He blinked. "They are abroad, are they not?"

She released a frustrated breath. "You do not bring news of my family? Why are you here?"

He smiled, showing his white, even teeth. "I call merely to inquire after your health—and to offer my condolences."

She did not believe him. "Condolences? I've been a widow for three-quarters of a year."

His expression turned sympathetic. "I thought it best not to cause comment by calling upon you sooner."

Such as during the brief time after the Queen had died when the newspapers had left her alone? "So you choose now when I am written of daily, with one man after another connected to my name?"

He gave no indication he perceived her barb. "I thought you might need a friend at this difficult time."

When Adrian had offered her friendship she had almost believed him. This man she believed not at all.

"Lord Crayden, I knew you only very briefly during my come-out." And then she'd refused his suit. "It is presumptuous of you to call upon me. Indeed, it makes me very unhappy. You expose me to more gossip I do not deserve."

A wounded look crossed his face. "My lady, my intentions are honourable, I assure you. I have always had a regard for you, as you well know—"

A regard for her dowry, he must mean.

"I have worried over your welfare and could not wait another moment to assure myself that you were in good health."

"Be assured, then, Lord Crayden, to what is none of your concern." Her tone was sharp.

She walked towards the door Dixon had left open. She trusted the butler was nearby.

"I am delighted to know you are well," Crayden continued, undaunted. "I shall rest easier at night."

"That is splendid," she said with great sarcasm, gesturing to the door. "You can have no other business here, then."

He bowed again. "I shall take my leave of you, my dear lady, but I fear you will not be gone from my thoughts."

She laughed drily. "I have become quite used to people thinking of me. Good day, sir."

As he walked past her to the door, he bowed again.

After he left, her biggest regret at his visit was that he'd not been Adrian.

Chapter Ten

All London waits for news of Lady W—. Before mid-night calls in the sixteenth day of August, Lady W—must give birth lest the world discover unequivocally that the child is not Lord W—'s progeny. *The New Observer* assures its readers it will keep a vigil up to the very stroke of midnight. In a Special Edition tomorrow morning, *The New Observer* will provide the answer.
—*The New Observer*, August 15, 1819

Samuel waited outside the gate of Lady Wexin's house. The night was warm and the haze that seemed to settle over London in the summer obscured the stars. Candlelight shone from the windows of the houses.

There were only two hours left for Lady Wexin's chance to give birth to a legitimate, and Samuel had planned this as-signation with Mary at this hour to discover whether Lady Wexin would make the time limit or not. The house had been quiet all day.

Through an open window he heard the faint chiming of a

clock. Ten o'clock. He peered into the darkness to see if he could spy Mary coming. His wait was short. The gate opened and she appeared.

"Mary," he greeted her in a low voice.

"Sam!" She hurried into his arms, warm and delightful.

"Ah, my love," he murmured, wasting no time in bending his face to hers and tasting her eager lips.

Their encounters became more and more passionate each time they met. Their last time together had been spent walking in Hyde Park where Samuel had found a secluded bench and nearly forgot to engage Mary in conversation. Even though pursuing the story of Lady W filled his days, thoughts of Mary consumed his restless nights. He wanted her more desperately than he had ever wanted a woman. What little conscience he still possessed kept him from bedding her.

Her kisses were driving away that fragile resolve. They could so easily walk into the garden to the bench nestled among the fragrant foliage…

He reluctantly broke away from her. "Tell me of your day," he murmured.

"We can sit in the garden," she whispered, taking him by the hand and leading him through the gate to the bench.

He sat her on his lap, her soft derrière so very tantalising and arousing. "Now, tell me how you fare. I want to hear all about your days since I saw you last."

Mary rested her head upon his shoulder. "I have spent the whole day fretting about my lady. She has remained in her bedchamber all day, not talking much, not eating. I know she is so worried and I am worried for her."

"No baby, I take it." He spoke the obvious.

"No baby." She sighed. "She's not even having pains."

"She'll not have the baby tonight, then?" He hoped she would say more.

She squirmed on top of him and he forgot that he wanted her to answer him. His hands slipped to her waist and he pressed her harder against him.

"Oh, Sam," she groaned, twisting to face him, straddling him.

He kissed her again, his hand cupping one of her pert little breasts. He slipped it under her dress and felt her soft skin, her firm nipple. All he need do was unbutton his trousers and he could couple with her.

"Sam," she murmured into his ear, her tongue tickling the sensitive skin there, "I want to do this with you. I'm sure of it."

He took his hand away from her breast and lifted her off him, feeling like a cad. She was young and fresh and virginal, and he was using her to get his story. How would she feel if he made love to her and then she discovered his real name and purpose?

"No, Mary." She reached for him again, and he moved her arms away. "You are too tempting. I want you, but we cannot do this."

She whimpered. "I know you are right. It is difficult, though."

He laughed softly and brushed her curls from her cheek. "Very difficult."

She took his hand in hers and laid her head against his shoulder. "I wonder if it was like this for my lady."

Samuel jolted back to his purpose. "What do you mean?"

"Well, she must have been with someone. Maybe it was difficult for her, too."

He tried not to sound eager. "Who was she with? Do you know?"

She sighed again. "I cannot think of anyone she could have

been with. She's been alone all this time, and it is so sad that her friends have left her. Even when she was going out a little, you know, after the Queen died. I can't remember a time she went out alone." She sat up straight. "Unless…"

His heart pounded. "Unless, what?"

She rested against him again. "It could not be. It is just that she went out once, before the Queen died, but it was on an errand, not to meet anyone."

"It might have been then, though?" he asked, forcing a conversational tone.

"It might have been, but she was going to—" She broke off, as if catching herself in something she ought not to say.

Just the sort of information he wanted to hear.

They had talked of this before, but she was always so careful of what she said, protective of her lady even with the man pretending to court her. Samuel kept hoping that she would say something or remember something that would lead him to the baby's father. Lord Chasey's claim had been a false one, not that Samuel had been surprised. After one of their reporters said Lord Crayden had called upon her, Samuel had checked on Crayden, as well, but there was no evidence he had called upon her before.

Mary rose from the bench. "I should go back to her."

Samuel stood as well, but was not quite as ready to end the conversation. "And you do not suspect anyone in the house." He'd asked her that before, as well.

She shook her head. "I would know if that happened. Besides, our men are not like that and neither is my lady."

He touched her cheek. "Indeed." He spoke as reassuringly as he could. "It is a mystery all London is wondering about, is it not?"

She collapsed into his arms again. "I hate that my lady has to read her name in all those awful newspapers."

"Indeed."

Samuel gave her one more kiss before she walked him back to the gate.

Adrian sat back in his chair at White's. It was past midnight and he'd spent the last three hours in the card room. He'd lost this night, not a great sum, but a loss, nonetheless.

He nursed a brandy, the first of the night. His parents would be proud that he had altered his behaviour of late. His parents' concern and his own alarm had jarred him out of a downward spiral.

Adrian took a sip of brandy and glanced around the room where other gentlemen sat at tables, drinking as he was. None of them seemed to notice he had changed, that his good cheer was forced, that his usual pursuits were boring him.

He closed his eyes, savouring the woody taste of the liquid and the warm feeling spreading in his chest.

Laughter roused him.

Levenhorne, seated at a table in the middle of the room, seemed to find something extremely amusing. A footman stood at his elbow. Levenhorne held a piece of paper in his hand.

"Listen, everyone!" Levenhorne stood and held the paper high in the air. "At midnight tonight the ten months was up! Lady Wexin did not produce an heir. The estate and title are mine."

"Bravo!" shouted one fellow. Others applauded.

Levenhorne bowed with a flourish.

"Dash it," one man said, "I wagered on her having a son."

Levenhorne clapped the man on the back. "You may still have a chance to win that wager. She has not yet given birth."

The other gentleman joined in Levenhorne's laughter.

Adrian's grip on his glass tightened.

Lydia had not had her baby. She'd wanted him to believe the baby was Wexin's, but now there was no chance at all.

Adrian rose and left the room. He retrieved his hat and walked out into the warm summer night.

He knew, had always known. Lydia's baby was his.

Blast her. She must have known it as well.

Adrian walked fast, the idea of his child being born a bastard filling his mind. Before he knew it he was on Lydia's street, in front of her townhouse. He stopped.

The reporters were gone.

They had probably dashed off to write their stories.

Adrian stared at her door for several seconds. It was an unforgivable hour upon which to call, but he suspected the household would still be awake on such a night.

He strode to the door and loudly sounded the knocker.

It did not take long for the door to open. "I told you all to bugger off—" Lydia's butler's fierce expression turned to surprise. "Oh! I—I beg pardon, my lord, I did not know…" The man peered at him. "What do you want, my lord?"

Adrian stuck his foot in the door. "I wish to see Lady Wexin."

The butler's brows rose. "Do you realise the hour, my lord?"

"I am very cognisant of the hour and of what has *not* taken place here this night." Adrian put pressure on the door. "I presume she is not sleeping. Tell Lady Wexin I wish to see her."

The butler still hesitated.

Adrian lowered his voice. "Listen, man. The reporters are gone. No one will know I've come. I beg you, announce me to Lady Wexin."

The butler opened the door and allowed Adrian entry.

* * *

Lydia sat in the rocking chair she'd had Dixon purchase for her. She'd hoped to be rocking her baby by this time.

It would be lovely if she could indulge in a fit of tears, yell and scream and pull at her hair, but instead there was only this cold stark terror inside her. By dawn, the world would know she'd become pregnant by another man, a man she'd lain with when her husband, vile man that he was, had been dead only a matter of weeks.

She would have to leave London. Go somewhere where no one knew her, where she could raise her child away from the newspapers and gossip-mongers. Her sister would surely not wish to see her; her parents, if they ever returned, would shun her as well.

How did one sell a house and its contents? Could she afford all the servants? Some would not wish to remain with her, she was certain.

"My lady, do you wish to get ready for bed?"

Mary sounded almost afraid to speak to her. Poor Mary. She had been so faithful, so good about not asking questions. Mary had been the only person who had known for certain this baby was not Wexin's. Now everyone knew.

"In a little while, Mary." Lydia tried to appear composed.

A knock sounded on her bedchamber door. Mary walked over and opened it a crack. "It is Mr Dixon."

Dixon stepped in, looking distressed. "My lady, there is a gentleman to see you."

Someone sent to verify that she had not given birth, she supposed. "Send him away."

"It is Lord Cavanley." Dixon wrung his hands.

Adrian stepped into the room.

"See here—" began Dixon.

Adrian ignored him and walked straight over to her. "Let us speak alone."

Lydia's heart pounded. She glanced from Mary to Dixon, both open-mouthed with shock. "It is all right," she said to them. "I will see him alone."

Dixon needed to take Mary by the arm to escort her out.

When the door closed, Lydia looked up at Adrian, so handsome in the lamplight. She continued to rock back and forth in her chair. "What do you want, Adrian?" she asked.

"Truth." His gaze slipped from her face to the round mound of her abdomen. "Is the baby mine?"

She turned her head away. "I suppose you have surmised that I am not carrying Wexin's child."

"I never thought you were." His voice was deep and angry. "Is the baby mine?"

Lydia glanced into his eyes, which were filled with pain. "Do you, like the newspapers, think it might be the child of a gypsy or a manservant?"

His gaze remained steady. "Answer my question."

She bowed her head. "The baby is yours, Adrian."

His anger, his pain, his very presence here confused her. She had already released him from any responsibility. Why had he come?

He stepped back. "Why, Lydia? Why keep this from me?"

The cold terror inside her was cracking like thin ice under his gaze. She did not wish to break apart in front of this man, who would be kind to her, as he had been before. His kindness was what had led her to seduce him, but that had been her doing, not his.

"I did not want you to know," she managed to respond.

"You did not wish me to know." He looked so wounded.

She could almost hear the crack-crack-crack of her control. Hot tears stung her eyes and her throat felt tight. She could not speak and so forced a shrug in response.

He swung away for a moment before turning back with a piercing gaze. "I offered you marriage, Lydia. I offered to acknowledge my paternity—"

She waved a dismissive hand and struggled to her feet. "You did your duty."

He came closer to her. "Yes, my duty, but you preferred my child to have a murderer's name."

Her cheeks stung as if he'd struck her. He spoke the truth and hearing it made her ashamed. "I—I did not wish to be married, Adrian." Her voice sounded too fragile, too vulnerable.

"Cut line, Lydia." His eyes flashed. "You did not wish to be married to me."

"I did not want to be married to anyone," she shot back.

He twisted away, making a sound of disgust.

She stepped towards him, placing her hand upon his shoulder. "Adrian, understand me. I thought I had a perfect marriage once. It was all lies, vile, evil lies. Do you really think I would trust any man after that?"

He straightened. "I am not Wexin."

She dropped her hand and wrapped her arms around herself. "Yes. Yes. You are not Wexin, but you are—"

He swung around. "A libertine?"

Lydia turned away, but he circled her so she was forced to look at him.

"You have made it very clear what you think of me, Lydia, and you made your choice, preferring my son or daughter be thought the progeny of a murderer rather than a libertine, but that matters little now, does it not?"

She tried to meet his eyes, but could not bear to see her shame reflected there. "I had a chance to be free of a man's control and I took it."

"You gambled with my son or daughter."

She inhaled a quick breath. She'd gambled and lost.

He took her chin in his fingers and lifted her face so she could not avoid looking at him. His touch, even in this circumstance, even in her condition, gave her a physical awareness of him.

"You cannot pretend my child is Wexin's now. What were you planning to do?" A muscle in his cheek flexed and he bent closer to her.

She shuddered. "I do not know."

He released her and stepped back from her.

She shook her head in confusion. "I expect nothing from you, Adrian. You are free. I take full responsibility."

He stood straight and tall in front of her. "The blood that flows through that child is mine. That makes the child my duty. My responsibility."

She rushed forwards, grabbing the front of his coat. "I will not allow you to take my child from me," she cried, feeling her emotions rise to hysteria. "I will deny you are the baby's father! You cannot have my child!"

His eyes widened briefly. He did not speak.

Lydia let go of his coat.

Finally, he spoke in a low and rumbling voice. "You misunderstand me, madam. My duty is to marry you, acknowledge the child and take responsibility for you both."

And then what? she wanted to add.

"I am waiting for your answer." He looked down at her.

She glanced up at him. "That was a proposal? You wish me to marry you and give you control of me and my child? To have your secrets kept from me? How can I put this plainer, Adrian? I have no wish to be married at all, let alone be married to a man such as you."

His eyes shot sparks. "Do not be so foolish, Lydia. This has nothing to do with what you want. Or what I want, for that matter. We must think of the child. If we marry in time, your son would be an earl some day. Your daughter would possess not only name, but fortune. No matter what you think of me, I offer a life of comfort, of advantage to our child."

Her heart pounded. "No, Adrian. Forget me. I will leave London and you will never hear of me again."

He stepped closer and seized her arms, leaning so close only inches separated their lips. "What of our child then, Lydia?" His eyes were like daggers. "You offer the child no name, no advantages, no protection, only the disgrace of being a bastard." His gaze did not waver and did not soften. "You must marry me."

She still could not speak.

He shook her. "For God's sake, Lydia. You must marry me."

She gasped and admitted her greatest fear. "You will be able to take my child away from me."

He released her. "Yes, as your husband I will have that right. I do not expect you to believe me, a mere rake, if I tell you I would never be so cruel to you."

"I cannot believe you, Adrian."

He recoiled. "Then I will not waste time trying to convince you of my character. Make your decision."

She sank back into the rocking chair and tried to soothe

herself, rocking back and forth. He stepped away from her and stood, arms folded over his chest, waiting.

His words offered so much. Comfort, safety, respectability. For her and their child.

Their child.

Would the child have his smiling mouth? The cowlick in his hair? His amber-coloured eyes?

She had no choice.

She took a deep breath. "Very well, Adrian. I accept," she whispered. "I will marry you."

It seemed a long time before he nodded. "I will go to Lambeth Palace today and procure the special licence. If I can snag a clergyman I will return here and we will be married right away."

As easy as all that, it would be done, and her life and the life of her precious child would be his to dictate. She felt as if she was giving up everything.

He had not professed love, as Wexin had done. He'd not professed devotion. He'd promised to do his duty to their child. Theirs would be a marriage of convenience—of necessity, rather.

She shivered.

He stared at her, so distant, so filled with an anger she could not begrudge him. All the fault in this situation was hers and hers alone.

"Have we come to an understanding, then, Lydia?" His voice actually shook.

She was not the only one overcome with emotion.

She extended her hand. "We have an agreement, sir."

He walked back to her, a masculine stride of grace and power. "An agreement, madam."

He grasped her hand. His hand was warm, his grasp strong, and, at his touch, her body again tingled with awareness of him. She wished she could be immune to this carnal yearning for him. It made matters worse.

He released her. "I will call upon you later today. May I suggest that your staff be prepared to allow me entry at your garden gate?"

To avoid the reporters who were certain to return. "I will have the gate attended after noon."

"After noon, then." He bowed.

He continued to gaze at her, but finally turned and walked towards the door.

"Adrian, wait!" She pushed herself to her feet.

He turned to her. The anger and pain remained in his face.

She took a deep breath. "May we—may we leave here? Leave London? I have no wish to give birth while reporters watch." The scandal was about to become so much worse.

She might have imagined a slight softening of his stiff posture. He nodded, almost imperceptibly. "I will arrange it."

A moment later he was gone.

Lydia buried her head in her hands and released the tension in a flood of tears.

Mary hurried back in the room. "My lady!" Mary rushed to her side, her questions unspoken.

Her maid and all the servants would wonder who was this Lord Cavanley to call upon her this night of all nights.

Lydia raised her head and, with her bare fingers, wiped the streaming tears from her cheeks. "Wish me happy, Mary." She stifled a sob. "I am to be married."

Chapter Eleven

Special Edition. Midnight arrived. Midnight passed.
Lady W—'s interesting condition remains interesting.
The child she wished the world to believe fathered by
the late Lord W— was not born by the deadline, prov-
ing she carries some other man's child. But who is the
father?—*The New Observer*, August 16, 1819

Samuel stood at the back of the newspaper offices, where the
two pressmen continued to run off copies of the Special
Edition, hanging the sheets over lines for the ink to dry. They'd
sold out once and hoped to sell another two hundred copies.

Samuel checked the pages that had hung the longest.
"These are ready. Let's get them out to the streets."

The men carefully pulled papers from the line and carried
them to the back door where hawkers waited to take them to
the streets. Only one story was printed in this edition—Lady
Wexin's failure to give birth within ten months. The columns
were filled with a rehashing of all the speculation that had
come before.

The rhythmic din of the printing press went silent, and the only sounds to be heard now were the shouts of the men outside. Samuel said a silent prayer that the hawkers would sell out and the pressmen would go to work again. Perhaps he and his brother might soon afford the steam-powered press that gave papers like *The Times* an edge.

Samuel intended to keep this story alive until some new scandal captured the public's attention. Then he would keep that scandal alive as well. His brother had been right. Scandal sold papers.

Today Samuel planned to call upon Lord Levenhorne. Levenhorne must have something to say about Lady Wexin's failure to produce Wexin's progeny. Samuel still hoped he could discover the truth about the child's paternity.

Through the curtain separating the press room from the office, he heard the front door open.

"Excuse me, sir." The voice was feminine. And familiar.

Mary!

"I am searching for a print shop," Samuel heard her say. "Can you give me the proper direction? I have walked up and down this street and I cannot find a print shop anywhere."

His brother, who had been working in the office, answered her. "We are the only printers on this street."

"There must be another," she insisted.

Samuel started to edge his way towards the back door, but his escape was blocked by the pressmen.

"My friend Samuel Charles works for a printer on this street," he heard Mary say.

Send her on her way, Samuel silently pleaded. *Do not say another word.*

"Samuel? You must mean my brother, Samuel Reed."

Damned Phillip.

"He is in the back. I'll fetch him." Phillip walked to the doorway and shouted through the curtain, "Samuel! Someone to see you."

"You are mistaken—" Mary protested.

Samuel's shoulders slumped. He crossed the room and slid the curtain aside.

"Samuel!" Mary cried, shock written on her face. "But—but—"

"I know, Mary." Samuel's voice filled with gloom. "You did not expect a newspaper office."

"This—this is *that* paper! The one that writes such nasty things about my lady." She blinked in confusion.

"I'll leave you two alone." Phillip sidled to the doorway and disappeared into the back.

Mary's huge luminous eyes fixed on Samuel. "I do not understand this."

He averted his gaze. "This is where I work, Mary." He inclined his head towards the curtain. "My brother and I own this newspaper."

"You *own* it?" Her eyes grew even wider.

He nodded.

"But—"

He shrugged, reasoning he might as well tell her the whole. "I wrote the stories about Lady Wexin."

"You?" Her voice squeaked.

"They sold newspapers, Mary."

She turned away from him. When she turned back, her eyes were filled with tears. "Did—did you befriend me to find out about my lady?"

Samuel nodded.

"And—and you p-pretended to be my sweetheart?" she stuttered.

Not all of it had been pretending. "Mary—"

She backed away from him. "Oh, no. Do not answer that! I will not believe you, whatever you say. You made me betray my lady."

"Mary, you never betrayed her." Mary had never told Samuel much of anything, but that had not kept him from wanting to see her again and again.

She shook her head. "You asked me a lot of questions, always. And I told you things. I thought you were interested in me, but you weren't." She shivered. "You just wanted me to talk about my lady!"

"Mary. Please. Listen to me." Although he was uncertain what he could say to her.

"No!" She clamped her hands over her ears. "I am going away. I came to tell you I am going away, but that is all I'm going to tell you."

He walked towards her. "Away? Where? Why, Mary?"

She reached the door and had her hand on the knob. "You only want to know because of Lady Wexin, but I won't tell you. Not another thing." She fixed her eyes, full of anguish and betrayal, on him. "Goodbye, Samuel."

She rushed out of the door, not even closing it. Samuel hurried after her, but she ran down the street and climbed into a hackney coach.

He watched the coach drive away and turn out of sight.

His worst nightmare had come true.

Mary had discovered exactly what a cad he really was.

Adrian arrived in a carriage at the side gate of Lydia's property promptly at one o'clock in the afternoon. He brought with him a special licence, a clergyman and a ring.

Lydia's footman waited to open the gate. This time when Adrian entered the house there were plenty of witnesses. The cook, a scullery maid and a housemaid all watched from the kitchen doorway. The butler led Adrian and the clergyman to the stairs, delivering them finally to the drawing room on the first floor.

"I will fetch m'lady." The butler bowed to Adrian.

While the reverend rocked on his heels, Adrian walked over to the window and peeked out. Several reporters stood outside, talking among themselves, looking bored, but showing no indication that they realised visitors had arrived. One man, unnoticed by the others, stared at the house. Adrian recognised Reed, the reporter who had accosted Lydia all those months ago and set into motion the events that had led Adrian here this day.

Lydia walked in the room and Adrian turned away from the window. Her maid and butler entered behind her.

She wore a pale pink dress with a high lace collar and matching lace cape. Its skirt was wide, but not too voluminous to conceal that she was big with child.

The reverend tossed Adrian a knowing look that made Adrian want to pitch him across the room.

Instead he stepped forwards to take Lydia's hand. "Our agreement stands?" he asked her in a quiet voice.

"It stands," she whispered back to him.

The clergyman approached her.

"May I present Reverend Keats to you, ma'am," Adrian said.

"Lady Wexin." The reverend bowed.

"Reverend." Her voice was barely audible.

She looked very pale, and Adrian wondered if she was ill, but, somehow, her health seemed too private a matter to discuss in front of the clergyman.

"Shall we begin?" Adrian said instead.

She cleared her throat. "Yes."

Reverend Keats glanced around. "But what of your witnesses?"

Lydia turned to her butler and maid. "Mr Dixon and Miss Shaw are my witnesses."

Keats looked down his nose at them and Adrian had a second wish to throttle him.

"I have no objection to these witnesses," Adrian told the reverend.

"Well, let us begin, then." Reverend Keats pulled out his prayer book from a pocket in his coat.

Adrian and Lydia faced him.

The reverend opened the book and read speedily, "Dearly Beloved, we are gathered together in the sight of God…"

The words barely made sense to Adrian. He felt as if he were watching from a great distance, seeing himself standing shoulder to shoulder with Lydia, noticing the tables and chairs in the room and the colours of blue and gold that predominated.

Reverend Keats asked, "Wilt thou take this woman…?" and Adrian heard himself answer, "I will." The reverend said, "Wilt thou take this man…?" and Lydia said, "I will."

Keats joined Adrian's right hand to Lydia's. Her skin felt smooth and warm in his palm. Her hand trembled. He glanced at her. She looked flushed and frightened and unhappy.

It plunged him into gloom. He'd never imagined marrying a woman who did not want him. Nor wishing so much that this woman felt differently.

"Repeat after me…" Reverend Keats said.

Adrian repeated, "I, Adrian Purdie—"

Her eyes darted to him when he spoke his middle name. Her mouthed twitched.

"My great-grandfather's name," he whispered to her.

"Take thee—" Keats raised his voice.

Her eyes momentarily filled with mirth and Adrian's spirits suddenly rose.

"Take thee, Lydia Elizabeth." He gazed at her when he said the next words, "To be my wedded wife—"

His depression returned. He wanted a marriage like Tanner's, like his parents', a marriage begun in joy. He wanted this marriage to begin in joy.

At Keats's signal Adrian released her hand and reached in his pocket and took out the ring he had purchased that morning from Mr Gray, the jeweller. He had also purchased all of the jewellery Lydia had sold to Mr Gray nine months ago.

He placed it on her finger. "With this ring, I thee wed…"

She gasped. The ring, with clusters of twenty-two diamonds, caught the light and shot it back like so many sparks against flint. Adrian nodded in satisfaction. At least the ring pleased her, if not the groom.

When Reverend Keats said, "I pronounce that they be Man and Wife together…" the words echoed through Adrian's brain. Man and wife. Man and wife. Keats rushed through the final prayers, reading so fast Adrian would not have caught the words even if he had been able to pay attention.

Man and wife.

The reverend grew silent. Lydia lifted her gaze to Adrian. Like that first day when he'd gazed upon her, she stole his breath away. He leaned down and touched his lips to hers very lightly, dutifully. She remained still, eyes still gazing into his.

It was done.

Her maid had tears streaming down her face. Her butler appeared as worried as a disapproving father.

Adrian took the Reverend Keats aside and placed a purse in the man's hand. "Thank you, sir." He gave the man a warning glance. "I have paid you very well to keep this wedding a secret. If I hear news of it before my announcement, I shall hold you responsible. I hope I am being quite clear."

The man nodded and cast an understanding glance towards the new Lady Cavanley. "I quite comprehend, Lord Cavanley. I have given you my solemn oath before God—"

Adrian could no longer even look at the man.

The footman appeared at the door, flanked by the cook and the two maids. He carried in a tray of champagne and three glasses. Before the man poured, Adrian asked that he fetch enough glasses for all the servants, which seemed to please Lydia.

When they each held a glass of champagne, the maids tittering as they took theirs, Adrian raised his glass in a toast.

"To happiness," he said.

Not more than an hour had gone by before Lydia and Mary were assisted into the Cavanley carriage that pulled up to the garden gate. First stop, the coachman deposited Reverend Keats at his church, where he would record the marriage in the registry. After the reverend left, Lydia and Mary were alone in the carriage, while Adrian rode beside the carriage on his horse.

Lydia leaned back against the soft red cloth that upholstered the carriage's seats. In what seemed the wink of an eye, her life had been totally altered. Again.

They were destined for an estate in Sussex near Eastbourne, Adrian had told her, but that was all Lydia knew of it. She shifted her awkward body, trying to find a comfortable position. The baby kicked wildly inside her, as if resenting being jostled about.

"Is anything amiss, my lady?" Mary asked, still looking as if she might burst into tears at any moment.

"Nothing amiss," she assured the maid. "I was just getting comfortable." Or trying to get comfortable.

Mary nodded and quickly averted her face, blinking rapidly.

Lydia glanced away, confused. She'd offered for Mary to stay in London to be near the young man she sneaked out to see in the evenings. Mary had refused.

The girl had gone out that morning to tell her sweetheart she would be leaving town. Lydia had not had a chance to discover if Mary had found him. She glanced back. "Were you able to get word to your young man about coming with me?"

Mary wiped her eyes and nodded and turned her head back to the window.

Her misery made Lydia's heart ache. "Are you certain you wish to make this journey?"

Mary nodded. "I am certain, m'lady."

"We could send you back to London, if you wish it. It is not too late."

Mary shook her head. "I do not wish it."

Lydia shifted her position and again the baby kicked in protest. Mary had brought several pillows along, and Lydia tried to position them to give her more comfort. "I would understand if you wished to stay with your young man."

Mary's head whipped around and her eyes were steady. "I wish to attend you, my lady."

Lydia sighed inwardly. She feared the girl had accompanied her out of loyalty, sacrificing her budding romance. Still, she was so very glad to have Mary with her.

Horse hooves sounded louder outside the carriage. Lydia glanced out of the window. Adrian—her *husband*—came alongside and leaned down on his horse so that his face was level with the window.

"We will stop soon," he told them. "We must change horses."

Lydia squirmed into another new position. "Thank you for telling us."

He nodded and spurred his horse forwards again.

Lydia watched him, his muscular thighs grasping the sides of the horse, his back straight and tall. She felt her skin flush.

She quickly leaned back in her seat. She must not lose her heart to this man who had married her out of duty.

The thought made tears come to her eyes, but she feared that if she started weeping, both she and Mary would never stop.

They would spend the night at an inn tonight, travelling no more than four hours today and at least as many hours tomorrow. Lydia doubted Adrian would share a bedchamber with her. There would, of course, be no consummating of their marriage, not with her so grotesquely huge, but she thought it would be lovely to fall asleep with his arms around her.

She shook away the foolish thought.

Lydia's back ached and her ankles were swollen by the time they pulled into the Old Crown Inn at Edenbridge.

Adrian appeared at the door to help her alight. "We will stay here for the night."

The sky was still light, but Lydia was glad they would not travel any farther. Adrian took her hand as she manoeuvred herself out of the door, her belly preceding her. He then assisted Mary.

"I rode ahead and arranged a parlour and a meal." He gave her his arm and walked with her across the yard to the inn's door on the street.

Before they entered, she said, "I should like to walk a little, if you do not mind." Her legs felt restless and she was certain the ache in her back would disappear if only she could move around.

Mary had already gone in a back door with Lydia's portmanteau.

Lydia glanced around. The street led to the bridge over the river. "I will only walk to the bridge and back."

Adrian frowned. "I will accompany you."

They walked in silence, their progress slow, because Lydia could not move fast these days. Still, moving felt much better than being cramped inside the carriage. Walking eased the ache in her back, as she had hoped. The air was fresh, and the village pretty with its mix of white Tudor, red brick and brownstone buildings.

They reached the bridge and leaned on its wall to watch the river flow under it.

Lydia's legs shook, but she was uncertain if that was due to being confined or because he had not spoken to her.

She took a breath. "Tell me about this house where we will be staying."

"Nickerham Priory?" He shrugged. "It was once the home of Augustinian monks until Henry VIII had the lands seized." He glanced down at the water flowing under the bridge. "Almost all the monks died of the plague, it is told, but at night when the wind is just right, you can hear their ghostly voices chanting."

She turned to him. "You are jesting with me."

There was a twinkle in his eye. "Perhaps. Perhaps not."

She inhaled a deep breath of fresh air and felt heartened by his good humour. "Has the property been in your family since Henry VIII?"

He shook his head. "Not at all." He paused. "It has been in Tanner's family that long, however."

She gasped. "Do you mean Lord Tannerton's family?"

"Yes. It is Tanner's property. He offered me the use of it for the summer."

"Oh, how awful," she groaned.

"Not awful." He sounded defensive. "It is quite a fine place."

"But I cannot impose on Lord Tannerton," she said. "Not after…" She almost said her former husband's name, a name she hoped never to speak aloud again.

He fixed his gaze on her. "Tanner does not hold you responsible for what Wexin did."

"He cannot consider me innocent." she said. "Surely his wife cannot."

He made a dismissive gesture. "Nickerham is a pleasant place, and no one will find us there. Tanner offered the house to me for the summer and even he knows nothing of our—connection."

She glanced away. Her wishes in this matter were, of course, of no account. She might never believe Lord and Lady Tannerton would welcome her anywhere, but the vow she had taken earlier meant she must obey her husband.

She stepped away from the bridge's wall. "I'm ready to go back to the inn."

Chapter Twelve

Lady W— has disappeared. Her servants claim they do not know her destination. Her natural child must be ready to be born any day. Has her mysterious lover whisked her away?—*The New Observer*, August 17, 1819

They were about an hour away from Nickerham Priory when the coachman stopped at a coaching inn for another change of horses. Adrian, dusty from the road, walked up to the carriage to assist Lydia.

This day's trip had not been as easy as the previous day. Lydia's face was pale and pinched and she had dark circles under her eyes as if she'd not slept at all the night before.

Adrian did not know if she'd slept or not, but she had been so exhausted when they'd stopped at the inn, he'd arranged a separate room for her and the maid. He had had their meal sent up to the room, as well. He spent his wedding night alone.

He worried she was ill. When he'd asked her, though, she vowed she was well. When they stopped this time, however, she looked even more fatigued.

He escorted her to the necessary, during which time they spoke the merest civilities to each other. He waited for her, gazing up at the blue sky.

At least the weather was fair.

Her maid approached him, not looking sullen for a change, but worried. "M'lord." She spoke in a quiet voice, her eyes downcast. "Do we have far yet to travel?"

"About an hour," he responded.

She bit her lip.

"Why do you ask?" Adrian supposed the maid was tired of the carriage, too.

She hesitated. "I—I think m'lady is having pains."

"Pains?"

The maid nodded. "She tells me 'tis nothing, but I think the pains come very regular."

He did not understand. "Regular?"

She gave him an exasperated look. "I believe m'lady is having birthing pains, my lord."

"Good God." He stared at the door of the necessary for a moment before striding up to it. "Lydia! Are you in distress in there?"

There was a pause before he heard a muffled, "No."

He considered pulling the door open to see for himself.

"I am coming out." She opened the door. "What is it, Adrian?"

He met her with hands on his hips. "Why did you not tell me you were having pains?" His voice came out sharper than he intended.

"Because…" She paused, wincing for a moment. "I thought it a mere trifle."

"A trifle?" He supported her with his arm around her. "Your maid says the baby is coming." With Mary on his heels he started to assist his wife back to the carriage, but stopped abruptly. "Maybe we should stay at the inn. Send for a midwife."

"No," Lydia protested. "The pains are bearable. We are close, are we not?"

He started for the carriage again. "An hour away. Less, if we make haste." If they abandoned the easy pace he'd set for them because of her condition.

The maid ran and climbed in the carriage ahead of her.

Adrian helped Lydia inside. "Are you certain you want to try to reach Nickerham?"

She positioned herself among the pillows. "Very—" A spasm seemed to seize her.

He reached for her. "That is it. We stay here."

She clasped his hand, but did not let him pull her out of the carriage. "No, Adrian. I do not want my baby born in an inn. We shall be forced to stay here for days, and someone is bound to discover who we are."

He stared at her, uncertain of what to do.

"Please, Adrian," she begged.

He shook his head. "Think of how it would be if you gave birth on the side of the road—"

She squeezed his hand. "If we have only an hour until we reach Nickerham, I can make it, but let us leave now."

He looked into her eyes, which pleaded with him. "As you wish, Lydia."

He released her and closed the door and ran to the front of the carriage. "We need to leave immediately," he said to the coachman. "Push the horses as fast as you are able."

"For what reason, m'lord?" The coachman was another of his father's old faithful servants who tended to look upon Adrian as the boy he'd once been.

Adrian levelled his gaze at the man. "The lady is in labour."

The man's eyes widened and he immediately turned to the men hitching the new team. "Hurry up, lads! We need to be off!"

Adrian swung his leg over the saddle of his horse and called to the coachman, "I'm going to ride ahead. Alert the household."

He ought to have sent advance word of their arrival, but in the haste of his marriage, he'd not thought of it. His visit was expected, but the servants knew not when, and not that he'd bring with him a wife in labour.

The coachman waved him on and climbed up on the box.

Adrian pushed his horse as much as he dared.

How ironic it was. If Lydia had gone into labour a mere two days earlier, she might have avoided marriage to him altogether.

It took Adrian only three-quarters of an hour to reach Nickerham. He galloped through the stone arch of the gatehouse and pulled his horse to a halt at the house. Bounding up to the door, he sounded the knocker. "Quinn. Answer the door!"

The butler, a burly man almost as tall as Adrian, opened the door a crack, surprised to see him. He swung the door wide. "Mr Pomroy— I mean, Lord Cavanley—we were not expecting you—"

Adrian entered the hall. "Surely Tannerton wrote to you?"

The man bowed in apology. "Forgive me, sir. Indeed the Marquess wrote to us. I meant we were not informed of what day you would arrive."

Adrian had no time for this. "Never mind that, Quinn. My wife will arrive in a moment—"

"Wife?" Quinn cried.

"My wife," he repeated. "You must immediately send for a midwife. She is in labour."

"Labour!" The man's eyes nearly popped out of his head. His hands fluttered in the air. "But—"

"Send for a midwife and alert Mrs Quinn." Mrs Quinn was the housekeeper. "Have her ready a bedchamber with all the—the—things a midwife needs."

Quinn rushed off, yelling his wife's name. Adrian hurried back outside to take his horse to the stables. By the time he'd finished handing the animal to the grooms, he heard the carriage in the distance. He ran to meet it as it arrived at the front of the house, the horses huffing and blowing from the hard ride.

Adrian opened the carriage door even before it came to a full stop. He lifted Lydia from the carriage. "Can you walk?"

"Yes," she replied in a breathless voice, but she doubled over in pain when he set her on her feet.

Feeling helpless, Adrian held on to her arm while she endured the pain, which seemed like several minutes but must have lasted only a few seconds.

She gave him a quick glance after it passed. "I'm all right. I can walk."

A bustling Mrs Quinn rushed from the house and before Adrian knew it, she, a housemaid and Lydia's maid took charge of Lydia, whisking her away. Adrian followed them into the hall and up the stairway to a bedchamber. Lydia glanced back at him right before the door closed and he was left standing alone in the hallway.

The midwife arrived about two hours after they'd arrived at Nickerham Priory. She was immediately admitted to the bedchamber from which Adrian could hear female voices and occasional moans. He'd been escorted to a parlour down the hall from the bedchamber, but he spent most of the next few hours pacing the hallway, staring at the closed door.

His wife was giving birth to *his* child in there. His wife. His child. Facing a battle of life and death. That's what childbirth was, Adrian thought, a battle of life and death.

Quinn or one of the footmen came from time to time to ask if he needed anything. He needed the waiting to be over.

Waiting alone in the parlour was too reminiscent of when he'd been ten years old and home on school holiday. His mother had been behind a bedroom door then, making sounds very much like Lydia's. The sounds became very loud, frightening, even to a lad who considered himself game for anything. Eventually someone remembered to come tell ten-year-old terrified Adrian that he had a little sister.

He remembered his feeling of wonder and pride when he'd been briefly allowed in his mother's room to see his sister, all small and pink and prunish. He'd touched her tiny little hand with his finger and she had stared up at him with blue eyes.

Adrian had gone from his mother's room to the old nursery, where he pulled out old toys from the cupboards, searching for a wooden rattle he remembered was there.

The next day, one of the servants came to tell him the baby had died. Adrian had only seen her once, touched her once. Adrian's mother had been ill a long time after that, and Adrian had feared she would die as well.

"Please, God, do not let this mother and child die," he prayed. "Not Lydia. Not this child." He felt like one of those friends who only appear on your doorstep when they need something. "Not for me, God," he added hastily. "Do it for Lydia and the baby. Not for me."

After several hours, the sounds coming from the room worsened, and it was like Adrian was ten years old again, frantic and frightened.

Lydia let out so loud a shriek Adrian rushed to the door.

He tugged it open. "What happened?" he cried. "Is she all right?"

He saw her lying on her back on the bed, her maid and Mrs Quinn flanking her.

Another maid hurried over to the door. "'Tis all right, my lord. She's doing well." She closed him out again.

Lydia's shrieks commingled with the raised voices of the other women. Adrian kept his hand on the door handle as the sounds intensified, Lydia's pain searing into him as if happening to himself, as if history was repeating itself.

He'd not expected to feel this helpless desperation, this terror of losing them, *his* wife, *his* child. He thought again and again that he was responsible for this. He'd impregnated her. He'd planted the seed from which the baby grew. If she died, if the baby died, he was responsible. "Please, God…"

Suddenly there was a cry of a different sort, and the women's voices turned joyful. Adrian opened the door.

The baby was in the midwife's hands, the cord still attached. Lydia was half-sitting and reaching for the baby. The maid ran to the door again and blocked his view.

"Congratulations, m'lord," the maid said. "You have a fine-looking son."

Lydia gazed with wonder at the wrinkled, squalling face of her son. Mrs Quinn wiped the child with a towel, and Mary cooed, "He looks lovely."

Lydia was speechless. She could not even compose a

mental prayer of thanks for this truly wonderful gift, but her heart soared with gratitude.

A son. Alive and healthy.

"Put the babe to your breast, dear," the midwife told her.

The baby searched around, limbs trembling until his lips closed over her nipple and he began to suckle.

"Helps with the afterbirth," the midwife added.

Lydia wanted to laugh with joy. He was so clever to reason it all out so soon. The sensation of nursing him was a surprise and a delight.

The afterbirth was delivered without mishap, and Lydia was hardly aware of the cutting of the cord. She had the illusion that nothing could hurt her as long as she could gaze at her lovely, handsome baby.

Soon she was all cleaned up, and the baby dressed as well. Before she knew it she was reclining on clean, dry sheets, in a clean, dry nightdress, holding her now-sleeping baby in her arms.

"My lady," Mrs Quinn said, "your husband is right outside the door. Do you wish to see him?"

Lydia was surprised he was not abed. The hour must be close to dawn. "Of course. Tell him to come in."

At his appearance the other women quietly left the room. He stood some distance from her. "How do you fare?"

She lifted her eyes to him and wondered if she, perhaps, fared better than he. He was in shirtsleeves, his waistcoat unbuttoned, his hair dishevelled, his eyes red.

"I feel remarkably well," she responded.

"And the child?" he rasped.

She smiled. "He is a son, Adrian, and he seems the very picture of health."

One of his hands shot out to brace himself on a nearby chair.

"Would you like to see him?" she asked warily, confused by the change in him.

He approached closer, close enough for her to be aware of his scent, familiar from their long-ago lovemaking, among all the new scents of baby.

He looked down at the child and was silent for a long time. "He's so small." His voice caught.

It felt like a criticism. "The midwife assured me he was big enough."

Still he stared at the baby. "I had forgotten new babies were so small."

"I think he is lovely," she said in defence.

She noticed then that the baby's lips were formed in that same shape as his. She glanced up at him to be sure. It pleased her that her child would have a perpetual smile, like his father.

He stepped back and rubbed his face. "And do you feel well?"

He had asked before. "Yes. I do."

He nodded and averted his gaze. "Is there something I can fetch for you or some service I can perform?"

"I cannot think of anything." She peered at him. "Did you not sleep, Adrian?"

"No." He looked down at the baby again.

"You should sleep," she said.

Adrian's behaviour unsettled her. He looked sad, even with his smiling lips. Sad and something more.

Perhaps he'd suddenly realised he was saddled with a wife and child.

"You look very tired," she added.

"I'll leave you, then." His voice did sound weary. He

backed away, pausing by the bedchamber door. "I am glad you are well," he said before he walked out.

The weeks of confinement were a hardship for Lydia. By even the day after her child was born, she'd felt like dancing around the room—and did dance around the room with the baby in her arms when no one was checking on her. She loved the time with her baby, loved nursing him, even loved changing his nappies, but the midwife had left strict orders for her to stay in bed. It was an order she could not help but disobey.

The bedchamber seemed too small to contain her happiness. When the infant was asleep, Lydia pined to walk outside in the fresh sea air that she inhaled in big gulps until Mrs Quinn came in and chastised her for opening the windows.

Sometimes from the window she saw Adrian gallop across the grassy land to the cliffs. She could spy the water in the distance, beyond where the land dropped off.

The smell of salty air reminded her of summers at Brighton. She, her sister and their governess had walked along the rocky beach or played at the water's edge, finding sea shells, and letting the water dampen their skirts as the waves washed in.

She would take her son to Brighton some day, she thought, and play at the water's edge with him.

Adrian visited her and the baby once a day. A duty visit, she thought of it. He never remained too long, but always asked after her health and the health of the baby. The baby stared at him when he spoke in his deep voice.

There was so much she avoided discussing with him, though. Naming the baby, for one. He never brought up the topic, and it was getting harder and harder for her not to attach a name to her darling baby. She called him her angel, her darling, her miracle, but those were not names.

There was also the whole problem of christening the baby. Finding godparents when you were hidden away and shunned by society would be difficult. She certainly knew of no one who would perform such a role for her.

Still, she loved the freedom of being away from anyone who knew her or anyone who wished to invade her home or sell her private matters to the newspapers and caricaturists.

Mary acted as baby nurse as well as lady's maid, although Lydia was rarely in need of another person caring for the baby. Poor Mary. She had once been so happy, but even Mary's melancholy could not put a tarnish on Lydia's joy.

Adrian had arranged for a physician to attend her and the man pronounced her and the baby the healthiest he'd seen in years. Lydia secretly thought it was due to her open windows and dancing around the room, the outward expression of her happiness.

As the weeks sped by Lydia tried very hard not to think about her marriage or her future, because she had no idea how she and Adrian would eventually get on together. Or how she could possibly endure it when her baby left for school and she would be alone again.

In the mere blink of a eye it was October and days consisted of crisp breezes; nights of frost. On one October day when the sun shone bright and the sky was blue, the physician came to call and pronounced her recuperation period to be at an end. The physician even approved travelling with the baby. After he left her bedchamber, Lydia felt like a prisoner released from Newgate. Leaving the baby under Mary's watchful eye, Lydia sought out Adrian in parts of the house she had never seen.

She found him in the library writing letters. She, too, had written letters during her recovery. To her parents to tell them of her marriage and baby, but she no longer felt optimistic that the letters would reach them. Worrying over the fate of her parents and brother was something she avoided, lest it spoil her happiness.

"Adrian?" She stepped inside the room.

"Lydia." He set down his pen and stood.

"The physician was here."

"I know," he said. "He spoke with me."

"Oh." She had not realised that the physician reported to her husband. "What did he say to you?"

He paused, as if deciding what to tell her. "He said your time of recovery is done. You can be up and about."

She nodded, uncertain why he spoke so hesitantly about something mundane. "He told me the baby and I could travel."

His expression stiffened. "Is there some place you wish to go?"

"Me?" She had not expected him to give her a choice. "I suppose if there were somewhere I need not impose on Lord Tannerton…"

He ran a hand through his hair. "I have assured you—"

"I know. I know." She held up a hand to stop him from assuring her one more time. "But you asked what I wished."

He nodded and seemed to wait for her to speak.

He never made it easy for her to talk to him, always so stiff and formal around her. She could hardly believe this was the same man who had charmed her when she'd been at her lowest point, who had shown her kindness and good humour.

And passion.

She flushed with the memory of making love with him.

But after all she had done, calling him a libertine, trying to pass off his child as another man's, *marrying him*, she no longer expected him to desire to make love with her.

Somehow the loss of lovemaking was worse for her knowing how splendid it could be.

She bowed her head. "Forgive me, Adrian. I disturbed you. Do sit and go about writing your letter. Forget my churlish remark. I—I've been so very tired of my bedchamber. I took my foul mood out on you."

She expected him to sit, but instead he walked out from behind the desk.

"Have you seen the house?" he asked.

She was taken aback. "Only what rooms I encountered before finding you."

"I could take you for a tour, if you like." He came closer. "Is the babe asleep?"

She nodded. "I just nursed him. He should sleep for a couple of hours."

"Then it is a good time to show you the house." He was close enough to touch now.

She looked up into his eyes and felt that jolt of awareness of him. Was she never to be near this man without thinking of bedding him? "I—I had thought to take a walk. I have yearned to be out of doors."

The day was sunny and warm and it would be soothing to feel the sea breeze upon her face.

"I will show you the garden, then," he said.

She blinked. "I had thought to walk to the sea."

"The sea, then," he said.

She hesitated. "Give me a moment to fetch my hat."

* * *

A few minutes later, Adrian watched Lydia descend the stairs looking as beautiful as when dressed in a ballgown and all men's eyes, including his, instantly turned to her.

Her dress was a simple one, pale blue and flowing loosely around her, but its bodice strained against her full bosom. The effect was erotic, as erotic as when he'd once come to visit her bedchamber and spied her nursing the baby. She'd been sitting on the bed that day, one leg exposed, her nightdress gaping open and the baby's tiny hand pressing into her breast as he suckled. Adrian had turned away and waited until the fire in his blood cooled before returning later to make his daily visit.

"We can walk through the garden," he said as she reached him and took his arm.

"That would be lovely." Her voice was breathless and her face tinged with colour as if she'd already spent an hour in the fresh air.

He escorted her through the small formal garden, and pointed out the stable and some outer buildings they passed.

She glanced towards where the sky met grass. "Is this the way to the sea?"

"It is." He had been walking at a slow pace for her sake. "It is some distance. Do you feel up to it?"

"Oh, yes!" She smiled.

She suddenly looked as if she could walk a dozen miles and show no more than a sparkle in her eyes.

"I have not walked so far in an age," she exclaimed, talking almost as if they were friends.

"Will you be able to do it?" The cliffs were a good quarter of a mile away. "We shall be gone an hour at least."

Her countenance darkened and she bowed her head. "Forgive me, Adrian. Will I keep you from something?"

He gave a sarcastic laugh. "Believe me, you will not."

This stay at Nickerham had been the very epitome of nothing to do. If he thought his life devoid of any meaningful employment previous to this, he had not appreciated the utter uselessness of fatherhood. He was needed for nothing here and had none of his usual distractions to help him forget it.

She became more subdued and he found his own mood depressed again. They walked in silence.

"It is not far now," he said finally.

The sound of waves heralded the sea, and the wind added an extra flourish, billowing Lydia's skirt and tugging at her hat. She paid no heed to it, broke away from him and ran to the edge of the cliff.

She stretched out her arms. "It is beautiful!"

"Indeed." His eyes were riveted on her as she twirled around and again faced the water.

The physician had made a point of telling him marital relations could be resumed. Before that moment, Adrian could at least pretend lovemaking would harm her when he left her sitting in her bed or seated in a chair in the dishabille of her thin nightdress. It had been easy to keep his distance when he told himself she needed to stay in her room and care for the baby.

Now she was silhouetted against the sky, the shape of her body revealed by the sun and wind. Most of all, her smile, her joy was an elixir, one he was uncertain he could resist. How the devil was he going to go on, filled with desire for a wife who'd not wanted him?

She joined him for dinner that evening for the first time, sitting adjacent to him, so close he could smell the lilac in her hair and the sweet scent of baby's milk. The meal was a simple one of poached cod, roasted potatoes and buttered parsnips, so there was no need for Quinn to attend the table. Adrian was left very much alone again with his wife.

"This is a pretty room," Lydia commented as they started to eat.

He'd never managed to show her the house. As soon as they had returned from their walk to the sea, the baby's wails could be heard echoing through the house. She had run up the stairs to tend to his needs.

"I hope the food is to your liking," he said. Perhaps they could get through the meal spouting polite platitudes.

"It is very nice."

He took a long sip of wine.

They fell into silence again, and the clinking of their cutlery against the porcelain plates seemed to reverberate in the room. Adrian had never been at a loss for words where women were concerned. Flattery and flirtation, so easy for him otherwise, seemed to utterly fail him now.

Lydia put down her fork and faced him. "I would like to select a name for the baby."

He nodded. At least she spoke, even if it was about a topic he had no idea how to discuss. "What name have you selected?"

She looked surprised. "I have not selected any name. I thought I must consult you."

Adrian had no idea how to name a child. "You must have names."

"I do not." She glanced away. "I suppose we could name him after my father, but it is not a very pretty name."

"I do not believe I've ever heard your father's given name." He took another sip of wine.

"Xenos."

He nearly sprayed the wine from his mouth. He coughed instead.

She rolled her eyes. "You may laugh. Everyone does."

"How the devil did he come by a name like that?" he asked.

"My grandfather apparently fancied himself a Greek scholar. Our estate is filled with antiquities."

He frowned. "I know you have sent letters to your father." He'd posted the letters himself in the village.

"I wrote to tell them of our—our marriage and the baby." She blinked. "I have had only one letter in a year. I do not know if my letters reach them."

"I'd heard they were abroad."

"A grand tour to India with my brother." She lowered her head. "But the letter I received was months ago. I fear something has happened to them."

Adrian took another sip of wine, vowing to send a man in search of her parents. He could at least discover their fate for her.

"Well." She seemed to compose herself. "I think you can agree Xenos is not a suitable name for our son."

Our son, she'd said. It cheered him to hear her include him.

He poured himself some more wine. "The name passed down in our family is Purdie."

She laughed, then covered her mouth. "I am sorry. I fear I almost laughed when hearing the name for the first time as well."

At their wedding, he thought.

She looked at him in alarm. "Do you wish to name our son Purdie?"

He could not help teasing her. "Perhaps."

"Well," she sputtered. "I suppose—if you insist."

He enjoyed her obvious dismay. "In that case, another family name must be added."

"What name is that?" Her eyes narrowed warily.

"Peterkin."

"Peterkin?" She winced.

"Peterkin." He made himself face her soberly. "How does Purdie Peterkin Pomroy sound?"

Her face paled. "Adrian…must we?"

A grin escaped. "No, indeed. I was thinking of, perhaps, Percival or Peregrine. Or perhaps, Parker."

She peered at him. "You are jesting, are you not?"

His grin widened. "Do you not like my choices? How about Piper or, even better, Pip?"

She laughed. "You *are* jesting! Can you think of any names that do not begin with the letter P?"

He sipped his wine and winked, enjoying this interplay with her. "Perhaps."

She placed a piece of parsnip in her mouth and, after swallowing it, slowly licked the butter from her lips.

Dear God.

He drained the contents of his wine glass.

"Seriously," she said, but still smiled, "we must choose a name."

He gazed at her. "Choose what suits you."

A wrinkle formed between her eyes. "I thought perhaps there was someone you would wish to name a son after."

"My father's name is Edmund."

She sobered. "Would he wish this child named after him?"

Adrian hoped his father would accept this son and eventual heir, but he truly did not know.

He poured more wine and lifted the glass to his lips. "We could name him Adam after Tannerton."

She blanched. "Oh, Adrian, please, no. I cannot name him after Lord Tannerton. Please."

"Why not?" At least he knew Tanner would be genuinely flattered by the choice.

She leaned towards him, the edge of the table pressing into her breasts so that it looked as if they would burst free of the confining dress. "It would be a cruelty to Lord Tannerton, would it not? To name *my* son after him."

He averted his gaze. She would likely think of her former husband every time she spoke her son's name. Adrian had no wish for that.

"Tell me." He met her gaze again. "If you had delivered the baby a few days before you did, would you have named him after Wexin, to make everyone believe he was Wexin's son?"

Her hands flew to her cheeks. "Never!" She shook her head. "Never! I am glad my baby has nothing of Wexin in him!"

Her vehemence gratified Adrian.

He tapped on his glass. "My grandfather's name was Ethan. We could name the boy Ethan Purdie Pomroy. That should solidify his place in the family."

She averted her gaze. "Ethan." Her eyes, looking dreamy, slid back and caught his. "Ethan." She reached for Adrian's hand and clasped it. "Ethan is perfect, Adrian. Perfect."

It seemed as if the air rushed out of his lungs. She was that breathtakingly beautiful.

Quinn entered the room to remove the dishes. "Some brandy, m'lord?"

It broke the moment.

"Very well, Quinn," Adrian said, somewhat sadly.

Another evening alone. Even drinking brandy gave no pleasure when alone.

Lydia glanced at Adrian through lowered lashes. "Perhaps—perhaps you might drink your brandy upstairs with me? We can continue our discussion there while I take my tea."

It was an invitation Adrian could not refuse.

Chapter Thirteen

Over two months have passed and still no news of the no-torious Lady W— or her fatherless child. No one has seen her. No one has heard from her. But one man must know. The mysterious man who whisked her away. Her secret lover, perhaps?—*The New Observer*, October 20, 1819

Lydia's heart beat wildly as she ascended the stairs, Adrian following her, carrying the decanter of brandy and a glass. The day had been full of pleasure, first walking to the sea, then sharing dinner. Even more gratifying, Adrian had actually talked with her about their son. It almost felt like a normal conversation between husband and wife. It had emboldened her to invite him to tea in her bedchamber.

Just to continue their conversation, she told herself.

She laughed nervously when she opened the bedchamber door.

Mary rose from the rocking chair, holding the baby. "He is starting to fuss, my lady."

Lydia hurried over and took the baby from Mary's arms. "Did you change him?"

"I did, my lady. I believe he is hungry."

Lydia stared down into the face of her son, who was squeaking and squirming. "Ethan," she whispered. She looked up at Mary, who had noticed Adrian's presence. "Thank you, Mary." Lydia smiled at her. "You must get your dinner. I will not need you."

Mary darted a glance at Adrian as she curtsied. She picked up the baby's soiled linen and hurried out of the room.

"Perhaps this is not a good time for tea and brandy." Adrian remained just inside the doorway.

Lydia swayed with little Ethan, who had quieted for only a moment at his father's voice. "Please stay. He needs nursing in a little while, but you can stay. I can nurse him very discreetly."

A small line formed between her husband's eyes. "Are you certain?"

She gestured to a cushioned settee near the rocking chair. He walked over to it, but remained standing, his bottle of brandy and glass still in hand.

"I'll be only a moment." Holding the baby, she grabbed the shawl that she'd worn on their walk. Mary had folded it and placed it on a chest near the bed.

As Lydia returned to the rocking chair, Mrs Quinn brought in the tea and placed it on the table nearby.

"How is the little lamb today, m'lady?" Mrs Quinn smiled at Adrian as well. Unlike Mary, the housekeeper saw nothing unusual in a husband and new father sharing after-dinner tea with his wife in her bedchamber.

"He is splendid, Mrs Quinn." She held the baby out so the older woman could see for herself.

The housekeeper tickled the fussing baby with her finger, but he only fussed the more. "He is a lusty boy, he is. And a hungry one." She chuckled.

Mrs Quinn left the room, closing the door behind her. Lydia settled in the rocking chair, draping the shawl around her before unfastening the bodice of her dress, all while holding the baby. "Ethan." She smiled at knowing his name at last.

Adrian sat and poured a glass of brandy. "Shall I pour your tea?" His voice was unusually low.

"In a little while, perhaps."

Little Ethan squirmed as she lifted him under the shawl and put him to her bare breast. They were both very skilled at this routine now, and she was free to transfer her attention to the man sitting across from her.

He took a sip of brandy and averted his eyes.

"Do I make you uncomfortable, Adrian?" she asked.

He glanced back at her. "I've not often been in the presence of a nursing mother." One corner of his mouth turned up. "Never before, in fact."

"Never?" She raised one brow. "A rake such as yourself?"

His smile disappeared and he took another sip of brandy. "Do you think I have left a long trail of bastards, Lydia?"

"Forgive me," she murmured. "It was a poor attempt at a joke."

He shrugged. "You would be surprised, then, that a *rake* such as I has always been careful about not fathering a child." He glanced at the lump under her shawl. "Except once."

She felt her cheeks go hot. She was indeed surprised to know this. "I am sorry, Adrian."

He poured himself more brandy.

She watched him. Even in this simple task he moved like

a man. Or, at least, the way he sat, the way he held his glass, the way he put it to his mouth made her think about him being a man. The baby suckling at her breast made her equally aware of being a woman.

She wanted him to touch her, to feel his hand sliding along her bare skin, to feel his lips upon her breast.

She took a quick breath. There could not possibly be a woman more wanton than she. It had been her wantonness that had trapped this man into marriage with her.

She positioned her shawl so she could gaze down at little Ethan. Her wantonness had also brought her this precious gift, a gift she would never regret.

She glanced back at Adrian, who seemed lost in his own thoughts. Desire surged through her again. What harm could it do to be wanton with him now? He was her husband, after all. He was a man as well, and men, everyone knew, enjoyed indulging in such needs. Perhaps Adrian, her husband, would not mind so very much coupling with her again.

She'd intended to sip tea and talk with him about the problem of having the baby christened, but any thoughts of church flew out of her mind. The baby pulled away from her nipple and, when she moved him to the other breast, she neglected to be certain the shawl covered her.

When he finally looked at her again, she let the shawl slip even further. "We do not know each other very well at all, do we, Adrian?" she murmured. "But we are married."

His expression was still hard. "You have married a rake, Lydia, but—" he glanced at Ethan "—you had little choice."

She blinked. "I am prepared to be a wife to you."

He gave a dry laugh and drained his glass. "Generous of you, Lydia."

She must close this distance between them, the distance she'd created.

"It is not so terribly generous of me, Adrian. You, more than anyone else, should know how—how selfish I am to indulge my own desire." She took another breath for courage. "You know that is my weakness."

He stared at her a long time. "Are you trying to seduce me, Lydia?"

She forced herself to look into his eyes. "Yes."

Adrian knew his brain was fuzzy with the amount of wine and brandy he'd consumed, more than he'd consumed since that long-ago episode at Madame Bisou's. Perhaps he would deduce on the morrow that he ought to have considered her frank invitation more carefully. But, what the devil, she was beautiful, desirable and willing.

And she was his wife. They'd already experienced the most profound consequence of indulging their desires. What more could happen?

The yearning in her eyes was as compelling this time as it had been that first time, except no longer did their lovely sapphire colour reflect pain and loneliness and confusion. Gone was the desperation of so many months ago. He'd eased all her problems. Why not reap some reward?

He reached across the table between them and pulled her shawl away. She gasped, but not with shame. With excitement.

Her chest was bare, her breasts swollen with motherhood. His son—his *son*—suckled at one, tiny fingers clutching her skin.

Adrian leaned back and watched. Lydia's breathing accelerated and her skin flushed pink. She gazed at him through lowered lashes, arousing him with her own growing excitement, deeply moving him with her devotion to the baby.

He watched in wonder as his son's lips slipped off the nipple, continuing to move as if suckling still.

Lydia looked up at him and smiled. "I'll put him in the cradle."

She rose, the shawl slipping from her shoulders, the bodice of her dress still open, exposing her breasts. She held the baby against her shoulder for a few moments, patting his back until a surprisingly loud belch escaped his lips.

Adrian followed her to the cradle. "How long does he sleep?"

The baby turned his head towards Adrian.

"He likes your voice, I think." Lydia smiled. "Would you like to hold him?"

"Me?" Adrian took a step back.

She held the baby out to him. "Here. Hold him. He won't break." She carefully placed him in Adrian's arms. "Ethan, meet your father."

Adrian stared down into his son's face, the wide, blue baby eyes gazing up at him. A pain seized his heart like he'd never felt before. His limbs grew weak and he feared he might drop this most precious of objects.

"Hello, Ethan," he managed.

His son's eyes remained fixed on his face, as if Adrian was the most important sight the infant had ever seen. A wave of protectiveness washed over Adrian, as well as a feeling of profound helplessness. His eyes blurred. What if Ethan fell ill? What if some accident befell him? What if Adrian could not keep him safe from every harm?

He glanced up at Lydia. "Is he healthy, do you think? Is he strong?"

Her expression was nearly as full of wonder as her son's. "He is healthy and strong."

He felt only a modicum of relief.

Lydia stepped closer and put her hand on Adrian's arm as she, too, gazed at this wonder they had created.

"He looks like you." She touched her finger to the baby's lips and the baby made more sucking movements. "He has your mouth."

Adrian glanced up at her and back to his son. "He does?"

She touched Adrian's lips in the same gentle manner. "Yes, he does."

Adrian grinned. He had a son, a son who looked like him.

Nothing bad will happen to you, my son, Adrian said silently. *Not if your father can prevent it.*

All of a sudden, the baby's mouth opened and he uttered a cry. His arms and legs shuddered. Adrian looked up at Lydia in alarm.

"He is tired, I think," she said.

"Shh, shh," Adrian murmured, rocking the baby. "Do not cry."

In no time at all, Ethan's eyes closed and he became still except for a twitching of his lips, lips that looked like Adrian's.

"Put him in the cradle," Lydia whispered.

Adrian bent down to do as she said, but he did not know how to get the baby out of his hands without dropping him. He gave Lydia a pleading look. "You do it."

Smiling, Lydia took the baby from Adrian's arms. With ease she gently placed him in the cradle and covered him with a blanket.

There was a tapping at the door. Lydia crossed the room, grabbing her shawl again and wrapping it around her. She opened the door a crack, spoke to her maid a moment, and closed it again. She returned to Adrian.

"I told her we would require nothing until morning." She had some difficulty meeting his gaze.

He glanced back at his son, who slept so peacefully Adrian felt his heart twisting again.

He was shaken by the emotions that had burst forth in him when he held his son. He suddenly wondered if his father had felt the same when first holding him, and his grandfather, when first holding his father. Adrian had felt his father's love for him his whole life. Had it begun at such a moment like this?

Adrian stared down at his son again and knew his love for this child would never waver.

After a long moment, he glanced up at Lydia.

There was disappointment in her eyes. "You have changed your mind, I think." She assumed a brave look. "It is all right. Truly, it is."

It suddenly became important to share with her what had just happened to him. She was a part of these new emotions, after all.

He met her gaze. "I once drove my phaeton in a race from London to Richmond, flying over roads so fast I nearly lost my seat a dozen times. At the end of it, I barely knew my name, the scenery flew by me so fast." His mouth widened into a smile. "That seems tame after holding my son."

She stared back at him. "Did you win the race?"

He laughed. "No. Tanner won and looked as if he'd just come from a leisurely turn around Hyde Park."

She grasped the bedpost and leaned her cheek against it. "If you think that was exhilarating, try knowing he came from inside your body." She took a breath. "You see? I do understand, Adrian, why the moment has passed for you. I do understand."

He stepped closer to her, so close only the bedpost was between them. He swept her cheek with the back of his hand. "If we created that life together, I suspect we can do anything. Even recreate a moment that has passed."

He pressed his lips to hers, a gentle kiss, not unlike the one he had given her after their wedding vows had been spoken. That kiss had been intended to reassure her that he would always do right by her. This one held the hope for some happiness together.

She deepened the kiss as if in confirmation of that hope.

His body caught up swiftly, flaring into arousal made all the more powerful by the knowledge he and this woman had created his son.

She moved away and climbed on the bed, kneeling so her face was even with his. "Do you wish to race with me, Adrian?"

He leaned towards her so that his lips were within an inch of hers. "That depends," he murmured. "Do I ride you, or do you ride me?"

She laughed, the sound lusty, her breath hot against his face. "Both," she rasped.

He seized her, crushing his lips against hers. She moved closer to him and buried her fingers in his hair. While parrying tongues with her, he peeled off his coat and waistcoat and tossed them on the floor. She broke away and hurriedly unfastened her bodice and pulled the dress over her head. Her hair came loose, raining pins as it tumbled to her shoulders like a flaxen waterfall. He kicked off his shoes and tossed away his shirt.

"I need help with my corset." She turned her back to him, holding up her glorious hair.

Adrian made quick work of the corset's laces. The garment was gone. That left only her shift and his trousers. He vaulted onto the bed while she lay back, welcoming him on top of her. He kissed her again, trailing his lips down her neck. She writhed beneath him, groping to unbutton his trousers.

He was already hard and wanting her urgently. It felt much like a race, each of them rushing as fast as they could for the pleasure they had only once shared together.

He slid off her only long enough to remove his trousers. At the same time she pulled off her shift. If this were a race, they remained neck and neck, both naked at once. This time she climbed on top of him, straddling him. Both as eager as quivering racers at the gate, he guided his length inside her.

He had forgotten this bliss, this feeling of connection to her. She felt like heaven, writhing on top of him, her head falling backwards, her eyes half-closed.

Let the flag drop. Let the race begin.

He set the pace, moving her, his hands grasping her waist. She gazed down at him, a smile of pleasure on her face as she caught the cadence of their contest.

"Faster?" he asked.

She laughed, and he was gone, lost to the race, sprinting to the finish, glorying in the fact that she kept up with him, that she wanted to win the race as much as he did.

The sensation built and thought failed him. There was nothing but the race and the woman who filled all his senses.

He felt her pulsate around him, an urgent moan of pleasure escaping her lips. His climax came a scant second later, his voice melding with hers. When the pleasure ebbed, she collapsed on top of him.

"Mmm." She rested her head against his heart.

His breathing and heartbeat slowly came back to normal. "Ahhh," he said.

She slipped off and nestled against him. "I won."

He turned on his side so their faces were an inch apart. "I think it was a draw."

She rose up on one elbow. "You are mistaken. I won."

He pulled her down again, turning to taste the tender skin at the nape of her neck. "There is only one thing to do, then," he murmured in her ear.

She squirmed beneath his lips. "What is that?"

He rose over her. "I demand a rematch."

Adrian jolted awake to the baby's shrill cry.

Lydia, illuminated by moonlight pouring in the window, held the baby in her arms.

"What is wrong?" Adrian sat up, his heart pounding.

She turned and smiled. "Nothing is wrong. He is hungry again."

Adrian frowned. "Should he be hungry again?"

She carried the baby to the bed and climbed up next to him. "Oh, yes. He may even wake again before dawn comes."

Adrian manoeuvred himself behind her and pulled her against him. With his arms around her he rested his chin on her shoulder and watched his nursing son. Lydia relaxed against him while the babe buried his nose in her breast and suckled energetically.

Adrian watched his son and a lump formed in his throat. With Lydia he'd finally accomplished something worthwhile.

When the baby finished nursing and Lydia returned him to the cradle, Adrian waited to embrace her again, to taste the sweetness of her lips, to experience the intense pleasure of making love to her.

He smiled as she approached him.

Marrying her might be his finest accomplishment, marrying her and giving his son his name. Perhaps this was just the beginning of wonderful things from their marriage, the beginning of meaning to his life.

It was something to hope for.

Samuel handed his brother the story he'd copied nearly word for word from the North Shields newspaper.

On Friday se'night an inquest was held at the George Tavern, Docwray Square, on the body of Joseph Cleckson, the unfortunate person who was killed upon the New Quay, during the riot—

"You ought to allow me to travel to North Shields, Phillip."

To Samuel these episodes of rioting, the sheer anger and discontent of the people, were the most important news events of recent times. There was unrest everywhere, and the gentlemen in the Lords and the Commons ought to be finding ways to put a stop to them. It had been their Corn Laws, after all, that had driven up the cost of bread, creating a hungry and angry populous.

Samuel went on, "I should like to interview some of the people affected."

"Don't be daft." Phillip skimmed Samuel's copy. "The North Shield's paper does the job for us." He handed the copy back to Samuel. "Send this on to the typesetters."

Samuel snatched the copy out of his brother's hand. "You are not heeding me."

Phillip shook his head. "We've been over this before, Sam.

Travel is expensive. Let us merely continue to copy what the out-of-town papers write." All the newspapers copied each other's stories, that was nothing new.

"Then let me take up the story here in London," Samuel persisted. "Let me discover what unrest is brewing here."

Phillip crossed his arms over his chest. "You are going to upset the royals with that nonsense. I thought we agreed not to do that."

Samuel leaned towards his brother. "It doesn't have to upset the royals."

Phillip turned back to the pile of papers in front of him. He lifted one to read. "We decided this long ago, Samuel. We'd stick to gossip and scandal, anything sensational. Leave the risky reporting to the other papers." He looked up at Samuel. "That reminds me, what ever happened to the Wexin widow?"

"She disappeared." Samuel felt a shaft of pain near his heart. He felt the pain every time he thought about Lady Wexin—and Mary.

"No progress discovering where they have gone?"

Samuel shook his head. "No one knows, it seems. Not even her servants." Nor had Lord Levenhorne known anything when he had called on him, heavy-hearted, after Mary had left town with Lady Wexin.

Phillip picked up another newspaper and buried his nose in it. "Then dig into some other *ton* scandal. Some earl or somebody must be sleeping with his brother's wife or his wife's sister. Everybody likes to read about that sort of thing."

Samuel had got wind of a wealthy widow who was plainly smitten with a much younger, impoverished gentleman. He supposed he could sensationalise their "accidental" encounters.

Somehow it did not excite him.

Samuel pictured how Mary's eyes would probably sparkle in joy at the older lady and her young gentleman falling in love, but she would cluck her tongue at reporting it in a newspaper.

He pressed his fingers against his forehead. It was pointless to think of Mary. Mary was gone. Disappeared with Lady Wexin, and Samuel would never see her again. He wagered they had fled to the Continent, where all notorious members of the *ton* fled to escape the consequences of their foolish actions.

He glanced at his brother. Would Phillip fund him the money to search for Mary—and Lady Wexin—in France? If he travelled to France, he had a chance of finding them. God knows he could not find them in Great Britain.

He blew out a disgusted breath. Phillip would never advance the funds for a trip to France. He'd just refused money for a jaunt to North Shields.

Samuel scraped his chair away from his desk and rose to deliver his copy to the typesetters, already busy at work on the next edition.

Chapter Fourteen

...the mob set no bounds to their rage. "Manchester over again!" "Blood for blood!" were vociferated incessantly. The window frames of the two lower storeys of the house were completely demolished...—*The New Observer*, October 21, 1819

"The London papers, m'lord." Quinn set them next to Adrian's plate. He glanced at the dates. Some of the papers were at least a week old.

Lydia and he were breakfasting in a sunny parlour with huge windows overlooking the garden. While these newspapers were making their way to Nickerham Priory this past, glorious week, Adrian had come to Lydia at night, and during the day she'd stolen more and more time away from baby Ethan to be with him. They took walks on the cliffs overlooking the ocean. They made quick trips into the village. They ate dinner together and made love all night. This was the first time they had shared breakfast together.

"You receive the London papers?" Lydia shivered. She would be happy to never see another newspaper again.

Adrian glanced up. "Did you wish to see them?" He handed one to her before she could answer.

"I do not." She pushed it back to him.

He opened one of the papers and was soon engrossed in it.

Lydia reached for her teacup. "What do you read?"

His eyes narrowed in concentration. "There was a disturbance in New Shields involving the keelmen. One man was killed."

She gasped. "How dreadful."

He made a sound of disgust. "There is a great deal of rioting lately."

Over the Corn Laws, she knew. The Corn Laws were intended to protect the profits of wealthy land owners by keeping grain prices high and restricting foreign imports. Unfortunately, they also made it very difficult for the poor to buy bread.

"At least writing of riots and such is the sort of news one ought to read in the newspapers. Not stories of me."

"There is nothing of you in the papers today." He smiled. "Thus far."

She took a sip of tea. "That relieves me."

"Your name rarely appears now," he assured her in a more serious tone.

"Rarely? That must mean there was much written at first."

"Well, there was," he admitted, looking back at the paper.

Her curiosity got the better of her. "What did they say of me, then?"

He lowered the paper. "That you had disappeared and were assumed to have fled to the Continent. There was a good deal of speculation about who accompanied you, however."

She groaned. "Those poor men, to have their names attached to mine."

He shook his head. "Spare them no pity. It was considered somewhat of a coup among the male set to be connected to you." He averted his gaze for a moment, as if thinking. "Perhaps I should feel insulted that my name was missing."

"Stop jesting about it," she cried, although he'd almost made her laugh. "It is horrible to be the object of such lurid speculation."

His gaze softened. He reached over and clasped her hand. "Do not credit what is written. It is not worth such worry."

She could almost believe him when he touched her so tenderly. "It is such a relief to be away from it all."

"I am certain it is, but you cannot stay away for ever." He spoke in a very matter-of-fact tone and turned back to the newspaper.

It was not a trivial matter to Lydia. "I see no reason for me to return to London."

He lowered the newspaper again. "Nonsense. You must return to London."

"It is not nonsense." Her heart pounded painfully at the thought. "Why can I not live in the country?"

"I have no place for you to live in the country, for one thing, and, as you have said before, we cannot impose on Tanner's generosity for ever." He stared at her. Disapprovingly, she thought. "Even without all that, we have obligations in London."

"*I* have no obligations in London," she retorted.

"You have a townhouse and servants to see to."

"You can see to them for me. You are my husband. They are your property now." A wife's property became her husband's upon marriage, unless special agreements were made beforehand. She had made no such agreements upon her marriage to Adrian.

He leaned forwards. "We must announce our marriage and see Ethan christened. We cannot do that in a place where we are unknown."

She did feel an obligation to have Ethan christened, but a christening in London would be fraught with problems. Who would be godparents? Who would come? Even her sister would consider her too scandalous to attend.

"I do not want to return to London." Her spirits plummeted.

Adrian gave her a level look. "We must, Lydia."

She turned her head away. Her throat constricted, and it became painful to breathe. She could not even think of returning to the unhappiness she'd endured in London. She felt near panic at the prospect.

She dug her fingernails into her skin, trying to be strong about this. Adrian was still buried in his newspaper and took no notice of her distress.

She tried again. "Adrian, you have no idea what awaits us if we return to town. Everyone will know of—of Ethan's birth. The newspapers…"

He placed the newspaper on the table. "Best to brazen it out. Face them all, and tell them to go to the devil. We have married and that should satisfy everyone."

Her insides twisted. "You cannot know what it is like, Adrian. There is no brazening it out."

"Ignore the papers, Lydia," he said firmly. "They will tire of you. We'll pay no heed to them."

Ignore them? Impossible.

He lifted the horrid newspaper again, placing it like a barrier between them.

"I do not want to return to London," she murmured again, but he was not listening.

"Good God!" He rose from his chair.

She jumped.

"Our decision is made for us." He pointed to the paper. "We must travel to London as soon as possible."

"No, Adrian—"

He held the paper out to her. "You do not understand. Your parents—"

Were dead? She just knew he would say her parents were dead. She stopped breathing. She wanted to cover her ears. Those hateful newspapers—they even brought her news that her parents were dead.

"Lydia, your parents, your brother, have returned to England. They are in London."

Alive? She felt like weeping with relief.

"We must pack up. Leave today, if we can," he said.

Her brief moment of relief vanished. "No!"

He gaped at her. "You must see your parents. Explain to them what has happened to you."

"We can write them a letter." She would much prefer writing them a letter.

It must take a few days for the newspapers to arrive from London and a few days more for her parents to send an announcement of their return. By this time her parents would have heard about Wexin. Someone was bound to have informed them. They would know about the baby, about him being conceived out of wedlock, and they would know she'd tried to pass him off as Wexin's.

They would know the whole sordid mess.

"My parents will not want to see me, Adrian." Not her

father, who was a stickler for proper behaviour. Not her mother, who put appearances before everything else.

"Of course they will want to see you." He looked at her as if she'd just sprouted horns.

She stood. "You do not know them! They will hate me now, like everyone else!" Her voice quavered as her panic rose. "Everyone hates me in London. They think I made Wexin kill his friend! They know I conceived a child who was not Wexin's. You know that! You cannot make me go back."

He grabbed her by the shoulders. "Lydia! Cease this immediately!"

She could not stop herself. She'd held it all in for so many months. It was like a dam breaking. "You cannot make me go back! The newspapers will write about me again. Tell lies about me. They will tear into every part of me. I cannot take that! I cannot take all those people reading about me, laughing at the pictures drawn of me..." She tried to pull away from him.

He held her shoulders firmly. "It will not be that way. You are married. Ethan is legitimate. Your parents will understand—"

She laughed like a maniac. "Do you think they will like my marriage to you? They will hate it. My father would never have allowed you to court me." She glared into his eyes. "Ours is a scandalous marriage. Wait until the newspapers get hold of it. I can see it—the scandalous widow marries the *ton*'s most notorious rake. Wait until you see your picture in a print-shop window! Wait until they write about you! You will regret this marriage as much as I do!"

He released her. "You regret this marriage?"

She turned her face away. She was breathing hard. All she wanted to do was return to her bed and weep into her pillow. "No. It makes Ethan legitimate, but it will make you and me miserable." She looked at him again, this time through a veil of tears. "Give me Ethan and let us live in the country. A cottage. A hovel. I do not care."

He seemed to have become very tall, very broad-shouldered suddenly. She felt dwarfed by him.

"We will leave for London today." His voice was as hard as granite. "You, me and Ethan. You will see your parents. You will attend social events. What you feel in private is your own affair, but, for Ethan's sake, we will present ourselves without apology. Do you understand?"

"You dictate to me?" She barely suppressed her outrage.

"I do dictate it. It is the only way." He gave her a firm nod and brushed past her out of the door.

She wished she were glass. She'd be shattered on the floor, then, and this pain and panic would be done with. As it was, she now had to endure the fact that she'd just told her husband he made her miserable and that she would rather live in a hovel than with him.

They left for London that day, as her husband had dictated, and the day after that Lydia stood in the bedchamber of Adrian's London townhouse holding Ethan while Mary unpacked her trunk. There was a connecting door leading to Adrian's room, she imagined, although she doubted he would wish to use it.

This room must have once been Adrian's mother's. It had expensive painted wallpaper, French-style furnishings, satin bed coverings and curtains. At least the colours favoured Lydia, all pale blues and whites and golds.

Lydia would have so much preferred staying at her own townhouse among the servants who meant so much to her, but she had not dared to make that request of Adrian. They had hardly spoken since her outburst.

She felt an ache that had settled inside her ever since she'd shouted at Adrian. She'd said horrid things to him, things that tore through the fragile fabric of their marriage. The previous night in her lonely bed in the inn, Lydia had missed him terribly, and the enormity of what she'd said to him washed over her.

By morning, however, she'd regained some of the fortitude that had seen her through the past difficult year. Things were not nearly as desperate as they once had been. She had food. Shelter.

A baby.

The baby made it all worthwhile.

Mary tripped while carrying clothing to the bureau, and the pile of folded clothes tumbled to the floor in a jumble. "Oh, no!" Mary cried as if she'd broken a piece of priceless Chinese porcelain.

"No harm done, Mary," Lydia assured her.

"I beg your pardon, my lady." Mary scooped up the clothing and set about folding it again. "I am so very clumsy."

"You are not at all clumsy." Lydia peered at her. "Do not look so upset."

Mary hung her head. "Beg pardon, my lady."

Lydia could not bear for them both to be in the dismals. She tried to cheer Mary up. "Perhaps you will see that young man again now that we are in London, the one who courted you. That would be nice, would it not?"

Mary's head whipped up. "I do not even think of him any more!"

Lydia drew back. "Very well, Mary."

Lydia had Mary's misery on her conscience as well as her own. Mary had never returned to her once-cheerful self while they'd been at Nickerham. Lydia had thought it was because she missed her suitor. She still thought so, no matter Mary's protests.

The maid loved caring for Ethan, at least. Mary had begged to be Ethan's nurse rather than continue as Lydia's lady's maid. It made no sense to Lydia for the girl to wish to lower her status in the household, but Lydia could not refuse her. It meant searching for another lady's maid, one who did not object to waiting upon a lady of scandal.

Ethan began fussing, and Lydia walked the room with him against her shoulder. "He is all at sixes and sevens, I think, from the carriage ride."

Lydia wandered to the window and looked out onto Curzon Street. Adrian had gone out almost immediately after they'd arrived, delaying only long enough to present his stunned servants to her.

He told Lydia he would call upon his parents. They'd known he had spent the last few months in Sussex; now they would learn the real reason why. Lydia was grateful Adrian had not compelled her to accompany him. Think what a reception she would be given.

She'd had a note delivered to her parents asking permission to call upon them. Better to warn them than to turn up on their doorstep. When it came to writing the note, Lydia could not think of what to tell them. She'd scribbled something hurriedly, and Adrian had dispatched a footman to deliver it and await a reply. The footman had not yet returned from the errand.

Lydia was convinced of what Adrian had yet to discover. Neither of their families would be happy about their marriage.

He would soon learn how it felt to be besmirched on the pages of newspapers as well. Eventually the newspapers would learn of her marriage and her return to London. Perhaps the reporters would appear on the doorstep by tomorrow. After enduring some of that harassment, perhaps Adrian would agree to send her and Ethan away. Far away.

Mary finished emptying the trunk, and Ethan finally fell asleep. Mary took him from Lydia's arms to carry him to the nursery, which seemed a great distance away, even though it was up only one flight of stairs.

And now Lydia had nothing to do except wait.

"You did what?" shrieked Adrian's mother. "Say it is not so."

"I will say it again." Adrian stood before both his parents in their drawing room. It was not the most convenient time to call upon them as they were bound for a dinner party. "I am married to Lady Wexin."

"Of all the foolish, addle-brained—" His father, dressed in formal attire, sputtered. "But she was to have some bastard child."

"My child," Adrian said in even tones. "My son."

"A son!" his father bellowed.

"My son," Adrian repeated, adding, "your grandson."

"But I am too young to be a grandmother!" his mother wailed.

His father gaped at him. "Do you mean it was you she had the affair with?" His expression turned indignant. "And you did not tell me of it?"

Adrian gave his father a withering glance. It was completely lost on his father, however.

His father laughed. "I'll be damned. It was my son who bedded her."

"This is all wrong, Adrian." His mother sniffed and dabbed at her eyes with her handkerchief. "I wanted to attend a wedding and a wedding breakfast and have all my friends present."

What might it have been like to marry Lydia in a church with family and friends around? Perhaps matters would be different between them.

Still, he could not regret that night of lovemaking, or assisting her later, or even their hasty marriage. They'd been briefly happy at Nickerham Priory. When he showed Lydia that the *ton* would accept them and the newspapers tire of them, perhaps they could grasp that happiness again.

His father crossed the room to give his wife a reassuring pat on the hand. "It is a damnable way to start a marriage."

To that statement, Adrian feared he could agree.

"Do not use vulgar language, Edmund," his mother chided.

"Mother." Adrian softened his voice "Will you call upon my wife? If you accept her, the *ton* will be hard pressed to cut her entirely."

She dabbed at her eyes again. "I shall be the laughingstock of all my friends."

"Please, Mother," he persisted.

She released a long, deep sigh. "Oh, very well. I will call upon her. We must put the best face on this that we can."

His father squeezed his wife's hand. "You are everything that is good."

Adrian walked over to her. "I agree." He leaned down and kissed her on the forehead.

His father clapped him on the back. "We shall do our duty by her, I assure you."

There could be no firmer commitment from his father. Adrian embraced him, his tears stinging. "I must take my leave. I have barely shaken the dust off from our journey."

After kissing his mother again, Adrian turned towards the door.

His father put his hand on Adrian's shoulder. "I'll walk you to the hall."

When they stepped out of the drawing room, the butler and footman, obviously listening, jumped to the side.

In the hall, while they waited for the butler to fetch Adrian's hat, his father leaned close to his ear. "Tell me, son, how did you accomplish it?"

Adrian gave him a puzzled look. "Accomplish what?"

"You know." His father smiled sheepishly. "How did you make the conquest of her when others did not? Your name was not even in White's book."

Adrian pulled away. "It is a private matter, sir."

His father went on as if he had no idea how outrageous it was for him to inquire about it. "Well, I confess I pine to know it. I know many a gentleman had the thought—"

Adrian gave him a direct look. "You are speaking of my wife, Father."

His father's face fell in disappointment. "Well, I merely wanted to know. You are my son—"

The butler appeared with the hat. Adrian took it. "Good day, Father."

His father opened his mouth to speak again, but seemed to think better of it. He smiled at Adrian and waved him off.

Stepping back onto the pavement, Adrian felt a surge of optimism. The interview with his parents had gone much better than he had expected.

Would it reassure Lydia?

He wanted desperately to reassure her all would be well in time. He'd badly mismanaged the whole episode between them when she'd gone into a panic over returning to London. He ought to have convinced her that she had done nothing to be ashamed of, that her one lapse—making love with him— had been at a desperate time for her.

Many *ton* marriages were hasty ones. He could have named some for her. Adrian had seen it over and over. When those couples spoke their vows, they were welcomed back like sheep to the fold. He'd be damned if he'd allow it to be any different for their marriage.

Adrian had one more stop to make before returning to his house, a stop he had not mentioned to Lydia. The newspapers had also reported that the Marquess of Tannerton was in town. Adrian intended to enlist his friend's assistance.

Tanner and his wife were intimately connected to the scandal that had brought such unwanted attention to Lydia— if they accepted her marriage to Adrian, who else would dare shun them?

Chapter Fifteen

It has been learned that the notorious Lady W—'s parents, Lord and Lady S—, who lately arrived from a lengthy tour abroad, learned about their daughter's murderous husband while in Bombay, India. The newspaper that found its way to the exotic land of the Maharajas was none other than *The New Observer*, newspaper to the world.—*The New Observer*, October 23, 1819

"It is so good to see you." Tanner gave Adrian an enthusiastic hug.

"Good to see you, too." Adrian had missed Tanner.

"Come see my son!" Tanner gestured for Adrian to follow as he bounded up the marble stairway.

They entered a pretty nursery with bright windows and a watchful nurse seated in a chair. Tanner pulled Adrian over to an ornately carved mahogany cradle that looked like it had served generations of marquesses.

"My son, William," Tanner whispered, looking down at a

peacefully sleeping infant, who looked of a size with Ethan, but was as dark haired as Ethan was blond.

"Fine fellow," Adrian responded.

As they tiptoed out of the room again, Tanner boasted of little William's lusty wails and strong grip. "He's a game one." Tanner grinned.

Would Tanner's grin fade when Adrian told him about his own son?

They made their way to the drawing room, about twice the size of his parents', but looking as if unchanged for two decades.

Lady Tannerton walked in behind them. "I've ordered tea."

"Tea!" cried Tanner. "I'd say we need some port first." He opened a cabinet and took out a decanter and two glasses. He gestured to his wife with a third glass, but she shook her head.

She turned to Adrian and extended her hand. "It is good to see you, Lord Cavanley."

"And to see you, ma'am." He accepted her confident handshake.

Tanner poured the port and handed a glass to Adrian. "Now tell me—what the devil were you doing at Nickerham Priory all this time?"

Adrian gave him a grave look. "That is what I must discuss with you."

Lady Tannerton broke in. "Would you prefer I leave you, then?"

Adrian stopped her. "Please remain, ma'am. I wish you to know about this as well."

Tanner and his wife exchanged questioning looks.

Adrian took a gulp of port and was about to plunge right in when the tea arrived. He waited until the footman had set the tea tray on a table and left the room. Lady Tannerton sat in one of the nearby chairs and poured a cup of tea for herself.

Adrian glanced at each of them in turn. "I am married."

Tanner and his wife exchanged looks again.

"I will explain."

Adrian began the story with his rescue of Lydia from the reporter, merely implying the events of which his father had been so curious. He skipped over Lydia's desperate financial situation and his secret assistance to her and spoke instead of the effect on her of all the newspaper stories and gossip. He told of how he learned of her pregnancy, and of how he married her. His voice trembled with emotion when he talked about the birth of his son at Nickerham Priory.

Tanner gazed at the floor much of the time or quietly sipped his drink. Lady Tannerton regarded him with a sympathetic expression. At least Adrian hoped it was sympathetic. He desperately wanted his boyhood friend to understand his choices and also for them both to understand the difficulties Lydia had endured.

Adrian stared into his port as he brought the story to an end with the reason for their return to London.

No one spoke.

He finally looked up, and Tanner broke into a smile. He crossed the room and clapped Adrian on the shoulder. "But this is splendid! Our sons will grow up together as we did!"

Lady Tannerton also smiled. "Why did you not bring Lady Wexin—I mean, Lady Cavanley—with you?"

Tanner held up his hands. "Wait a moment. You two are driving me mad with this 'Lady' this and 'Lord' that. By God, we are all friends."

Lady Tannerton laughed and looked up at Adrian. "Do call me Marlena."

He bowed. "Then I am Adrian to you."

"What do we call your wife?" Tanner said.

Adrian liked the natural way Tanner said *your wife*. "She is Lydia."

Marlena smiled. "What of Lydia? Why did you not bring her?"

He slid Tanner a glance. "I needed to be certain of your feelings first."

"Pom." Tanner addressed Adrian as he'd done all their years together. He would probably be the only one who would ever do so. "We have always been sympathetic to her. That cursed Wexin left her in a terrible position."

"You must tell her of our feelings," Marlena insisted.

"I have," he assured her. "But she blames herself for Wexin's actions."

"Fustian," Tanner responded.

Adrian shrugged. "You must understand, she has endured so much ill treatment, she is reluctant to believe anyone would feel sympathetic towards her. She fears her own parents will shun her. She is to see them tomorrow."

"Surely they will understand!" Marlena glanced aside. "It must have been so difficult for her, being so alone. And then to wait for her baby to be born…"

"Indeed," Adrian felt suddenly as if a weight was off his shoulders. He had not realised how worried he'd been about Tanner's reaction. "Our marriage should put everything to rights. I'm convinced the newspapers and the *ton* will tire of the gossip if we re-enter society and ignore everything they write."

Tanner raised a finger. "You need an entrée. I believe you need a marquess making a show of welcoming her."

Adrian's response was restrained. "I had hoped to beg you for that."

"No need to beg, Adrian," Marlena said. "Of course we will welcome her."

He decided not to mince words. "Would you be willing to be our son's godparents?"

His friend smiled wider. "We would be honoured."

"In fact," Marlena added, "Tanner and I intended to ask if you would be our son's godfather, but now your wife can be godmother as well."

This was more than Adrian could have desired. "Are you certain of this?"

"Of course we are." Tanner lifted his glass to Adrian.

"We should arrange to christen them together," Marlena mused. "As soon as possible, I think. With a dinner afterwards." She turned to Tanner. "Do you think the Duke of Clarence would attend if you asked him to?"

The Duke of Clarence was the Prince Regent's younger brother and, since the death of Princess Charlotte, third in line to the throne.

"Brilliant idea!" Tanner slapped his hand on the table. "I am certain His Royal Highness and his princess would attend. He may even agree for them to be godparents to both boys. No reason why our sons cannot have more than one set of godparents. It would start things off splendidly."

Adrian stared at him. "If you are able to contrive that, Tanner, you will earn my eternal gratitude."

Tanner laughed. "You always say that when I get you out

of a scrape." He added, "Leave it all to me. I will arrange it for the next Sunday, if at all possible."

"I will call upon Lydia tomorrow," Marlena said. "To welcome her back to town."

When Adrian took his leave a short time later, Tanner walked him to the door. "How do you fare, Pom?" he asked as they crossed the hall. "This marriage cannot be a comfortable one, not with the way it came about."

Adrian did not answer right away. There was too much to say and no time to say it. Indeed, he was not yet certain how much he ought to confide in his friend.

He might have told Tanner that he'd briefly thought his marriage might turn into something quite special. Since his quarrel with Lydia, Adrian did not know if he could ever scale the breach between them.

"I am determined to do my best by her," he finally answered.

"I would expect no less from you." Tanner briefly gripped his shoulder.

Adrian said goodbye and stepped outside. The hour was later than he thought and the sky was already dark. Turning up his collar against the evening chill, he set a brisk pace down South Audley Street. Soon Adrian would show Lydia that the gossip would cease. Soon she would be able to return to the life she'd been born to.

When he reached his townhouse the butler attended the door.

"Lady Cavanley received an answer to her letter," Bilson told him when he crossed the threshold.

From her parents. Adrian's brows rose. "And?"

Bilson frowned and shook his head.

"Thank you, Bilson," Adrian said.

Adrian found Lydia in her bedchamber, seated in a chair facing the window, the letter in her hand.

"You received word." It was not a question.

She turned and stared at him with blank eyes. She handed him the letter.

He read:

Dear Daughter,
Your father and I are pleased to find you in excellent health; however, the scandal and notoriety in which you have embroiled yourself during our absence prevents us from receiving your call on the morrow. The accounts of your behaviour, of which we have now been fully apprised by unimpeachable sources, are not the sort our family can condone.
Yours, etc.,
Catherine Strathfield

He threw the letter down. *Those damned heartless idiots.*

"Lydia." His voice came out harsher than he intended.

She did not even glance at him. "I told you they would not want to see me."

"They will change their minds."

Her gaze slid to him, but her eyes still showed no emotion. "Now it will be written that my parents refuse to see me."

And she blamed him for it.

This battle might be harder won than he thought. "Your parents will come around."

She turned her face away. "I suppose your parents greeted the news of our marriage with great joy."

"They were quite reasonable," he told her. "My mother will call upon you."

She gave a mirthless laugh. "Such enthusiasm."

"I made another call, Lydia." She still did not look at him. "I called upon Tanner. He and his wife have agreed to be Ethan's godparents, and I accepted that we would be godparents to their son."

Her eyes widened.

"They will arrange a double christening to take place in St George's in Hanover Square as soon as possible."

"Why did you not discuss this with me beforehand?" she rasped.

"I took the father's prerogative of arranging the christening, nothing more," he countered.

She glared at him. "How dare you put me in this position, Adrian? How can I be a godparent to Lord and Lady Tannerton's child? How can I? And how can I ask them to be Ethan's godparents?"

"Who better?" Adrian's patience was fraying. "Who else, for that matter? Tanner remains my friend whether you are easy with it or not, and I do not know who else we might have asked. It is more than generous of him to do this for us." He moved closer to her and leaned into her face. "I'll brook no argument on this matter, Lydia. We will have the christening. Tanner and his wife will host a dinner party afterwards, and no one will dare refuse an invitation."

"That is splendid, Adrian." Her voice dripped with sarcasm. "Force people to associate with me. That will be so pleasant for everyone." She whipped her face away.

He straightened and walked out of her room before this discussion eroded into the shouting match they'd had in Nickerham, and before they again said things to each other that were better left unspoken.

The next morning when Adrian sat down to a breakfast of muffins, butter and potted beef, Bilson informed him that Lydia had requested her meal in her room.

"Thank you, Bilson." He schooled his expression to look bland.

He tried to convince himself that she merely needed time to accustom herself to all the changes in her life. Eventually they would have to find a way to deal comfortably with each other. They could not avoid one another for ever.

At least she would not ask him what he meant to do today. He'd rather not quarrel with her over the tasks he intended to accomplish as soon as the hour permitted it.

He wiled away the time reading the newspapers. *The New Observer* was the only paper that wrote about Lydia. The paper reported that her parents were so shocked at reports of her behaviour that they intended to banish her from the family.

Adrian stuffed the paper in his pocket. No need for Lydia to read that drivel.

Ironically, one of his errands was to send an announcement to a newspaper, telling London of his marriage and of Ethan.

The other was a more difficult task.

When Adrian finally went out, the weather was crisp as befitted the autumn day. He walked several hundred yards to a row of houses that faced Hyde Park. Lord and Lady Strathfield's townhouse. Lydia's parents.

He sounded the knocker and was admitted.

"Lord Cavanley to speak to Lord Strathfield. Lady Strathfield, too, if she wishes." He handed his card to the butler.

In a sonorous voice the man asked, "May I inform my lord and lady as to the purpose of this call?"

"Tell them I wish to speak to them about their daughter."

The butler's brows rose. He bowed. "Allow me to escort you to the drawing room."

Adrian cooled his heels in the drawing room, which was adorned by Indian statues and silks undoubtedly purchased on their lengthy tour.

Lord and Lady Strathfield soon entered.

"Cavanley?" Lord Strathfield said by way of greeting. "I expected your father." Both he and Lady Strathfield looked on guard.

Adrian bowed. "Good morning, to you, Lord Strathfield. Lady Strathfield. My father is Earl of Varcourt now."

"Old Varcourt died?" Strathfield coughed.

"He'd been ill a long time," Adrian said hurriedly.

"I cannot fathom why you should call," Lady Strathfield said.

"It is about your daughter." Adrian pulled their letter to Lydia from his pocket. "This letter states that you refuse to see her."

"Why do you possess that letter?" Lord Strathfield's tone was sharp.

"She gave it to me." Adrian looked directly into their eyes. "I urge you to reconsider your decision to cut her. Not only is it cruel, but it is completely foolish—"

"Now see here—" Strathfield broke in.

Adrian talked above him. "Listen to me."

"Reconsider?" cried Lady Strathfield. "After she has dragged our good name through the newspapers? Married to a murderer, for heaven's sake. Parading lovers in and out of her house? Trying to foist her bastard off as—"

"There were no lovers." He tried to remain calm. "The

newspapers printed falsehoods. She deserves your pity for all she has been through."

"Bearing a bastard does not deserve my pity," Lady Strathfield said hotly. "I am mortified at her complete moral lapse." She lifted her gaze heavenwards. "My husband called upon Levenhorne and learned of her little scheme, to pass the baby off as Wexin's."

"My dear, I do not think it wise to discuss our private affairs so openly," Strathfield broke in. He turned back to Adrian. "You, young man, are a fine one to moralise. Your reputation is well known, I assure you."

His wife gave a tight, false smile. "I suppose you were one of her many men. You are an acknowledged rake, are you not? Is she in your keeping? Is that why you have the letter?"

"She is not in my keeping." Adrian's voice turned low.

Strathfield seized the floor again. "Then why are you here, sir? Whether we acknowledge our daughter or not can be no affair of yours."

Adrian looked from one to the other. "As her husband, it most certainly is my affair."

"Husband?" the Strathfields cried in unison.

"Husband," he repeated. He narrowed his eyes. "Did she not explain that in her letter?"

"She most certainly did not!" her father retorted.

He nodded, supposing he ought to have expected that. Perhaps she thought announcing her marriage to a rake would not gain her entrée to her parents' house.

"The child is mine as well." He fixed a steady gaze on Lady Strathfield. "And he is no bastard."

Lydia had watched her husband leave the townhouse that morning, just as she settled down to nurse Ethan.

Her emotions had been in a turmoil since knowing she must come to London. How nice it would be to be back at Nickerham Priory walking along the cliffs with Adrian.

She must not think of that brief happy time between them. It would be impossible to regain it in London.

She dreaded the christening. Dreaded it. The *ton* would not welcome her. Her own parents refused to see her.

Would it have made any difference to her parents if she'd told them she was married? She'd only scribbled a quick request to call upon them, giving no details at all.

No matter what she had told Adrian, she had truly believed her parents would see her and had harboured a secret hope they would understand all she'd been through.

Lydia shook her head. How foolish of her.

Her throat tightened. Soon the newspapers would learn of her presence in Mayfair and of her marriage to Adrian. The reporters would return.

Ethan finally fell asleep, and Lydia rose from the chair to carry him to the nursery. When she entered, Mary was there folding a basket of baby linen that had been laundered upon their arrival the previous day.

"He is sleeping," she told the maid. "And I am at liberty to watch him today." Because she would not be calling upon her parents, of course. "You could visit your mother, if you like."

She'd hoped Mary would smile at this prospect. The maid had not seen her mother since June.

The girl merely nodded. "As you wish, my lady. I am certain my mother would like that very well."

"Go, then," Lydia told her.

Mary curtsied and left her. Lydia fetched her sewing from her bedchamber and brought it back to the nursery. She wandered about the room. It had been a guest bedroom turned into a nursery when the cradle and rocking chair were brought down from the attic the day before. She sat in the rocking chair and picked up a piece of white dimity with which she was sewing a new shirt for Ethan. He'd already outgrown his other clothes.

A few minutes later the butler came to the door, sounding out of breath. "M'lady." He stopped for a moment. "The Marchioness of Heronvale and the Marchioness of Tannerton have called."

She rose, dropping her sewing on the chair. "They have called? To see Lord Cavanley?" Why would those ladies call upon Adrian?

The butler shook his head. "To see you, my lady. They are waiting for you in the drawing room. I took the liberty of ordering tea."

"Thank you, Bilson." He'd ordered tea. She could not refuse the visit if he'd already ordered tea.

Lydia looked down at herself, still in an old morning dress stained from her milk and Ethan's lusty burps. She was an appalling sight.

She collected her wits. "Send one of the maids to help me dress and another to watch over the baby. He'll sleep."

Bilson bowed and rushed out of the room.

Lydia managed to be half-dressed by the time the maid came to assist her. She pinned up her hair while the maid did her laces, and within ten minutes she was hurrying down the stairs to the drawing room.

This must be about the christening, she thought. It made some sense that Lady Tannerton would wish to speak to her about the christening. Perhaps to ask her not to appear at the ceremony. Sometimes mothers did not attend christenings.

But why would Lady Heronvale come? Lydia had no more than a nodding acquaintance with that lady.

She took a breath and walked into the drawing room. "My ladies. Forgive me for keeping you waiting." She curtsied to each of them. "Lady Heronvale. Lady Tannerton."

"Why, you look lovely!" exclaimed Lady Heronvale.

What did she expect? That she would be scarred from the scandal?

Lydia remembered that Lord Heronvale was Levenhorne's brother-in-law. Perhaps Lady Heronvale had been sent to spy on her.

Lady Heronvale smiled. "Let me present you to Lady Tannerton."

Lydia curtsied again. She dimly remembered Lady Tannerton from her first Season, before her first marriage.

Lady Tannerton extended her hand. "I am so very glad to have the pleasure of knowing you at last." She shook Lydia's hand warmly.

"We came to welcome you back to town." Lady Heronvale spoke as if this were the most normal thing in the world.

"And to talk to you about the christening," added Lady Tannerton. "Serena has very kindly agreed to assist with the guest list. I probably know less than you about who we ought to invite."

Lydia did not know of anyone who would want to come.

The tea arrived.

"Won't you have tea? I will pour." Lydia gestured for them to sit.

Lady Heronvale smiled prettily. "Oh, before we have tea, may I be so presumptuous as to ask to see the baby?"

"Oh, yes!" agreed Lady Tannerton. "May we see the baby?"

Lydia had no choice.

She led them up the flight of stairs to the nursery. The maid attending Ethan stood and curtsied and moved into a remote corner of the room.

The ladies peered into the cradle. Ethan's little pink mouth moved as it often did when he slept. Lydia always supposed he was dreaming of nursing. He clutched his blanket with one hand. The other hand rested on the lace of his cap.

"Oh, he is precious!" exclaimed Lady Heronvale. "He is so fair!"

What had she expected? Was she searching for clues to the baby's paternity?

Lady Tannerton gently stroked the baby's forehead with her finger. "I believe he is every bit as big as my son." She glanced up at Lydia. "My son is about one month older."

"And I have a daughter the same age." Lady Heronvale laughed. "Your boys will be rivals over her!"

Lydia remained guarded. This affability could not be genuine, especially from Lady Tannerton who had suffered so much because of Lydia.

Lady Tannerton gazed back at Ethan. "No one seeing this boy will dare question his paternity. Not with that little mouth." She gave Lydia a steady look. "He is the very picture of your husband."

Lydia stiffened. "Did you come to discover if my baby was indeed my husband's?"

"Oh, no!" exclaimed Lady Heronvale.

Lady Tannerton did not waver. "We came here to offer our

friendship and our help. I assure you, I have experienced too much of life to ever judge another woman's difficulties."

"And I assure you, there are secrets in our family as well," Lady Heronvale added. She gazed down at the baby and her voice turned dreamy. "But when you look upon something so precious as a little baby—this dear little one—what does anything else matter?"

Lydia looked from one lady to the other. "I do not believe this."

Lady Tannerton put a hand on her arm and looked her directly in the eyes. "Believe us."

Lady Heronvale tore herself away from gazing upon the baby. "Yes, and there is much to do. We have a christening to plan! We shall not leave so important a task to the fathers." She linked arms with the other two ladies. "Do you know who Marlena says we must invite?"

"Who?" asked Lydia suspiciously.

"The Duke of Clarence!" Lady Heronvale laughed again. "He may even agree to be your son's godparent!"

Lydia's jaw dropped.

"It is true," Lady Tannerton said. "He is another friend of my husband's, and Tanner intends to ask him if he and Her Royal Highness, Princess Adelaide, would be our sons' godparents. Tanner said the Duke has always been fond of your Adrian, so he is confident the answer will be yes."

Lydia felt as if she'd run a great distance. "The Duke of Clarence?" she whispered.

Chapter Sixteen

Marriage Announcement. Viscount Cavanley to The Lady Wexin, formerly Lady Lydia Strathfield, August 16, in Mayfair... Birth Announcement. August. The Viscountess Cavanley, a son and heir.—*The Morning Post*, November 1, 1819

"This is an outrage!" Phillip Reed shot to his feet, sending the chair to his desk clattering to the floor.

Samuel nearly suffered an apoplexy. "What is it?"

Phillip held up a newspaper. "It is *The Morning Post*, that is what it is! An announcement. Two announcements!" His face turned an alarming shade of red. "They've stolen the story right from under us, and I want to know why the deuce we did not know this first."

Samuel walked over to him. "What? What story?"

"Lady Wexin!"

Samuel froze.

Phillip thrust *The Morning Post* into Samuel's hands.

Samuel read for himself. "Lord Cavanley?" The one man Samuel knew the lady had seen.

He'd found no indication of any other encounter between Cavanley and Lady Wexin. Cavanley had spent more time at Madame Bisou's gaming house than anywhere else. He'd given up on the man. Prematurely, it seemed.

Phillip picked up the chair and threw it down again. "Why did you not discover this? You were following the story. What the deuce have you been doing?"

Samuel had been looking into the presence of unrest in the various guilds in the city to gauge if the level of discontent would spawn an assembly the size of Peterloo or a riot like that at North Shields, but he'd best not admit that to Phillip.

"I have been out and about, with my ear to the ground for any news of the lady. I've been speaking to her parents' servants regularly. I have heard nothing." Of course, he had not checked for a couple days.

"Well, *The Morning Post* certainly heard," Phillip huffed.

Samuel glared at his brother. "Do not plague me with this! Those were announcements! Someone brought them to the *Post*."

Phillip put his fists on his hips. "Blast it, you should have known before the announcement was made! It is your story, Sam, the best story we've ever had. What happened to your source inside her house? Could you not worm the information out of that servant?"

"How dare you question my skills at reporting? All you do is sit here and select what to steal from other newspapers." Samuel grabbed his hat. "I'll endure no more of this." He stormed out of the office.

Samuel strode down the street, not really heeding where

he was headed, angry at Phillip for ringing a peal over his head, angry at himself for slacking off on the story and missing out.

Phillip was right. He should have known that Lady Wexin had returned to town as soon as her feet alighted from the carriage. He should have sensed it in the air.

Because Mary would be with her.

Samuel reached the line of idle hackney coaches and grabbed the first one.

"To Mayfair," he said to the jarvey.

Samuel had the hack stop at Hill Street, alighting in front of the Wexins' townhouse. A reporter from another paper was just stepping away from the door.

The man shook his head at Samuel. "You've seen the *Post*, then, have you? Some surprise, eh?" All the reporters knew this was Samuel's story. "She's not here, though. I'm off to Cavanley's place."

Samuel walked with the reporter to the Cavanley house, where others had already gathered. The reporters engaged in some good-natured ribbing at Samuel's expense about *The Morning Post* breaking his story.

"What do we know?" he asked.

"She's in there," one of the men said. "She's married to him. One of the neighbour's servants said the Marchionesses of Heronvale and Tannerton called on her yesterday. Her mother-in-law, Lady Varcourt, came today."

Lady Tannerton had called upon Lady Cavanley? That was interesting, Samuel thought, but, more importantly, had Mary come to London with her?

"Cavanley's been out, but not her," another man said.

Samuel nodded. He hung around with the others for a

while, but, as soon as he could contrive to do so, he slipped away and walked around to the garden gate, peering through its cracks at the back of the house. He saw no one.

His spirits plummeted, but what had he expected? Even if he could see Mary, she would not speak to him. And there was nothing he could say to her that would make any difference at all.

Still, he just wanted to see her, to glimpse her trim figure, her pretty round face, her huge, expressive eyes. He just wanted to see her.

He made his way back to the front of the house. His colleagues were all abuzz.

"What happened?" he asked.

"Wouldn't you like to know?" one of them muttered. The others drifted away.

Samuel paced back and forth, thinking Phillip would kill him if he did not discover what this latest piece of information was. He sidled up to one of the younger lads, there to run errands for his newspaper's reporter.

"Interesting news, eh?" he said.

The young fellow nodded. "You can never guess with the Quality, can you?" Then he peered at Samuel. "I thought you didn't know."

Samuel shrugged. "I knew about it yesterday."

"Go on," he said. "You couldn't have."

Samuel rocked back and forth on his heels. "I did." He gave the fellow a sideways glance. "In fact, I know more than you do."

"Y're bamming me."

"I'm not," Samuel said. "I'll make a wager with you. If I don't know more than you, I'll give you a shilling."

The lad grinned. "A shilling?"

Samuel pulled a shilling from his pocket and held it up. "You must convince me you know what I just heard, however."

The lad stared at the shilling. "That the Cavanley baby and the Tannerton baby are to be christened together at St George's in Hanover Square, do you mean?"

Samuel handed the shilling to the fellow and walked off.

The christening took place one week later on Sunday, 7 November, with the Duke of Clarence and his new wife, Princess Adelaide, standing up as godparents to both infants. The sunny, cool day, as well as the presence of the Royal Duke and perhaps sheer curiosity, resulted in a full church. Only a very few invitations had been regrets.

Lydia had hastily commissioned her old modiste to make a new gown for the event. After a tearful reunion with the dear woman, which surprised Lydia almost as much as the welcome from Ladies Heronvale and Tannerton, the modiste outdid herself in creating a stunning gown. The design was elegant and the fabric a perfect complement to Lydia's colouring, pale yellow muslin with threads of gold running through it so that it caught the light and shimmered. Lydia's hat was a matching confection woven with strands of gold, and decorated with ribbons and flowers and lace. The ensemble cost a fortune.

Perhaps Adrian would object to the cost of keeping her in London.

At least the dress gave Lydia a small measure of confidence. She knew she looked the part of a tasteful and wealthy wife and mother. Adrian had said nothing when he saw her in the gown, and Lydia had been unable to interpret the intense expression on his face.

She'd done well, she thought, greeting people who could not

quite meet her eye, pretending not to notice whispers behind gloved hands. She made herself focus on Ethan, her son, remembering that this was *his* day, not the day the notorious Lady W—now the notorious Lady C—came out of seclusion.

Lydia had attended St George's Church in Hanover Square many times, but, after a year's absence, it felt unfamiliar to her. The parents and godparents were gathered around the baptismal font. Lydia held the Tannerton infant, named William after the Duke of Clarence, and Lady Tannerton held Ethan. When the water was poured over little Ethan's head, he gurgled with pleasure, as if he'd known he must charm everyone to assist in improving his mother's reputation. William, the son of the Marquess, wailed in outraged protest.

When the ceremony ended, Lydia handed baby William to his nurse and soon found herself walking down the aisle next to the Duke of Clarence.

She took the opportunity to speak to him. "I wish to thank Your Royal Highness for the extreme honour you have done my son. I hope it has not caused you or Her Royal Highness any distress."

To her surprise he grasped her hand and squeezed it fondly. "My dear lady, I know something of being the object of gossip and a great deal of falling in love. And I know, too, that we are devoted to our children no matter how they begin life."

The Duke of Clarence had lived for many years with a woman he could not marry, the actress Mrs Jordan, and they had several children together. Even though the Duke and Mrs Jordan had been estranged in later years, it was said the Duke grieved deeply at news of her death only three years ago.

"Thank you, Your Royal Highness." Lydia curtsied.

The Duke smiled at her. "I wish you every happiness in your marriage, my dear."

A wish Lydia feared had already become impossible. "I wish the very same to you and more," she told him.

The Duke of Clarence had lately married a German princess half his age, young enough to bear him legitimate children. When the Regent's only child, the Princess Charlotte, had died in childbirth two years ago, all the unmarried royal dukes rushed to marry and breed, to secure the succession. Although the royals' illegitimate progeny were numerous, the only legitimate child had been born to the Duke of Kent the previous May, Her Royal Highness Princess Victoria.

The Duke spied his young wife. "I must go to her," he said, patting Lydia's hand.

Lydia emerged from the church and stood alone among its columns until Adrian appeared at her side. The large group formed itself into a procession of sorts to walk to the Tannerton townhouse. The Duke's attendants led, followed by the Duke and Duchess. Tanner and Marlena walked behind the Duke, and Lydia and Adrian behind them. Mary and the other nurse followed with the babies. The air was cool, the sky free of clouds, and the walk was rather pleasant after being inside the church.

Once within the house, the ladies took each other's babies again, and, with their husbands and the Royal Duke and his Duchess, they stood in a reception line. Marlena, as the Marchioness of Tannerton insisted Lydia call her, stood on one side of her and Adrian on the other. Any unkind remarks or behaviour would be witnessed by the Marquess and his friend, the Duke. No one dared. If anyone tried to escape the receiving line, Lady Heronvale—Serena—pulled them over to admire the babies.

"Look!" she would say each time she brought someone up to see Ethan. "Does he not favour his father?" She made it seem the most natural thing in the world to do, and Lydia was still not certain why she was doing it.

Lydia glanced down the line and inhaled a quick breath. Her family approached. Adrian stepped a bit closer to her, brushing against her. She glanced at him. She had forgotten how handsome he looked in formal attire. Women's heads turned to admire him.

Serena walked up to Lydia's parents at the crucial moment. "Is he not the finest baby?"

"Oh, yes, indeed." Lydia's mother spoke with a little too much expression in her voice.

A moment later her mother was suddenly in front of Lydia.

"Lydia, darling." Her mother made as if to press her cheek against Lydia's, but did not quite make the contact. "How *good* to see you."

Adrian brushed against her again.

"Mother," she managed.

Her father nodded at her. "Lydia."

Her sister murmured, "Lovely baby," but did not look her in the eye. Her brother-in-law merely shook hands, and her brother gave her a bored look, muttering something about events such as this being tedious. It was an odd reunion of people she had not seen in over a year, but Lydia breathed a sigh of relief when they had passed.

Adrian leaned into her ear. "My parents now."

She glanced at Lord and Lady Varcourt as they chatted with Tanner. Adrian's father was nearly as tall and straight-backed as his son, but his hair, though still abundant, was fading into grey.

Adrian's mother had called upon Lydia, an interview that had been tense and uncomfortable, but blessedly short. Lydia did appreciate her gesture, and Lady Varcourt had genuinely oohed and aahed over Ethan. Lydia had forgotten how stunning Adrian's mother was, with hair so white it looked as if she'd powdered it, a clear complexion free of lines, and, most surprising of all, the same smiling mouth her son and grandson possessed.

In the reception line Lady Varcourt took Ethan out of Marlena's arms, rocking him and talking nonsense to him and showing him to her husband. Lydia noticed Adrian gazing proudly at her.

After Lady Varcourt gave the baby back, she and Lord Varcourt turned to Lydia.

"How are you, dear?" Lady Varcourt said loudly, embracing Lydia with exaggerated affection. "So good to see you again. And what a lovely party this is!"

"Ma'am," Lydia responded.

Adrian's father looked at her with a gleam in his eye that made her feel uncomfortable rather than welcome. "Well, well, well."

Adrian addressed them. "I am delighted you could attend, Father. Mother." His mother presented her cheek for him to kiss.

"But of course we would attend!" cried his mother loud enough for others in the room to hear.

After Adrian's parents passed through, the crush of people waned a bit. Lydia spied a man in a dark brown suit standing near gentlemen all dressed in black.

She gasped. "Adrian." She forgot they were barely speaking. "That reporter is here."

He looked to where she indicated. "Reed." He left the line to speak to Tanner.

When he returned to her, he leaned down to her ear. "Tanner invited one representative from each of the newspapers. Better to have them report the truth than make up stories of the event, he said."

Rather like letting the fox in among the chickens, Lydia thought. Reed wandered through the crowd. He glanced in her direction, caught her eye, and immediately looked away.

Two gentlemen worked their way down the receiving line. One was a man whom she did not know. His neckcloth and collar were so high he could not turn his head. His coat so perfectly fitted his body that he could barely lift his arms.

He was soon in front of her.

Adrian turned towards her. "Let me present Lord Chasey."

"Charmed, m'lady." His eyelids fluttered and his gaze seemed aimed at the space between her and Adrian. "Charmed."

He passed Lydia and shook Adrian's hand, or rather he allowed Adrian to grasp his limp fingers before he quickly moved away.

"I cannot think he was invited," Adrian murmured.

The second gentleman moved down the line.

Lord Crayden, her one-time suitor and the man who had called upon her when she was pregnant and the newspapers wrote about her daily.

"He was not invited," she whispered.

Adrian surprised her by responding, "I dare say not."

As Crayden passed Marlena and stepped towards Lydia, she saw Tanner and Marlena exchange questioning looks.

"My dear lady," Crayden said, gazing into Lydia's eyes.

"Lord Crayden," she responded in a flat voice. "You were not expected here."

He gave her a wide smile that only pretended to be

charming. "I confess, I could not stay away." He leaned closer, nearly smothering the Tannerton baby in her arms. "The chance to see you again—"

Baby William started to cry, and Lydia glared at Crayden. "Now see what you have done."

Little Ethan, who had been so good through this whole evening, sputtered into a wail as well.

"Oh, dear!" Marlena said to Lydia. "I think we had better retire for a moment."

Lydia followed her up an elegant marble stairway into a large nursery. Mary and the other nurse took the babies and changed their linen while the ladies collapsed into chairs.

"My feet are so sore." Marlena groaned. "I wish I had worn my half-boots."

Lydia smiled, still feeling uncomfortable around this woman. "I think the babies did well."

Marlena laughed. "Ethan was a real champion; our William, I fear, did not do nearly as well."

"He did not like the water."

They nursed the babies and chatted about the party as if they were friends, but to Lydia it still felt unreal, as if she was play-acting. Afterwards, they left the babies in the care of Mary and the other nurse and returned to the party.

Marlena was soon pulled from Lydia's side, and Lydia found herself alone. She tried to glance around the room in a serene, not frantic, manner and spied Adrian in a far corner surrounded by both gentlemen and ladies. Serena and Heronvale chatted with Lord and Lady Levenhorne, and Lydia certainly did not wish to approach them.

She decided to seek out her parents or sister, who could be depended upon to continue their familial show of affection, at least while the *ton* watched. To her dismay, Lord Crayden stepped in her path.

"My dear lady, what service might I perform for you?" He had the affront to thread her arm through his.

She pulled it away. "I can think of nothing." This man's attentions were mystifying.

He pursed his lips in disappointment. "I should like nothing more than to be in your company a little longer." He darted a glance to where Adrian stood. "I see your new husband does not need you. He is among friends."

Lydia noticed interested looks in her direction. She would have to tread a thin line with this gentleman, neither looking impolite nor friendly. "I am certain my husband has many friends with whom he wishes to speak."

Lord Crayden laughed and leaned into her ear. "Many lady friends," he whispered. Straightening, he added, "But you knew that, surely. I take it he plans to continue his friendships, then." He cocked his head towards Adrian again.

Lady Denson, a pretty young widow whose elderly husband had died several years ago, gazed up at Adrian and laughed at something he said.

Lydia turned away.

"I confess," the loathsome Crayden went on, "I am surprised she was invited."

Lydia met his eyes. "Perhaps she entered without an invitation, as you did." She walked away from him and did not look back.

Her family had disappeared from where they had been standing, so Lydia was forced to make her way through the room, the eyes of the guests upon her. She crossed into another room to look for them. The Tannerton townhouse was elegantly decorated, if not in the most modern style, very tastefully done. Huge *jardinières* of flowers everywhere enhanced the beauty.

As Lydia walked through the rooms, some guests smiled at her and some felt free to cut her now that they were away from the watchful eyes of a marquess and a royal duke.

She was about to give up her search when she nearly collided with her sister.

"Oh," her sister exclaimed. "It is you."

They were alone. "I am glad we have this moment, Joanna."

Her sister's eyes darted to and fro, as if to be certain they were indeed alone.

"I have long wanted to thank you," Lydia told her. "I do not know how you accomplished it, but I cannot be more grateful to you for coming to my rescue when—when things were so bad for me." Her throat constricted with emotion. "I do not know what I would have done without your assistance."

Her sister stared blankly. "What are you talking about?"

"The money," Lydia explained, shaking her head in confusion. "Paying my debts. Restoring my portion."

Joanna looked shocked. "I did no such thing. My husband forbade me to assist you and, I assure you, even if he had not, I would not have done so."

"But—"

Her sister bustled away before Lydia could say another word. *Who had helped her, then?*

It took a moment for her to catch her breath. She did not know what to think. Someone else had paid that enormous sum, but who?

When she could fill her lungs with air again, she glanced

up and saw Mr Reed, the reporter, staring at her. She straightened and bravely met his gaze. He bowed to her and walked away.

Lydia forced herself to return to the drawing room, where Adrian still stood tête-à-tête with Lady Denson. She felt her cheeks flame. She turned in another direction but was stopped by Lady Varcourt, Adrian's mother.

"I was looking for you." Lady Varcourt's expression turned distressed. "Oh, dear. What do I call you?" Her gloved fingers fluttered at her chest.

Lydia understood the dilemma. What, indeed, ought she to call her mother-in-law?

"Call me Lydia," she answered her.

Lady Varcourt formed a smile. "Lydia." She gave Lydia a serious look. "Dear, I saw you talking to Crayden and I thought I should warn you about him." Lady Varcourt glanced over to where Crayden stood conversing with another gentleman. "I could never like him. His smiles are so false—"

On that they could agree. At least Lady Varcourt's smile seemed...dutiful.

Adrian's mother went on, "Crayden has been toadying up to anyone who might lend him money. Do beware of him, would you, please?"

"I will do so, ma'am," Lydia replied.

Lady Varcourt went on, "In any event, do tell me, *Lydia*—" she put extra emphasis on the name "—when did you and my son—how shall I put it?—get together? To make this—this child of yours, I mean." She added with a happy sigh, "My grandson."

Lydia could not believe her ears. "I beg your pardon, ma'am?"

Lady Varcourt continued as if she'd not spoken. "I merely wondered, because Adrian gave us no inkling of it. My husband told me Adrian's name was not even in the betting book at White's—"

"The betting book?" Lydia gasped.

"I see you are getting acquainted, Mother." Adrian came to Lydia's side.

She turned to him, her voice tight. "Your mother was telling me of the betting book at White's."

"Tell me you were not." Adrian's eyes flashed back to his mother.

"Not at all," Lady Varcourt responded. "I was asking her how you—er—met…"

From his spot in the doorway Samuel watched the exchange between Lady Varcourt, her son and Lady Cavanley. Something the Countess had said shocked Lady Cavanley and outraged her son. Samuel ought to burn with curiosity as to what had been said, but instead he felt like a veritable Peeping Tom.

Heronvale had instructed that the reporters must merely observe. No speaking to the guests, and, above all, no approaching Lady Cavanley. Samuel followed the Marquess's rules, but he did watch Lady Cavanley most of the time. He'd seen all manner of things about her—the pain in her eyes when someone cut her, the surprise at whatever her sister said to her, and now this horror at whatever her mother-in-law told her.

To Samuel, Lady Cavanley had always seemed like one of the caricatures drawn of her, the kind displayed in print-shop windows. In one she was drawn as a fool, in another, a strumpet, another, a spendthrift—but always mere line and ink. In person, though, she was a living, breathing, feeling woman. In person she was rather as Mary always described her.

Mary.

Samuel's heart had almost stopped when he had seen Mary in St George's Church. With the baby in her arms, he thought she had never looked so pretty.

The butler walked to the doorway and announced, "Dinner is served."

The most top-lofty of the guests headed towards the dining room, where they would join the Marquess and the Royal Duke. Lesser folk went to sit at tables that footmen were now setting up in other rooms.

Samuel had been told there were fifty invited guests, but there were more than fifty people strolling through these rooms. This was the time those uninvited guests would slip out before anyone noticed there were no seats for them at the tables. Reporters were supposed to leave now, as well.

Samuel waited for all the guests to be seated, then made his way to a servants' staircase at the back of the house. He climbed one flight of stairs and emerged into a hallway. Listening carefully for voices, he stealthily made his way down the hall.

Lady Tannerton and Lady Cavanley had come to this floor with their crying babies earlier in the evening. The nursery ought to be on this floor, and if Mary was caring for the Cavanley baby, she would be on this floor.

He listened at closed doors until behind one he heard female voices. Holding his breath, he rapped on the door.

A maid answered. "What do y'want, sir?"

He tried to peek in the room. "I would like to see Mary for a moment, if that is possible."

She disappeared, closing the door, but he could just make out her saying, "Someone t'see you."

The door opened again and through its gap he saw Mary.

Her large eyes grew huge. "Samuel!" She glanced behind her and quickly stepped out into the hall, closing the door. "You shouldn't be here, Samuel."

"I had to see you." His heart pounded in his chest.

Her expression turned to outrage. "What are you doing here? Are you spying on my lady?"

"No, I—"

She did not allow him to finish. "I don't want them to find you talking to me. I'll be dismissed."

He reached for her, but she stepped back. "I was invited, Mary," he tried to explain. "The Marquess invited reporters."

Her eyes flashed. "Then he's a daft one. He ought to know better, seeing all the lies you write. How you hurt my lady." She turned her head away and wiped tears from her eyes. "I don't know what she'd have done if it hadn't been for his lordship." She clamped her mouth shut and refused to look at him. "There you go again. Tricking me into talking to you. Well, I won't say another word, so go away, Samuel."

"Please, Mary," he begged. "Listen to me. I miss you. I care about you more than anything. Meet me. Let me make amends. Meet me next Saturday at one o'clock. At Gunter's Tea Shop. One o'clock."

She shook her head as if she could not bear hearing his words. She opened the door and stepped back into the room.

"One o'clock," he cried as she closed the door and disappeared from his view.

Chapter Seventeen

His Royal Highness, The Duke of C—, and Her Royal Highness, The Duchess of C—, stood as godparents to both infants, the son of the Marquess of T— and the son of Viscount C—. The dinner party hosted by the Marquess was an elegant affair, with the finest of the *beau monde* attending. Curiosity was rampant for the new Lady C—, who was resplendent in yellow and attended by one former suitor, while her new husband doted upon the lovely widow, Lady D—…—*The New Observer*, November 9, 1819

Samuel pulled one of the sheets of paper from its drying line and skimmed the copy.

"What?" He read again and stormed into the office.

His brother Phillip sat with his feet on his desk, reading another of the newly printed pages by the light of a lamp. It was not yet dawn, but they wanted to be first to get the paper out that morning.

Samuel slammed his copy on the desk. "This is not the story I wrote."

Phillip looked up idly. "I edited it a bit."

"Edited it? You put in information that I did not give you. What is going on, Phillip?" Samuel snatched up the copy again and pointed to the story. "See? This part about a suitor and Lady Denson—"

"Is it not true?" Phillip asked.

Samuel sputtered. "Yes—yes. In its way it is true, but—"

Phillip shrugged his shoulders. "There you are, then. Nothing to fret about."

Samuel jabbed his finger at the paper again. "I did not write this. Everyone knows this is my story, but I did not write this. They will think I did."

Phillip placed his feet back on the floor. "Before you fly into a pet, tell me this…" He leaned his elbows on his desk and gave Samuel a direct look. "Were you in attendance at that party? Because I could have written the drivel you handed me if all I possessed was a copy of the guest list. Where were you while all this intrigue was taking place?"

Samuel stiffened. He had seen Crayden approach Lady Cavanley, and he had seen Lady Denson corner Lord Cavanley. He'd also seen Lady Cavanley extricate herself from Crayden as soon as she was able, and Lord Cavanley casting gazes out into the crowd as if he were searching for his wife.

Samuel glared at his brother. "I wrote a respectful piece about a social event involving a royal duke and a marquess."

Phillip slapped his palm on the desk. "Exactly. And the story was tedious in the extreme."

Samuel secretly agreed, but he still protested. "It was respectful of the Royal Duke."

His brother waved a dismissive hand. "Everyone knows the Duke of Clarence is off to Hanover any day now. Can't afford to live in England, poor fellow." He laughed. "And as far as the Marquess is concerned, you could have made more of the connection between him and Lady Cavanley's first husband."

Yes, Samuel could have reminded the readers of the sordid events that bound the Marquess, his wife and Lord Wexin, but it seemed churlish to do so on what was supposed to be a happy occasion.

He'd be damned if he'd admit that to his brother, though. "So, from where did you steal your information about the party? There cannot possibly be anything printed before our edition."

Phillip grinned. "I have a source."

"A source?" Samuel blinked in surprise. "Who?"

His brother put his feet upon the desk again. "I will tell you once I am certain he is worth the money I pay him."

"Why not tell me now?" Samuel's voice rose.

One of the pressmen stuck his head through the curtain on the doorway. "The ink is dry."

Phillip stood up. "Excellent! You have made excellent time." He followed the man into the back.

Samuel lowered himself into a chair and buried his face in his hands. How was he to make amends to Mary now?

Adrian came out of the dining room, looking for Bilson. He found the butler below stairs taking inventory of the wine cellar.

"M'lord." Bilson looked surprised to see him.

"Where are the newspapers, Bilson?" He was used to reading the papers at breakfast.

Bilson stared at him. "Lady Cavanley took them, sir."

Lydia? Blast it. He'd wanted to read what was written about the christening before she did.

"Thank you, Bilson." He climbed the stairs again and entered the hall.

He'd been proud of her at the christening two days ago and he'd told her so in their brief carriage ride home afterwards. She'd done everything well. Not only had she been the most beautiful woman present, but she also had held herself proudly, even when some of the guests had behaved badly.

Yesterday had been a reprieve. The party had broken up too late for the morning papers and there was only a brief mention in the afternoon ones. It had not been a pleasant reprieve, however.

Lydia remained in her room or in the nursery and had begged off dinner. Rather than spend the evening staring at four walls, Adrian had gone off to White's, where he played cards until the wee hours, with some winnings, but no enjoyment.

Adrian rubbed his eyes as he passed the table in the hall. On the table were a stack of invitations.

He smiled.

They'd done it! They'd faced society and won. One appearance together had been all it took. He bounded up the stairs to tell Lydia.

He knocked on her bedchamber door.

"Who is it?" he heard her say.

"Adrian."

The door burst open and she stood in the threshold, thrusting a newspaper at him. "I told you it would be this way!"

He had no choice but to take the paper. "What is it?"

She swung away and walked towards the window. "Read it."

Adrian glanced at the masthead. *The New Observer.*

He read:

Curiosity was rampant for the new Lady C—, who was resplendent in yellow and attended by one former suitor, while her new husband doted upon the lovely widow, Lady D—.

He had not *doted* upon Lady Denson. His brow wrinkled. Who was Lydia's former suitor? He greatly disliked the idea of another man paying addresses to his wife.

"It has started," she said, pointing to the window. "They are out there already."

He looked up. "The reporters have been around since the marriage announcement appeared."

She whirled on him again. "Well, they have not disappeared, have they?"

It may have been premature of him to think matters resolved. He took a breath. "What of the other papers?"

She began pacing. "They are less blatant, but have patience. They will soon try to outdo the *Observer.*"

Adrian glanced back at the story. "This is Reed's paper."

"Whom your friend, Tanner, *invited,*" she reminded him.

He looked back at the article and frowned. "Former suitor—who did he mean?"

She threw up her hands. "He could mean anyone!"

"You must have some notion," he insisted. He'd like to call the man out, although he somehow doubted he could fight a duel merely because a man courted her.

She glared at him. "I assure you I do not, but I suspect you know precisely who he meant by *Lady D*."

"Lady Denson, I presume." He tried not to sound defensive.

"You *presume*?" She laughed, then narrowed her eyes. "You really must be much more circumspect in your flirtations, Adrian, if you wish to avoid gossip."

"It was not a flirtation," he protested. Too loudly.

She turned away.

He came after her and touched her arm.

She flinched, but turned her head to look at him over her shoulder. "If you insist on continuing this foolish charade, you must at least pretend to be the devoted husband."

"Lydia!" His voice rose, but he clamped his mouth shut. Self-rightous protests would not help the situation, especially since her point was well taken. He ought never to have left her side.

"I will remember that," he said quietly.

She faced him, eyes wide with surprise.

He tried to smile at her. "I must learn to be a husband and not a rake, must I not?"

Her brow creased as if confused.

He wanted to reach for her, to comfort her by holding her close, but she took a step back and crossed her arms over her chest.

He looked down at the newspaper again. "I am sorry for this, Lydia, but it changes nothing. We are making progress. There are a stack of invitations that have arrived. Let us discuss which to accept. Perhaps you will join me in the library in an hour and we will attend to it."

She just stared at him.

He tried to think of more to say. "You looked splendid the

other night. Do you have more new gowns coming? You must order as many as you need."

She looked down at the old, rather shabby morning dress she wore, then lifted her chin. "I have ordered new gowns."

"That is good," he murmured.

They stood just a few feet apart in this room that was unchanged since his mother had lived here. It was all he could do not to take Lydia in his arms. He yearned to rekindle the passion they had so briefly shared together, but she was still so angry at him he dared not make any attempt.

Finally Adrian said, "In an hour, madam."

Lydia's stomach was in knots when Adrian walked out of the bedroom. She felt worse than after she'd read *The New Observer*. She'd expected him to rage at her as she'd raged at him, but he'd been reasonable, and now she was no longer certain he had been indulging in a flirtation with Lady Denson, as it appeared. Perhaps he meant what he said about learning to be a husband instead of a rake.

She pressed a hand against her stomach. She was afraid to believe in him, afraid to believe in anything except that the reporters would seize upon whatever she did and make something sordid out of it.

That was no excuse for her to behave badly towards Adrian, though. It was wrong of her to blame him for what the reporters wrote and for how the fine members of the *beau monde* acted towards her—some of them, at least. It was wrong of her to blame Adrian for her own confused emotions.

Lord and Lady Tannerton ought to despise her the most and yet they professed to offer friendship and support. Lady Heronvale's efforts to be helpful were equally as mystifying.

Other people had treated her kindly, as well. Even Adrian's parents were trying to be nice to her.

Yet Lydia's own parents could barely look at her, and her sister openly rejected her and denied ever helping her.

Who had given her the money?

And had Adrian—her husband—truly been flirting with Lady Denson?

Lydia's new lady's maid rapped on the door and entered. "Pardon, my lady. Your new gowns have arrived."

The new woman was an experienced lady's maid who preferred the formality of being addressed by her last name, Pratt. Luckily for Lydia, Pratt had been too desperate for employment to refuse working for a lady embroiled in scandal. It did not mean the woman felt compelled to be friendly towards Lydia.

"Thank you, Pratt."

The woman crossed into Lydia's dressing room to put away the rainbow of muslin, lace and silk draped over her arms.

Lydia followed her. "I believe I will change. Is there a new day dress for me to wear?"

"There is indeed, my lady."

Lydia would at least appear presentable when she answered Adrian's directive to meet him in the library.

When she entered at the appointed hour, Adrian had a stack of invitations in his hand. They sat in adjacent chairs and considered the invitations, one by one.

Lydia tried to remain civil to Adrian while they discussed each invitation. One was for that very evening, to attend the theatre with Lord and Lady Tannerton. Tannerton had secured a box in the Theatre Royal, a distance away in Richmond. A comedy was to be performed, its title ironic to Lydia: *Man and Wife; or, More Secrets Than One.*

It would mean a long carriage ride each way, confined with Tanner and Marlena, the two people who were almost killed because of her. But she would not readdress that issue with Adrian.

It would also mean being away from Ethan for several hours and that thought made her ache inside. Ethan regularly slept during the hours they would be gone, but what if their carriage overturned? What if he became ill? Neither of those matters were very likely, not likely enough to refuse the invitation.

She suspected few people who knew her would travel as far as Richmond for a play. For that reason alone, it seemed the best invitation to accept.

That evening Lydia took care in her appearance, choosing one of her new gowns in an ice-blue silk. Pratt threaded matching blue ribbons through her hair. The paisley shawl she carried was an old one, but it matched beautifully.

When the Tannerton carriage came to pick them up, Lydia soon learned that the Levenhornes would be part of their party, travelling with Lord and Lady Heronvale, who also would share the theatre box. She wondered if Adrian had known that all along.

The carriage ride was not as dreadful as she had imagined it would be. Tanner and Adrian entertained her and Marlena with stories of their schoolboy antics. Lydia learned her husband was the more reckless of the two, the instigator of wild schemes, such as releasing a flock of chickens in the headmaster's room or sneaking out at night to watch the older boys kissing tavern girls at the local pub.

Adrian did not mention whether he had also kissed tavern girls when he became the older boy.

The time passed quickly. When they arrived at the theatre, Adrian helped Lydia down from the carriage, taking her hand and looking directly into her eyes. He held her arm as they entered the theatre and climbed the stairs to Tanner's box.

Lord and Lady Heronvale and Lord and Lady Levenhorne were already there.

Lady Heronvale greeted Lydia as if they were bosom bows. "Lydia! How wonderful to see you!" She grasped Lydia's hands and surveyed her. "You look stunning. I defy anyone to say otherwise. Now, do tell how little Ethan is doing."

Lady Levenhorne smiled at her. "Your dear little baby is such a darling!"

The same baby who, had he been born two days earlier, would have stolen her husband's inheritance, Lydia thought, but she answered the ladies' questions politely and asked politely after their children.

She glanced at Adrian, standing with the other gentlemen. He looked over at her, raising his brows as if to ask if all was well. She nodded to him. It reminded her a little of the silent communication she'd witnessed between Tanner and Marlena, the sort of communication married couples ought to have.

"I have champagne." Tanner lifted up a bottle from a table that had been set up with wine bottles and glasses. Champagne was an extravagant choice.

"Come, let us sit. Tanner will pour for us." Marlena gestured to the chairs in front.

Serena sat next to her. "I was curious to know how you thought the christening went."

"It was a beautiful ceremony," Lydia replied. "And a lovely dinner."

Serena made a face. "That is not what I meant. I meant for you. How did you think it went for you?"

Lydia fixed a smile on her face. "I had a lovely time."

Marlena broke in. "Well, I thought you did splendidly, Lydia. Most people want to wish you well, you know, and the others you handled with exceptional grace."

It was one of those moments that made it seem as if these two ladies offered genuine support, but why would they? Why would anyone wish her well? And she certainly did not feel she had *handled* anyone. It was more a matter of maintaining her composure. Like tonight.

"Thank you, Marlena," she said.

She glanced out into the theatre and was surprised by how small it was compared to King's Theatre or Covent Garden, which she'd attended last.

Over a year ago.

The theatre was lit with candles and had only two tiers of boxes. King's Theatre had five. This theatre could not seat many more than two hundred. Lydia was stunned to see that there were probably that many people in attendance tonight, and far too many people she recognised.

"I cannot believe it, but this has suddenly become the event of the evening. It looks as if all Mayfair is here," Lady Levenhorne said. "My husband told me only yesterday that no one he spoke to was planning to attend. I suspect he was wrong."

People had turned towards their box, pointing and laughing and whispering to each other.

"Did your husband say I would be among your party?" Lydia asked her.

Lady Levenhorne blinked. "Why, I believe he did."

It became quite obvious the people in the other boxes

were staring at Lydia. She shrank back in her chair, but it did no good. Tanner had chosen a box with a prime view of the stage and that meant the whole house had a prime view of Lydia.

Marlena put a steadying hand on Lydia's arm. "Pay them no heed, Lydia."

Lydia spied her parents in a box on the right, her sister and brother-in-law sitting with them. Her mother stared directly at Lydia and whispered something in her sister's ear.

Adrian brought her a glass of champagne. She glanced into his eyes, and he must have seen her distress. His gaze swept the house and he bent down to her ear, so close she felt the warmth of his breath. "You look beautiful, Lydia. Who would not stare at you?"

She glanced into his eyes again and felt the same jolt of attraction that had first occurred so long ago. It greatly surprised her. She thought she had killed off her own attraction when she so thoroughly killed off his with her rash and cruel statements.

He returned to his friend Tanner. As the other ladies chatted around her, Marlena kept her hand on Lydia's arm. Lydia drank her champagne faster than was typical of her.

Soon the announcement came that the performance was ready to begin. The Irish melodist, Mr Webb, was the star performer in the comedy this night, but it mattered little who performed. Lydia was the main attraction.

Someone sat in the seat behind her, and Lydia knew without turning around it was Adrian. Her senses were heightened to him, as if he'd chipped a hole in a dam and now all the water had broken through.

Someone else noisily took the chair next to Adrian. "Good

God," she heard Tanner say, "I hope this is less tedious than that blasted *Don Giovanni*. I endured that opera twice."

The music started, the curtain opened and Mr Webb came out on stage. Lydia tried very hard to concentrate on the comedy and on Mr Webb, whose voice was pleasant and who delivered his lines in a humorous manner. Lydia might not have laughed out loud, but the play made her smile a few times.

Too soon it was over and the audience clapped and cheered. An intermission was announced and it seemed as if everyone instantly got up to go somewhere else.

"That was lovely, was it not?" exclaimed Serena. "I enjoyed it very much."

Lydia had, too, she realised.

Adrian put his hands on the back of Lydia's chair as he rose, his fingers brushing the nape of her neck. She felt the touch as acutely as if he'd branded her with a hot iron.

"Ned," Lady Levenhorne called to Lord Heronvale, her brother, "I see Helen in one of the boxes. We must make her a visit." She looked over to Lydia. "Helen is our sister. Lady Rosselly."

Lydia knew that. She'd only been estranged from the *ton* for a year. Everyone knew everyone else.

"I suppose we must," said Lord Heronvale.

"Yes, I suppose we must," grumbled Levenhorne.

"Shall we stretch our legs as well?" Tanner asked his wife.

Marlena stood. "I would like that."

Adrian glanced at Lydia, who rather hoped to hide away. Her breasts were full of milk and they ached, making her wish she'd stayed in the nursery with Ethan.

"Come, Lydia," cried Tanner. "Come with us. Don't let them keep you confined."

All the curious onlookers, he meant. She glanced at Adrian.

"It is up to you," Adrian said.

"Do come, Lydia," Marlena chimed in. "We shall walk together and show them all we are great friends."

When they stepped out of the box, the hall was a *mélange* of people all in a hurry. Lydia took hold of Adrian's arm, but Tanner and Marlena were soon separated from them, and Lydia could no longer see them in the crowd.

"This is ridiculous," Adrian said after they had pushed their way through throngs of people. "We should return to the box."

"Yes," Lydia agreed. "Please." She was enduring far too many ill-mannered stares from young men staggering from too much to drink.

With difficulty, they reversed direction.

A woman's voice called out, "Cavanley!"

Adrian turned quickly to see who it was, and Lydia's grip on his arm loosened. At that same moment a young buck seized her other arm and pulled her away.

"The notorious Lady W!" he cried. "I recognise you!"

"Release me!" Lydia tried to pry his fingers loose from his vicelike grip.

"Not yet." He grinned insipidly, and she smelled drink on his breath. "Must show the fellows I'm with the notorious Lady W! The Wanton Widow! What else d'they call you?"

"Lady Cavanley," she said in a firm and haughty voice. "Release me before my husband finds you."

The young man laughed. "Oh, he's over there. He's occupied well enough."

Through the crowd she spied Adrian's back. He was with Lady Denson, who had seized him by the arm as well.

"C'mon." The young gentleman pulled at Lydia.

She saw her parents approaching. "Father!" she cried, but he turned his head away.

Her mother gave her a scathing look. "Scandalous!"

They passed her by.

It was too much. Lydia ceased resisting her inebriated captor and rushed at him instead. He let go of her in surprise, and she shoved him so hard he fell against the wall. The people around her gasped, but she pushed through them and headed back to the theatre box.

Someone else touched her arm and she whirled on the man.

It was Lord Crayden. "Lady Cavanley, I came to offer you assistance."

"I need nothing," she cried, hurrying to Tanner's box.

Crayden stayed with her and was next to her when she put her hand on the doorknob. At that same moment, Adrian and Lady Denson walked up.

"Lydia!" Adrian sounded alarmed.

Lydia supposed it was because he saw her with Lord Crayden.

Lady Denson laughed. "He was worried about you, but I told him you would come to no harm." She glanced at Crayden, amusement in her eyes. "I think we have interrupted something private, Cavanley. You'll just have to come with me."

Lydia could not even look at this woman taking possession of her husband, but opened the door of the box and went in, slamming it behind her. Her heart still beat so fast that she thought it would spin right out of her throat. She retreated to the wine table at the back of the box and grabbed an open bottle of champagne. She poured herself a glass and downed it in one gulp.

She felt something cool and damp on her chest and looked down at herself. The front of her gown was stained with milk.

She almost laughed. She'd been abandoned by her husband and her parents, accosted by a stranger, and now even her own body was betraying her. She quickly wrapped her shawl around her to cover up the soaked front of her gown.

She closed her eyes to compose herself, but all she could see was Lady Denson on Adrian's arm.

Adrian pried Lady Denson's fingers away. "That was badly done, Viola."

She grabbed on to him again. "I was only making a jest!" She glanced at Crayden, who stood with a smirk on his face. "Was it not a mere jest, Crayden?"

"I took it as such," Crayden said.

Adrian pried her fingers away again. "Stop this. I must attend to her at once."

He reached the doorknob before she could re-attach herself to him and opened the door and went inside. She followed him.

He turned on her. "Go, Viola."

She made a helpless gesture. "I cannot. I have no escort."

He strode to the door and opened it, but Crayden, who would have made an adequate escort, had gone.

"You may take her back, Adrian," Lydia said from the recesses of the box. "I do not need you."

He walked up to her. "I suddenly lost you."

She stepped away from him. "Yes, well. No harm was done."

Lady Denson came to Adrian's side. "Do forgive me, Lady Cavanley," she said in a sweet voice. "I truly was making a jest. I assure you—" she gave Adrian a meaningful glance "—as soon as your husband lost you, he was quite distressed.

I was at a loss as to how to comfort him. We came searching for you at once."

Adrian waved her away. "I could not see. What happened to you?"

"Nothing happened to me," Lydia said. "When we were separated, I merely came back to the box when Crayden approached me."

The alert sounded for the audience to return to their seats.

"I must go back now, I'm afraid," Lady Denson said.

"Take her," said Lydia.

Adrian felt he had no choice. He strode to the door and Lady Denson skipped after him.

When they were out in the hall, walking towards her box, Adrian spoke to her. "You kept me from pursuing her, Viola. You put her at risk and made a jest of it."

When Lydia had slipped from his arm, Adrian had turned to go after her, but Viola had stopped him, delaying him, and he'd lost sight of Lydia completely.

Viola drew him aside. "I am sorry, Cavanley." She sounded quite sincere. "You know how I enjoy seeing you. I quite forgot everything else."

He glared at her. "I do not want your regard. Do you understand? I am married—"

She broke in. "But you had to get married. Everyone knows that. She accused you of being the father of her baby!"

He shot back, "I am the father of her baby."

She gave a sad smile. "Oh, that is dear of you to be so noble, but you deserve happiness, Cavanley, and I can give it to you." She threw her arms around him and kissed him.

He had to pry her away. "Where is your box?" He pulled her along by the arm.

"We have passed it," she said.

He retraced their steps. "You had better tell me which it is or I will leave you right now."

She told him.

When they reached the box, he released her and stormed away, not even waiting to see if she entered safely.

Out of the corner of his eye he saw Crayden.

When Adrian returned to Tanner's box, he wanted only to explain to Lydia how it had happened that he'd lost her. He wanted to assure her that Viola was a nuisance to him, nothing more.

As luck would have it, the whole party had returned, and Lydia was again seated with the other ladies. She did not even look over when he entered.

"Where the devil were you?" asked Tanner.

"On a blasted errand," Adrian replied.

Tanner's brows rose.

"It is a long story." Adrian took his seat behind Lydia.

He watched the farce, *The Sleeping Draught*, although he paid no attention to it. He was attuned to his wife, who sat with her hands folded in her lap and did not move a muscle. He, on the other hand, had a strong urge to fidget.

When the performance ended and goodbyes said to the Heronvales and Levenhornes, Lydia behaved with perfect cordiality. In the carriage, she answered anyone who spoke to her, but said as little as possible. Adrian doubted she wanted to say anything to him.

Eventually Marlena fell asleep on Tanner's shoulder while Lydia gazed out of the carriage window into the darkness. Although the inside of the carriage was only dimly illuminated by the carriage lamps on the outside, Adrian could see Tanner's worried expression.

"I'm going to be at White's tomorrow at around three," Tanner said. "Will I see you there?"

It was an invitation to tell him what was going on. "Perhaps," Adrian responded, glancing towards his wife.

Chapter Eighteen

Can anyone expect more from marriage between a rake and a wanton woman? In their first appearance in society they continue their dissolute ways.—*The New Observer*, November 9, 1819

Adrian and Lydia no sooner stepped into the hall than Lydia ran up the stairs. Adrian quickly gave the attending footman his hat and gloves and went after her.

She was not in her bedchamber.

He heard the baby crying and he bounded up another flight to the nursery.

Lydia was unfastening the front of her dress and Mary was holding the baby in one arm and assisting Lydia at the same time. They both looked over when he entered.

Lydia quickly looked away, turning her back to him. "I need to nurse Ethan." She took the baby from Mary and sat in the rocking chair, wrapping her shawl around her exposed skin and concealing the nursing baby.

Adrian turned to Mary. "Leave us."

Mary paused a second, looking uncertain before curtsying and walking out of the door.

"This is not a good time for a discussion, Adrian," Lydia said. "Not while I am nursing Ethan."

He stood over her. "I will not rest until I speak to you."

She looked up and he saw far too much in her eyes—pain, anger, distrust, humiliation and, worst of all, resignation. He felt responsible for it all.

She lowered her head. "When I am finished, I will speak with you."

"In my bedchamber," he said.

Her gaze flew back to him. "If you insist."

"I insist."

Adrian left her with their son and felt as estranged from both of them as he'd felt the day of Ethan's birth.

He guessed she would have preferred a discussion in a sitting room or the library, but he wanted a place more private. When he walked into the bedchamber, dominated by the large four-poster bed, he realised she might fear he had something else in mind.

Good God. She could not think he would impose his marital rights on her if she were unwilling?

His valet awaited him, and it was easier to allow the man to ready him for bed than it was to explain that he wanted a moment with his wife first. So Hammond set about the routine of assisting Adrian out of his coat, standing aside as Adrian removed his other clothes, holding up Adrian's old figured silk banyan until he slipped his arms into its wide sleeves and wrapped it around himself. Hammond gathered Adrian's shirt and underclothes to launder, his coat and breeches to brush, and his boots to polish. He headed for the door.

"Bring me a bottle of sherry, would you, Hammond?" Adrian asked him. "And two glasses."

"Very good, sir," Hammond said in a tone that sounded more like approval than agreement.

Adrian lit every lamp so that it looked less as if he was arranging a seduction, even if he wore a robe and nothing else. He pulled two comfortable chairs and a small table away from the bed and arranged them in a cosy seating area. When Hammond delivered the sherry, Adrian placed the bottle and glasses on the table he'd set between the chairs.

He surveyed the room.

It still was dominated by the large four-poster bed, and, worse, it still looked like a room belonging to his father. Sitting in one of the chairs, he poured himself a sherry and decided that some money ought to be spent on redecorating the house. Perhaps Lydia would enjoy the project.

A few more long minutes passed. Adrian was in the midst of taking a sip of sherry when Lydia knocked on the connecting door between their rooms. She opened it before he could tell her to come in.

"You are dressed for bed." Her voice was tight.

He placed the glass on the table and stood. "You are not," he replied.

She still wore her blue gown and was wrapped in her shawl.

He gestured for her to sit. "Hammond was waiting to assist me. It seemed easiest to just let him proceed." It was the sort of excuse he might have come up with if he had been bent on seduction.

She eyed him suspiciously as she walked to the chair.

"Some sherry?" he asked as she sat.

She glanced at him. "This is not a social call, Adrian. It is a summons."

He poured her a glass and set it in front of her. "It was a request, Lydia. Not a summons. A request to talk to you, nothing more."

"It was a summons," she repeated, but more to herself than to him.

She reached for her sherry and the shawl slipped off her shoulders, exposing the bodice of her gown, which had two dark spots staining the fabric over her breasts.

"What happened to your gown?" He gestured to the stains.

She looked down at herself. "My milk came while we were at the theatre."

His brows rose. "It did? Such a thing can happen?"

She gave a dry laugh. "Well, it did happen, so the answer is, yes."

He took his seat. "Is that why you rushed away from me in the theatre?"

Her eyes flashed. "I did not rush away from you. An inebriated young man pulled me away and tried to drag me off to show to his friends."

"No." Adrian half-rose. "Did—did he injure you?"

"It is more likely I injured him." She lifted the glass to her lips and sipped. "But not until my parents walked past me. You were busily occupied with Lady Denson, and even Crayden stayed back until I had freed myself."

He sat down again, averting his gaze. "I ought never to have let her detain me."

"Indeed." Lydia spoke as if she was holding in a great deal of emotion. "But you made the choice."

The wrong choice.

He leaned forwards. "Are you certain you are unharmed?"

She lifted her glass again. "There are no visible marks."

He bowed his head. Just invisible ones.

His head shot up again. "Your *parents* walked past?"

She pressed her lips together tightly before answering. "They saw what they wished to see. 'Scandalous', my mother said."

"Curse them. And Crayden as well. Why did he not assist you?" He looked at her again with regret. "Forgive me, Lydia. It was I who ought to have assisted you."

She avoided looking at him. "I suppose if the young man had not recognised me, nothing would have happened. I would have remained at your side and Lady Denson would have been disappointed."

"He recognised you?" Adrian leaned forwards again. "Is he known to you?" *Give me a name*, Adrian thought, *and I will call him out*.

"He was not known to me," she snapped. "He recognised me. From the prints of me or from being pointed out in the theatre box, I do not know which, but he called me the notorious Lady W and the Wanton Widow, so he knew who I was."

Adrian's grip tightened on the arm chair.

She added, "He knew me from the gossip about me, nothing more."

He closed his eyes and saw the people in the pit and the theatre boxes all pointing at her. She'd endured it with admirable fortitude. Then he'd taken her out into the theatre's hallway, oblivious to the danger that awaited her. He'd allowed another woman to distract him and he'd turned away from his wife. He had abandoned her to the rowdy crowd.

She interrupted his self-recrimination. "I thought there was something important you wished to discuss." This time her voice trembled with emotion. "If not, may I leave now?"

He opened his eyes. "Lydia," he whispered, "do not leave."

She averted her gaze.

He did not know what to say to her. Being sorry he had failed her was not enough.

Silence loomed between them, and all Adrian could think was that his father was right about him. Perhaps all he was fit for was to have a good time, to play games, with cards, with women. He professed to accept responsibility for a wife, but he shirked it at the first opportunity.

She broke the silence. "Well, if you are not going to speak, perhaps you will answer my question?"

"Of course," he said, his gaze meeting hers again. "What is it?"

Her eyes narrowed. "I want you to answer truthfully. Do not mince words with me."

"I will answer truthfully." He could at least speak the truth.

She took a breath as if gathering courage, then kept her gaze steady. "Do you wish to pursue a liaison with Lady Denson?"

It was not the topic he expected. *"What?"*

She went on. "We have been out in society together a mere twice, and both times you have attached yourself to Lady Denson. You told me this morning that you were not engaged in a flirtation with her, but men sometimes say one thing and mean another." She glanced away and back again. "I do wish you would tell me the truth now." She blinked and shook her head. "Because if you do wish for a liaison with her, I cannot prevent you. I would simply ask that you allow me to live somewhere where I need not see it or read about it."

Ah, she wished to live apart from him. That was the crucial matter. "Do you ask so you might move to the country?"

Her eyes flashed with pain. "Please just answer me, Adrian."

"I do not desire a liaison with Lady Denson," he stated as emphatically as he could. "I have never desired a liaison with her."

She turned her head away. "I do not know if I can believe you. I saw you with her."

He rubbed his face. "Lydia, how do I convince you?" He leaned forwards suddenly. "Perhaps appearances deceived you. Your parents were deceived when they passed you in the theatre. They did not see your distress."

Her eyes narrowed. "That was different."

"Not so different," he said. "Lady Denson sets her cap at first one gentleman, then another. I am merely the next in line, and my value has increased with the rivalry of a wife. She makes it appear to you that the contest is already won."

"You place the blame on her?" Her tone was accusing.

He shook his head. "Not entirely. I allowed myself to be distracted by her, but not for the reason you think. Not for a liaison."

"For what reason, then?"

He thought about it. "I do not know precisely. Habit, I presume." He gave a wan smile. "A woman calls a rake's name and he responds."

She waved a dismissive hand. "This is a silly discussion. I do not care about Lady Denson. You will have many Lady Densons, I expect. A man does not change just because he marries."

Adrian tried to think of continuing the life he'd led, the life of a rake. Of leaving her side to play cards the whole night, to be off to the races or hunting or travelling whenever the whim struck him, to set up a new mistress and be seen with her about town.

None of it appealed.

He leaned over to her, trying again to convince her that he spoke the truth. "Listen to me, Lydia, and please believe me. I do not want Lady Denson or any other woman. I am ready to be your husband and Ethan's father."

She looked at him with scepticism. "You were forced to marry me."

"I was not forced," he countered. "I chose to marry you. I chose to make love to you that night and I chose to marry you. You were the one who did not have a choice."

She met his gaze. "I chose to seduce you."

That fateful choice. "Perhaps we can look on that as a fortunate choice, the choice that brought us together. Perhaps even that event is subject to perception. We can see it the way we want to see it."

Her parents had perceived the very worst of her. If people erroneously perceive the very worst, why could they not turn it around and see the very best?

She gazed at him very intently. "What do you propose, Adrian?" Her voice turned low.

He returned her gaze with as much sincerity as he could convey. "Let us decide to enjoy this marriage of ours, Lydia, as we did once, so briefly."

Her breath quickened and her eyes flashed with fear.

He backed away. "This is not coercion. It is not a dictate. I speak the truth when I say I want a marriage with you." He paused. "But if you do not want me, tell me now. I'll find you a home in the country if you wish it."

He waited for a long time for her answer.

Finally she said, "Very well, Adrian. We will try this a

little longer, but next time I ask to leave, you must promise to let me go."

It was his turn to pause. "I promise to let you go," he finally said, "if you so request it."

He extended his hand to seal the bargain with a handshake. She held back at first as if reconsidering, but eventually she did clasp her hand to his. Her hand was soft and warm and he was reluctant to let go.

They stared into each other's eyes, hands clasped but still, as if they'd become bound together. It was what he wanted, Adrian thought. He wanted to be bound to her.

Lydia felt captured in his gaze, so intent, so unwavering, so earnest. She could feel the air moving in and out of her lungs. If she could trust her judgement, she would say she saw truth in his eyes, but she could not trust herself.

She *perceived* him to be telling the truth, that was it, but perception was not truth, not proof of what was real.

Her senses told her the strong grasp of his hand was real. His smooth palm, the spattering of hairs on the back of his hand. Those were real.

Her eyes darted away, but landed on the bed in the centre of the room. Its covers were turned down and she could imagine how cool they would feel against her bare skin. How warm he would be in contrast.

The air rushed into her lungs at a faster rate.

She gazed at him again. His eyes were dark and yearning now, an emotion she, too, well understood.

She ought to snatch her hand back and run to the safety of the bedchamber on the other side of the connecting door, but she did not wish to let go of his hand, the hand that was making her senses sing, making her body flare to life in a manner it only had done with him.

He bowed his head and let her hand slip from his. She felt bereft. He expected her to leave.

She started to turn away, but caught sight of the bed again. She turned back.

"Do you wish for a real marriage, Adrian?" Her voice felt raw in her throat.

His brows rose. "What do you mean?"

"Do you intend to assert your marital rights?"

He stood perfectly still. "I would do nothing you did not wish me to do."

She averted her gaze. "And if I wished it?"

"You have only to ask," he replied.

She turned and looked at him through lowered lashes. "Must I always ask?"

A smile flashed across his face. He gently touched her hair and plucked out the pins, one by one. Her hair tumbled onto her shoulders. He pulled the blue ribbon from her curls and used his fingers as a comb, smoothing the tangles. The sensation was so lovely Lydia sighed with the pleasure of it. Next he pulled away her shawl, almost tentatively, as if half-expecting her to flee after all, but she did not wish to flee.

It made no sense for her to want his lovemaking after such a dreadful evening, but his touch never failed to ignite her desire, to fan it into a white-hot heat. Her desire was as real as the sensation of his fingers in her hair, his hand on her skin.

His hand slipped down her neck to her breasts, skimming the stained silk fabric, making her need more urgent. He searched for the complicated fastenings of her bodice, making her wish he would just rip the fabric away.

She stilled his hand and undid the bodice, pulling the gown over her head.

"You must have another gown made like this one," he murmured to her, caressing her neck and quickly untying the laces of her corset. "You looked beautiful in it."

She could only hope his words were not mere flattery.

He unlaced her corset with ease and soon she was free of all clothing but her shift.

He took her hand once more. "I am asking this time, Lydia," he murmured, leading her to the bed.

"Yes," she breathed.

He lifted her hand to his lips, placing his kiss in her palm like a gift.

She untied the sash of his banyan and slipped her hands underneath, feeling the firm muscles of his chest, the peppering of his hair. She rested her hand against his heart and felt it beating.

This was real, not perception.

His scent filled her nostrils, clean and male and, like an aphrodisiac, instantly enveloped her in carnal desire.

He released her hand and lowered his head to place his lips on hers, his kiss gentle, reverent and real.

Uncertainty plagued her, but there was nothing uncertain about Adrian's touch, his lips, his waiting body. She wrapped her arms around his neck and pressed herself against him, savouring the taste of him, the feel of him.

He splayed his hands around her waist and lifted her onto the bed, shedding his banyan and climbing up next to her. She rid herself of her shift and met him on her knees for another, less gentle, more demanding kiss.

He stroked her naked skin, his touch familiar from their

too-brief moments of bliss, like revisiting a place with happy memories. He kneaded her skin, ran his thumbs across her nipples and lowered his mouth to her breast, his tongue hot and wet.

He laughed against her. "I believe you taste of milk."

She kissed the top of his head, holding him as he tasted her again.

His lips were not perception, nor his laugh, nor the rigid male part of him that told of his desire for her.

He laid her down and entered her. She vowed to savour every sensation, every tangible thing, not only the growing urgency he created as he moved inside her, but also the sheen of perspiration on their skin, the sound of his breathing, the press of his weight upon her. She felt the smooth fabric of the bed linen against her back and the rough texture of the hair on his legs.

All real.

Lydia abandoned herself to the experience, feeling her need grow with each stroke, feeling it build as his breath came faster. Sounds, uniquely his, escaped his mouth. He brought her closer and closer, yet made her want to beg him to hurry.

Her release came in a sudden burst and she cried out. While she still throbbed with exquisite pleasure, he spilled his seed, and she felt truly joined to him, as if they were for ever connected.

But that was perception, she thought, as her pleasure ebbed and reason returned. *Illusion.*

He slid off her and nestled her against him while she felt his heartbeat and breathing return to normal. His lips found tender skin on the back of her neck.

"Stay with me tonight," he murmured.

She did not think herself capable of leaving him.

* * *

The room was light with the first stages of dawn when Adrian opened his eyes, suddenly aware that Lydia was no longer at his side.

She was moving about the room, gathering her clothing.

"Lydia?" He'd hoped she would not leave him.

She started, but turned to him. "Ethan's crying," she said. "I must go to him."

Crying? Adrian strained to hear and could just barely make out Ethan's sounds.

She disappeared through the connecting door.

It was not until breakfast that he saw her again, but for her to share breakfast with him seemed like a huge step forwards.

As their lovemaking had been.

He almost dared to hope all would be well between them.

She was filling her plate from the side board, when Bilson brought in the morning newspapers. Both he and Lydia froze. She sat stiffly, pouring her tea as Adrian picked up *The New Observer* and looked for the section filled with gossip.

He looked up at her. "It is not so bad. A mere rehash of the christening and a promise of more tomorrow."

Lydia frowned.

He put the paper down. "Remember. It is all perception. We act as if the newspapers do not even mention us, and the stories will be discounted. People will believe what they see."

"Or they will see what they wish to see," she added in a strained voice.

He skimmed through the other papers, but they merely mentioned that he and Lydia were in town and expected to rejoin the social scene. Had the reporters known that he and

Lydia were to attend the theatre in Richmond? he wondered. It had certainly seemed as if all the *ton* knew.

He gazed at Lydia as she sipped her tea. She was distant again, reserved. Nothing like the warm, passionate woman who had shared his bed and his lovemaking the night before. He wondered if that warm, passionate woman would return to him tonight. He could only hope.

At least her anger had gone.

"How is Ethan this morning?" he asked.

Her expression revealed a ghost of a smile. "He is well. Hungry and dear as ever."

"I must pay him a visit." Adrian had missed spending time with his son.

"He will probably be awake soon," she said.

It was practically an invitation.

He was emboldened. "After I visit him, would you like to walk around the house with me and talk about what you might want to change about it?"

She looked up at him. "The house is adequate as it is, Adrian."

He gave her a wry smile. "I should like your advice on changing it. Everywhere I look I think I am in my parents' home."

She glanced down at her plate, spreading butter on a piece of toasted bread. "Very well. If you wish."

If he went slowly, he said to himself, he might be able to break down her careful reserve.

They passed a pleasant morning spending time with Ethan and walking around the house, discussing pieces of furniture, wall paper and curtains. It was a bit difficult to draw out her opinion, but if he was patient, she shared her ideas.

In the middle of their tour she stopped him.

"Do you have the money to pay for all this?" she asked him.

"I do, Lydia," he answered her. "My allowance has always been generous and I have wealth of my own." In fact, he'd done a fair job of repaying himself the money he'd secretly given to her.

"But you gamble a lot," she added.

He faced her. "Not as much as I used to, and, I promise you, Lydia, I am not a reckless gambler. I never wager more than I can afford to lose."

They walked into a small sitting room at the back of the house.

She looked at him again. "You will tell me if I need to economise." She gazed away, seeming to survey the room. "My first husband spent extravagantly and left me in terrible debt."

"I remember." He turned away so that she could see nothing on his face of how well he knew about her debt.

She was quiet for a long time while Adrian pretended to examine items in the room.

Suddenly she swung back to him. "It was you!"

He looked up. "What was me?"

"You. It was you." She shook her head. "Of course it was you. You were the only one who could have known of it."

"Known what?" His heart pounded.

She met his gaze. "I thought my sister had rescued me. Restored my finances, but at the christening she denied it." She glanced away and back again. "Very vehemently denied it. I could not imagine who would have put out so much money for me, but, now that I think of it, you were the only one who could have possibly known how desperate matters were."

He simply stared back at her.

"Tell me, Adrian." Her voice turned more serious. "Was it you?"

He paused, but finally answered her. "Yes."

"How?" she cried. "Why?"

He shrugged. "I had a great deal of money and you were in need. You'd let your servants go and were conserving candles. I surmised that your circumstances were desperate. I followed it up with Mr Coutts who sent me to Mr Newton."

"They told you of my debts?"

He nodded. "I believe they were very anxious to see restored to you what ought to have been your due."

She continued to gape at him.

He added, "Your parents were abroad and it seemed no one else had assisted you, so I did."

She swung away. "That was an outrageous thing to do."

So much for gratitude. "You were not supposed to know."

She shook her head. "I am so beholden to you." She made it sound like an evil he'd done her.

"Lydia, there is no obligation to me at all. It was a secret gift and I would not have told you, except that I promised to always answer your questions with the truth."

She raised her eyes to his. "You saved my life."

The discovery that he had been her benefactor only seemed to increase her discomfort with him. They ended the tour of the house and she made the excuse that she needed to be with Ethan, who was sleeping.

Adrian told her he was going to White's to meet Tanner, but that information seemed to create even more distance.

Baffled, he walked out of the door of the townhouse and the reporters rushed towards him. He'd forgotten about them. They were yelling questions at him all at once, about Lady

Denson, about Lydia. He pushed through, resolving to hire some burly fellows to keep them away. He was surprised he had not thought of it before.

When he reached the street he spied Reed at the fringe of the group, just watching, arms across his chest.

Adrian felt he ought to walk over and put a fist in the man's face for whipping the gossip about Lydia into a frenzy. He'd do it, too, if he could be certain Reed would not use it for more scandal in the paper.

Reed was not among the reporters who followed him to White's. Adrian ignored them, knowing they could not cross the threshold of that private club. Let them hang about outside all day, if they so wished.

Tanner awaited him at a corner table. He had an extra glass of brandy waiting as well.

Adrian pointed to the glass of brandy as he joined him. "What would you have done if I had not shown up?"

Tanner grinned. "Drunk it, of course."

Adrian took a sip. "Glad I came."

Tanner's expression turned serious. "I am also glad you came. What happened last night?"

Adrian frowned, wondering how much to tell. "A great deal happened." He began with the events in the theatre.

"Not a good evening after all," Tanner said when he'd finished.

Adrian lifted his glass to his lips, intending to tell Tanner at least a little of how it was between himself and his wife.

Tanner spoke instead. "I've heard talk here today, Adrian. A version of what you have described, except they are saying you ran off with Lady Denson at the theatre last night, while your wife cavorted with a wild crowd."

Adrian rose from his chair. "It is not true!"

Tanner bade him sit. "Of course it is not true, but three people have made a point of telling me about it and asking for more details."

Adrian glanced around the room and noticed that the other gentlemen were looking his way. "This is the outside of enough. Who is spreading such lies?" The answer came to him. "Crayden. The weasel. I'll wager a pony he is the one. He was at the christening and at the theatre, and he was watching both Lydia and me. I will deal with him immediately." He started to rise.

Tanner put a stilling hand on Adrian's arm. "Wait. Will that not cause more scandal? Why not allow me to handle Crayden, Pom? I would consider it an honour."

Adrian sat again, thinking of Tanner's proposal. "It would give me great satisfaction to throttle him myself, but I fear you are correct." He released a breath and drummed his fingers on the table. "There must be some way to counter the gossip. I wish there were some way I could keep it from Lydia." He glanced up at his friend. "How the devil do I tell her about it?"

Chapter Nineteen

Their infant forgotten at home, the notorious Lady C—
and her new husband sought entertainment in Richmond, attending the theatre, where, it is authoritatively
said, Lady C— dressed as a harlot, and, during the intermission, romped shamelessly with an unidentified gentleman. Her husband, meanwhile, was spied in a
passionate embrace with Lady D—, his latest paramour.
—*The New Observer*, November 11, 1819

The next morning Lydia entered the dining room for the
single purpose of reading what was written in the papers. After
Adrian had returned from White's the previous day, he'd
warned her that the events of that night had become public
knowledge and would likely appear in this morning's paper.

She'd spent a sleepless night and not in Adrian's bed. She
had all but made her request to move to the country. He had
begged her to give it more time.

Adrian was seated with the paper in his hand.

"Is it very bad?" she asked him.

His face looked ashen. "It is highly exaggerated."

She extended her hand and he placed the paper in it.

She read it.

"It is horrible!" She threw the paper down, the words *scandalous*, *romping* and, worst of all, *passionate embrace* spinning through her head.

Adrian skimmed the other papers. "These also write of the event, somewhat more moderately."

She stared at him, more wounded than she could ever expect. "What was this *passionate embrace*?"

He looked up. "It was not a passionate embrace."

But some sort of embrace, she surmised. Lydia's throat felt tight. And she'd almost believed his protests.

"Lydia." His expression was a plea. "Believe me."

It felt hard to breathe. "I cannot stand this, Adrian. I have been through this nightmare once. It is even worse now."

"It must pass," he insisted. "It cannot go on. We must stay the course, Lydia. Show them the newspapers are false." He leaned towards her. "We should go to the shops today. Ride in Hyde Park. We need to be seen together."

They already had accepted an invitation to a musicale at Lord Heronvale's, but the idea of facing anyone, whether at the shops, in the park or at an evening event, made Lydia feel sick.

Nonetheless, within the hour they were bound for St James's Street and Piccadilly. At Adrian's insistence they left through the front door.

As they stepped out, a footman accompanying them, the reporters rushed forwards, shouting questions. The footman pushed the men away. Lydia noticed Reed standing nearby. He had not approached them.

"I shall hire some men to keep them from our door,"

Adrian said. "But today we make use of them. They have seen us leave the house together."

Some of the reporters followed them, but the footman kept them from coming close. They soon crossed Old Bond Street, pretending to glance into shop windows. The streets were crowded, and people Lydia did not recognise turned around to point at them. People she knew pretended not to see them at all. Adrian kept up a conversation with her as if nothing were amiss.

"Shall we look for furniture next week?" he asked. "Perhaps we should add some chinoiserie, like the Regent has used in Brighton."

She mumbled replies to his questions as they strolled towards Piccadilly and tried to appear as if they were a contented married couple.

They stopped in Hatchard's Bookshop, where Lydia retreated behind a bookshelf in the corner. She heard someone approach and took down a book, pretending to read. Two ladies stood on the other side.

"Can you imagine?" one of them said. "How can they show their faces?"

"Did you see her?" the other one replied. "She is said to be quite beautiful, although, living as she does, her looks will never last. He certainly is handsome." The lady sighed. "A terrible rake, they say."

The first lady added, "Lady Denson is no better than she ought, but you knew he had to eventually succumb. What rake would not? Imagine being married to a man like that."

Her friend responded, "I suppose if you live the same sort of life, you would hardly notice."

"They must condone the practice of free love like that Shelley fellow," the first lady said.

"Well, I predict their marriage will not even last as long as Lord Byron's, but I'll wager she is the one banished to the Continent, not he." The two ladies giggled.

Lydia stepped out from behind the bookshelf, making it obvious she'd heard everything they said. The ladies gasped.

They had spoken as if they knew everything about her. She nodded to them and walked away with as much dignity as she could.

Adrian had remained in the front of the bookshop near the window so that he would be visible to passersby and anyone entering the shop.

He smiled when he saw her, a pained smile. "Did you find a book?"

"No, but I'm ready to leave." She was more than ready.

He insisted they visit Fortnum and Mason next door.

"We are not rushing away," he whispered to her.

They browsed through the store with its dried fruit, preserves and its newest novelty—tinned foods. Adrian selected some jams for their table. Finally they could walk back, the footman trailing behind with the packages.

Some of the reporters continued to track them, noting their every move, Lydia suspected. It made them even more of a spectacle. As they walked, she noticed that the women they passed gazed at Adrian.

Finally they reached Curzon Street. The reporters who had remained came towards them again, but they managed to get in the townhouse.

As soon as they stepped into the hall, Bilson hurried up to them. "Your father has called. He is waiting in the drawing room."

"My father?"

Lydia put her hand on the banister, eager to retreat to the peacefulness of the nursery and her baby Ethan. Adrian stopped her.

"Come with me," he said. "This is bound to involve us both."

She started to protest, but both Bilson and the footman watched to see what she would do. She nodded and followed Adrian to the drawing room.

"Good morning, Father," Adrian said when they entered the room. "We have just returned from the shops."

"Are you mad?" His father, who looked as if he'd been pacing, turned to face them. When he saw Lydia, he gave a disapproving frown. "Going to the shops after all this." He inclined his head. "I would speak with you, son."

Adrian gestured to Lydia. "You have neglected to greet your daughter-in-law."

"It is of no consequence, Adrian," Lydia said.

"It is common courtesy." He turned to his father and waited.

Lord Varcourt finally bowed. "Good morning, ma'am." He glanced back at his son. "I would speak with you, Cavanley. Now." He looked at Lydia as if to dismiss her.

Adrian held her arm. "Does this involve my wife?"

His father snapped, "Of course it does. Is your head buried in sand, boy?"

"Then she shall stay." His grip became firmer.

"Adrian—" Lydia protested.

Adrian leaned to her ear. "Whatever this is, hear it from my father's mouth, rather than from me later."

"Do not whisper," his father snapped.

"Just tell us what this is about." Adrian's voice was impatient.

His father pulled out a piece of paper and shoved it at his son. "This was in the print-shop window."

They had not passed a print shop on their walk. Lydia looked to see what it depicted.

It showed a caricature of her in a drunken orgy with a group of men, and Adrian in a lewd embrace with Lady Denson. In the corner was a baby, naked and wailing.

Lord Varcourt huffed. "They are in great demand, the fellow said."

Lydia pressed a hand to her stomach.

Lord Varcourt glared at his son. "Your mother had an attack of the vapours about all this. She's quite ill over it."

Adrian shoved the print back at him.

His father moved away. "I do not want the thing."

Adrian pointed to the print. "This is all fabrication, Father. It is not true."

His father gave a sardonic laugh. "Nonsense. It must be true. Or true enough." He snatched it back. "Look at it. It is too specific to be fabrication." He threw it down again and it fluttered to the carpet. "Besides, everyone knows Lady Denson—"

Lydia flinched at the lady's name.

Adrian broke in. "There is nothing to know about Lady Denson."

"Witnesses saw you kissing her," his father countered.

Lydia backed away.

"What they saw was not me kissing her," Adrian shot back.

Lord Varcourt snorted.

"It is abominable that you speak of such matters in front of Lydia," Adrian went on.

"You wished her to be present," his father reminded him, but his father did turn to Lydia and add, "I do beg your pardon, ma'am." He actually sounded as if he meant it.

He faced Adrian again. "Please, son, this is getting out of hand." He put a hand on Adrian's arm. "Go to Cavanley House as soon as possible. Stay there until the newspapers forget you. Leave now and you could be there before nightfall."

Lydia could only think, *a kiss is a kiss*.

"We will stay," Adrian replied.

"Then you are an idiot," his father muttered.

Adrian stiffened. "It will pass if we simply all ignore it."

"Son—" Lord Varcourt looked earnest "—it will only get worse."

Lord Varcourt is correct, Lydia thought.

His father sighed and bowed to Lydia. "Good day, ma'am." He walked past Adrian. "Heed me, son." He strode out the door.

Adrian glanced at her.

She lifted her chin. "You neglected to tell me the part about kissing Lady Denson."

"It only looked like I kissed her." He sounded defensive.

She laughed. "Perception again?"

"Yes," he said tightly.

She backed away. "I believe I have had enough, Adrian. Your father is right. This is only going to get worse, and it is already too far out of hand." She gestured to the outside. "Your father offers Cavanley House. Send me and Ethan there."

He did not answer her.

"Adrian." She gave him a level stare "You promised I could leave if I so desired."

"Give it more time, Lydia," he said. "Give *us* more time. This Lady Denson thing is nothing—"

She put up her hands to stop him, feeling as if she wanted to weep. "Do you not see, Adrian? It has gone too far.

Whatever the newspapers say is what people will believe. Even you and I believe it."

"I do not believe what the papers say." He looked offended.

"You believed there had been some former suitor of mine at the christening. You believed it because the newspaper said it."

He glanced away.

"I cannot dismiss what happened with you and her," Lydia whispered. She cleared her thoughts and spoke in a stronger tone. "In any event, we cannot ignore the fact that this affects other people as well. Our families—"

"Do not say it." His eyes flashed. "Your family has behaved abominably to you. They should rally around us. Instead they believe the lies."

She shook her head. "We cannot entirely blame them. Everyone believes the stories about us. You saw it. You saw them staring at us and whispering about us."

And gossiping between the bookshelves, she thought.

Lydia crossed the room and picked up the caricature. She brought it back to Adrian. "Look. They have started on Ethan, too. Do you wish your son to grow up with this sort of attention?"

His eyes turned pained.

"Very well." He sounded resigned. "We will go to Cavanley House."

Her heart pounded at what she was about to say. "Leave Ethan and me at Cavanley, Adrian."

He stared at her. "You do not wish me to come with you?"

She gazed at him. He was her champion, rescuing her every time she needed him, even when she had not known it. It was impossible not to love him and loving him made all the difference.

Loving him made not trusting him, worrying about every

woman who looked at him, so much worse. She'd been betrayed by a man once, she could not bear being betrayed again.

Especially by Adrian.

She took a breath. "You promised that if I asked, you would send me away, Adrian." Her voice seemed as if it came from another person. "I am asking now."

He stared back at her, looking as if she had slapped him across the face. Finally, he shook his head. "Cavanley is only about a four-hour carriage ride away. Pack your things. I'll escort you there today and get you settled." He looked at her with pained eyes. "I will not stay."

Samuel remained at the edge of the group of reporters, who were all buzzing about the Cavanleys' walk to the shops and what Cavanley's father might have said to him, what made him look so angry as he pushed his way through them a short time ago. They began taking wagers as to what entertainment the couple would attend that evening, or whether they would go out at all.

None of it mattered to Samuel.

He stood in front of the house because he had nowhere else to go.

He and Phillip had had a row after the morning paper appeared. Phillip had tricked him and switched the story he'd written with one Phillip had written from his mysterious source. Phillip had done it all in secret.

Samuel had stormed out of the newspaper office and had come here, where Mary was near.

He stared at the windows of the upper floors, hoping to see her peek out. He'd not had even a glimpse of her, but he could hope.

One of his colleagues laughed and money was passing hands. Samuel felt someone walk up behind him.

"Samuel?" a sweet voice said.

He spun around. "Mary!"

She was not dressed for out of doors, wearing a cap, but no bonnet, an apron still covering her dress. He took her arm and led her away from the other reporters.

"I came through the garden, Samuel, and I'll be dismissed if my lord and lady see me talking to you."

"Why did you come, Mary?" he asked.

She handed him a crumpled copy of the morning newspaper. "I want you to stop writing such things about my lady."

"Mary, I—"

The story had sickened him. Having seen Lord and Lady Cavanley together, he could not imagine those events occurring. He could imagine Lady Cavanley looking wounded and shamed.

And he could imagine the look on Mary's face, the look she showed him now.

How was he to tell her he had not written the story and have her believe him?

"How could you write such things?" She looked down at the newspaper. "I can read, you know. I fetched it after my lord and lady left the house." Her eyes rose to meet his. "I am asking you to stop this. It is hurting them very much."

"I cannot stop it, Mary," he said truthfully, wanting to explain.

Her eyes flashed. "At the christening, you professed to care about me. If you do care, you will stop this."

"Mary." He took a step towards her. "I cannot stop the stories. I do not have the power to stop them."

Her eyes widened and she made a mournful sound. "I thought you would not agree." She turned away. "I have to go back." She paused before turning away. "I will not be at Gunter's on Saturday after all."

He watched her hurry around the corner, his spirits plummeting to new depths.

Any chance he might have had for her forgiveness was gone because of a story another man had written.

Chapter Twenty

Sent by his father into exile to the family estate, Lord
C— and his scandalous wife have no new antics to report. Lady D— has been seen soothing her wounded
heart with a certain wealthy nabob, Mr G—. —*The New
Observer*, November 26, 1819

Adrian had been true to his word, remaining only one day
to make certain Lydia and Ethan were settled at Cavanley. So
close to London, the Cavanley staff had read all the newspapers and did not precisely greet them with open arms. He hated
to leave her in that atmosphere, but he kept his promise to her.

He'd not returned to London, though, but had ridden on
horseback through the countryside, staying at inns, trying to
sort out the disorder of his life.

His first impulse had been to drink and play cards, but the
liquor tasted foul and the card games bored him. Some tavern
maids eyed him hopefully, one offered herself blatantly, but
Adrian could not bear the thought of bedding a woman not
his wife. Not Lydia.

There was no returning to the life of a rake for him, but, without Lydia and Ethan, he had no other life at all.

On the third day, perhaps forty miles from London, he rode by a house, once a fine Tudor manor house, now crumbling and abandoned.

Like him.

The house called to him like the mythical Sirens. He saw it not as it was but as it could be. He almost laughed. There in front of him was a task he wanted to complete, a useful way to spend his time. He would purchase this property and bring it back to its past glory, make it into a home.

He'd been waiting for his father to bestow upon him a property to manage and all this time all he had to do was purchase one.

The property included the house, some equally dilapidated outer buildings, and, best of all, land that ought to be growing crops.

Adrian rode back to London to make the arrangements to purchase the property from the family who'd not had funds enough to support it. When he arrived at the townhouse, he sent a note around to Tanner to tell him he was in town, but would remain secluded most of the time. When the footman who delivered the note returned, Tanner was with him.

Tanner and Adrian sat in the library, sharing a bottle of brandy, and Adrian told Tanner how things stood with Lydia, how the newspaper had spoiled what they might have had together.

"I cannot see any remedy for us," he told Tanner. "If we had been left to ourselves, we might have had a chance." He lifted his brandy and took a long sip.

Tanner's forehead creased and his eyes followed the brandy glass. "What will you do now?"

Adrian gave a knowing smile and held his glass high. "You fear I'll succumb to the pleasures of the bottle again." He lowered the glass and stared at its contents. "I tried. The first night I left her, I'd planned to do exactly that." He smiled wryly. "The innkeeper's brandy was vile, however."

Tanner's expression remained wary.

Adrian shook his head. "Truly, I hated that muzzy-headed feeling. I stopped before imbibing too much."

"I am glad," Tanner said. "It solves nothing."

"I felt the same about playing cards," he added. "The thought of sitting at a card table bores me."

"By God!" Tanner feigned alarm. "What will you do with yourself?"

Adrian smiled again. "It took me a few days of wandering, but I have found something to interest me."

Tanner frowned again.

Adrian laughed. "Do not fear. It is not a woman."

Tanner relaxed. "You read my mind. If not a woman, then what?"

"A property." He leaned forwards. "In Berkshire. Not far from your estate, come to think of it."

"And?"

Adrian took another sip of brandy. "And I have taken steps to purchase it. It is in sad shape, but that is the joy of it. There will be much work to occupy me there. It can be restored to something fine again, I am certain of it, and once it is done, perhaps…" He let his voice trail off. He did not say that perhaps Lydia and Ethan would come to live with him there.

"It sounds splendid, Pom."

They discussed the cost of renovating, the possible uses of the land, how many workers he would need. Tanner wanted to see the place and they talked of when that might be accomplished.

When Tanner poured them each a second glass of brandy, he changed the subject. "I should apprise you of my dealings with Crayden."

Adrian averted his gaze. He felt the twinge of jealousy upon hearing Crayden's name. On his long rides over the English countryside, he'd obsessed over the fact that Crayden had once been Lydia's suitor. His father had told him so long ago.

He turned back to Tanner. "Go on."

Tanner paused, even though Adrian had given him permission. "He, of course, denied being the person who informed the newspaper of what happened in Richmond. Or at the christening. I do not believe him."

"It must have been Crayden." Adrian narrowed his eyes.

"I did discover that Crayden is dipping his toes in the River Tick. He owes a great deal of money and is having difficulty repaying."

Bilson entered.

"A man to see you, m'lord," he said. "I told him you were occupied with Lord Tannerton, but he insisted I tell you he is here. He was certain you would wish to see him."

"Who is it?" Adrian asked.

"Mr Reed, sir."

He and Tanner exchanged glances.

"What the devil can he want?" Tanner said.

Adrian said, "How the devil did he know I was here?"

Bilson's complexion reddened very slightly.

Adrian stood. "Bilson, did you inform Reed I was here?"

The butler lifted his chin. "I did take that liberty, m'lord, but it was with good reason."

Adrian's anger flared, but he held it in check. "Show Mr Reed in," he said tightly. "I will deal with you later."

Bilson bowed. "Very good, my lord."

When Mr Reed walked in, both Adrian and Tanner were standing, ready to face him. Adrian's muscles were taut with anger, and it would not take very much from Reed before he let that anger off its leash.

When Reed appeared, however, he looked dreadful, pale and gaunt and with dark circles under his eyes.

"Thank you for seeing me, my lord." Reed bowed to both men.

"Are you ill, Reed?" Adrian asked, forgetting his anger.

Reed glanced at him in surprise. "Why, no."

Adrian waved a dismissive hand. "Never mind, then. Get on with it. You wished to see me."

Reed bowed his head. "I fully understand the harm I have done you and Lady Cavanley—" he began.

Adrian broke in, "I doubt you know the extent of it."

Reed nodded. "I do not ask for your forgiveness, because I do not deserve forgiveness. I do wish to convey how profoundly I regret the words I wrote about you."

"It is my wife you maligned," Adrian snapped.

"I know it." Reed winced as if in physical pain. He pulled a letter from his pocket. "There is no reason you should agree, but I would beg you to send this letter to your wife, as your own letter, so she will open it. Not a letter in my name."

"You expect me to allow you to write to my wife?"

Reed looked chagrined. "Well, I have written a brief note to your wife, but the letter is really for Mary."

"For Mary!" Adrian stepped back in surprise.

"Who is Mary?" Tanner asked.

"Lydia's maid." Adrian still felt dumbfounded. He turned to Reed. "What do you want with Mary?"

Reed stared at his letter and silently handed it Adrian. "I did not seal it. Please read what I wrote to Lady Cavanley and to Mary."

Adrian unfolded the paper, and Tanner looked over his shoulder to read along with him. The note to Lydia was an apology and a plea to make certain Mary read his letter. The letter to Mary was a profession of love, primarily, but in it Reed also apologised to her and made a complicated explanation of not being the author of stories that had appeared since the christening.

He ended the letter saying, "I no longer write for the newspaper, but whatever employment I may find, my standard of behaviour shall always be, 'What will my Mary think?'"

"You no longer write for the paper?" Adrian and Tanner said at the same time.

"No." Reed gave a wan smile. "My brother pays some society fellow to feed him information and my brother writes the stories."

"I'll be damned," said Tanner. "Crayden, again. The cursed fellow is selling his lies to the paper."

Adrian stared at the letter, rereading Reed's profession of love.

"My lords," Reed said, "if I could print a retraction of the vile things that were written, I would do it, but I no longer have any control over the paper."

"Your brother won't agree to it?" asked Tanner.

Reed shook his head. He looked at Adrian. "Will you send the letter in your name?"

Adrian's mind was spinning. If the newspaper created this story, the newspaper could kill it as well.

He glanced at the letter again. "You must print that retraction."

"I said I cannot, sir." Reed protested. "My brother—"

"We'll get your brother's co-operation." His plan was already forming, a plan that might just put everything to rights.

"You will never convince my brother," insisted Reed.

"I know a surefire way to convince him," Tanner said.

"What is it?" Reed asked.

"Bribery," Tanner and Adrian said together.

Tanner grinned. "Bribery will work on Crayden as well."

"You are going to pay them to be silent?" Reed sounded shocked.

"Well," Tanner admitted, "perhaps it is a bit more like extortion. A lot more, actually. Wait until I get my hands on Crayden."

Adrian's excitement increased. "We'll have your brother print the retraction. We'll expose Crayden. Get him to admit he was lying." He gave the reporter an intent gaze. "But you must print an interview with me as well."

Reed looked as if his head had been twisted around, but he only murmured, "The issue will sell very well."

It was six days before they could accomplish it all, but Tanner's extortion did the trick. Neither Crayden nor Reed's brother wanted to be exposed for printing lies about peers.

Both Adrian and Tanner were at the office of *The New Observer* when the first copies of the Special Edition came off the press.

They each read it over carefully. Tanner grinned. "This should do the trick."

Adrian glanced over to see Reed waiting for him. "We are off, then. Wish me luck."

Tanner clapped him on the shoulder. "Good luck."

Chapter Twenty-One

Editorial. Falsehoods have abounded in the pages of this newspaper, your editor has learned, all the perfidy of one man, Viscount Crayden. Crayden sold to this paper an exclusive view of society events, but it has lately been discovered that he sold sensational lies. Peruse the whole story in this issue, we beg of you. An exclusive interview with Lord C—, husband of the notorious Lady C—, finally provides the true story.— *The New Observer*, December 3, 1819

Lydia leaned over Ethan's cradle and watched him shake a rattle, making excited cooing sounds at the same time. He'd changed so much in these last few weeks. Lifting his head, kicking his legs, grasping the rattle.

She'd found the rattle in a box on a high shelf in the nursery and all she could think of was that Adrian had probably held the same rattle in a tiny hand. He'd probably shaken it just as energetically.

Even though Adrian had been true to his word and left her,

his presence was everywhere at Cavanley. A box of baby clothes was discovered in the attic. She knew they had been Adrian's. The nursery contained his toys and books. The servants related stories about him, prompted by Ethan, his little son who looked so like him. Worst of all, there were portraits of him throughout the big house. Miniatures on side tables or forgotten in drawers. Paintings of him. With his mother when a mere toddler. An impish-looking schoolboy. A rascal of a youth. And one full-length portrait that must have been painted when he was in his twenties. He stood next to his horse, his hand casually on the saddle, a young man in his prime, full of virile energy and so handsome she could not help but stare. His image stared back, so real he looked as if he really could see her and as if he might break into an amused smile at any moment.

That portrait haunted her. She could not sit in that room, because it felt as if his eyes were always upon her. She avoided even entering the room, and yet, three times already she had woken during the night and carried a lighted candle down the white marble staircase to gaze at the portrait.

Once away from him and the relentless newspaper stories, Lydia realised what she had thrown away. He had always done the right thing by her, every time. She'd allowed the newspapers and the gossip and her own fears of betrayal to colour her perceptions of him, about what she knew in her soul about him.

And now it was too late.

A maid entered the nursery. "Newspapers from London." The girl's dimples twitched on her cheeks.

Odd for the girl to bring the papers up to this room. They

were usually left in the library. Lydia avoided reading them, except skimming them for mention of Adrian.

"The messenger said you must read them right away, m'lady," the maid said.

The messenger? Why must she do what some messenger said?

"And the housekeeper wishes to see Mary, my lady." The maid looked as if she were a cat who had eaten a canary.

"Me?" Mary said from the corner of the room where she sat mending.

"Indeed," the girl replied. "You are to come right away." As she turned to leave, she pointed to the newspapers. "The messenger said to read them!"

Mary followed her out of the door.

"Oh, Ethan," Lydia sighed, "I do not wish to read newspapers."

"Oooo," said Ethan and he shook the rattle.

The servants at Cavanley had been cool to her from the moment she arrived and watchful around her. Lydia supposed it was because they had read all the London gossip about her. Perhaps there was some mention of her the servants wanted her to see.

Or mention of Adrian.

She stepped away from the cradle and walked to the table where the maid had left the papers. *The New Observer* was on top.

Would she never escape that paper? "Special Edition," it said. She picked it up and glanced at it.

"What?" Not believing her eyes, she held it closer to her face.

The Special Edition was about her and Adrian.

She read about Lord Crayden fleeing to the Continent, his

creditors pursuing him. She read about *The New Observer* paying him for his sensational news stories. *The stories are completely false*, the newspaper now said.

She read about "Lord C" with even more interest. "Oh, Ethan," she exclaimed.

Adrian had given the paper an interview, to tell the true story about Lord and Lady C. In the paper he stated he had married her for love and was now grieving the necessity of them being apart. It said that Adrian had loved her from the first time they had met, but that her marriage to Wexin had made her frightened of love and marriage.

This "true" account was not entirely true. She knew Adrian had not *loved* her from that first moment, but now it seemed possible that he might have loved her later on, perhaps when he restored her widow's portion and gave her back her home.

The account put a touching, beautiful interpretation on everything that happened. Even if not wholly true, it made for a very romantic story.

"Perception," she whispered, "can be positive."

She put down the paper and moved across to Ethan, who greeted her with a shake of the rattle.

She scooped him up in her arms and twirled around. "Ethan," she cried, "we are going to London. We are going to see your papa!" She must go to him this very day. Tell him how wrong she'd been, tell him she loved him, too.

A voice came from the doorway. "Does the newspaper meet with your approval, then?"

She turned.

Adrian stood there, framed by the doorway, looking as if his portrait had come to life.

"Adrian."

He stepped inside the room. "I know the account is not entirely true, but it paints a prettier picture than had been painted previously." He paused and his eyes burned into her. "The part about me loving you—that part is true."

"Oh, Adrian." She closed the distance between them, their son still in her arms.

He enfolded them both in an embrace.

"I have missed you," she said. "I have been so entirely wrong about everything."

"You have not been entirely wrong. You were right about facing the newspapers. We ought to have stayed away." He kissed her, careful not to squeeze Ethan. When his lips reluctantly parted from hers, he added, "I do not believe I ever told you that I love you, that meeting you and marrying you and fathering Ethan are the best things that have ever happened to me."

He took Ethan from her and lifted him high in the air. Ethan broke into a huge smile and made a noise that sounded like a laugh.

"He smiled at you." She wrapped her arm around Adrian and leaned her cheek against his shoulder. "You made him laugh." She pulled Adrian over to the cradle. "Come see what else he can do!"

She took Ethan from Adrian and placed him in the cradle, holding the rattle near his hand. Ethan grabbed it and shook. "Oooooo!" he cried.

Adrian laughed and reached in the cradle to run his finger over Ethan's soft cheek. "Clever boy."

Lydia hugged her husband from behind. "You are the clever one," she murmured against his back. "To use the newspaper this way."

He turned around and held her in his arms. "I could not have done it without help. Reed helped write the article. He gave me the idea, really."

"Reed?"

Adrian grinned. "Reed is the urgent reason the house-keeper summoned Mary."

She was mystified.

He laughed. "Lydia, Reed was Mary's suitor. He courted her at first to learn about you, but he fell in love with her. Wrote a lovely letter telling her. That is what gave me the idea."

She gaped at him. "Mary and Reed?"

"I hope they are this very minute doing what I am about to do."

He leaned down and kissed her again, a soft and reverent kiss, a kiss full of hope.

Hope surged through her, not the glimmer of hope she'd experienced from time to time since meeting him, but a torrent of hope that their lives would always be as happy as this moment.

"You've created a beautiful world for us, Adrian. No man could ever have achieved a more beautiful world." She gazed into his eyes. "And I love you for it. I will always love you for it."

His eyes filled with emotion and he wrapped his arms around her, holding her as if he never wished to let her go.

Epilogue

Lord and Lady C— continue to summer at Nelbury House, Berkshire, where they are expected to remain for several weeks. —*The New Observer*, August 24, 1821

"Curr'cle, Mama! Look. Curr'cle!"

Ethan, who had just turned two years old the week before, pulled on Lydia's skirt and excitedly pressed his nose against the parlour window.

A shiny new curricle pulled by two snowy-white horses made its way up the carriage path. Lord Tannerton held the ribbons, and Marlena sat next to him with little William on her lap.

Ethan, however, only had eyes for the dashing vehicle. "*Two* horses," he added knowledgeably.

"Yes, I see," Lydia replied, mimicking his enthusiasm. "Two *white* horses."

"*Black* curr'cle, Mama. Black."

Lydia was amazed at this small creature who was her son. He seemed to learn new things every day.

"Let us go and meet our callers, shall we?"

Ethan would have run had Lydia not caught his hand and held him to a fast walk to the hall.

This was Tanner and Marlena's first visit to Nelbury House, the Berkshire property Adrian had purchased. The Tannerton estate, only two hours away, was palatial in comparison.

Lydia could not love her house more.

Adrian had spent the last year and a half seeing to the restoration of the old Tudor property. There was still much to be done, but at least enough of the house was habitable for them. They already had tenants on the property, a small flock of sheep, and enough swine and poultry to make this a working farm. Adrian and Lydia and Ethan moved into Nelbury House a few days after the King's coronation in July.

In the hall Dixon stood ready to attend the visitors.

A smile tugged at Dixon's lips at sight of the eager Ethan. "Your father is already outside, Master Ethan."

"Papa?" Ethan tugged harder.

Lydia smiled. "The father is as eager as the son, is it not so, Dixon?"

"Indeed, my lady." Dixon opened the front door for them.

Dixon, Cook and Thomas, the footman, had come to Nelbury House with Lydia from her London townhouse, still as faithful to her as they'd been in her darkest time.

Lydia and Ethan stepped outside.

Adrian stood shaking hands with Tanner, who clapped him on the back. Adrian glanced over at her and smiled. Lydia's heart leapt as it always did when she saw him. Tanner's tiger drove the curricle to the stable, and Thomas carried in the few items the Tannertons had brought with them, gifts for Ethan among them, no doubt.

Little William tried to pull away from his mother to go and chase the chickens that had escaped their coop. Marlena held tightly on to William's hand.

Lydia bent down to Ethan. "See. William has come to see you."

The carriage was safely away, and Marlena released William, who dashed after the chickens.

Ethan ran after him. "Curr'cle, William!"

Marlena embraced Lydia. "It is good to see you."

Lydia returned the hug. She was becoming accustomed to the friendship Marlena unfailingly offered. "Welcome to our home."

Another carriage turned into the property and both Lydia and Marlena dashed to again grab the hands of their little boys.

"Papa's gig," Ethan informed William excitedly.

William ignored him in favour of the chickens.

"This must be Mary and Samuel," Lydia said. Mary and Samuel were coming for a visit of several days. "Adrian's coachman has fetched them from the London coach."

Lydia's joy over her life with Adrian was increased by knowing that Mary, too, had found happiness. Mary wed Samuel Reed over a year ago and had her own pretty set of rooms near Lincoln's Inn Fields. Mary also was expecting a baby.

Lydia turned to Marlena. "I do hope it does not offend you that Samuel and Mary will also dine with us. We had little notice that they had changed their day to arrive."

A Marchioness had every right to object to sharing a meal with a former maid, but Adrian had insisted Tanner and Marlena would not stand on such formalities. Lydia sent a message informing Marlena just to be certain.

"We do not mind at all," Marlena assured her. "In fact, I believe Tanner wishes to discuss business with Mr Reed."

Tanner had purchased *The New Observer* newspaper, making him boss over the Reed brothers. Tanner quipped that it seemed the easiest way to keep *The New Observer* from printing gossip about them.

Lydia's name still appeared in the newspapers, although in a kinder manner. What entertainments she attended, what clothing she wore, what shops she patronised, all found their way into the columns. Her mother actually liked her daughter receiving this kind of attention. Lydia's status as a leader of all things fashionable gave her entire family a certain cachet and had done much to mend the breach between them. Secure in her husband's love, Lydia could even forgive her family their superficiality. It helped that her parents genuinely doted on Ethan.

"Gig, Mama!" Ethan cried.

The gig pulled up and Mary almost did not wait for it to stop. Samuel assisted her down from her seat.

"My lady, it is so wonderful to see you!" Mary curtsied, but Lydia gave her a one-armed hug, the other arm busy holding Ethan.

"We have missed you, Mary."

"Mary!" Ethan cried, pointing to the carriage. "Papa's gig."

Mary scooped him up and kissed him on the cheek. "Are you not clever to know that?"

Samuel stepped over to Lydia. "Good day, my lady. It is an honour to be here." He always looked at her with apology in his eyes.

"You are most welcome here, Samuel." As far as Lydia was concerned, Samuel's devotion to Mary was enough to redeem him to her.

Adrian's voice rose. "Let me take you on a quick tour of the property, before you brush off the dust of the road."

Lydia smiled. Her husband could not wait to show off all that he'd accomplished.

He provided all the details as he led them around to the back of the house from where the outer buildings and the vegetable garden were visible. In the distance were the white sheep grazing on a hillside.

After the tour, Ethan's nurse took the boys to the nursery, and the adults sat down to their meal, Dixon overseeing and Thomas and another newly hired footman serving.

As the lively meal progressed, Lydia took in the sight, the Marchioness being so kind to Mary, the Marquess arguing politics with a newspaperman, her husband showing himself a happy, contented man. Her breast swelled with emotion.

Adrian looked over at her and smiled. She knew his thoughts were much like her own, grateful for the company of friends at their table, grateful for their new home, for their son, for each other.

The talk at the table seemed to fade, and it felt as intimate as if she and Adrian were alone. He lifted his wine glass to her. "I love you," he mouthed.

Tears of joy stung Lydia's eyes. She nodded in reply.

Their friends conversed, oblivious to the toast Lydia and Adrian drank to each other and to their bright and happy future.

Lydia could imagine how Samuel, had he been paying the least bit of attention, once might have written about it in *The New Observer*:

Lord and Lady C— shockingly ignored their dinner guests to pass longing looks at each other. Dear Readers, are we to assume that the rake and the notorious widow have found happiness at last?

* * * * *

Gallant Officer,
Forbidden Lady

In memory of my father, Colonel Daniel J. Gaston,
who showed me the honour of soldiers

Prologue

Badajoz Spain—1812

Jack Vernon dodged through the streets and alleys of Badajoz as if the very devil were at his heels. Several devils, in fact.

Drunken, marauding British soldiers poured out of doorways and set buildings afire, the flames illuminating their gargoyle-like faces. Bodies of their victims littered the pavement, French soldiers and ordinary citizens, men, women and children, their bright-hued Spanish clothing stained red with blood. Jack's ears rang with the roar of the fires, screams of women, wails of babies, but no sound was as terrible as the laughter of madmen with a lust to rape, plunder and pillage.

Jack gripped his pistol in his hand while several red-coated marauders chased him, hoping for the few coins in his pockets. These were the same men at whose sides he'd scaled the walls of Badajoz earlier that day while French musket fire rained down on them. Now they would impale him with their bayonets for the sheer sport of it.

The men were consumed with bloodlust, a result of the desperately hard fighting they'd been through that left almost half their number dead. A rumour spread through the ranks that Wellington had issued permission for three hours of plunder. It had been like a spark to tinder. The rumour was untrue, but once they had begun there was no stopping them.

The real nightmare had begun.

After the French retreated to San Crisobal and the looting started, Jack's major ordered Jack and a few others to accompany him on a patrol of the streets. 'We shall stop the looting,' his commanding officer had said.

The plunderers almost immediately turned on Jack's patrol, who ran for their lives. Separated from the others, all Jack wanted now was a safe place to hide until the carnage was over.

He ran through the maze of streets, turning so often he no longer knew where he was or how to get out. Finally the pounding of feet behind him ceased, and he slowed, daring to look back and to catch his breath. He proceeded slowly, flattening himself against the ancient walls, and hoping the sound of his laboured breathing did not give him away. All he needed to find was an open door or a nook in an alley.

Shouts and screams still echoed and dark figures ran past him like phantoms in the night. The odour of burning wood, of spirits, blood and gunpowder, assaulted his nostrils.

Jack sidled along the wall until he turned into a small courtyard. From the light of a burning building he could see a British soldier holding down a struggling woman. A boy tried to pry the man's hands off her, but another soldier plucked the boy off and tossed him on a nearby body. The man laughed as if he were merely playing a game of skittles.

A third soldier picked the boy up and raised a knife, as if to slash the boy's throat. Jack charged into the courtyard, roaring like an ancient Celt. He fired his pistol. The soldier dropped the knife and the boy and ran, his companion with him. The man attacking the woman seemed to give Jack's attack no heed.

Fumbling to undo his trousers, he laughed. 'Come join the fun. Plenty for you, as well.'

Jack suddenly could see this man wore the red sash of an officer. The man turned and revealed his face.

Jack knew him.

He was Lieutenant Edwin Tranville, aide-de-camp to Brigadier-General Lionel Tranville, his father. Jack grew up knowing them both. Before Jack's father had been dead a year, General Tranville had made Jack's mother his mistress. Jack had only been eleven years old.

He stepped back into the shadows before Edwin could recognise him. He'd always known Edwin to be a bully and a coward, but he never suspected this level of depravity.

'Leave the woman alone,' Jack ordered.

'Won't do it.' Edwin's words were slurred. He was obviously very intoxicated. 'Want her too much. Deserve her.' A demonic expression came over his weak-chinned face and his pale blond hair fell into his eyes. He brushed it away with his hand and pointed a finger at the woman, 'Don't fight me or I'll have to kill you.'

Jack stuck his pistol in his belt and drew his sword, but the woman managed to knock Edwin off balance and now stood between Jack and her attacker. She pushed at Edwin's chest, driving him away while the boy vaulted on to his back. Edwin cried out in surprise and thrashed about, trying to pull the child off. He knocked the woman to the ground and finally managed to seize the boy by his throat.

Jack gripped the handle of his sword, but before he could take a step forwards, the woman sprang to her feet, the runaway soldier's knife in her hand.

'*Non!*' she cried.

She slashed at Edwin like a wildcat defending her cub. Edwin backed away, but the drink seemed to have affected his judgement.

'Stop it!' he cried, the smile still on his face. 'Or I'll break his neck.' He laughed as if he'd made a huge jest. 'I can kill him with my hands.'

'*Non!*' the woman cried again and she lunged towards him.

Edwin stumbled and the boy squirmed out of his grasp. The woman sliced into Edwin's cheek with the knife, cutting a long gash from ear to mouth.

Edwin wailed and dropped to his knees, pressing his hand against his bleeding face. 'I'll kill you for that!'

The woman shook her head and lifted her arms to sink the knife deep into Edwin's exposed back.

She was suddenly grabbed from behind by another British officer.

'Oh, no, you don't, *señora*.' He disarmed her with ease.

A second officer joined him. They were a captain and a lieutenant wearing the uniforms of the Royal Scots, a regiment Tranville had once commanded.

Edwin pointed to the woman. 'She tried to kill me!' He made an effort to stand, but swayed and collapsed in a heap on the cobblestones, passed out from drink and pain.

The captain held on to the woman. 'You'll have to come with us, *señora*.'

'Captain—' the lieutenant protested.

Jack sheathed his sword and showed himself. 'Wait.'

Both men whirled around, and the lieutenant aimed his pistol at Jack's chest.

Jack held up both hands. 'I am Ensign Vernon of the East Essex. He was trying to kill the boy and rape the woman. I saw it. He and two others. The others ran.'

'What boy?' the captain asked.

A figure sprang from the shadows. The lieutenant turned the pistol on him.

Jack put his hand on the lieutenant's arm. 'Do not shoot. It is the boy.'

The captain held the woman's arm while he walked over to Edwin, rolling him on to his back with his foot. He looked up at the lieutenant. 'Good God, Landon, do you see who this is?'

'General Tranville's son,' Jack answered.

'You jest. What the devil is he doing here?' the lieutenant asked.

Jack pointed to Edwin. 'He tried to choke the boy and she defended him with the knife.'

Blood still oozed from Edwin's cheek, but he remained unconscious.

'He is drunk,' Jack added.

The boy ran to the body of the French soldier. '*Papa!*'

'*Non, non, non, Claude,*' the woman cried, pulling away from the captain.

'Deuce, they are French.' The captain knelt down next to the body and placed his fingers on the man's throat. 'He's dead.'

The woman said, '*Mon mari.*' Her husband.

The captain rose and strode back to Edwin. He swung his leg as if to kick him, but stopped himself. Edwin rolled over again and curled into a ball, whimpering.

The boy tugged at his father's coat. '*Papa! Papa! Réveillez!*'

'*Il est mort, Claude.*' The woman gently coaxed the boy away.

The captain looked at Jack. 'Did Tranville kill him?'

Jack shook his head. 'I did not see.'

'Deuce. What will happen to her now?' The captain gazed back at the woman.

Shouts sounded nearby, and the captain straightened. 'We must get them out of here.' He gestured to the lieutenant. 'Landon, take Tranville back to camp. Ensign, I'll need your help.'

Lieutenant Landon looked aghast. 'You do not intend to turn her in?'

'Of course not,' said the captain sharply. 'I'm going to find her a safe place to stay. Maybe a church. Or somewhere.' He glared at both his lieutenant and at Jack. 'We say nothing of this. Agreed?'

'He ought to hang for this,' the lieutenant protested.

'He's the general's son,' the captain shot back. 'If we report his crime, the general will have our necks, not his son's.' He tilted his head towards the woman. 'He may even come after her and the boy.' The captain looked down at Edwin, now quiet. 'This bastard is so drunk he may not even know what he did.'

'Drink is no excuse.' After several seconds, the lieutenant nodded his head. 'Very well. We say nothing.'

The captain turned to Jack. 'Do I have your word, Ensign?'

'You do, sir.' Jack did not much relish either father or son knowing he'd been here.

Glass shattered nearby and the roof of a burning building collapsed, sending sparks high into the air.

'We must hurry,' the captain said, although he paused to extend his hand to Jack. 'I am Captain Deane. That is Lieutenant Landon.'

Jack shook his hand. 'Sir.'

Captain Deane turned to the woman and her son. 'Is

there a church nearby?' His hand flew to his forehead. 'Deuce. What is the French word?' He tapped his brow. '*Église?*'

'*Non,* no *église, capitaine,*' the woman replied. 'My…my *maison*—my house. Come.'

'You speak English, *madame*?'

'*Oui, un peu*—a little.'

The lieutenant threw Edwin over his shoulder.

'Take care,' the captain said to him.

The lieutenant gave a curt nod, glanced around and trudged off in the same direction they had come.

The captain turned to Jack. 'I want you to come with me.' He looked over at the Frenchman's body. 'We will have to leave him here.'

'Yes, sir.'

'Come.' The woman, with a despairing last glance towards her husband, put her arm around her son's shoulder and gestured for them to follow her.

They made their way through the alley to a doorway facing a narrow street not far from where they had been.

'My house,' she whispered.

The door was ajar. The captain signalled them to stay while he entered. A few moments later he returned. 'No one is here.'

Jack stepped inside. The place had been ransacked. Furniture was shattered, dishes broken, papers scattered everywhere. The house consisted only of a front room, a kitchen and a bedroom. He kicked debris aside to make room for them to walk. Captain Deane pulled what remained of a bed's mattress into the front room, clearing a space for it in the corner. The woman came from the kitchen with cups of water for them. The boy stayed at her side, looking numb.

Jack drank thirstily.

'Can you keep watch?' the captain asked after drinking his fill. 'I'll sleep for an hour or so, then relieve you.'

'Yes, sir,' Jack replied. He might as well stand watch. He certainly could not sleep. Indeed, he wondered if he would ever sleep again.

They barricaded the door with some of the broken furniture, and Jack salvaged a chair whose seat and legs were still intact. He placed it at the window and sat.

The captain gestured for the woman and her son to sleep on the mattress. He sat on the floor, his back leaning against the wall.

Outside the sounds of carnage continued, but no one approached. Jack stared out on to a street that looked deceptively innocent and peaceful.

Perhaps by morning the carnage would be over, and Jack would be able to return to his camp. Perhaps his major and the others in their patrol would still be alive. Perhaps someone, before this war was over, would put a sword through Edwin Tranville's heart for his part in this horror.

Jack reloaded his pistol and kept it at the ready. In the stillness, images flooded into his mind, over and over, flashing like torture, forcing him to relive the horror of this day.

His fingers itched to make the images stop, to capture them, imprison them, store them away so they would leave him alone.

The sky lightened as dawn arrived, but Jack still heard the drunken shouts, the musket shots, the screams. They were real. Even though it was day, the plundering continued.

Captain Deane woke and walked over to Jack, standing for a moment to listen.

'By God, they are still at it.' The captain rubbed his face. 'Get some sleep, Ensign. We'll wait. Maybe things will quieten down soon.'

Jack gave the captain his seat. He glanced at the corner of the room where the woman and boy lay. The boy was curled up in a ball and looked very young and vulnerable. The woman was awake.

Jack surveyed the room and started picking up the sheets of paper scattered about the floor. He examined them. Some sides were blank.

'Do you need these?' he asked the woman, holding up a fist full of paper.

'*Non.*' She turned away.

Some of the sheets appeared to contain correspondence, perhaps from loved ones at home. Jack felt mildly guilty for taking them, but his notebook was stored safely in his kit back at his regiment's encampment and he'd not realised how badly he would need paper.

He found a wide piece of board and carried it to a spot of light from another window. Sitting cross-legged on the floor, he placed the board on his lap and fished in his pockets for his wooden graphite pencil. Jack placed one of the sheets of paper on the board, and heaved a heavy breath.

He started to draw.

The images trapped in his brain flowed from his fingers to the tip of his pencil on to the paper. He could not get them out fast enough. He filled one, two, three sheets and still he was not done. He needed to draw them all.

Only then, after he'd captured every image, would he be free of them. Only then could he dare to rest. Only then could he sleep.

Chapter One

London—June 1814

It was like walking in a dream.

All around him, history paintings, landscapes, allegories, portraits hung one next to the other like puzzle pieces until every space, floor to ceiling, was covered.

Jack wandered through the exhibition room of the Royal Academy of Art, gazing at the incredible variety, the skill, the *beauty* of the works. He could not believe he was here.

His regiment had been called back to England a year ago. Napoleon had abdicated, and the army had no immediate need for his services. Jack, like most of the young officers who'd lived through the war, had risen in rank. He'd been promoted to lieutenant, which gave him a bit more money when he went on half-pay. This gave him the opportunity to do what he yearned to do, *needed* to do. To draw. To paint. To create beauty and forget death and destruction.

Jack had gone directly to Bath, to the home of his

mother and sister, the town where his mentor, Sir Cecil Harper, also lived. Sir Cecil had fostered Jack's need to draw ever since he'd been a boy and he became Jack's tutor again. Somehow the war had not robbed Jack of the ability to paint. At Sir Cecil's insistence, he submitted his paintings to the Royal Academy for its summer exhibition. Miraculously the Royal Academy accepted two of them.

They now hung here on the walls of Somerset House, home of the Royal Academy, next to the likes of Lawrence and Fuseli and Turner, in a room crowded with spectators who had not yet left the city for the summer.

Crowds disquieted Jack. The rumble of voices sounded in his ears like distant cannonade and set off memories that threatened to propel him back into the nightmare of war.

A gentleman brushed against him, and Jack almost swung at him. Luckily the man took no notice. Jack unclenched his fist, but the rumble grew louder and the sensation of cannons, more vivid. His heart beat faster and it seemed as if the room grew darker. This had happened before, a harbinger of a vision. Soon he would be back in battle again, complete with sounds and smells and fears.

Jack closed his eyes and held very still, hoping no one could tell the battle that waged inside. When he opened his eyes again, he gazed up at his sister's portrait, hung high and difficult to see, as befitted his status as a nobody. The painting grounded him. He was in London, at Somerset House, amid beauty. He smiled gratefully at her image.

'Which painting pleases you so?' a low and musical voice asked.

At Jack's elbow stood a young woman, breathtakingly lovely, looking precisely as if she had emerged from one of the canvases. For a brief moment he wondered if she too was a trick his mind was playing on him. Her skin was like silk of the palest rose, beautifully contrasted by her rich auburn hair. Her lips, deep and dusky pink, shimmered as if she'd that moment moistened them with her tongue. Large, sparkling eyes, the green of lush meadows and fringed with long mink-brown lashes, met his gaze with a fleeting expression of sympathy.

'Do say it is the one of the young lady.' She pointed to his sister's portrait.

Tearing his eyes away from her for a moment, he glanced back at the painting of his sister. 'Do you like that one?' he managed to respond.

'I do, indeed.' Her eyes narrowed in consideration. 'She is so fresh and lovely. The rendering is most life-like, but that is not the whole of it, I think—' she paused, moistening her lips, and more than Jack's artistic sensibilities came alive with the gesture '—it is most lovingly painted.'

'Lovingly painted?' Jack glanced back again at the canvas, but just for a second, because he could not bear to wrest his eyes from her.

'Yes.' She spoke as if conversing with a man to whom she had not been introduced was the most natural thing in the world, as if she were the calm in this room where Jack had just battled old demons. 'The young lady's expression. Her posture. It all bespeaks to emotion, her eagerness to see what the future holds for her and the fondness the artist has for her. It makes her even more beautiful. The painting is quite remarkable indeed.'

Jack could not help but flush with pride.

He'd painted Nancy's portrait primarily to lure commissions from prospective clients, but it had also given him the opportunity to become reacquainted with the sister who'd been a child when he'd kissed her goodbye before departing for the Peninsula. Nancy was eighteen now and had blossomed into a beauty as fresh and lovely as her portrait had been described. The painting's exquisite admirer looked to be no more than one or two years older than Nancy. If Jack painted her, however, he'd show a woman who knew precisely what she desired in life.

She laughed. 'I ought not to expect a gentleman to understand emotion.' She gazed back at the painting. 'Except the artist. He captures it perfectly.'

He smiled inwardly. If she only knew how often emotion was his enemy, skirmishing with him even in this room.

Again her green eyes sought his. 'Did you know the artist has another painting here?' She took his arm. 'Come. I will show you. You will be surprised.'

She led him to another corner of the room where, among all the great artists, she had discovered his other work.

'See?' She pointed to the painting of a British soldier raising the flag at Badajoz. 'The one above the landscape. Of the soldier. Look at the emotions of relief and victory and fatigue on the soldier's face.' She opened her catalogue and scanned the pages. '*Victory at Badajoz*, it is called, and the artist is Jack Vernon.' Her gaze returned to the painting. 'What is so fascinating to me is that Vernon also hints at the amount of suffering the man must have endured to reach this place. Is that not marvellous?

'You like this one, too, then?' Jack could not have felt more gratified had the President of the Academy, Benjamin West himself, made the comment.

'I do.' She nodded emphatically.

He'd painted *Victory at Badajoz* to show that fleeting moment when it felt as if the siege of Badajoz had been worth what it cost. She had seen precisely what he'd wanted to convey.

Jack turned to her. 'Do you know so much of soldiering?'

She laughed again. 'Nothing at all, I assure you. But this is exactly how I would imagine such a moment to feel.' She took his arm again. 'Let me show you another.'

She led him to a painting the catalogue listed as *The Surrender of Pamplona*. Wellington, who only this month had become Duke of Wellington, was shown in Roman garb and on horseback accepting the surrender of the Spanish city of Pamplona, depicted in the painting as a female figure. The painting was stunningly composed and evocative of classical Roman friezes. Its technique was flawless.

'You like this one, as well?' he asked her. 'It is well done. Very well done.'

She gave it a dismissive gesture. 'It is ridiculous, Wellington in Roman robes!'

He smiled in amusement. 'It is allegorical.'

She sent him a withering look. 'I know it is allegorical, but do you not think it ridiculous to depict such an event as if it occurred in ancient Rome?' Her gaze swung back to the painting. 'Look at it. I do not dispute that it is well done, but it pales in comparison to the other painting of victory, does it not? Where is the emotion in this one?'

He examined the painting again, as she had demanded, but could not resist continuing the debate. 'Is it not unfair to compare the two when the aim of each is so different? One is an allegory and the other a history painting.'

She made a frustrated sound and shook her head in dismay. 'You do not understand me. I am saying that this artist takes all the meaning, all the emotion, away by making this painting an allegory. A victory in war must be an emotional event, can you not agree? The painting of Badajoz shows that. I much prefer to see how it really was.'

How it really was? If only she knew to what extent he had idealised that moment in Badajoz. He'd not shown the stone of the fortress slick with blood, nor the mutilated bodies, nor the agony of the dying.

He glanced back at his painting. He'd not deliberately set about depicting the emotion of victory in the painting of it. He'd meant only to show he could do more than paint portraits. With the war over, he supposed there might be some interest in military art. If someone wished him to paint a scene from a battle, he would do it, even if he must hide how it really was.

Jack glanced back at his painting and again at the allegory. Some emotion, indeed, had crept into his painting, emotion absent from the other.

He turned his gaze upon the woman. 'I do see your point.'

She grinned in triumph. 'Excellent.'

'I cede to your expertise on the subject of art.' He bowed.

'Expertise? Nonsense. I know even less of art than of soldiering.' Her eyes sparkled with mischief. 'But that does not prevent me from expressing my opinion, does it?'

Jack was suddenly eager to identify himself to her, to let her know he was the artist she so admired. 'Allow me to make myself known to you—'

'Ariana!' At that moment an older woman, also quite beautiful, rushed up to her. 'I have been searching the rooms for you. There is someone you must meet.'

The young woman gave Jack an apologetic look as her companion pulled on her arm. 'We must hurry.'

Jack bowed and the young woman made a hurried curtsy before being pulled away.

Ariana. Jack repeated the name in his mind, a name as lovely and unusual as its bearer.

Ariana.

Ariana Blane glanced back at the tall gentleman with whom she had so boldly spoken. She left him with regret, certain she would prefer his company to whomever her mother was so determined she should meet.

She doubted she would ever forget him, so tall, well formed and muscular. He wore his clothes so very well one could forget his coat and trousers were not the most fashionable. His face was strong, chiselled, solid, the face of a man one could depend upon to do what needed to be done. His dark hair was slightly tousled and in need of a trim, and the shadow of a beard was already evident in mid-afternoon. It gave him a rakish air that was quite irresistible.

But it was that fleeting moment of emotion she'd seen in him that had made her so brazenly decide to speak to him. She doubted anyone else would have noticed, but something had shaken him and he'd fought to overcome it. All in an instant.

When she approached him his eyes held her captive. As light a brown as matured brandy, they were unlike any she had seen before. They gave the impression that he had seen more of the world than he found bearable.

And that he could see more of her than she might wish to show.

She sighed. Such an intriguing man.

He had almost introduced himself when her mother interrupted. Ariana wished she'd discovered who he was. She was not in the habit of showing an interest in a man, but he had piqued her curiosity. Now she might never see him again.

Unless she managed to appear on stage, as she was determined to do. Perhaps he would see her perform and seek her out in the Green Room afterwards.

Her mother brought her over to a dignified-looking gentleman of compact build and suppressed energy. Her brows rose. He did not appear to be one of the ageing men of wealth to whom her mother persisted in introducing her. You would think her mother wished her to place herself under a gentleman's protection rather than seek a career on the London stage.

Of course, her mother had been successful doing both and very likely had the same future in mind for her daughter.

'Allow me to make you known to my daughter, Mr Arnold.' Her mother gave her a tight smile full of warning that this introduction was important. 'My daughter, Miss Ariana Blane.'

She needn't have worried. Ariana recognised the name. She bestowed on Mr Arnold her most glittery smile and made a graceful curtsy. 'Sir.'

'Why, she is lovely, Daphne.' Mr Arnold beamed. 'Very lovely indeed.'

Her mother pursed her lips, not quite as pleased with Mr Arnold's enthusiastic assessment as Ariana was. 'Mr Arnold manages the Drury Lane Theatre, dear.'

'An explanation is unnecessary, Mama.' Ariana took a step forwards. 'Everyone in the theatre knows who Mr Arnold is. I am greatly honoured to meet you, sir.' She extended her hand to him.

He clasped her fingers. 'And I, you, Miss Blane.'

Ariana inclined her head towards him. 'I believe you have breathed new life into the theatre with your remarkable Edmund Kean.'

Edmund Kean's performance of Shylock in *The Merchant of Venice* had been a sensation, critically acclaimed far and wide.

The man smiled. 'Did you see Kean's performance?'

'I did and was most impressed,' Ariana responded.

'You saw the performance?' Her mother looked astonished. 'I did not know you had been in London.'

Ariana turned to her. 'A few of us came just to see Kean. There was no time to contact you. We returned almost immediately lest we miss our own performance.'

Arnold continued without heeding the interruption. 'Your mother has informed me that you are an actress.'

Ariana smiled. 'Of course I am! What else should the daughter of the famous Daphne Blane be but an actress? It is in my blood, sir. It is my passion.'

He nodded with approval. 'You have been with a company?'

'The Fisher Company.'

'A very minor company,' her mother said.

'I am acquainted with Mr Fisher.' Mr Arnold appeared impressed.

Four years ago, when Ariana had just turned eighteen, she'd accepted a position teaching poetry at the boarding school in Bury St Edmunds she'd attended since age nine. She'd thought she had no other means of making a life for herself. At the time her mother had a new gentleman under her roof, and would not have welcomed Ariana's return. Fate intervened when the Fisher Company came to the town to perform *Blood Will Have Blood* at the Theatre Royal, and Ariana attended the performance.

The play could not have been more exciting, complete with storm, shipwreck, horses and battle. The next day Ariana packed up her belongings, left the school, and sought out Mr Fisher, begging for a chance to join the company. She knew he hired her only because she was the famous Daphne Blane's daughter, but she did not care. Ariana had found the life she wanted to live.

'What have you performed?' Mr Arnold asked her.

'My heavens, too many to count. I was with the company for four years.'

With the Fisher Company she'd performed in a series

of hired barns and small theatres in places like Wells-next-the-Sea and Lowestoft, but she had won better parts as her experience grew.

She considered her answer. '*Love's Frailties, She Stoops to Conquer, The Rivals.*' She made certain to mention *The Rivals*, knowing its author, Richard Brinsley Sheridan, still owned the Drury Lane Theatre.

Her mother added, 'Mere comedies of manners, and some of her roles were minor ones.'

'Oh, but I played Lucy in *The Rivals*.' Ariana glanced at her mother. Why had she insisted upon her meeting Mr Arnold only to thwart every attempt Ariana made to impress the man?

'Tell me,' Mr Arnold went on, paying heed to Ariana and ignoring the famous Daphne Blane, 'have you played Shakespeare?'

'The company did not perform much Shakespeare,' Ariana admitted. 'I did play Hippolyta in *A Midsummer Night's Dream*. Why do you ask, sir?'

Mr Arnold leaned towards her in a conspiratorial manner. 'I am considering a production of *Romeo and Juliet*, to capitalise on the success of Kean. If I am able to find the financing for it, that is.'

Ariana's mother placed her hand on Arnold's arm. 'Will Kean perform?'

He patted her hand. 'He will be asked, I assure you, but even if he cannot, a play featuring Daphne Blane and her daughter should be equally as popular.'

Her mother beamed at the compliment. 'That is an exciting prospect.'

Arnold nodded. 'Come to the theatre tomorrow, both of you, and we will discuss it.'

'We will be there,' her mother assured him.

He bowed and excused himself.

Ariana watched him walk away, her heart racing in excitement. She might perform at the Drury Lane Theatre on the same stage as Edmund Kean, the same stage as her mother.

Hoping for another glance at Ariana, Jack wandered around the room now, only pretending to look at the paintings.

Could he approach her? What would he say? *I am the artist whose work you admired.* He did want her to know.

The war's demons niggled at him again as he meandered through the crowd. He forced himself to listen to snippets of conversations about the paintings, but it was not enough. He needed to see her again.

On his third walk around the room, he found her. She and the woman who'd snatched her from his side now conversed with an intense-looking gentleman. Jack's Ariana seemed quite animated in her responses to the man, quite pleased to be speaking to him. Even from this distance he could feel the power of her smile, see the sparkle in her eyes.

When the man took leave of them, the older woman walked Ariana over to two aristocratic-looking gentlemen. Ariana did not seem as pleased to be conversing with these gentlemen as she had with the intense-looking fellow, but it was clear to Jack he could devise no further encounter with her.

He backed away and returned to examining the paintings, this time assessing them for the presence or absence of emotion.

Someone clapped him on the shoulder. 'Well, my boy. How does it feel to have your work hanging in Somerset House?'

It was his mentor, Sir Cecil.

'It is a pleasure unlike any I have ever before experienced, my good friend, and I have you to thank for it.' Jack shook the man's hand. 'I did not expect you in London. I am glad to see you.'

Sir Cecil strolled with him back to the spot in the room where Nancy's portrait hung. 'Had to come, my boy. Had to come.' He gazed up at the portrait. 'This is fine work. Its place here is well deserved. Unfortunate your sister cannot see her portrait hanging in such honour.'

'She has seen it,' Jack responded. 'She is here. She and my mother. They are this moment repairing a tear in my mother's gown. They should return soon.'

'I am astonished.' Sir Cecil blinked. 'It is unlike your mother to come to London, is it not?'

His mother had not been in London since his father died, so many years ago. 'She wished to be here for this, I think.'

That was only part of the reason. The truth was, his mother had come to London because Tranville, the man who'd made her his mistress, had also come to town.

When Jack's father, the nephew of an earl, had been an officer in the Life Guards, the whole family lived in London. John and Mary Vernon were accepted everywhere, and Jack could remember them dressed in finery, ready for one ball or another. All that changed with his father's death. Suddenly there were too many debts to pay and not enough money to pay them. Jack's mother moved them to Bath where Tranville took notice of the pretty young widow and put her under his protection.

Jack's mother always insisted Tranville had been the family's salvation, but as Jack got older, he realised she could have appealed to his father's uncle. The earl would not have allowed them to starve. Once his mother chose

Tranville and abandoned all respectability, his great-uncle washed his hands of them.

Sir Cecil patted Jack on the arm. 'It is good your mother and sister have come. How long do they stay?'

Jack shrugged. 'It depends.'

Depends upon how long Tranville remained in London, Jack suspected. Jack's mother was a foolish woman. Tranville had been no more faithful to her than he'd been to his own wife. He did return to her from time to time, between other conquests.

Matters were different now. Tranville had unexpectedly inherited a barony and become even more wealthy than before. Shortly thereafter, his wife died. Since suddenly becoming a rich, titled and eligible widower, he'd not called upon Jack's mother at all. There was no reason to expect him to do so while she was in London.

Jack cleared his throat. 'My mother and sister have taken rooms on Adam Street, a few doors from my studio.'

'You have established a studio?' Sir Cecil beamed with approval. 'Excellent, my boy.'

Tranville's money paid for his mother's rooms. Practically every penny she possessed came from him. He had thus far kept his promise to support her for life. His money had kept her and her children in great comfort. It had paid for Jack's education and his commission in the army. Jack swore he would pay that money back some day.

'The studio is not much,' Jack admitted to Sir Cecil. 'Little more than a room to paint and a room to sleep, but the light is good.'

'And the address is acceptable,' added the older man, thoughtfully.

The address was not prestigious, but it was an area of town near both Covent Garden and the Adelphi Buildings, which attracted respectable residents.

'I should like to see it,' Sir Cecil said. 'And to call upon your mother. I am in London for a few weeks. My son, you know, is studying architecture here at the Academy.'

'I hope to see you both, then.' Jack spied his mother and sister searching through the crowd. 'One moment, sir. My mother and Nancy approach.'

Nancy caught sight of him and waved. She led their mother to where Jack stood. Sir Cecil greeted them warmly.

'Jack.' Nancy's eyes sparkled with excitement. 'I cannot tell you how many people have asked me if I am the young lady in your portrait. I told them all the direction of your studio.'

His mother lifted her eyebrows. 'I would say some of those enquiries were from very impertinent gentlemen.'

Jack straightened and glanced around the room.

'Do not get in a huff, Brother.' Nancy laughed. 'I came to no harm. It was mere idle curiosity on their part, I am certain.'

Jack was not so certain. He worried about Nancy in London. With her dark hair, fair complexion and bright blue eyes, she was indeed as fresh and lovely as the incomparable Ariana had said. Jack worried about Nancy's future even more. What chance did she have to meet eligible gentlemen? What sort of man would marry the dowerless daughter of a kept woman?

He frowned.

His mother touched his arm. 'I confess to being fatigued, my son. How much longer do you wish to stay?'

He glanced around the room. The crowd was suddenly thinning. The afternoon had grown late and many of those in attendance would be heading to their townhouses in Mayfair. Some of them, perhaps, would take their carriages for a turn in Hyde Park before returning home. It was the fashionable hour to ride through the park.

Jack, his mother, and sister would walk to Adam Street.

'We may leave now, if you like.' Jack glanced around the room again, hoping for one more glimpse of Ariana.

Luck was with him when he and Sir Cecil escorted his mother and sister to the door. Ariana appeared a few steps ahead, but there was no question of approaching her. She and her companion walked with two wealthy-looking and attentive gentlemen.

Jack pushed aside his flash of envy. Instead, he focused on the way she carried herself, the graceful nature of her walk. He watched how her pale pink gown swirled about her legs with each step, how the blue shawl draped around her shoulders moved with each sway of her hips.

Jack watched her as they reached the outside and crossed the courtyard. No more than five feet behind her, he might as well have been a mile. Her party continued to the Strand where a line of carriages waited. In a moment Jack would have to head towards home. This would be his last glimpse of her.

She turned and caught sight of him. Her face lit up and took his breath away. His gaze locked with hers, and he thought he sensed the same regret in her eyes that was gnawing at his insides.

One of the gentlemen accompanying her took her arm. 'The carriage, my dear,' he said in a proprietary tone, apparently unaware of Jack staring at her.

She turned back one more time and found him again. 'Goodbye,' she mouthed before being assisted into a shiny, elegant barouche.

Jack watched her until he could see the barouche no more. He tried to engrave her image upon his memory but could feel it fading with each moment. He needed to reach his studio. He needed paper and pencil. He needed to draw her before the image was lost to him as well.

Chapter Two

London—January 1815

This chilly January night, Jack escorted his mother and sister to the theatre. His latest commission, a wealthy banker, offered Jack the use of his box to see Edmund Kean in *Romeo and Juliet*.

Jack had acquired some good commissions because of the exhibition, until the oppressive heat of August drove most of the wealthy from London. The banker, Mr Slayton, was his final one. Jack's mother and sister also returned to Bath, but they came back to London with the new year. Jack had placed an advertisement seeking some fresh commissions in the *Morning Post*, but, thus far, no one had answered it.

Jack tried to set his financial worries aside as he assisted his mother to her seat in the theatre box. Sir Cecil's son, Michael, was also in their company attending Jack's sister. Michael, as kind-faced as his father, but tall, dark-haired and slim, continued with his architectural studies and had again become a frequent addition to

Jack's mother's dinner table now that she and Nancy were back in London.

As Nancy took her seat, it was clear she was already enjoying herself. 'It is so beautiful from up here.'

They'd attended the theatre once the previous summer, but sat on the orchestra floor with the general admission. From the theatre box the rich reds and gleaming golds of the décor were displayed in all their splendour.

Nancy turned to Jack. 'Thank you so much for bringing us.'

He was glad she was pleased. 'You should thank Mr Slayton for giving me the tickets.'

'Oh, I do.' She turned to their mother. 'Perhaps we should write him a note of gratitude.'

'We shall do precisely that,' her mother agreed.

'Well, I am grateful, as well.' Michael stood gazing out at the house. 'This is a fine building.'

Nancy left her chair to stand beside him. 'You will probably gaze all evening at the arches and ceiling and miss the play entirely.'

He grinned. 'I confess they will distract me.'

She gave an exaggerated sigh. 'But the play is *Romeo and Juliet*. How can you think of a building when you shall see quite possibly the most romantic play ever written?'

He laughed. 'Miss Vernon, I could try to convince you that beautiful arches and elegant columns are romantic, but I suspect you will never agree with me.'

'I am certain I will not.' She nodded.

'I remember coming here in my first Season.' Jack's mother spoke in a wistful tone. 'Of course, that was the old theatre. There were not so many boxes in that auditorium.'

That Drury Lane Theatre burned down in 1809.

Nancy surveyed the crowd. 'There are many grand people here.'

The play was quite well attended, even though most of the *beau monde* would not come to London for another month or so. Perhaps Jack's commissions would increase then. Of course, with the peace, many people had chosen to travel to Paris or Vienna and would not be in London at all. Still, the theatre had an impressive crowd. Edmund Kean had been drawing audiences all year in a series of Shakespearean plays.

Nancy leaned even further over the parapet. 'Mama, I see Lord Tranville.'

'Do you?' Jack's mother's voice rose an octave.

'There.' Nancy stepped aside so her mother could see. 'The third balcony. Near the stage.'

'I believe you are correct.' Her voice was breathless.

Tranville stood with another gentleman in a box close to the stage, the two men in conversation while surveying the theatre. If Tranville spied his former mistress in the crowd, he made no show of it.

The curtain rose and Nancy and Michael sat in their chairs. Nancy's gaze was riveted to the stage, but their mother's drifted to the nearby box where Tranville sat.

Jack's jaw flexed.

Edmund Kean walked on.

'He is old!' Nancy whispered.

Shakespeare had written Romeo as a young man who falls in love as only a young man could. Kean's youth was definitely behind him. Still, Kean made an impressive figure in the costume of old Verona, moving about the stage in a dramatic manner. It would be a challenge to capture that movement in oils, Jack thought.

Artists such as Hogarth and Reynolds painted the famous actors and actresses, Kemble and Garrick, Sarah Siddons and Daphne Blane. The portraits were engraved and printed in magazines and on posters in order to entice people to the theatre. Jack straightened. Perhaps the theatre could provide him with a clientele. He might not get commissions for the principal actors, but maybe the lesser known ones, or maybe he could depict whole scenes as they occurred on the stage. If he could paint the action of battle, he could easily paint the action of a London stage.

The idea took firm root in Jack's mind. His studio was quite near to Covent Garden, so it would be convenient for the actors. Or he could easily come to the theatre. He began to imagine the scene onstage as he might paint it. He was ready to assess every scene for its artistic potential.

Romeo spoke the lines about planning to attend the Capulets' supper. He left the stage, and Lady Capulet and the nurse entered, looking for Juliet.

Jack's fingers itched for a pencil, wishing to sketch Lady Capulet and the nurse with their heads together.

'See,' Nancy whispered to her mother. 'Lady Capulet is Daphne Blane. Her natural daughter is playing Juliet.'

Jack had the notion he'd seen Daphne Blane before. Of course, she was a notorious beauty whose conquests were as legendary as her performances on stage so he might have seen her image somewhere. The birth of her natural daughter had been the scandal of its day with much speculation on who the father might be. Many artists had painted Daphne Blane's portrait. Why not Jack?

Juliet made her entrance. 'How now? Who calls?'

'Your mother,' the nurse replied.

Juliet faced the audience. 'Madam, I am here…'

Jack nearly rose from his chair.

Ariana.

Juliet was Ariana. From this distance, her features were not clear, but she moved like Ariana, sounded like her. He'd found her. He'd despaired of ever doing so.

His eyes never left her while she was on stage. His fingers moved on the arm of the chair as if he were drawing the graceful arch of her neck, the sinuous curves of her body.

The intermission was almost torture, because he could not record her on paper and he had to act as if his world had not suddenly tumbled on its ear. As the curtain closed on the actors' final bows, Jack remained in his seat, staring at the curtain.

Michael gave his hand to Jack's mother to help her rise, and Jack noticed his mother glancing in the direction of Tranville's box.

Nancy sprang to her feet, her hands pressed together. 'Was it not splendid? I mean, it was so sad, but so lovely, did you not think?'

Jack smiled at her, still partially abstracted. 'You enjoyed it, then?'

Her blue eyes shone with pleasure. 'I adored it.' Michael helped her on with her cloak. 'Well, perhaps not Romeo. Mr Kean was not my idea of Romeo, I assure you.'

Michael grinned. 'Was he not romantic enough?'

'He was *old*.' Nancy made a face.

Jack's mother glanced over her shoulder once more as they all made their way to the door. Once they were out in the noisy, crowded hallway, Jack would lose his chance to talk to them.

He placed a hand on his mother's arm. 'I should like your permission to part from you here.'

His mother shook her head. 'Forgive me, Jack. What did you say?'

'I would bid you goodnight here.' He turned to Michael. 'Would you escort the ladies home?'

'I would be honoured and delighted,' Michael replied. 'But this is a surprise. Why do you leave us?'

Jack's primary reason was to go in search of Ariana, but he had no wish to tell them that. He'd give them a partial truth. 'I had the notion that I might paint the actors performing their roles. I want to seek out the manager and give him my card.'

'You would paint the actors?' Nancy exclaimed. 'Why, that would be splendid! The print shops are always full of prints of actors. How perfect since you are so close to the theatre.'

'My thoughts precisely,' he responded, knowing this was not true. It was far less complicated than explaining about Ariana, however. 'I should be able to offer a reasonable price.'

Nancy nodded. 'Very sensible, Jack.'

'Proceed, my son,' his mother said. 'We will manage without you.'

His mother rarely complained, not even when Tranville failed to call upon her. It had been a year since he had bothered.

'Then I bid you all goodnight.' He leaned over and kissed his mother's cheek.

Nancy smiled. 'Thank you for bringing us, Jack.'

Michael made as if fighting with a sword. 'Do not fret. I shall scare off any foes who dare to cross our path.'

Nancy giggled. 'What nonsense. We shall take a hackney coach.'

Michael put his arm around her. 'Yes, we shall, and I shall pay for it.'

Out in the hallway, they made for the theatre door and Jack for the stage. He did not know the location of the Green Room, where the actors and actresses gathered after the performance and where wealthy gentlemen went to arrange assignations with the loveliest of the women, but he suspected that would be where he would find Ariana.

Backstage he followed a group of wealthy-looking gentlemen, some carrying bouquets of flowers. Jack walked behind them, but suddenly stopped.

Tranville stood to the side of the door.

He still retained his military bearing, even though he was attired in the black coat, white breeches and stockings that made up the formal dress of a gentleman. His figure remained trim and only his shock of white hair gave a clue that he was a man who had passed his fiftieth year.

Tranville, unfortunately, also saw Jack.

'Jack!' He stepped in the younger man's path. 'What are you doing here? Why are you not in Bath?'

Jack bristled. He'd never been able to disguise his dislike of this man, although when a child he doubted Tranville had even noticed. A few adolescent altercations with Tranville's son Edwin had made the animosity clear and mutual. Jack never initiated the fisticuffs, but he always won and that rankled Tranville greatly.

Jack straightened and looked down on the older man. 'I have business with the theatre manager.'

'You?' Tranville eyed him with surprise. 'What business could you have with Mr Arnold?'

Jack felt an inward triumph. He now knew the manager's name. 'Business to be discussed with Mr Arnold.'

Tranville's jaw flexed. 'If it is theatre business, you may tell me. I am a member of the committee.'

'The committee.' This meant nothing to Jack.

Tranville averted his gaze for a moment. 'The subcommittee for developing the theatre as a centre for national culture.'

Jack remembered it. Control of the theatre had been wrested from the debt-ridden owner, Richard Brinsley

Sheridan, and given to a manager and a board of directors. A subcommittee of notables had been appointed, but Jack doubted they had access to the purse strings. Nevertheless, if Jack had encountered any other member of the subcommittee he would have spoken of how his art work could further the committee's goals. This was Tranville blocking his way, however.

Jack maintained a steady gaze. 'My business will not concern you.'

Jack would wager Tranville's theatrical interests were in fostering liaisons with the actresses, not fostering national culture. Actresses and dancers encouraged the attentions of wealthy lords who wanted to indulge them with jewels and gowns and carriages.

He frowned. He had nothing to offer Ariana.

He told himself he merely wanted to renew their brief acquaintance. He wanted her to know *he* had been the artist whose work she so admired.

Two gentleman approached the door and Tranville was forced to step aside for them. Jack took the opportunity to follow them.

Tranville grabbed his arm. 'You cannot go in there, Jack. You do not have entrée.'

Jack shot him a menacing look. 'Entrée?

Tranville did not flinch. 'Not everyone is welcome. Do not force me to have you removed from the building.' He glanced towards two muscular stagehands standing nearby.

Had Tranville forgotten Jack had also been on the Peninsula? His was the regiment that captured the Imperial Eagle at Salamanca. Jack would like to see how many men it would take to eject him from the theatre.

More *gentlemen* approached, however, and Jack chose not to make a scene. It would not serve his purpose.

Tranville smiled, thinking his intimidation had succeeded. He dropped his hand. 'Now, if you wish me to speak to Mr Arnold on your behalf, you will have to tell me what it is about.'

The other gentlemen were in earshot, the only reason Jack spoke. He made certain his voice carried. 'A proposition for Mr Arnold. To paint his actors and actresses.'

'Paint them?' Tranville's brow furrowed.

'I am an artist, sir.' Jack wanted the other gentlemen, now looking mildly interested, to hear him.

With luck one of them might mention to Mr Arnold that an artist wanted to see him. That might help gain him an interview with the manager when Jack called the next afternoon.

Convincing Mr Arnold to hire him to publicise his plays would serve both Jack's ambitions: to earn new commissions and to see Ariana again.

Tranville made an impatient gesture. 'Well, give me your card and I will speak to Arnold.'

Jack took a card from his pocket. 'Tell him Jack Vernon has a business proposition for him. Tell him my work was included in last summer's exhibition.'

The most curious of the onlookers appeared satisfied. They had heard Jack's name, at any rate.

Jack nodded to the men. He was resigned. These men would see Ariana tonight. He would not.

And all because of Tranville's interference. Jack's hand curled into a fist.

Tranville snatched the card from Jack's other hand and stuck it in his pocket without even looking at it. Jack turned to leave.

Tranville stopped him. 'Tell me, Jack—how is your mother?'

The question surprised him. 'In good health.' He added, 'She was at the performance. Did you not see her?'

Jack meant it as a jibe, to show his mother doing well without Tranville's company, but instead the man cocked his head in interest. 'Was she?' He spoke more to himself than to Jack. 'So Mary is in London.'

Another man walked past and opened the door to the Green Room. Tranville emerged from his brief reverie. 'I must go.'

Jack was more than ready to be rid of him.

Still, he would have tolerated even Tranville's presence if it meant seeing Ariana again. Instead Tranville had prevented him.

Another reason to despise the man.

The next day, Jack, wearing only an old shirt and trousers, both spattered with paint, put the finishing touches on Mr Slayton's portrait. There was a rap on the door.

Before he could put down his palette and don a coat, the door opened and Tranville strode in.

'Jack—' Like many military men, Tranville apparently had not lost the military habit of rising early.

'What is the meaning of this?' Jack stepped out from behind his easel. 'You cannot just walk in here without a by your leave.'

Tranville, looking perfectly at ease, removed his hat and gloves and placed them on a table by the door. 'You work in this place?' He glanced around with disdain.

White sheets covered the furniture, wooden boxes and rolls of canvas littered the floor, but Jack had no intention of apologising to Tranville for the clutter. He tidied the place when he had sittings scheduled.

'Tell me why you intrude or leave.' Jack crossed his arms over his chest.

Tranville wandered over to the easel and examined Mr

Slayton's portrait. He shrugged and turned back to Jack. 'You do seem to have some skill. More than one fellow told me so after I left you last night.'

He'd been discussed? Remembered from the exhibition, perhaps? Jack hid his pleasure. He hoped these admirers mentioned him to Mr Arnold as well. 'You have not told me why you are here.'

Tranville's lips curled. 'I want to hire you for a commission.'

Jack did not miss a beat. 'No.'

Tranville's brows shot up. 'You've heard nothing about it.'

'I do not need to hear. I am not interested in painting you. The reasons should be obvious.' He headed to the door.

Tranville, remaining where he stood, laughed. 'If I were to commission a portrait of myself, I'd hire Lawrence or someone of his calibre. No, this portrait would be of someone else. A woman.'

Jack's eyes narrowed. He ought to have guessed. 'Most emphatically no.'

It sickened Jack that Tranville would ask him to paint a woman. Who else could it be but Tranville's latest conquest? Not if he were down to his last shilling, would Jack do such a thing.

He opened the door, but Tranville ignored the demand to leave. 'I checked with my man of business this morning—'

Rousing the poor man from his bed, no doubt.

'He gave me your mother's direction. A few doors up from here, eh?' Tranville's tone was pleasant, but Jack did not miss the hint of menace beneath it.

He gripped the door knob. 'Speak plain, sir.'

Tranville smiled, and Jack recoiled in disgust. 'Why, I thought I would call upon her. That is all.'

Jack's nostrils flared.

Tranville's smile fled. 'Surely you have no objection.'

Jack had a barrelful of objections, but none he could voice. As much as he despised the idea, his mother would desire the visit. 'It is my mother's decision.'

Tranville sauntered towards the door, retrieving his hat and gloves. As he passed Jack, he paused and leaned close. 'I always get my way, Jack.'

The rumble of imaginary cannon fire sounded in Jack's ear. A battle loomed, Jack would wager, this time in his London rooms and not on the battlefield.

It took Jack an hour before he could again focus on Mr Slayton's portrait, attending to its finishing touches. Better to concentrate on the tiniest brush stroke than to dwell upon Tranville visiting his mother.

He peered at the painting before him. He'd posed Mr Slayton at a desk with a pen in his hand. It would have been faster to merely paint the banker's head on a dark background, but Jack preferred some context to his painting, some sense of movement. Whether it had emotion, he could not tell. The emotion Ariana had seen in his two paintings at Somerset House had been unconsciously done.

He picked up a small brush and stared at the painting, but saw Ariana instead. Thoughts of her were the best antidote to the encounter with Tranville. He might see her today. He planned to visit the theatre this afternoon.

Another knock sounded at the door. Jack braced himself for a further intrusion by Tranville, but the person knocking apparently did not feel entitled to burst in as Tranville had done. The knock came again. Jack put down his palette, wiped his brush and crossed the room to open the door.

'Jack!' Nancy entered. 'Mama wishes to see you.'

'What has happened?' What has Tranville done? he meant.

She pinched his arm. 'Nothing terrible.' She smiled. 'Lord Tranville called upon her.'

He frowned. 'Did he upset her?'

Nancy looked puzzled. 'Of course not. She was in raptures. You know how Mama feels about him.'

Yes, but he could not fathom it. 'Then why does she wish to see me?'

'I am not certain.' Nancy removed her cloak and hung it on one of the pegs by the door. 'I did not remain with them above a few minutes. Lord Tranville said very pretty things to me. And to Mama. It was quite a pleasure to see him.'

'Is he still there?' If so, Jack preferred to avoid him.

She shook her head. 'He left, and then Mama asked me to fetch you.'

Jack walked over to his easel to clean his brushes. He covered his palette with a cloth so that the paint would not dry and wiped his hands. 'Give me a moment to change my clothes.'

A few minutes later he and Nancy walked the short distance to his mother's set of rooms on Adam Street. Jack liked having his family near after the long separation of war, and Tranville's money could well pay for rooms in both London and Bath, but his mother would have been far wiser to save that money for Nancy's future.

Nancy paused mid-step. 'Do you think Lord Tranville has asked Mama to marry him? Perhaps that is why she wants to see you?'

He gave a dry laugh. 'That is a ridiculous notion, Nancy.'

She pursed her lips. 'Why is it ridiculous? He is an eligible man now.'

He shook his head. 'He has not seen fit to call upon her for over a year. That is hardly prelude to a proposal.'

Nancy gaped at him as if he'd lost his wits. 'Surely Lord Tranville was concerned as to how it would appear to see Mama so soon after his wife died. He was being protective of her reputation.'

Jack resumed walking. 'He was never so protective of her reputation before his wife died.'

She hurried to catch up. 'You do not understand it at all. Now that he is an eligible man of rank, it becomes more important to protect her from talk.'

Jack bit his tongue. He'd always tried to shield Nancy from the sordid reality of Tranville's relationship with their mother. He wasn't about to change now.

'I do not understand why you dislike Tranville so.' Nancy looked wounded.

Jack never intended for Nancy to think well of Tranville, merely to prevent her from thinking ill of their mother. 'I suppose I dislike him because he is not our father.' And because he so quickly replaced their father in their mother's bed.

She squeezed his arm. 'I cannot remember our father like you do. I only remember that Tranville helped our mother when we were so poor.'

They had never been so poor that their mother would not have had a chance for a respectable second marriage. Tranville ruined that for her.

They arrived at his mother's door, but Nancy held him back. 'Can you not perceive the situation between Mama and Lord Tranville as romantic?'

'Romantic?' He could not lie. 'No, I cannot.'

'Well, I can.' Her tone was definite. 'They have loved

each other for so many years, but because Lord Tranville was married, they could not be together. Even so, he loved her with such a passion he could never stay away completely.'

He gave her a disapproving look. 'A passion?'

She lifted her chin. 'I am not a child any more. I know what happens between a man and a woman.'

Jack put his hand on the doorknob. 'What happens between a man and a woman is not necessarily romantic, my dear sister.'

Nancy stood her ground. 'He *must* love her. He pays for everything for her. Our food. Our house. Everything.'

'He has done so.' It was the only thing to Tranville's credit and it had always puzzled Jack. A man of Tranville's character would cut funds the minute he tired of a woman.

'Why would he spend that money on her if he did not love her?' Nancy asked.

'I confess, I do not know,' Jack responded honestly, turning the knob and ending the discussion.

When they entered the rented rooms, their mother's manservant, Wilson, appeared in the hall to take Nancy's cloak and Jack's hat and gloves. 'Your mother awaits you in the parlour.'

Jack opened the parlour door for Nancy and followed her in.

His mother stood by the fireplace and turned at their entrance. 'Jack, I am pleased you could come right away.'

He crossed the room and kissed her on the cheek. 'Mother.'

Slanting him a somewhat determined look, she gestured for them to sit. Jack waited for her to lower herself in a chair.

Her hands nervously smoothed the fabric of her skirt. 'I am certain Nancy has told you Lionel—Lord

Tranville—called upon me.' Her eyes flickered with a momentary pleasure.

'He informed me of his intention to call.' Jack tried to keep his voice even.

'We had a lovely time,' his mother went on.

'Indeed.' Jack fought sarcasm.

His mother took a breath. 'Well, I suppose I should just say that Lionel told me he offered you a commission.'

'He did.'

'He did?' Nancy sat forward in surprise. 'You never said. How exciting.'

Jack turned to her. 'I did not accept it, Nancy.'

His mother broke in. 'The thing is, Jack, I want you to accept it.'

'I will not.' She must be mad.

'Ja-ack.' Nancy drew out his name, sounding disappointed.

Jack stared at his mother. 'A woman, Mother.'

She shot a glance to Nancy and back to Jack with an almost imperceptible shake of her head. Very well. He would not delve into why he presumed Tranville wished him to paint a woman, even though his mother was not deluded about it.

His mother answered calmly, 'He is financing a production of Shakespeare's *Antony and Cleopatra* and wishes the portrait to be used in advertisements. It is precisely what you said you wanted last night.'

'I did not say I would work for Tranville.'

'But, Jack—' Nancy inserted.

'Do not be foolish, my son,' his mother went on. 'He offers you a good price—better, I dare say, than you have earned on your other paintings.' She named the price Tranville had offered. It was a staggering amount.

Jack gritted his teeth. 'I do not want his charity.'

Lines formed between her brows. 'This animosity does you no credit.'

He shrugged.

He'd tried to explain before, telling her of Tranville's harsh treatment of his men during the war while toadying to his superiors, of how Tranville turned a blind eye to his son avoiding combat, but sent better men to their deaths.

'You know what sort of man he is.'

'Say no more.' She lifted both hands to halt further discussion. 'I accepted the commission for you.'

He stood. 'You did not!'

She regarded him with a steely glance. 'You will paint this portrait for *me*, Jack, because I wish it. I ask little of you, but I ask this.'

He remained standing, looking down at her. She'd aged since he'd left for war. Her brown hair was streaked with grey and tiny lines had formed at the corners of her eyes and her mouth. Still, he thought her as beautiful as when he'd been a boy and she'd been young and carefree. He wished he could paint that memory.

She continued, 'And I insist you do not cross him. Treat Lord Tranville with civility for my sake, because it is important to me.' Her eyes pleaded. 'It is important to me that you have this work, the money it will pay, and it is important to me that Lionel succeed in gaining his desires. He wishes to make this play a success and, therefore, I wish it for him.'

Tranville wished to make a conquest of this actress, if he was not bedding her already. Who was it? An actress as sought after by men as Daphne Blane? Jack would not put it past Tranville to try to buy his way into her bed by financing a play. He'd bought his way into his mother's bed, after all, and now his mother wanted her son to paint this woman? It was absurd.

Jack narrowed his eyes. 'Did he threaten you? Threaten to withhold your funds or some such thing?'

She looked surprised. 'Threaten? Of course he did not. Lionel has always paid my quarterly allowance. I ask merely out of my gratitude for all he has done for us.'

Jack averted his gaze and stared into the carpet whose pile had worn thin in places.

'Say you will do this for me, my son,' his mother murmured.

He wanted to refuse, but his mother so rarely asked for anything, certainly nothing from him. Jack slowly nodded. 'For you, Mother, I will do as you ask.' He raised his chin. 'But only for you.'

Only for his mother would he would paint her lover's new conquest.

Chapter Three

Ariana descended the stairs at the boarding house on Henrietta Street where she and other actresses and actors lived. The rooms were comfortably furnished and the company, excellent. The landlady of the establishment was an accommodating woman, a stickler for propriety, if one desired, or equally willing to ignore propriety completely.

Today Ariana chose propriety. Betsy, the maid, had announced that Lord Tranville had called. Had he not been funding Drury Lane's production of *Antony and Cleopatra*, selecting her to play Cleopatra, she would have refused to see him. She kept him waiting in the drawing room a full ten minutes to discourage any notion he might have about how far her gratitude might reach.

She had no doubt her mother had told him where she resided. Her mother believed in patronage above all things.

Ariana wrinkled her nose.

What was her mother thinking? The gentleman was old enough to be her father, at least fifty years old, ten years older than her mother, even.

She swept into the drawing room. 'Lord Tranville. What a surprise.' She extended her hand, thinking he would shake it.

Instead he grasped it and brought it to his lips, actually placing a wet kiss upon it. 'My dear Miss Blane.'

She grimaced and pulled her hand away as soon as she could. Gone was any hope his interest was confined to her acting ability. She sighed. It would require skill to remain in his good graces while discouraging his advances. She'd managed it with other gentlemen; she could do it with him.

She made no effort to look at him directly. 'I am astonished you are here. Have you come on theatre business?'

He smiled wide enough to show all his white teeth. At least he had teeth, one point in his favour. 'I hoped my desire to gaze upon your loveliness would be reason enough to call upon you.'

With effort she kept her expression bland, staring blankly at him, as if waiting for him to stop spouting nonsense.

He fiddled with his watch fob. 'My—my visit does involve the theatre. In a manner of speaking.'

'Oh?' Only then did she gesture for him to sit. He chose one of the sofas. She lowered herself on to a chair, making a show of brushing off an invisible piece of lint from her sleeve.

Finally she looked at him again. 'Do tell me why you have called.'

He leaned towards her. 'I have a notion to advertise your role in *Antony and Cleopatra*.'

She lifted a brow.

He went on. 'If you are agreeable, an artist will paint you as Cleopatra. We shall have engravings made that can be printed for advertising. In magazines. On handbills. It will increase your success, I am certain.'

She looked at him with a wary eye. 'Who will pay for all this?' Surely not the theatre.

Mr Sheridan had run Drury Lane Theatre into terrible debt. Kean's performances, so very popular, helped to ease the burden, but that did not mean the theatre would expend money on behalf of a new actress whose popularity had not yet been established. Her performance had been barely mentioned when the critics gave *Romeo and Juliet* a very unfavourable review, greatly criticising Kean's performance.

'I will pay for everything,' Tranville said. 'And, if it pleases you, I will make the portrait my gift to you.'

She wanted no gifts from him, but she did need this play to be a success.

He tilted his head in a manner he probably thought charming. 'If it is convenient, the artist can see you this afternoon to discuss the painting. I will be honoured to escort you.'

She had no plans for the afternoon. 'Where is this artist?'

'On the corner of Adam Street and Adelphi.'

'Near the Adelphi Terraces?' It was only a few streets away.

'Yes.'

A good enough address and nearby. 'Who is the artist?'

He leaned even closer to her. 'His name is Jack Vernon.

Ariana gaped at him, 'Jack Vernon!'

Tranville looked apologetic. 'I realise he is not as fashionable as Lawrence or Westall, but he did have some paintings in the Royal Exhibition, I've heard tell.'

How well she remembered. She'd used her admiration of Vernon's paintings to brazenly approach the tall, handsome, solitary young gentleman whose inner struggle of some sort had fascinated her. Sadly, she had never learned who he was.

She resisted another sigh. What good was it to dwell on what was gone? Here was an opportunity to meet the artist and be painted by him.

'I will do it, my lord,' she told Tranville. 'But there is no need for you to escort me such a short distance. Merely give me the exact direction and tell me the time I am expected.'

His lower lip jutted out. 'I would be delighted to escort you.'

Her hand fluttered. 'Do not trouble yourself.'

'But—'

She gave him a level look. 'I prefer going alone. It is daylight. The streets are full of people. No harm will come to me.'

'I insist.' He persisted.

Her brows rose. 'Is your escort a condition of this agreement? I will not do it if there are conditions to which I must comply.' Ariana knew better than to make herself beholden to any man.

'No, no conditions—' he blustered.

'Good.' She rearranged her skirt. 'Tell me when I am expected.'

An hour later Ariana stood at Mr Vernon's door, her heart thumping with anticipation. She looked down at herself, brushing off her cloak, pulling up her gloves, straightening her hat. She took a quick breath and knocked.

Almost immediately the door opened.

Framed in the doorway was the handsome gentleman she'd met in Somerset House, the one she'd thought she would never see again.

'You!' She gasped. 'I—I have an appointment with Mr Vernon.'

He looked equally surprised. It took him several seconds before he stepped aside.

As she brushed by him she felt a flurry of excitement. She'd found him, the man who'd so intrigued her at the Summer Exhibition. He was taller than she remembered, and his sheer physical presence seemed more powerful than it had been in the crowded exhibition hall. In the light pouring through the windows, his brown eyes were even more enthralling and every bit as beset with private demons.

'Is Mr Vernon here?' she asked.

He slowly closed the door behind her. 'I am Vernon.'

'You are Vernon?' The breath left her lungs.

His frown deepened. 'I—I did not know you would be coming.'

He did not seem happy to see her. In fact, his displeasure wounded her. 'Forgive me. Tranville said I was expected at this hour.'

He stiffened. 'Tranville.'

She began to unfasten her cloak, but stopped. Perhaps she would not be staying. 'Did you desire him to accompany me?'

His eyes were singed with anger. 'Not at all.'

He confused her with his vague answers. She straightened her spine and put her hands on her hips. 'Mr Vernon, if you do not wish me to be here, I will leave, but I beg you will simply tell me what you want.'

He ran a hand through his thick brown hair and his lovely lips formed a rueful smile. 'Tranville told me to expect an actress. I did not know it would be you.'

His smile encouraged her. 'Then we are both of us surprised.'

His shoulders seemed to relax a little.

He stepped forwards to take her cloak, and as he came

so close she inhaled the scent of him, bergamot soap and linseed oil, turpentine and pure male.

He seemed unaware of her reaction and completely immune to her, which somehow made her want to weep. Only once before had she wanted to weep over a man. He took her cloak and hung it upon a peg by the door, moving with the same masculine elegance that had drawn her to him when she first caught sight of him. He had been the first man to ignite her senses in years, a fact that surprised and intoxicated her even now.

He faced her again, and she hid her interest in a quick glance around the studio, all bright and neat, except for where an easel stood by the windows, a paint-smeared shirt hanging from it. She removed her hat and gloves and placed them on a nearby chair.

He did not move.

So she must. She walked to him. 'Let us start over.' She extended her hand. 'I am Ariana Blane.'

He shook it, his grasp firm, but still holding something back.

Her brows knit. 'Why did you not tell me, that day, that you were the artist? That you were Jack Vernon?'

He averted his gaze. 'I intended to, but the moment passed.'

'Come, now.' She tried smiling and shaking her finger at him. 'You allowed me to rattle on for quite a long time without telling me.'

He turned his intense brown eyes upon her. 'I wanted your true opinion of my paintings. You would not have given it, had you known I had painted them.'

She laughed. 'Oh, yes, I would. I am never hesitant to say what I think.'

Indeed, she had half a mind to ask him why he scowled when looking at her. He made her senses sing with pleasure. She longed to feel the touch of his hand against her skin, but he seemed completely ill at ease with her.

There had been no unease between them in that first, fleeting, hopeful encounter.

She cleared her throat but disguised her thoughts. 'What happens now, Mr Vernon? This is my first time having my portrait painted.'

He walked over to a pretty brocade upholstered chair and held its back. 'Please be seated, Miss Blane. I will bring tea.'

She sat down, very aware of his hands so near to the sensitive skin of her neck. When he released her chair, she swivelled around to see him disappear behind a curtained doorway to a small galley in the back. A moment later he returned, tray in hand.

He placed the tray on a small table in front of her chair.

She touched his arm and his gaze flew to her face. 'Allow me to pour,' she murmured, as affected by the touch as he appeared to be. 'How do you like your tea? Milk and sugar?'

He lowered himself in the chair on the other side of the table. 'I grew accustomed to going without both on the Peninsula.'

'You were in the war?' she asked as she poured his tea and handed him the cup.

His gaze held. 'In the infantry.'

Her voice turned low. 'Now I comprehend why your history painting had such authenticity.'

He looked away.

Ariana poured her own tea, adding both milk and sugar. She gazed at him when she lifted the cup to her lips. A barrier had risen between them, one that had not existed when they had met at the exhibition. That conversation had been exhilarating; this one dampened her spirits.

She placed her teacup on the table. 'So, how do we proceed with this portrait?'

A crease formed between his brows. 'I need to know what you would like it to be.'

She waved a hand. 'I have no notion. I first heard of this idea an hour ago.'

He glanced away and his brooding expression intensified. 'I first heard this morning.'

'Lord Tranville has been busy,' she murmured, taking a sip of tea.

He made a sound of disgust, pausing before looking back at her with shrouded eyes. 'I did not expect you to come alone. If you desire it, I shall ask my sister to be present. She is but a few doors away.'

What maggot had taken up lodging in his brain? 'Why did you think that?' Actresses did not require chaperons.

He continued to stare at her. 'Tranville is not with you. Perhaps you would like another woman to be present.'

'Tranville?' Why did he persist in bringing up Tranville? He wasn't her father. Who else would care if she were chaperoned?

Suddenly her brows rose. He thought Tranville was her lover.

Jack Vernon would be surprised to know she'd had only one lover, a long time ago. Yes, she'd been deceived once, even though she ought to have learned of men's fickle natures at her mother's knee. Never again. In fact, she'd not even been tempted—until meeting the mysterious stranger at the Summer Exhibition.

In spite of his present behaviour, he still tempted her with his sorrowful eyes holding wounds of the past.

She gave herself a mental shake and made an effort to retrieve their conversation. 'I require no chaperon, Mr Vernon. No one expects propriety from actresses. There is some freedom in that.'

He merely sipped his tea.

She took a breath and tried again. 'Shall we discuss the portrait?'

'You and I must decide how you are to appear as Cleopatra.' He spoke as if all emotion had been leached out of him.

Except from his eyes.

'I am not at all certain how to do that,' she murmured.

He shrugged. 'We try different poses. I sketch you, and we select the best image.'

This struck her as insufficient, like trying to prepare for a play by guessing one's lines.

'Have you read the play?' She rubbed one finger on the arm of the chair. 'It might provide you with some ideas.'

'Not since school days.'

He glanced at her hand, and she curled her fingers into her palm. 'I have my copy in my rooms. Let us get it so you can read it.'

He blinked. 'There is no need. Bring it tomorrow.'

'Then we will be delayed another day. My residence is nearby. It will take no time at all.'

He stared at her and the moment stretched on. 'Very well,' he finally said.

He went into another room to get his top coat, and a minute later they were outside in the cool, breezy air.

She took his arm and glanced at the street ahead. 'Which of the "few doors away" is your sister?'

'Not far.' As they passed, he pointed to it. 'This one.'

'And is there a wife behind those doors, as well?' Please say no, she thought.

He shook his head. 'I am in no position to marry. My sister lives with my mother in those rooms.'

Her heart skipped a beat.

'You have seen my sister,' he said to her as they walked on.

She glanced at him in surprise. 'I have?'

'Hers was the painting you admired at the exhibition.'

She stopped. 'Of course it was. Now I understand.'

'Understand what?'

She met his eyes. 'Why it was such a loving portrait.'

His colour heightened and she sensed him withdrawing from her again.

And they'd almost returned to the comfort between them at the exhibition.

Ariana asked more questions about his sister, hoping she'd not lost him again. She asked his sister's age, her interests, how she'd been educated, anything she could think of that seemed safe. The short walk, a mere few hundred yards to her residence on Henrietta Street, was by far the most pleasant she'd had in an age.

When they entered the house, he turned towards the open drawing-room door.

She pulled him back. 'Come up to my room.'

His brows rose. 'To your room?'

She waved a hand. 'No one will mind, I promise.'

She chattered to him about how she came to live at this place, about the other boarders who lived there as well, anything to put him at ease, to put her at ease, as well.

When they entered the room, Ariana pointedly ignored the bed, the most prominent piece of furniture and the one that turned her thoughts to what it might be like to share it with him. It unsettled her that he could so quickly arouse such dormant urges in her. If she'd learned anything from her former lover, it had been that her senses were not always the best judge of a man's character.

She took off her cloak and flung it over a chair. He removed his hat and gloves, but not his top coat.

He glanced about the room. 'Where is your copy of the play?'

'On the table.' She pulled off her gloves and gestured to a small table by the window.

He picked up the small, leather-bound volume. 'I will have it read by tomorrow.'

He opened the book and flicked idly through the pages. Quickly snapping it closed, he slipped the book into a pocket of his top coat.

Which passage had caused that reaction? she wondered. Antony's line, perhaps?

There's not a minute of our lives should stretch;
Without some pleasure now.

He seemed to gain no pleasure from her company. 'I should return to my studio.'

She had not moved from the doorway. 'When should I come and sit for you tomorrow?'

'At the same time, if it is convenient.' His manner was stiff.

'Tomorrow, then.' She nodded.

He strode towards her. As he passed, she caught his hand. 'I would greatly desire our time together to be pleasant. We started as friends. May we not continue that way?'

Again that mysterious distress flashed through his eyes. What bothered him so?

He stared into her eyes. ''Til tomorrow, Miss Blane.'

She released his hand and he hurried out of the door. From the hallway she watched him descend the stairs and walk through the front door, not even pausing to put on his hat and gloves.

When Jack reached Adam Street he was still reeling with the unexpected pleasure of being in Ariana's company again, as well as the crushing knowledge that she was Tranville's actress.

Jack walked with his head down against the chilly wind from the river. It was even more appalling that Tranville had chosen an actress young enough to be his daughter.

Instead of going back to the studio, Jack called upon his mother. He found her alone in her sitting room doing needlework by the light of the window.

She looked up as he entered. 'Jack, you are back again.'

He glanced around the room. 'Where is Nancy?'

'She and our maid went to the market.' His mother's smile was tight. 'I fear Nancy finds these four walls tedious. She takes every opportunity to venture out of them.'

He did not respond, but stared blankly at the carpet.

'Sit, Jack.' She indicated a chair. 'Tell me why you are here.'

He wandered over to the mantel, absently moving one of the matched pair of figurines flanking a porcelain clock.

Finally he looked at her. 'Did Tranville tell you that his actress is almost as young as Nancy?'

She stabbed her needle through the cloth. 'That is no concern of mine, and ought to be no concern of yours, Jack.'

'No concern!' He swung away, then turned back to face her. 'Does it not trouble you? How can it not? How are you able to insist I paint this portrait?'

Her eyes creased in pain. 'It is what he wishes.'

He felt his face flush with anger. 'You do not have to do what he wishes, Mother. He treats you abominably.'

Her expression was stern. 'That is your opinion. In my opinion he has enabled me to live in comfort, to rear my children in comfort, to give them an education, a future.'

He gave a dry laugh. 'I could debate what sort of future he's provided Nancy with, but, that aside, have you not more than paid him for what he has done for you?'

She merely pulled her needle through the cloth.

Jack paced before walking to her chair and crouching down so that he was at eye level with her. 'Mother, I will make a living as an artist. I will earn more commissions. If we economise I will have enough to care for you and Nancy. You do not need to accept another shilling from Tranville. You can tell him to go to the devil.'

She gazed directly into his eyes. 'I will not do that.'

He blinked. 'Why not? I promise I can take care of you.'

She went back to her sewing. 'I am certain you will be very successful, my son, but I still will not spurn Lionel.'

Jack stood. 'He has spurned you. In the most insulting way.'

She gazed up at him again. 'I do not need to explain myself to you and I have no intention of doing so. I will not change my arrangement with Lionel.'

It was no use. Where Tranville was concerned his mother was blind and deaf.

'Do you stay for dinner?' she asked, breaking the silence. 'It is not for a few hours yet, but you are welcome to stay. If you are hungry now, I'll send for tea and biscuits.'

He shook his head. To sit down at dinner and pretend this day had not happened would be impossible. 'Do not expect me for dinner. I have much to do tonight.'

She smiled wanly. 'You are still welcome if you change your mind.'

He walked over and kissed her. 'I must go.'

She patted his cheek, but her eyes glistened with tears. 'I hope we will see you tomorrow.'

Once he stepped back out into the winter air, he hurried to his studio and let himself in. He leaned against the door with visions of Tranville hopping from his mother's bed into Ariana's.

Throwing down his gloves and hat, he crossed the room to a bureau where he kept paper. Pulling out several sheets, he grabbed a piece of charcoal and began sketching.

The lines he drew formed into an image of Ariana.

Chapter Four

That evening Ariana sat at a mirror applying rouge to her cheeks and kohl to her eyelids to make her features display well to the highest box seats of Drury Lane Theatre. The dressing-room doors were open wide, so that she and the other actresses could hear their cues to go on stage. In a half-hour the curtain would rise on the evening's performance of *Romeo and Juliet*, and backstage was its usual pandemonium. People shouted. Pieces of set were moved from one side to the other. Actors, actresses and the ballet dancers who entertained between acts ran here and there in all states of dress and undress.

Ariana loved the commotion. She vastly preferred being among it to walking up the stairs to the private dressing room usually reserved for the leading actress. Her mother had demanded that dressing room, and Ariana had not minded in the least. The backstage bustle energised her.

Her mother's reflection appeared behind her in the mirror. Dressed for the comparatively minor role of Lady Capulet, her mother glared at her. 'Have your wits gone begging?'

Ariana set down the tiny brush she'd used to darken her lashes. 'Whatever do you mean, Mama?'

Her mother gestured dramatically in the direction of an invisible someone. 'Lord Tranville pays for your portrait and an entire play and you refuse his escort. You would not even walk with the man.'

Ariana replied to the image in the mirror. 'I was under the impression his financial investment was meant to benefit the theatre, not his vanity.'

Her mother threw up her hands. 'Then you are a bigger fool than ever I imagined.'

Ariana was no fool. She knew precisely what Tranville had hoped to purchase.

She averted her gaze from the mirror. Even if Tranville's motives had merely been gentlemanly, Ariana would not have welcomed his company. She liked being alone with Jack Vernon. She liked the intimacy of it, liked that he could look at her without anyone else as witness.

Ariana held her breath, imagining him raking her with those eyes and rendering on paper what he saw. It felt akin to him touching her.

Her mother tugged at her shoulder, interrupting her reverie. 'Tranville has a great deal of influence here in the theatre. You cannot treat him so shabbily without penalty. You profess to wanting success, but, the way you are bound, you will ruin matters for both of us.'

Ariana did indeed wish for success, success as an actress, not as Tranville's plaything.

The renowned Daphne Blane enjoyed above all things the adoration of men. Her acting career was merely the means of putting herself on display, and her fame came more from the numbers of men with whom her name had been linked over the years than from her roles on stage.

Her single-minded interest in winning the attention

of the most prestigious gentlemen had left Daphne Blane little time to be bothered by a daughter. Ariana had been cared for by others. Theatre people were the ones who showered her with attention. They had dressed little Ariana in costumes, painted her face, even allowed her to walk on stage as part of a scene. The theatre had been where she was happiest. She loved it so much she'd walk on any stage, in any role, merely to be a part of it all.

Ariana drew the line at bartering herself to lustful men, even if they would help her acting career. If that was the price of success, it was too high and too false. She wanted to rise on the merits of her skill, nothing more. She wanted to earn the best roles, the best reviews, the most applause, because her performance deserved it.

Her mother, however, had made one valid point. Ariana might not wish to share Tranville's bed, but she ought not to alienate him completely. He could wield his influence in this theatre for both good and ill.

She turned to look her mother in the eyes. 'Put your mind at ease, Mother. I am well able to manage Lord Tranville. I've managed others like him before.'

'Oh?' Her mother placed fists on her hips. 'Eighteen years old and you are such an expert on men?'

Ariana inhaled a weary breath. 'I am twenty-two, older than you were when you gave birth to me.'

Her mother's eyes scalded. 'Well, one can be very foolish at twenty-two. If I'd had more sense I never would have given birth to you.'

Ariana flinched.

She covered the sting of her mother's words with a tight smile. 'I learn by your mistakes.'

Her mother glanced away, gazing at a tree that seemed to cross in front of the door. Scenery for Act II. 'Well,

Tranville attends the performance tonight. Be nice to him in the Green Room.'

Ariana turned back to the mirror and dipped a huge feather puff into the face powder. 'I am always nice to gentlemen.' She merely did not bed them.

Mr Arnold appeared at the dressing room door. 'Ah, there you are, Daphne, my dear. You look lovely as usual.'

Ariana's mother beamed. 'Such flattery. I am dressed as a matron.'

'Nothing could diminish your beauty.' He squeezed her hand and glanced to Ariana. 'Your daughter has inherited every bit of your loveliness. She makes a fine Juliet. Beauty and an acting skill that rivals your own. You must be proud.'

Ariana's mother still smiled, but Ariana caught the hard glint in her eye. 'Yes, I *must* be proud, mustn't I?'

Early the following morning, Jack woke to a messenger bringing him Tranville's first, quite generous, payment of the commission. At least Tranville's money enabled Jack to replenish his supplies. He walked the mile to Ludgate Hill where Thomas Clay's establishment offered the finest pigments and purchased enough for several paintings. He returned in time to set up the studio for Ariana's arrival.

As he waited for her, he looked over the several images of Ariana he'd sketched from memory, including the ones he'd drawn after that first fleeting contact with her. The night before he'd filled page after page with her profile, her eyes, her smile; when the light had faded to dusk, he read *Antony and Cleopatra* by lamplight.

She knocked upon his door promptly at two. Jack rose from his drawing table, hastily stacking the sketches. When he opened the door, her face was flushed pink from the winter air.

'Good afternoon, Mr Vernon.' She smiled and her eyes shone with pleasure.

Their impact forced him to avert his gaze. 'Miss Blane, I trust you are well.'

'I am always well,' she responded cheerfully.

He had the presence of mind to assist her in removing her cloak, too aware of the elegant curve of her neck and, beneath her bonnet, the peek of auburn hair at its nape.

'Were you able to read the play?' she asked, pulling off her gloves and untying the ribbons of her bonnet.

He hung her cloak on a peg. 'I read it all last night.'

She placed her hat and gloves on the table nearby and faced him, still smiling, looking eager for whatever was to come.

His sketches had not done her justice, he realised. He'd not captured that spark of energy, that vivacity that was hers alone. His fingers itched to try again.

But he must attend to the civilities. 'I will make us some tea.' He started for the galley, but she reached it ahead of him.

'I'll do it.' She swept aside the curtain covering the doorway and glanced around the galley. 'There is very little for me to do. You've prepared everything.'

He'd placed the kettle on the fire before she arrived. The tea was in the pot. She poured the water.

'You must allow me to carry the tray,' he said.

She looked up at him with an impish grin. 'Must I?'

He stepped into the space. 'I insist.'

There was no room for both of them, but he thought of that too late. Their arms brushed as she tried to move past him and the mere contact with her caused Jack's senses to flare with an awareness of more than her physical beauty.

She faced him, their bodies almost touching. Reaching up to his face, she gently rubbed his cheek with her finger. 'You have a black smudge.'

Charcoal from his drawings.

He grabbed a cloth and rubbed where she had touched, but he could not erase the explosion of carnal desire she aroused in him. He turned from her and picked up the tray. She followed silently as he carried it to where they'd been sitting the previous day.

She sat in a chair as if that moment of touching had never happened. 'Where do we begin? Do we discuss how to depict Cleopatra?'

Jack murmured, 'It seems a good way to start.'

She poured the tea and handed him his cup. 'What did you think?'

'Of Cleopatra?'

'Yes.' She lifted her tea.

He placed his cup on the table. 'I was struck by her political ambition. I had not remembered the play that way from my school days.'

She smiled. 'Perhaps you were too romantic as a boy.'

He laughed drily. 'I dare say not, but I understand more of life now. Antony was motivated by passion, but Cleopatra was motivated by ambition.'

She nodded. 'I do agree. She betrays Antony twice. And I doubt she killed herself out of love for him.'

He moved his cup, but did not lift it. 'But his love for her led to his death.'

'And to hers,' she reminded him. 'One could say she was a woman alone merely trying to make her way in the world and that his passion for her led to her downfall.'

He thought of his mother's situation. 'The world has not changed much.'

'Indeed,' she said with a firm tone.

He glanced into her face, remembering it was Tranville who played the role of Antony in her life, not he. The sun from the window shot shades of red through her auburn hair.

The look she gave him in return was soft and companionable.

Jack had to glance away. 'It is an odd play. More a history than a romance.'

She laughed. 'It is a good thing. There is enough romancing from Mr Kean in the play as it is.'

He glanced at her in surprise. 'You do not like Kean as your leading man?'

She shook her head. 'Not at all. He smells of whisky and he is too short.'

'The celebrated Mr Kean?'

Her face puckered as if she'd eaten a lemon. 'I dare say he shows more favourably in the theatre boxes.'

Her frank tone made him relax and pushed thoughts of Tranville out of his mind. He felt as if they'd returned to Somerset House.

They began discussing how Cleopatra might be depicted and if she should be seated or standing. Jack was impatient to draw her.

She put down her teacup and sat on the edge of her chair. 'Shall I pose now? Perhaps as Cleopatra on her throne?'

She straightened her spine and raised her chin, instantly transforming herself into a haughty queen who looked down on the rest of the world.

He was intrigued. 'Hold that pose.'

He moved his drawing table closer to her chair and placed a clean sheet of paper on its angled surface. He sketched quickly, using charcoal and pastels, not thinking, allowing the image to come directly from his eye to his hand.

She remained very still, almost like a statue.

He put that sketch aside and replaced it with a fresh piece of paper. 'Stand now and move.'

'Move?'

He twirled his hand as an example. 'Move around in front of me. Like Cleopatra would move.'

The natural quick and graceful movements that had entranced him heretofore were replaced by a regal step, back and forth.

He sketched hurriedly.

'I feel a bit silly,' she said as she crossed in front of him.

'You do not look silly,' he responded. 'This is precisely what I need.'

He tried her in other poses, seated and standing, producing ten pastel drawings that gave him ideas of how a final painting might appear.

He looked through them.

'May I see?' She walked over to stand beside him at the drawing table, bringing with her the scent of rose water. She examined each drawing, one after the other.

'Remarkable!' She looked through them again, setting three of them side by side. 'You were drawing so fast, I never dreamed you could make them look so much like me.'

He sorted through them again. 'They are still not right. I am not sure why.'

He'd set his earlier sketches of her on the floor next to the drawing table. She saw them. 'What are these?'

She picked them up and went through them. When she came to the ones he had done after Somerset House, she looked up at him with a puzzled expression.

'Some sketches I made earlier,' he replied, deliberately vague.

'These are different from the others.' She stared at them. 'I look…' She paused. 'Alluring.'

He did not respond.

She broke into a smile. 'You drew these after the exhibition, did you not?

He would not lie. 'I did.'

'I like them,' she said simply and he felt himself flush with pleasure. 'You make me look enticing.'

'It is not enough.' He was glad she did not question him about why he'd drawn her that day; he was uncertain he could answer her.

She looked at him as if she could see into his thoughts to all he'd felt about her that day, feelings forbidden him now, but he would not think of that. Today he merely wished to paint her.

'Cleopatra must look enticing.' She looked around the room and found a *chaise-longue*. She pushed it closer to his writing table and reclined upon it, propping herself on one arm and turning to face him directly. The effect was both sensuous and regal.

Jack's breath hitched at the sight of her.

She dropped her role as Cleopatra. 'You do not like this one?' She started to change position.

He held up a hand. 'Do not move. Let me draw you that way.'

She resumed her pose. 'We are doing well today, are we not?'

'Yes.' He concentrated on the lines he was drawing.

'I feel we are rubbing together as well as when we met at the exhibition.'

He glanced up at her, but did not respond.

She went on. 'What happened yesterday, do you think? I was convinced you were unhappy with me. Will you tell me now what it was?'

He stopped. 'There was nothing.'

She tilted her head, then seemed to remember why she was there and returned to her original pose. 'I did not imagine it. My presence distressed you.'

He focused on his drawing. 'Perhaps my mood was due to something else not concerning you.'

'Then tell me what made you unhappy,' she said in a kind, genuine tone.

'I cannot recall now,' he lied. 'Likely it was nothing.'

She remained quiet for a while and Jack filled in the colour of her dress, the flawless tint of her skin.

'Do you have many friends in London?' she asked after a time.

'Not many,' he answered. 'I am from Bath.'

'Are you?' she said brightly. 'I played *The Beggar's Opera* in Bath. Did you see it? That was two years ago.'

He shook his head. 'I would have been in Spain.'

Her expression turned sympathetic, but she did not pursue that topic. 'I do not have many friends in London either,' she said instead.

'Does not your mother live here?'

She waved a hand, then remembered to return to her pose. 'My mother is not precisely a friend. One needs friends for entertainment.'

Jack had little room in his life for entertainment. 'Entertainment.'

'You know. Walks through the park, visiting the shops, sharing an ice at Gunter's—things like that.' She paused. 'There are my theatre friends, of course, but most of their entertainment involves taverns.'

Jack let her conversation wash over him like the water of a clear spring on a summer day. It kept him from concentrating too hard on his work and allowed the lines of the drawing to flow. He replaced one paper with another and began to draw just her face, filling the page with it.

'You and I should be friends,' she went on.

His hand stopped and he stared at her again.

She smiled at him. 'Then I could call you Jack. And you could call me Ariana.'

Before he could form a response, there was a rap at

the door. Jack put down his pastel to answer it, but the door opened.

Lord Tranville walked in. 'Well, well, well.' He removed his hat and bowed to Ariana. 'Good day, my dear.' He turned to Jack. 'I thought I would stop by and see how things were progressing.'

'Tranville.' Jack went rigid. 'It is the second meeting. What progress did you expect?' He placed the sketch of her on the *chaise-longue* on the bottom of the pile.

'I should like to see.' Without waiting for permission, Tranville stepped behind Jack's drawing table.

Jack kept his hand on the stack of drawings, so that Tranville could see only the one on top, one of Ariana seated upon the chair.

Tranville glanced over at Ariana. 'You make a lovely model, my dear.'

She did not respond.

He examined the drawing again and shook his head. 'You look nothing like Cleopatra, however.' He turned to Jack. 'For God's sake, she needs to look Egyptian.'

Jack's fingers flexed into a fist.

Ariana spoke up. 'Gracious, my lord. You expect too much of a first day of posing. Did you think I would be in full costume and theatre paint?'

Jack felt fully capable of defending his work to the likes of Tranville. He resented the older man's intrusion, but resented more the reminder of his claim on Ariana.

Tranville smiled at Ariana, and Jack noticed his eyes flick over her reclining form. 'If you are happy with the sitting, my dear, then I am content.'

Jack twisted away, hiding the disgust on his face he knew he could not disguise.

'Jack, when do you finish for the day?' Tranville asked. 'I am here to escort Miss Blane home.'

Jack's shoulders stiffened.

Ariana sat up. 'That is not necessary, sir.'

'I cannot allow you to walk alone.' Tranville tossed Jack the sort of glance that passed between men when they expected to make a conquest.

That Tranville would flaunt his affair with Ariana to the son of his former mistress made Jack's blood boil. Only his promise to his mother kept him from grabbing Tranville by the collar and tossing him out on to the cold pavement.

'We are not finished.' Ariana resumed her Cleopatra pose.

Tranville walked over to a chair and sat. 'I do not mind waiting.'

Jack stacked the drawings and put his pastels back in their box. He would not draw another line with Tranville there. 'We are finished.'

Ariana shot to her feet and glared at Jack. Without a word she picked up the teacups and tray and carried them into the galley.

'You must not do that,' Tranville said. 'It is servant's work.'

'I do not mind.' She used the same inflection Tranville had used previously.

Jack followed her in to the galley. 'I will see to the tea things.'

'We were not finished. Why did you say we were?' She spoke quietly, but seemed to bristle with annoyance.

'I cannot work with him watching.'

She crossed her arms over her chest. 'When do I return, then?'

He shrugged. 'Tomorrow?'

'Very well. I'll arrive at two, if that will be convenient for you.' Her voice was clipped.

'Two o'clock, then,' he responded in kind.

She pushed past him, back into the studio.

Tranville stood with her cloak, ready to assist her. He draped it over her shoulders, his hands lingering.

Jack turned away, pretending to see to his dishes. He did not turn back until he heard the door close behind them.

Chapter Five

Ariana reluctantly took Tranville's arm. The pleasantries he uttered as they walked to the end of the street were no more than an annoying buzz in her ears.

She trembled, so full of anger she could barely contain herself. She did not know who made her angrier, Tranville for intruding or Jack for not tossing him out.

She thought of him as Jack now, already feeling an intimacy with him even though he had only begun to relax in her presence. It had been a most curious experience to sit for him. She felt his every glance, but also felt that the paper, the colours, the lines kept him at a distance from her.

If only Tranville had not swept in—

'What time do you pose for Jack tomorrow?' she heard Tranville ask.

She avoided answering the man, asking a question of her own instead. 'You seem on very familiar terms with Mr Vernon. What is your connection with him?'

He gave a trifling laugh. 'Jack is the son of a friend. I have known him most of his life.'

'Oh?' she said, truly interested. 'Are you a friend of his father?'

Tranville paused for a moment. 'His mother, actually, although I was acquainted with his father before the man's untimely death.'

'I see.' A friend of the mother and merely acquainted with a deceased father? She pumped him for more information. 'When did Mr Vernon's father die?'

He waved a hand, as if the man's death had no importance at all. 'Sixteen—seventeen years past or some such.'

'I would have been only six years old.' Let him be reminded of the differences in their ages. 'Mr Vernon must have been quite young as well.'

He frowned. 'Indeed.'

Had Jack's mother been a conquest of Tranville's? It might explain much about Jack's seeming animosity towards the man. They crossed Maiden Lane. Almost home, thank God.

'You did not tell me what time you were expected at Jack's.' He sounded as if he were trying to disguise his annoyance.

'Two o'clock.' She hated answering him.

'I will come to escort you,' he said.

She halted and released his arm, facing him directly. 'Sir, I would beg you not come at all and certainly do not intrude on the sitting again.'

He looked affronted. 'I beg your pardon?'

'Do not come,' she repeated, saying each word slowly and clearly. 'You ruined the sitting. It broke Mr Vernon's concentration. Could you not see that?'

His face turned red.

Forcing a charming smile, she changed tactics. 'Now do not become cross with me. Anyone entering at that moment would have done the same.' She took his arm again and they began walking. 'I am very cognisant of how much you wish this portrait to be a success for the theatre. In order to achieve that end, the artist will need privacy.'

'Did Jack tell you that?' His arm tensed.

She made herself laugh. 'Indeed not! But anyone who knows anything about posing for portraits realises that privacy is paramount.' She, of course, had only a day's knowledge of sitting for a portrait, but she trusted Tranville knew even less.

Ariana spied a pretty young woman glancing at them from across the street. The young woman's companion was an equally young and handsome man who gazed upon the young woman as if the sun rose and set upon her.

Ariana envied them.

Tranville spoke again. 'Surely I might walk you to Jack's with no disruption.'

Ariana hated that she must cater to this man, merely because of the power he wielded. She sighed inwardly and looked up at Tranville. 'Very well, you may call for me a quarter of an hour before two and walk me to the artist's studio.'

His mouth widened into a broad smile.

She shook a finger at him. 'But you must not arrive to walk me back home, because it is never certain precisely what time we shall finish.'

His brow creased. 'If the hour is late, it will not be safe for a young woman—'

She cut him off. 'If it is late, I shall insist Mr Vernon walk me home.' She made her voice sound as if this was not the circumstance she most desired. 'I dare say it is the least he can do for all that you must have paid him.'

'Very well.' This time he stroked her palm with his thumb. 'I will do as you wish of me.'

She withdrew her hand. They were finally at her door.

'Good day, sir,' she said with a curtsy.

He obviously hoped to be invited inside. He reached for her hand again, but she opened the door.

'Wait.' He gripped the door. 'Will I see you tonight in the Green Room?'

'Perhaps.' She plastered on a smile and hurried inside.

Jack begged off dinner at his mother's again that evening. After seeing Tranville's manner toward Ariana, Jack could not face his mother. He spent the rest of the afternoon staring at the drawings he'd made of Ariana, forcing himself to think of the task as an artistic challenge.

He finally set them all aside and donned his top coat, needing the brisk winter air to cool his emotions. He burned with anger and resentment.

Head down against the wind, Jack crossed the Strand and strode toward Covent Garden, avoiding Henrietta Street and memories of Ariana's bedchamber and fears that Tranville might have visited it. All he desired was a meal of mutton and ale in some noisy tavern smelling of ordinary men partaking of ordinary pleasures. He wandered to Bow Street and found such a place, seating himself at a small table against one wall.

The man seated at the next table insisted upon befriending him. The man turned out to be an actor, no great surprise since Drury Lane was only a few streets away.

'I perform with Kean and the incomparable Daphne Blane,' the man said. 'You must come to see me perform. I'll get you in.'

It meant seeing Ariana as Juliet again. Jack accepted the invitation.

No one questioned the actor's new friend when they entered the theatre. The man told Jack to stand at a spot in the wings with an excellent view of the stage, albeit a sideways one. Before the play began Jack looked around, expecting at any moment to glimpse her. He saw Ariana in the wings on the other side, but she did not see him.

Jack's newfound friend played Abraham, a Montague servant who had a few lines and a swordfight in Act I. No longer on stage, he stood next to Jack, watching the performance.

'This is an excellent portrayal of Juliet,' the man whispered to Jack. 'Best I've ever seen. Ariana is Daphne Blane's daughter so her acting skill is no surprise.' He laughed quietly. 'The word is that Daphne does not know which of the many gentlemen bedding her at the time sired the girl.'

Everyone knew that theatre people lived by very loose standards, with no expectations to mix in polite society, but Ariana's story seemed a sad one.

Jack watched her on stage, playing a beloved daughter. She was completely convincing as an innocent, trusting young girl about to be thrown into a cauldron of passion and family strife. When Ariana had posed as Cleopatra, she'd been equally convincing, turning herself into a jaded, cunning, sensuous queen.

He wanted his portrait also to reveal what was uniquely her. That she was forthright, unafraid and determined.

He frowned. Perhaps that was merely the role she played with him. Did she play another sort of woman for Tranville?

He ran a hand through his hair. He must not allow himself to care about her. She was a commission, nothing more. He need only create a decent painting.

On stage she recited the lines, '*My bounty is as bound-less as the sea, My love as deep; the more I give to thee, The more I have, for both are infinite—*'

Jack closed his eyes. Her words fired his senses. Ever since Spain, he'd numbed himself against disappointment, loss and horror. Ariana threatened to cut through those defences and make him feel again.

Jack suspected his theatre companion could take him to the Green Room if he requested it. But if Tranville was there and fawning over Ariana, Jack could not stomach it.

The play was over and his companion joined the final bows on stage. Afterwards he invited Jack, not to the Green Room, but to return to the tavern for more drink. Some of the other young actors joined them. As they walked out of the theatre, Jack came close enough to Ariana to reach out and touch her. Her mother had her in tow and was so busy talking to her that Ariana did not see him.

He let the opportunity pass.

At the tavern Jack was content to observe his companion with his friends. Jack was included in round after round of drink, but was not really a part of their circle. As he watched, the drink rendered them quicker to laughter, to anger, to maudlin sentimentality. He made note of the expressions on their faces, their gestures, their postures, all tinted in shades of brown in the dim tavern light.

Jack felt the haze of too much drink and eventually bade them goodnight. He walked out to the street and turned the corner into an area that was dark and narrow. Sounds of the tavern's revelry echoed against brick walls.

Suddenly it was as if he was back in Badajoz. The shadowy figures crossing the street in front of him, darting into alleys or standing in doorways, suddenly seemed about to attack. The good-natured laughter from distant taverns sounded like the demented laughter of Badajoz. Happy bellowing turned into screams. Jack plastered himself against the cold wall of a building and pressed his hands over his ears.

He was not in Badajoz, he told himself, but his senses refused to listen. His heart pounded, his muscles tensed, and a voice in his head shouted, 'Run!'

He ran. Ran as if drunken soldiers pursued him as they had in Badajoz. Ran as if he were escaping visions of carnage and brutality and violent lust.

His lungs burned by the time he reached his studio and pulled the key from his pocket. Panting, he opened the door and stumbled inside. Visions of the soldiers holding down the French woman returned. Again her son wailed for them to stop. Again Jack saw the face of Edwin Tranville, smiling drunkenly.

'Come join the fun,' the spectre said. 'Plenty for you, as well.'

Jack staggered into his bedchamber and pulled out the chamber pot. Kneeling over it, he vomited until nothing was left but dry heaves.

The next morning he woke with a start. His mouth tasted foul, his head throbbed with pain, and the room stank of vomit.

He rose, still dressed in the clothes of the previous night, and picked up the chamber pot, retching as he carried it out back to clean it.

Afterwards, he pumped clean water into a large pitcher. He used the water to rinse out his mouth, brush his teeth and wash himself, all the while his head reeling and his stomach threatening to rebel.

After he managed to change into clean clothes, he made his way to his mother's residence to beg for breakfast and pots and pots of tea to rid himself of the hammer and anvil in his head.

Wilson let him in and he went directly to the dining room, expecting to see food set out to eat.

He did not expect to see Tranville seated at the table, cup in hand, reading a newspaper.

'Jack.' Tranville nodded in greeting. He was alone in the room.

Jack put a hand on the doorjamb to steady the growing rage inside him. He did not nod in return.

Tranville chuckled and returned to his newspaper.

The need for food and to prove Tranville could not intimidate him prevented Jack from turning around and walking out. He went to the sideboard and found it more generously filled than usual, kippers and slices of ham, in addition to the usual cooked eggs and sliced bread. The kippers made his stomach reel almost as violently as Tranville's presence. Jack chose two eggs and slices of bread, spreading them with butter and raspberry jam.

He chose the chair directly opposite Tranville and poured himself a cup of tea from the pot in the centre of the table.

'You are asking yourself if I did indeed spend the night here.' Tranville popped a forkful of kipper into his mouth. 'I spent a very pleasant night.'

Jack glared at him, but refused to be baited.

Tranville tried again. 'I did consider your sister's presence, if you are wondering.' He lifted his tea cup to his mouth. 'But I decided she is old enough to know what is what. Old enough for a husband, I dare say.' He laughed again. 'Besides, she had already retired when I arrived. I came after the play was done.'

After the play? Tranville had not spent the night with Ariana, then. Despite his resolve to think of Ariana as merely a commission, Jack expelled a relieved breath. It was quickly replaced with anger that Tranville had come to his mother instead. 'It is a wonder you considered anyone's feelings but your own.'

Tranville's eyes burned with anger. 'Your mother did not mind.'

Jack gripped the edge of the table. He held Tranville's gaze. 'Take care how you speak.' Even a promise to his mother had its limits.

Tranville made a placating gesture. 'Now, now. You know I have the highest regard for your mother.'

'Regard for her?' Jack looked daggers at him.

Tranville's voice turned low. 'What passes between your mother and me is none of your affair and you would do well to remember that.'

Those were almost the exact words his mother had spoken to him.

Tranville slapped his palm on the table. 'Know your place, boy,' he said with more energy. 'Do not question a peer of the realm about his affairs.'

Jack leaned forwards. 'I will not see my mother hurt by you.'

Tranville adopted the expression of a reasonable man. 'Your mother understands my needs, boy. That should be the end of it for you.' He stuffed a piece of ham into his mouth and chewed.

Jack's gaze did not waver. 'She knows you are bedding Miss Blane?'

Tranville gave a half-smile and lifted a finger in the air. 'Ah, but I am not bedding Miss Blane. Yet.' He took a swallow of tea. 'Otherwise I should not be here.'

Tranville had not bedded Ariana? At all? This news stunned Jack. For a moment he felt paralysed. Until he realised Tranville was using Jack's mother to slake his lust for Ariana. It was enraging on all accounts.

Jack pushed his chair back, ready to vault across the table and lunge for Tranville's throat, when his mother swept into the room. 'Why, Jack, I did not know you were here.'

Still trembling with rage, he stood and gave his mother a kiss. 'For breakfast.'

She patted his cheek. 'You are always welcome.'

She walked over to Tranville, who also stood. 'Good morning, Lionel.'

He kissed her on the lips, sliding a glance to Jack as he did so. 'My dear, allow me to serve you from the sideboard.'

He held a chair for her and she lowered herself into it gracefully. 'I would be most grateful. Just an egg, I think.'

He brought her the egg and returned to his seat to pour her tea for her.

Beneath the table Jack's hands were clenched into fists.

Nancy walked in, rubbing her eyes. Never cheerful in the morning, she peered at Jack and mumbled, 'Morning.' Then she noticed Tranville. 'Oh!'

He stood and bowed. 'Good morning, Nancy, my dear. Will you allow me to serve you?'

She looked confused. 'I can do it. Please sit.'

When she returned to the table, Tranville popped up and pulled out a chair for her. 'Did you sleep well?'

'Yes, thank you,' she responded politely.

As she ate, Nancy glanced from her mother to Tranville and back. She turned to Jack, her expression questioning.

He shrugged.

Nancy finished one cup of tea and poured herself another. 'Lord Tranville, I saw you on the street yesterday afternoon. Who was the young lady with you?'

Jack darted a glance to his mother, who merely stared down at her plate.

With no hesitation Tranville responded, 'It must have been Miss Blane. I escorted her back from Jack's studio.'

Nancy shook her head in bewilderment. 'From Jack's studio!'

Jack broke in. 'Lord Tranville commissioned me to paint Miss Blane's portrait.'

Nancy's eyes widened. 'It was the younger Miss Blane, the actress who played Juliet. I thought she looked familiar.'

Tranville leaned towards Nancy. 'I am convinced the young Miss Blane will be a great success, as great as her mother. She will be an asset to the theatre.'

'I see,' murmured Nancy, but she looked uneasy.

Jack rose and put another piece of bread on his plate.

Tranville pulled out his watch, an expensive gold time-piece, and checked the time. 'It is late. I must be off.'

Jack returned to his seat.

'Must you leave so early, Lionel?' Jack's mother appeared crestfallen.

Tranville leaned down and kissed her on top of her head. 'Business, my dear. I'll call upon you again, I promise.' He put his hand on Nancy's shoulder. 'A pleasure to see you again.' He nodded to Jack and walked out of the room.

Jack could not even look at his mother.

Nancy seemed to force a smile. 'Well. It is the younger Miss Blane who sits for you. Tell us, is she as pretty up close as she was on stage?'

Jack fought to keep his expression bland. 'I would say so.'

Nancy went on, sounding determinedly cheerful. 'How exciting. How is the painting progressing?'

'I have hardly begun.'

She kept on. 'I should like to see her up close. When does she next come for a sitting?'

'Today at two.'

'May I come and meet her?' She gave him a look that

dared him to refuse her. 'I promise I will not stay and distract you.'

Jack glanced at his mother, whose face had become pinched.

'I can think of no reason to object,' their mother said, looking as if she wanted anything else but to give her daughter permission to meet the woman who was to replace her in Tranville's bed, a woman in the freshest bloom of youth and beauty.

Jack could think of no excuse to keep Nancy away. 'Very well.' His glance went from his mother to Nancy. 'Come at two.'

Chapter Six

Nancy picked through the bundled herbs at the Covent Garden stall, selecting a bunch of lavender and holding it to her nose before placing it in the basket her friend Michael held for her. She reached in her reticule for her coin purse.

'I will pay,' Michael gave the vendor a coin. 'It will be my gift to you.'

'Thank you, Michael. You are too good.'

'It is my pleasure,' he said.

They strolled past vegetable and fruit stalls tended by red-cheeked vendors bundled in wool, their breath making clouds as they hawked their wares.

'Thank you for taking me out, too,' Nancy said. 'I sometimes think I shall go mad sitting in the drawing room all day watching Mama do needlework.'

'Again, the pleasure is all mine.'

She sighed and glanced away as they walked.

'Something is troubling you,' he said.

'Troubling me?' She glanced back at him.

Michael was not quite as tall as her brother. He was thinner, as well, but to Nancy he was a dependable friend and much too perceptive.

'Nothing troubles me,' she stated emphatically.

He threaded her arm through his and looked upon her with his kind blue eyes. 'You cannot fool me, you know.'

His face was so dear, so open and earnest, but she was not even certain she could put into words what troubled her.

'Are you concerned about your mother?' he asked.

She pulled away. 'Why do you think I would be concerned about Mama?'

His smile turned conciliatory. 'A mere guess.'

They walked on in silence, no longer touching. Nancy stopped in front of a stall holding cages of hedgehogs, popular as pets because they ate the beetles that plagued London houses.

She leaned down and touched the snout of a baby hedgehog poking through the slats of his cage. She liked how Michael never pressured her to speak, like Mama sometimes did, wanting to know anything that distressed her. Her mother, like Michael, would also have perceived her upset and she certainly could not confide in her mother.

Nancy glanced up at Michael, who merely smiled with unspoken sympathy. She stood again. 'Oh, Michael.' She slipped her arm through his and they strolled on. 'I am not certain what upsets me.'

He merely squeezed her hand.

They passed by a flower stall. He stopped and purchased a small bouquet of flowers and handed them to her. She smiled. He was always giving her small things. He was her very best friend and the only friend she had in London. Even though she only really met him last summer, she felt as if she'd known him her whole life. Perhaps she could talk to him a little.

'How much do you know of my family?' she asked him.

He did not answer right away. 'I know your father died when you were very young. I know that—' He hesitated and took a breath. 'I grew up in Bath. I know that Lord Tranville...supported your family.'

He said it without censure and it gave her the courage to go on. 'It was very wrong for my mother to accept Lord Tranville's help, but I am convinced it is due to the grand passion they have for each other.'

She glanced at him to see if he wore that same sceptical look as Jack. Michael seemed only to be listening.

She went on. 'I was used to his—his visits to my mother from time to time, but last night—' She swallowed. 'I think he spent the night with her because he was at the breakfast table this morning. It bothered me.'

'Did it?' Michael remarked.

She stopped him and looked up into his face. 'Remember yesterday when we saw him with that young lady?'

He nodded.

'That bothered me, too.' Her throat tightened. 'It was that actress, the one who played Juliet. It is she Jack is painting.'

'Jack is painting her?' He sounded surprised.

She nodded. 'Lord Tranville commissioned the portrait. I—I think she may have some designs on Lord Tranville.'

'What makes you think so?' His calm tone soothed her.

'Oh—' she sighed again '—just a feeling. When I mentioned seeing her with Lord Tranville everyone started acting strangely. Jack was there, too, and he acted strangest of all.'

Michael reached up and brushed a lock of hair off her cheek, tucking it behind her ear. 'There is likely some other explanation, but let us formulate a plan to discover what the true reason may be.'

She felt all the tension leave her. 'You will help me?'

He smiled at her. 'Of course I will.'

She took his arm again and started walking. 'What are you doing today at two o'clock?'

Shortly before two, Nancy and Michael rapped on Jack's door.

Jack was still in his shirtsleeves when he answered it.

'I hope you do not mind I brought Michael.' Nancy crossed the threshold and took off her cloak.

'Indeed not.' Jack shook Michael's hand. 'No classes today, Michael?'

'Not today.' Michael set the basket on the table near the door. 'I was at liberty to escort your sister to the market.'

'We brought a tin of biscuits for tea.' Nancy hung up her cloak. 'Shall I put a the kettle on?' She took the tin from the basket and handed it to him.

'You are staying for tea?' Jack did not look happy.

The plan she and Michael had concocted was that they would stay for tea so Nancy would have a better opportunity to assess Miss Blane. 'It will enable us to have a real chat.' She walked to the galley.

Jack followed her. 'You merely wanted to meet Miss Blane, you said.'

She smiled sweetly at him. 'It would be impolite not to chat with her.'

Michael approached Jack. 'My father sends his regards. I received a letter from him yesterday.'

How like him to create a diversion. Nancy gave him a grateful look.

Jack answered him. 'He is well, I hope.'

'In excellent health.' Michael gestured toward a stretched canvas on the floor. 'Do you need any help with that? I'm accustomed to it with my father.'

'No help. I have finished. It only lacks tidying up.' Jack brought out a broom and swept up the scraps of linen and wood that were on the floor.

'I'll get those.' Michael took the dustpan from Jack's hands. 'Is there somewhere for this outside?'

'Out of the door in the galley.' Jack picked up the stretched canvas and set it against the wall.

Michael brushed past Nancy on his way to the door. 'How are we doing?' he asked in a low voice.

'Splendid so far.' Nancy leaned her head out of the galley doorway. 'I can only find three cups,' she called to Jack.

'Look behind the jars of pigment,' Jack responded.

She rummaged through the cabinet and found the extra cups, setting one on the tray. 'Will Miss Blane be prompt? I can pour the hot water now.'

Jack did not look pleased. 'She was on time yesterday.'

Nancy took a breath, refusing to be daunted.

'I need to finish dressing.' Jack disappeared into his bedchamber.

Michael came in from outside. 'We are staying for tea, I gather.'

Nancy grinned. 'We are indeed.' She carried the tea tray into the studio. 'Help me rearrange the furniture.'

They pushed four chairs into a cosy group with the tea table in the centre. Nancy took out the flowers Michael had purchased for her. 'I'm going to put these out. I'll take them home later.' She found an empty jar to use as a vase and placed the flowers on the table. 'Thank you, Michael. We should have plenty of time to take her measure.'

Jack emerged from the bedchamber still buttoning his

coat. He surveyed the scene. 'You cannot stay long, Nancy. I've work to do.'

A knock sounded at the door and Nancy's heart jumped into her throat.

'I'll answer it.' She reached the door before Jack could protest.

When she opened it, it was Lord Tranville she saw first. He stood with Miss Blane on his arm.

'Lord Tranville!' Nancy's spirits fell. This seemed a confirmation of her fears.

'Nancy, my dear.' Tranville gave her a peck on the cheek and stepped aside so Miss Blane could enter.

Miss Blane looked at Nancy and broke into a smile. 'You are the sister—'

'Jack's sister,' Tranville broke in.

Her attention was on Nancy. 'I remember your portrait from the exhibition.' She extended her hand. 'I am Ariana Blane.'

She remembered the portrait? Nancy could not help but be complimented. She curtsied. 'I am Miss Vernon.'

'I am so pleased to meet you.'

Lord Tranville was poised to assist her with her cloak, but Miss Blane took it off herself and hung it on a peg next to Nancy's.

Jack stepped forwards. 'Allow me to present our friend to you.' He gestured to Michael. 'Lord Tranville, Miss Blane, this is our friend Mr Harper.'

'I am honoured.' Michael bowed.

'How nice to meet you,' Miss Blane said, sounding as if she really meant it. 'I believe I saw both of you on the street yesterday. Is that not a coincidence? Oh, look, you have tea.' She turned to Jack. 'You should not have gone to so much trouble.'

'My sister did it all,' he responded.

Lord Tranville immediately chose the best chair and held it out for Miss Blane. 'I cannot stay long.' He took the chair next to her for himself.

Michael fetched a fifth cup and chair while the others sat and Nancy started to pour.

Conversation predictably began with the weather and how they all hoped February would bring warmer temperatures.

Miss Blane turned to Nancy. 'Let me say again how glad I am to have seen the lovely portrait of you. I do not know when I have been so impressed.'

'She's a very pretty girl.' Tranville spoke as if Nancy were not seated across the table from him. 'I believe her looks will bring her excellent marriage prospects.'

Nancy lowered her head in embarrassment.

Jack glared. 'That, sir, is family business.'

Tranville gave him an ingratiating smile. 'Jack, my boy, you know that what concerns your family, concerns me. You may rest assured that I will be on the lookout for suitors for your sister. My position gives me an advantage. I know the best people. I dare say I can discover more than one man who will find her acceptable.'

Nancy's cheeks grew hot.

Miss Blane laughed. 'You jest, sir, surely. It is very plain that Miss Vernon can attract her own suitors.'

Tranville gave her a patient look. 'She looks well enough, indeed. Her looks and youth will make my job easier, I am certain.'

Jack looked as if he would explode. 'It is not your job, sir.'

Even Michael looked angry.

'Stop talking nonsense, Tranville,' Miss Blane ordered in a good-humoured voice. 'Your joke is falling flat. If you were onstage, I would close the curtain and bring out the ballet dancers.'

Tranville looked about to defend himself, but Miss Blane quickly turned to Nancy. 'Tell me, Miss Vernon, have you seen any fashion prints for this month? There seems to be a tendency for dresses to have ruffles at the hem, which I adore. I must order one.'

She had deliberately altered the subject, Nancy realised. 'I think it makes for a pretty change.' Nancy turned to Michael. 'Do you not think so, Michael?'

Michael looked as surprised as Nancy, but he rose to the occasion. 'It is rather like the embellishments one sees in the decorative arts these days, I would say. A new trend.'

Jack seemed also to be staring at Miss Blane in astonishment.

'Michael is a student of architecture at the Royal Academy,' Nancy explained to Miss Blane.

Jack turned to Lord Tranville, but his expression was still rigid. 'Mr Harper is Sir Cedric's son. You know Sir Cedric, the portrait artist in Bath?'

'The fellow who got you into this business?' Tranville's tone was deprecating. 'Paints the people who come for the waters?'

'He is a member of the Royal Academy.' Jack looked thunderous again.

'Hats…' Miss Blane turned to Nancy again. 'What do you know of the latest in hats?'

Nancy knew nothing of the latest in hats, but she babbled on about ribbons and lace and different shapes until Lord Tranville stood.

'I must be about a matter of important business.' He bowed to Nancy, but more pointedly to Miss Blane. 'Do forgive me for leaving.'

Jack stood, but made no effort to walk him to the door. Miss Blane continued to chatter about hats. When the door closed behind Lord Tranville, she abruptly abandoned the topic.

When Jack sat again, Miss Blane lifted her cup. 'Well, this is lovely.' She took a sip and slid a glance towards Jack. 'Have you showed your sister and Mr Harper our work so far?'

'I have not.' Jack still frowned.

'Oh, do show them,' she pleaded. 'I should like their opinion.'

'I would like to see them,' Nancy added.

Jack was still fuming inside at Tranville's comments about Nancy. The audacity of the man to assume he had any right to arrange Nancy's life. He rose reluctantly. 'The sketches are in the back room. I'll get them.'

He strode into his bedchamber.

Tranville thought some man of his choosing would find Nancy *acceptable*? Jack remembered the men Tranville befriended in the army, men like Tranville himself, more concerned with their own ambition than with the welfare of the men serving under them.

Jack opened the large trunk where he kept his drawings. He riffled through the stack he'd produced the day before, selecting only ten of them. When he put back the rest, he noticed the corner of a large leather envelope peeking out from beneath many other drawings he'd produced. It was the envelope containing his drawings from the war, from Badajoz.

He closed his eyes as images of that night flashed in his mind, as they had so vividly the night before. Edwin deserved to be punished for it and Tranville deserved the shame of having such a son.

Jack slammed the lid of the trunk. He, Deane and Landon had chosen to keep that secret. Jack had given his word.

He wondered again what had happened to the French

woman and her son. Had Deane managed to find them a place of safety? Had they survived the war? Did they dream of that night like he did?

Jack shook the thoughts from his mind and picked up yesterday's drawings and carried them into the studio. Michael removed the tea tray and flowers and Jack placed the drawings on the table.

He showed them one by one and the lively discussion that ensued helped bring him back to the world that was his refuge. The world of his art.

'I like the reclining figure,' Michael said. 'Its composition is pleasing. Very reminiscent of Titian's Venuses.'

Miss Blane laughed. 'Mr Harper! Those paintings showed Venus without clothing. I've seen the engravings.'

Michael turned red. 'I meant in the composition, the pose.'

She placed her hand on his. 'I know that is what you meant.' She turned to Jack. 'Imagine if your work was compared to Titian.'

Jack shook his head. 'I very much doubt that would happen.' He stared at his sketch of the reclining Ariana. God help him, he was picturing her as Titian's nude Venus.

'You are good enough,' Ariana said.

He raised his head and his gaze met hers.

Nancy pointed to the picture. 'It is very nice, but there is nothing in it to say this is Cleopatra. I thought you were to paint her as Cleopatra.'

Her comment was very close to Tranville's the previous day. 'This is merely the first step,' he said tightly.

Ariana picked up the sketch. 'I have no idea how an Egyptian queen would appear.' She turned to Jack. 'Would it not be splendid if I truly looked the part?'

Nancy said, 'You must have such a costume in the theatre.'

'I dare say such costumes exist.' She gazed away in

thought. 'I should love to look as if plucked directly from an Egyptian vase.'

As they spoke the painting was beginning to form in Jack's mind. Ariana draped in fine linens, gold jewellery adorning her neck and wrists, her *chaise*, an Egyptian sofa, pyramids in the background.

'There are prints of Egyptian friezes and sculptures we could view at the Royal Academy,' Michael said. 'If you wish, we could view them today.'

'You could arrange that?' Ariana asked him.

'Of course, he could!' Nancy jumped to her feet. 'Let us go right now. May we, Jack?'

He liked the idea of using real images from the period to inform the work. 'Give me time to get my sketchbook and pencil.'

Soon they were walking down The Strand toward Somerset House, the wind from the Thames fluttering the ladies' skirts and threatening to whip Jack's hat off his head. Michael and Nancy were ahead, their heads together in deep conversation.

Jack heard a snippet of it. 'It was not at all what I expected…'

Nancy spoke about meeting Ariana, he suspected. Jack should have anticipated Tranville would be with her. This portrait was merely a part of Tranville's pursuit of her, no doubt. Had Tranville bestowed other gifts upon her?

Ariana's manner towards Tranville was a puzzle. She seemed to ignore him, except when deflecting his talk of arranging nuptials for Nancy. The damned audacity of the man.

Ariana held Jack's arm as they walked. 'Those two seem very happy,' she remarked. 'I dare say matchmaking for Nancy's sake will be unnecessary.'

'What do you mean?' It was as if she'd heard his thoughts.

'Those two.' She inclined her head towards Nancy and Michael. 'Surely they are sweethearts.'

He gaped at them. 'They are friends. Michael is our only friend in London.'

'Not your only friend,' she murmured.

'Who else?' he asked.

She gave him a disappointed look, and they walked on.

After a while she asked, 'Is Tranville not your friend? He says he is.'

Jack stiffened. 'He is no friend.'

She shook his arm. 'Jack. Jack. You make me want to ask you what is between you and Tranville, but I doubt you would tell me.'

He gritted his teeth. 'It is a private matter.'

The mood that had been lightening between them darkened again. Jack could not shake the picture of Tranville seated at his mother's breakfast table from his thoughts. It had not been the first time Tranville had so used Jack's mother, only this time she must have had no illusions about it.

Jack walked on, mouth clamped shut.

Ariana broke the silence. 'Every time Tranville appears in person or in conversation, you turn dark and sullen. Did you know that?'

He turned to her and spoke with deep sarcasm. 'Forgive me. I shall endeavour to be more entertaining.'

She hit his arm. 'Stop it. I do not want that.' They walked a few more steps before she added, 'I like you, Jack. I wish to be your friend. If we might be friends, think how enjoyable our time together will be.'

He broke in. 'This is a matter of business between us. Nothing more.'

'It is more to me,' she countered. 'It is my future. Yours, as well, I think. I want this painting to help make me a sensation on the London stage. You must be counting on it to bring you commissions. We both want the money and attention the painting can bring.'

'That is still business, Ariana.'

Her eyes widened and a smile flitted across her face. He realised, then, that he'd called her by her given name, belying all his talk of business.

'Jack.' She spoke his name as if confirming his slip. 'Your drawings are good, but they are not exceptional. You are holding back. I look flat in them, like I am nothing more than a doll. You can do better; I've seen you do better, but we must get over this—this barrier between us.'

'Nonsense. There is no barrier.' Inside he knew she was correct.

'The barrier is Tranville,' she said.

'Then it is an insurmountable barrier,' he shot back. 'Tranville is paying for the portrait. He is as much a part of it as you and me.'

She stepped in front of him, causing him to stop. 'Money doesn't make him part of it.' She put both hands on his arms. 'He is nothing to me, Jack.'

The hood from her cloak fell away and her face was bathed in a soft light, diffused by clouds obscuring the sun. Wisps of auburn hair beat against her cheeks and eyes he knew to be green had turned grey from the sky's reflection. Her eyes pleaded and she raised herself on tiptoe, bringing her face even closer.

His gaze fell to her lips. He tried to memorise their colour in the overcast afternoon, more violet than pink. His head dipped and he noticed the length and curl of her dark lashes.

His hands closed around her waist.

A carriage clattered by and Jack stepped away, shaken out of his reverie.

He glanced past her to see that his sister and Michael had put a great deal of distance between them.

'We had better walk on,' he said.

She held him back. 'Can we be friends, then? Forget about Tranville when we are together and enjoy ourselves?'

He stared down at her, knowing at this moment he wished for more than friendship with her.

Forgetting Tranville would be difficult, but far easier than resisting the desire she aroused in him, yet she looked so earnest, so compelling, he could refuse her nothing at this moment.

'Very well, Ariana.' He looked into her eyes again and again felt the rush of desire for her. He bit down on his resolve. 'I shall try.'

Chapter Seven

Ariana walked out of Somerset House with Jack at her side feeling she could not be happier. Only on stage did she feel similar exhilaration.

True, she had not convinced Jack to confide in her, but he had used her given name, more than once. And he had almost kissed her. It was enough to send her spirits soaring to the heavens.

Inside Somerset House Jack had quickly sketched from print after print of Egyptian art. He'd been so totally absorbed that she, his sister and his friend might well have been invisible. Ariana did not mind. It was fascinating merely to watch him work.

Now that their lovely time at Somerset House had ended Ariana could not bear her day with Jack to come to an end.

They strolled back to Adam Street talking about Egyptian prints.

'I did not like all that I saw,' Ariana said as she walked between Jack and his sister. 'The women looked so strange.' She shuddered, recalling one print depicting a bas relief of a bare-chested queen nursing a boy almost as tall as she.

Michael grinned at her. 'Do you mean you do not wish to be painted in profile with some strange symbol resting on top of your head?'

'I want to look regal and exotic.' She gazed at Jack, who had lapsed into silence again. 'What do you think, Jack? Am I to be in profile?'

'Not necessarily.' He seemed to be only half-listening.

Michael went on. 'At the Academy we practise designing classical architecture, but we are expected to create buildings suitable for modern use. Jack might use the same principles.'

'Meaning I do not have to be in profile?' Ariana arched a brow.

Jack finally smiled down at her. 'You do not. Cleopatra will be as exotic and regal as you desire.'

His smile made Ariana feel like warm honey inside. She was quite in danger of becoming completely besotted with him.

'Well, I am glad the Egyptian ladies wore their hair down,' Nancy remarked pragmatically. 'You have such lovely hair. It will make a very pretty display.'

Ariana smiled at her. 'Why, thank you, Miss Vernon. What a nice compliment.'

She liked Jack's sister, so fresh and young and full of hope, exactly like the portrait Jack painted of her. It was obvious to Ariana that Michael shared her opinion of Nancy and more.

Ariana turned back to Jack. 'Perhaps you might come with me to look through the theatre's costumes and props for something that will befit our Egyptian queen?'

'That is an excellent idea,' Michael agreed.

'What fun to rummage through theatrical costumes!' Nancy looked at her brother. 'You should do it.'

Jack's gaze touched Ariana again. 'If you wish it.'

Her heart fluttered.

They reached Adam Street, and Nancy pulled at Michael to hurry him on. 'Mama will wonder what has happened to us. It is almost time for dinner.'

Michael was evidently an invited dinner guest.

Nancy and Michael said their goodbyes and hurried off. She was alone with Jack.

'Will you walk me home?' Ariana asked.

'Of course,' he replied without hesitation.

It made her heart soar. 'I enjoyed myself today.'

He did not respond.

She jostled his arm. 'Here now, Jack. There is no harm in telling me you enjoyed yourself as well.'

He looked down at her and his mouth slowly widened into a smile. 'I did enjoy myself.'

She *was* besotted with him, she thought.

When they crossed Maiden Lane, it was all she could do to not dance for joy. What harm would there be if she opened her heart to Jack? She was not the green girl she'd been at nineteen.

When they arrived at her door, she grabbed his hand. 'Come in for a little while.'

He did not ponder long. 'For a little while.'

She opened the door, still holding his hand, giddy with excitement.

Betsy stepped into the hall, carrying folded laundry. 'Miss Blane, there is a gentleman to see you.'

'A gentleman?' She glanced at Jack, who already seemed to have retreated from her. 'Who is it?'

'Lord somebody.'

Her insides turned leaden.

'Tranville,' Jack said.

'I'm sure I don't know, sir,' the maid responded. 'I wasn't the one who let him in. He's been here over an hour, though.'

Ariana felt as if she'd plummeted down a well. 'Is he in the drawing room?'

'That he is,' the girl repeated and hurried up the stairs.

Jack moved toward the door. 'Good day, Miss Blane.'

She still had his hand. 'No, come upstairs with me, just for a little while.'

He glanced toward the closed drawing-room door. 'You have a guest.'

It felt as if a stone wall had suddenly been erected between them.

'He can wait,' she pleaded.

'He must not be reckoned with, Ariana.'

'I will send him away,' she insisted.

He shook his head.

It was no use. 'You will still come to look at the costumes tomorrow, will you not?'

He again glanced at the drawing room door.

'Oh, do not refuse, Jack. Please,' she whispered.

He put his hand on the front doorknob. 'Select any costume you desire and bring it to the studio.'

She covered his hand with her own. 'Please, Jack.'

He looked into her eyes. 'There is much at stake for both of us. You said so yourself. It is best this remain a business matter.'

She tossed her head. 'I can manage him.'

His expression hardened. 'Do not underestimate what that man can do.'

He turned the knob, her hand still touching his. She reluctantly released him as he opened the door.

'Come to the studio tomorrow afternoon whenever you choose.' He turned away and was gone.

Ariana closed the door, her throat tightening. She made a frustrated sound as she tore off her cloak and hat and pulled off her gloves, throwing them down on a nearby chair. She paced the hall for a few minutes, trying to calm herself enough to face Tranville.

Jack was mistaken about Lord Tranville. He was merely full of his own consequence and ruled by carnal desire rather than a rational assessment of his attraction to a woman less than half his age. She could manage such a man.

She squared her shoulders and entered the drawing room.

Tranville sat in a chair, his legs extended and his head bobbing against his chest.

She cleared her throat.

He uttered a loud snort, opened his eyes and sprang to his feet. 'Miss Blane!'

She remained just inside the doorway and spoke in her coolest voice. 'Lord Tranville.'

He took a step forwards. 'My dear, where have you been?'

She lifted an eyebrow, but did not answer him.

He halted. 'I was concerned something had happened to you.'

She gave a shake of her head. 'Why?'

'I stopped by Jack's studio, but there was no answer. Naturally I thought you had come home—' his tone was matter of fact '—so I decided to call upon you.'

'You stopped at the studio?' She was shocked. 'I asked you not to.'

'Oh, I had given you plenty of time. I actually thought I would see Jack.'

Her breathing accelerated. '*You* gave me plenty of time? I did not realise my time was yours to give.'

He answered with a laugh. 'You misunderstand me. I merely happened to be in the neighbourhood and I wanted to see what progress Jack had made.'

'Happened to be in the neighbourhood,' she repeated.

'Indeed.' It now seemed to be dawning on him that she was not pleased. 'So, where were you? Where did you go?'

Ariana walked to the window, pressing her lips together so she would not say something she would later regret.

'You expect me to account to you where I go, what I do?' Her voice rose to a higher pitch.

'Not at all.' his tone was almost cheerful. 'I just wanted to know.'

She swung around to stare at him. This man deserved the biggest dressing down she could deliver.

Her mother's voice—and Jack's—sounded in her head, warning her not to make an enemy of him.

Even so, she must make clear to him he had not purchased *her* along with the portrait. Gentlemen assumed actresses, singers and dancers were like trinkets in a shop, awaiting purchase. Ariana's mother had been a high-priced ornament, but as soon as some new glittering ornament had appeared, gentlemen cast her aside.

Ariana wanted none of that. She just wanted to act.

She turned to Tranville. 'Sir, do sit.'

He had not moved far from the chair in which he had been napping. He lowered himself on to it.

She chose a chair not too nearby. 'I am distressed.'

'Distressed?' He sat forwards in his chair, immediately solicitous.

She wished she could shrink back.

Instead she put on a patient smile. 'I perhaps misunderstood you.' It was always better to act as if the fault was on her part, not the gentleman's. 'I thought you said this portrait placed me under no obligation to you—'

He interrupted her. 'It does not, I assure you—'

She silenced him with a hand. 'And I thought you agreed not to come to the studio.'

He straightened. 'I agreed not to interrupt you at the studio while you were sitting for the portrait, which I assure you I had no intention of doing.'

She tilted her head as if pondering a question beyond her means of comprehension. 'And if I had been there when you knocked, would that not have been an interruption?'

He coloured, but she feared it was not in embarrassment, but in anger. 'But you were not there.'

She must tread carefully. 'The point is, sir, that I either misunderstood you or you are not a man of your word.' She made herself smile again. 'And I cannot believe you are not a man of your word.'

His eyes flashed. 'Of course I am a man of my word.'

She stood. 'Excellent!'

He rose as well.

'Then I may continue to sit for the portrait.' She smiled again. 'Without your assumption that you have purchased my attentions—'

His eyes bulged. 'Purchased your attentions!'

'—and I have your word you will not come looking for me at the studio and intrude on what I consider a most serious endeavour?' An endeavour she wished to make very private.

He had no recourse but to nod his head in agreement, although she could see he did not like it.

She took a few steps towards the door and then stepped aside.

He gaped at her as if not believing she expected him to leave. He did not march out as contritely as she had hoped.

Instead, he walked up to her, his eyes hard as flints. He took her hand and raised it to his lips, and spoke in a smooth voice. 'My dear, I have the highest, the deepest esteem for you. Anything I did, I did because of my regard for you, my desire to fulfil your every wish.'

He still did not believe she was serious.

She curtsied, gently pulling her hand away. 'I am complimented, sir, but I must speak very plainly. My affections are not secured by what favours a gentleman performs for me. I must refuse the portrait if you expect some compensation from me in return for it.'

This was a gamble. If he pulled out of the portrait, she would lose that valuable exposure for her acting career and Jack would lose his commission.

He looked affronted. She'd wounded his vanity, and men whose vanity was wounded were very prone to retaliation.

Placate him, she told herself. Don't lose Jack's commission.

She touched Tranville's arm. 'It is not you, sir. It is merely that I value myself too highly to sell my attentions to anyone. You know how the theatre is. How gentlemen are. In my opinion, it cheapens me to give my heart to the highest bidder.' She spoke honestly. 'I never accept a gift if an obligation is attached.'

His brow wrinkled as if he was pondering what, to him, must seem a mystifying statement. An actress not willing to sell herself to the highest bidder? Was this possible?

'You may still sit for the portrait—'

'Thank you, sir.' She smiled, genuinely grateful she had not lost her gamble. She extended her hand to him. 'I look forward to seeing you at the theatre.' Perhaps he would get the message that his visits to her residence were as unwelcome as his visits to the studio. 'And I shall be happy to share your conversation there.'

He clasped her fingers a bit too tightly. 'I will bid you good evening, then.'

'Good evening, sir.'

He bowed and walked out without another word.

Rid of him at last. She would have felt some joy if not for the fact that Tranville had already driven Jack away.

That evening Tranville walked up the narrow steps leading to Daphne Blane's dressing room, a room that Tranville thought ought to have been given to her daughter who had the lead female role.

He paused, inhaling a deep breath at the thought of Ariana. Such a beauty. Like a fresh, spring day. He felt young again just gazing upon her, and she fired his blood unlike any woman since he'd first set eyes on the youthful Mary Vernon.

It was indeed fortunate Mary was nearby. She had secured Jack's co-operation, but, more than that, she had indulged his needs. Otherwise he might have been forced to visit a brothel. Ariana's coquettish behaviour had him in a constant state of frustration. The girl drove him mad. He must have her, there was nothing else for it.

Daphne Blane was bound to have influence over her daughter. She was a woman who knew the value of a gentleman's attentions.

He reached her door and knocked.

A maid admitted him.

Daphne Blane lounged on a red brocade sofa, wrapped in a silk robe festooned with peacocks. 'Do sit, Tranville. I am delighted you have come to me.'

She leaned forwards a little and the top of her robe gaped open enough to reveal quite impressive *décolletage*. Her daughter resembled her in that regard, but with breasts young and firm…

'It is always a pleasure to see you, Daphne, my dear.' He took the wooden chair that was nearby, turned it around and straddled it so that he could lean his arms on the chair's back. 'I have come to you for assistance.'

She moved again, exposing a bit of bare ankle. 'My assistance?'

He nodded. 'With Ariana.'

'Ariana.' She leaned back and tightened her robe. 'What has Ariana done now?'

'She is acting as if she will spurn me.' His voice grew low.

She looked aside. 'Spurn you?'

He laughed. 'Values herself too highly, she says.'

Daphne frowned. 'Foolish girl.'

'Intervene with her.' He leaned forwards, but spoke as if ordering his soldiers.

She sighed and tapped a long fingernail on the wooden table next to her. 'The little fool. She is no better than she should be. She plays a game with you, sir.'

His brow wrinkled. 'I detest games.'

Her eyes flashed. 'Oh, I suspect she thinks she is being clever. I dare say she will come running if she feels you have lost interest.'

'I have not lost interest.' He pounded on the back of the chair. 'I am more determined than ever. Tell her I will purchase some jewellery for her, something made up from Rundle and Bridge. Tell me what sort of bauble will tempt her.'

She shook her head. 'You act too eager, sir.' Her eyes shifted in thought. 'You need to teach her a lesson. Stay away from her.'

He began to rise from his seat. 'That is out of the question. I've half a mind—' He broke off.

She seized his arm. 'I am telling you what will work with her. Make her jealous. Give jewellery to some other woman.' Her expression turned shrewd. 'Me, if you like. Let her think you are interested in me. She wants my roles in the plays; she will want you, as well.'

He pondered. The girl was ambitious. He could make things happen for her if she would allow it. He already had.

Daphne crossed her arms over her chest. 'She came to London to take my place on the stage. Without her here, I might have played Juliet. I might have had the role of Cleopatra.'

Daphne had fought hard with Mr Arnold for the role that went to her daughter.

He straightened in the chair and inclined his head to her. 'Help me and I will help you.'

She looked thoughtful.

He put on a pleasing face. 'I would be indebted to you. The next play is yours if you make my desires come true.' As long as her daughter did not want the role, that is.

She considered. 'I will help you, but you need to follow my advice. Let her think she has lost you.'

There was a knock on her door. 'Ten minutes, Miss Blane.'

He stood. 'We have a bargain, my dear. I will not stay for the performance tonight.'

She extended her hand to him. 'Excellent, sir. Have patience. All will come out right.'

He clasped her hand and brought it to his lips. 'Thank you, dear lady.' When he dropped her hands he hardened his voice. 'I am determined to have your daughter, but I will not be toyed with. She will find me a generous bene-factor, but a formidable enemy.'

Daphne returned a look equally as hard and deter-mined. 'I am also not without influence, my lord, if you trifle with me.'

He understood her. They were two of a kind, both used to having matters go their way.

Tranville bid her adieu and hurried down the stairs. Not

wishing to encounter Ariana, he slipped through the backstage, where people were running to and fro preparing for the curtain to rise. He refused to be publicly snubbed by the silly chit.

Let her think he was succumbing to her wishes by failing to show up for her performance. *Romeo and Juliet*'s run would be over soon. Then Ariana would begin preparing for the April opening of *Antony and Cleopatra*, and Jack would be finishing her portrait. When the portrait was completed and it became his gift to her, he would make his move.

Just to show her his kindness, he'd sweeten the deal with some diamonds or emeralds, diamonds to dazzle her and emeralds to match her eyes.

Tranville walked outside to where the carriages delivering the fashionable theatregoers were moving away. His frustration was so high it needed relieving. When his coach rounded the corner and stopped in front of him, Tranville called to the coachman, 'Adam Street.'

Chapter Eight

The next day Jack delivered Mr Slayton's portrait to the man's bank on Fleet Street. He walked back to save on the coach fare. As he turned onto Adam Street from the Strand, a hackney coach pulled up to his building's entrance.

Ariana emerged—alone—juggling two large band-boxes. She placed them on the pavement and handed some coins to the coachman. Jack watched her retrieve the boxes again and start for his door. He quickened his step.

Her face lit up when she saw him approach. 'Hello, Jack.' The cheerful tone of her greeting made it seem as if the last words they'd shared had not been strained. She lifted the boxes. 'I have raided the costume room.'

He took them from her. 'I see,' was all he could muster.

She followed him inside, unfastening her cloak and hanging it on the peg. As she took off her gloves and hat, she asked, 'Would you like to see the costumes?'

She seemed determined to pretend that nothing had happened between them. No attraction. No invitation to her room. No intrusion by Tranville.

'I would.' He could pretend as well. He carried the boxes to the *chaise-longue* before removing his own outerwear.

She opened one of the bandboxes. 'This one has the gowns.'

She pulled out three gowns and laid them out on the *chaise*. They were made of cloth so thin it floated until resting on the *chaise* in graceful folds. One gown was shimmery yellow silk. The other two were white muslin.

She pointed to the yellow one. 'I thought this looked almost like gold. Gold cloth would befit a queen like Cleopatra.' She rearranged the skirts of the other two. 'These could look like classical gowns, I thought.'

The one looked like no gown at all, but more like a chemise made of a light, sheer fabric that would cling to her body. If Cleopatra wore that gown with nothing underneath, the muslin would reveal the blush of her bare skin, the deep rose of her nipples. The tantalising idea took hold and the artist in him yearned for the challenge of painting such a transparency. The man in him had no business thinking such thoughts of her.

He turned to the other box to distract himself. 'What is in this one?'

She opened it and brought out a golden collar, long lengths of gold chain necklaces, two bejewelled crowns and an assortment of colourful shawls. The chains and crowns were cheaply gilded, the jewels mere glass.

'I thought this might have an Egyptian air to it.' She placed the collar over one of the white gowns, creating the sort of circular collar that adorned the clothing on the Egyptian prints. 'Or perhaps Cleopatra could wear a great deal of jewellery.' She draped the gold chain necklaces over the other muslin dress.

She seemed careful to confine her attention to the costumes, barely looking at him, acting in exactly the business-like manner he'd requested of her. It ought to have put him at ease.

It did not.

Had he gone with her to the Drury Lane Theatre and searched through trunks of costumes, he might have seen her eyes sparkling at each discovery. He might have witnessed her excitement at finding the gold collar. Perhaps she would have held up the jewelled crowns, letting their cut-glass gems glitter in whatever light the costume room possessed. They might have debated which gowns to select. They might have laughed together.

He had missed that chance.

She stood back and surveyed her arrangement of the gowns. 'What do you think?'

He hid his reaction. 'Any of them will do.'

She made a face. 'Any? I was hoping you would tell me which was best.' She touched the yellow cloth again. 'I confess, I could not decide.'

'I do not know.'

He knew. His choice was too scandalous to consider. Only one gown suited him, both the artist and the man. 'Would you be willing to try them on?'

Her determinedly impersonal attitude faltered a bit as she returned his gaze. 'Certainly.'

She gathered the gowns and he opened the door of his bedchamber for her.

As she walked into the room and placed the gowns on his bed, she looked over her shoulder. 'I fear I shall have to ask you to unlace me.'

Had she said the words with any hint of seduction, he would have refused, but she spoke as if he were her maid.

Jack found the hooks at the back of her dark blue carriage dress. As his fingers undid them he brushed the soft skin of her neck. She moved under his touch, like a cat being petted. When he untied her laces, her head lolled against her shoulder.

Desire shot through him at her reaction to his touch. It also brought a surge of pleasure he ought not to allow himself to feel.

As soon as he finished, she stepped away. 'Thank you, sir,' she said brightly. The moment passed.

He left the room and paced the length of the studio until she emerged wearing the yellow gown. 'I need your help again.' She presented her back to him.

He tied the laces, his fingers now trembling a bit.

She stepped back and twirled around in front of him. 'Well?' The yellow silk swirled around her, creating pretty patterns of light and dark.

He took in a deep breath. 'Try the collar and the jewellery.'

He brought over the full-length mirror he sometimes used when he needed to draw from a reflection. She tried on the collar first and then the jewellery and surveyed herself in the mirror with each.

They repeated this performance with the sheer muslin dress, which tantalised Jack more than he wished to admit, even though it was her shift and corset visible beneath it, not the pink skin he yearned to see, not the image lodged in his brain so vividly it aroused him.

Ariana remained carefully impersonal, enabling him to maintain control over himself.

The second muslin gown was little more than two gathered pieces of cloth joined at the shoulders and tied with a simple cord at the waist. As she walked in it, the muslin billowed like clouds around her legs.

'I love how this gown feels.' She danced in front of him, the fabric moving with her. 'It would be perfect onstage.'

She caught him watching her and stopped, the ghost of a smile on her face.

He glanced away. 'Try it with the collar.'

She picked up the collar and brought it to the mirror. 'I have an idea for this.' She pushed the neckline of the dress lower so that her shoulders were bare and fastened the collar over it. When done, she looked at herself in the mirror before lifting her gaze to his reflection behind her. She waited for his reaction.

He nodded. 'I like that.' It made a perfectly acceptable costume.

'I do as well.' She untied the cord around her waist and replaced it with the gold chain necklaces, looking up to see if he approved.

He nodded.

She smiled and reached up to take the pins out of her hair. Her auburn locks tumbled halfway down her back.

He drew in a breath.

She gathered her hair in her hands. 'I think I can roll it under so it looks more Egyptian.'

As she fussed with hairpins, the light caught in her curls, creating gold highlights that rivalled the gold of the collar and chains. Jack's fingers twitched, wishing to be buried in her curls.

'Leave it loose,' he murmured.

She looked at him through the mirror and he felt the passion flare between them.

He took another breath. 'It wants only a crown.'

He handed her the simplest crown, the one that came to a single point in the front. Three large red jewels decorated it, one at the peak and two lower, enhancing the triangular shape of the gold.

He placed the crown on her head and they both examined the result in the mirror. His hands came to rest on her bare shoulders and their gazes met through the reflection and held.

She whispered, 'Jack?'

The brief contact begged for more. The connection between them could not be denied, only resisted.

Reluctantly he removed his hands and took a step back. 'We have Cleopatra.'

Her expression flickered first with disappointment, then turned into a determined smile. 'I approve. What now?'

He closed his eyes, better able to deal with an image of Ariana on the canvas than the flesh-and-blood woman. He pictured her in white against white. White linen draping the *chaise*, white marble walls behind her and a window showing white buildings in the distance. Hieroglyphics lining the wall would provide some contrast, but the tones would be white, grey and black, except for Ariana, who would shine like the gold of her collar and crown.

'Pose on the *chaise*.' He pushed his writing table over. 'I want to sketch this idea.'

She climbed on the *chaise* and assumed the position he'd drawn before. He took a piece of charcoal and started to draw.

Several minutes passed before she spoke. 'Did Tranville call upon you today?

Tranville again. The mere mention of the man's name broke Jack's concentration. 'He did not.'

'Good.'

They fell silent again, and Jack wondered why she had asked. He did not request an explanation, however; he merely tried to concentrate on his sketch.

After a time she said, 'I told him not to interfere.'

He looked at her. 'Told him?' Tranville did not take well to being told anything.

She explained, 'I reminded him that I'd accepted this portrait with the understanding that it would place me under no obligation to him. I reminded him that my affections were not for sale.'

Jack glanced at her, not quite believing what she said.

She sobered. 'Not every actress wants the attention of gentlemen in the Green Room.'

He nodded, even though he doubted any actress could avoid such attention. 'What was Tranville's reaction?'

She shrugged and the collar slipped lower on her shoulder. 'What could he say? He had given his word to me. He merely needed convincing that I meant to hold him to it. I told him he must not interfere and I am delighted that he seems to have listened to me this time.'

His eyes narrowed. 'Ariana, he is not a man who gives up what he wants.'

She shrugged again. 'He is a man.'

'A ruthless man.'

She stared at him. 'How do you know that?' She held up a hand. 'Wait. I don't suppose you will tell me, will you? What connection you have with Tranville?'

He did not answer immediately. 'He is connected to my family.'

'A friend of your mother's, he told me.'

Jack frowned. 'He told you that? A friend?'

'Yes.'

'A friend is one way to put it,' he said tightly. 'Or at least he once was such. You may then comprehend his connection to me.'

She nodded, clearly understanding his meaning. 'But there is more, is there not?'

He went back to his drawing before speaking again. 'On the Peninsula, he was ruthless in his ambition, caring more for his own consequence than for the welfare of his men.'

'He was a soldier?' She sounded surprised.

'A brigadier-general. Before he inherited his title.'

'A general?' She laughed.

He was puzzled at what amused her.

Her eyes sparkled. 'Forgive me, but it seems a silly thing for a general to suddenly become such an enthusiastic patron of the arts.' She giggled. 'I suspect he is more interested in the actresses than in preserving the cultural significance of the theatre.'

He could not help but smile. Not at her accurate measure of Tranville's character, but at how lovely she looked when filled with mirth.

She gazed at him. 'That is nice.'

'What is nice?' He sobered again.

'You smiled.'

He returned to the sketch, selecting pastels to add colour to her skin and to the gold.

Ariana watched his face as he drew. His concentration on his work was as intense as it had been at Somerset House. This time it felt as if he'd retreated again to that place she could not reach, that place somehow connected to Tranville. It frustrated her and made her sad.

She had indeed become besotted with this moody artist who kept so much inside, yet showed so much in his art. She wanted to unlock the mystery of him and to be someone with whom he could share confidences and engage in little adventures, as their excursion to Somerset House had been.

'Jack, we should visit the Egyptian Hall. Have you been there?' The building on Piccadilly had a façade in the Egyptian style. It would be a treat to explore it with him.

He hesitated. 'I have not been there.'

'We should try to see it, do you not think so? To complete our research.'

He merely continued drawing, using his thumb to smear something on the paper.

She tried again. 'Perhaps your sister and her Michael would like to come with us.'

He stopped drawing, as if he were actually considering her request. 'My sister has few outings. She would enjoy it.'

She smiled. 'Then say yes.'

He paused and it took him a long time to meet her gaze. 'Yes.'

Her insides danced with happiness.

She smiled. 'That is splendid. Will you make the plan? My days are free and soon my nights, as well, when the play ends.'

'When will that be?' he asked.

Some of the ease they'd built together the previous day seemed to have returned. 'Three more performances, the last on Saturday night. Will you come to that performance? As my guest?'

'No.' His expression turned dark. 'Tranville will be there, no doubt.'

She had pushed for too much. It contented her that he agreed to visit the Egyptian Hall.

'Make the plans for our outing. I'm sure I will have nothing to conflict with it.' She would not allow anything to do so.

He put down his piece of chalk and stood back, looking from her to the drawing and back, his elbows akimbo.

Finally he said, 'Come and look.'

She slid off the *chaise* and walked over to stand beside him.

'Oh, my!' In his drawing, he'd transformed the room into an Egyptian palace, complete with an Egyptian view out of a window. She was in the foreground, full body lounging on the chaise. The only colour on the paper came from her skin and features and the gold adornments she wore. As a result, he'd shown her off in a remarkable manner. Still…

'It is but a quick sketch,' he said apologetically.

'It is good.' She gazed at it again, her brow creasing. 'For a sketch.'

He examined it again. 'Speak plain, Ariana.'

She stepped back and turned her head towards him. 'It has no emotion.'

He stared at it again. 'It is merely a sketch.'

'You will make it a marvellous painting, I am certain.' It only wanted the life he could bring to it.

She clasped his arm and squeezed and to her surprise he put his arm around her for a moment as they stood together.

His mantel clock chimed six.

She knew he would say it was time to leave.

'I have already begun to prepare the canvas,' he told her. 'It must dry, so there is no need to meet tomorrow.'

She was bitterly disappointed, not wanting to go a day without seeing him. She averted her head so he would not see.

'Unless,' he went on, 'Nancy wishes to see the Egyptian Hall tomorrow. It would be a good day to do that since we cannot work.'

She turned back to him, trying not to show how happy the idea made her. 'That would do very nicely, would it not?'

'If you are at liberty to wait, I will take a few minutes to go and see if the plan is agreeable to Nancy.'

'Shall I come with you?' She was perfectly willing to persuade Nancy, if necessary.

'No,' he said sharply. 'No,' he repeated in a softer voice. 'My mother—it is best I dash over there. I can arrange a hack for you while I am out.'

She nodded and wondered if Jack's mother knew of Tranville's interest in her. If so, his mother would certainly not want to encounter her. Ariana's mother resented every man who had left her and every woman who'd replaced her, especially if the woman was younger.

Ariana made herself smile. 'I will change back into my dress. Will you lace it again before you go?'

His eyes darkened. 'Of course.'

She hurried into his bedchamber and quickly took off the crown and the voluminous costume. She donned her carriage dress and returned to the studio. Jack stood at the window, his arms crossed over his chest.

'I need my lady's maid,' she joked, lifting her hair and presenting her back to him.

He made quick work of tying the laces and fastening the hooks.

As soon as he was done he walked over to take his top coat from its peg. 'I will return shortly.'

He seemed in a hurry.

She smiled. 'Take your time.'

After he left, she pinned up her hair and returned to tidy the bedchamber where she'd left the costumes in disarray. She picked up the bandboxes and carried them into the room. Smoothing out the fabric as best she could, she folded the gowns and placed them back in the bandbox. She repacked the crowns and the gold chains into the other. No need to return them to the theatre until her portrait was completed. After she closed up the boxes, she sat on the bed, fingering the coarse blanket that covered Jack when he slept.

An image of him, all tangled in the blanket, flew into her mind. How lovely it would be to lie next to him, to feel his warm skin all along the length of her, to fall asleep nestled in his arms. She'd always thought that one of the nicest parts of being with a man. If the man were not a scoundrel, that is.

She quickly stood. It would not do to dwell on such matters, especially because things between her and Jack seemed so fragile and tenuous. Best she simply be glad he was willing to make a visit to the Egyptian Hall with her.

She glanced around his room, which was sparse of furniture. The simple bed. A chest of drawers with a pitcher and bowl on it. The room seemed to double as a storeroom with a big trunk in one corner and several paintings leaning against the wall. She placed the bandboxes next to them and could not resist a peek.

All the paintings were of battle. Not the glory of victory like the painting he'd exhibited at the Royal Academy, but paintings of soldiers fighting. She turned them around and lined up three of them side by side.

They were not pretty. The men's faces were distorted with fear and violence and pain. They stabbed at each other with swords and bayonets. Blood flowed everywhere. But, in each painting, Jack had also included something that contrasted to the horror. One painting showed a beautiful church in the background. In another, green fields dotted with sheep. In a third, white stucco buildings on a pretty village street. The street was stained with rivulets of blood, but, even so, something of beauty remained.

She thought her heart would break for him. How awful war must have been.

She squatted so she could better examine the skill with which he'd created the images. He certainly depicted emotion in these paintings, complicated emotion. Such as including the face of a terror-stricken child in one of the village windows.

'What are you doing?' She looked up to see Jack in the doorway, a black expression on his face.

She'd not heard him return, but could not even think of answering his question, not in the presence of these wonderful works of art. 'These are marvellous, Jack. I am in awe of them. Why are they here against the wall? You should display them.'

He crossed his arms over his chest. 'I did not paint them to display them.' His voice was tight.

Why did this disturb him? 'Why did you paint them?' she asked almost in a whisper.

He glanced away from her before walking into the room and facing the paintings. 'It is difficult to explain.'

She did not waver. 'I am capable of comprehending difficult things.'

He reached for the frame of the painting with the church and turned it back against the wall. 'When I came back from war I could not rid myself of what I'd seen. So I painted it.'

'You painted how it felt.' She thought her heart would break for all he'd gone through. She gestured to a cluster of soldiers slashing at each other. 'I cannot see how you endured it.'

His voice dropped deeper. 'These do not show the half of it. I have sketches—' He waved a hand. 'Never mind the sketches.'

'I should like to see them,' she murmured.

He shook his head and turned to the doorway. 'We must go. The hackney coach is waiting outside.'

She followed him out to the studio. He held out her cloak for her and put it around her shoulders.

She fastened it, greatly desiring to dispel the grim mood she'd created by looking at his work. 'Did you find Nancy at home? Did she agree to the outing?'

He barely looked at her. 'She agreed and will ask Michael this evening if he can join us.'

She felt her spirits lift. She would not miss a day with Jack.

'We will meet you at your residence at eleven o'clock, if that is acceptable.'

She tied the ribbons of her hat under her chin. 'At my residence?'

He looked puzzled. 'Should we not?'

She did not know how to answer that. 'Your mother did not mind Nancy coming to a house where actors live?'

'I still do not comprehend.'

She thought it was self-evident. 'Actors and actresses are not respectable, you know.'

He laughed drily. 'Neither are we Vernons.'

He waited at the open door for her to walk through. She could see the hack waiting for her.

She brushed past him, but suddenly turned and looked up into his eyes. 'I do not wish our day together to end.'

His eyes darkened.

'Come with me, Jack,' she murmured, trying not to show how much she yearned for him to say yes. 'Spend the evening with me. Come to the theatre. Be my guest.'

He glanced towards his mother's door. 'I am not expected elsewhere.'

She smiled and touched his cheek. 'Then come with me.'

She watched the ultimate decision form on his face. 'Give me a moment to lock my door.'

Chapter Nine

Jack turned the key in the lock and returned to the street where Ariana waited. She smiled like a child giddy at receiving a much desired toy.

He doubted his company was worth celebrating, but he simply wanted to remain with her, to hold on to her company for as long as he could. That had been his motivation for the Egyptian Hall outing as well. He'd included Nancy as a chaperon. For him.

It occurred to him again that they had no chaperon in the studio, and that he had already engaged in the intimacy of undoing her laces. In the studio he had his work. His art was the chaperon.

Tranville had been at his mother's house again, his mother delighted at his company. It sickened Jack, but helped him make his decision to spend the evening with Ariana. If he remained with her, he would not be thinking of his mother.

Jack assisted Ariana inside the hack and climbed in next to her. 'I told the driver to take us to Henrietta Street.'

'Perfect.' She tucked her arm around his. 'We can eat dinner there and go to the theatre afterwards.'

Tranville had announced that he was not attending the theatre that night. Ariana and Jack would be free of the sight of him.

Jack was surprisingly comfortable sitting close to Ariana during the brief ride to Henrietta Street. After he paid the jarvey, Ariana took his arm again and they walked up to the door. In the evening light, her features were muted in grey, but every bit as lovely as in sunlight. What would it be like, he wondered, to paint her in all different kinds of light?

'I am so glad you came,' she said as they entered the house. 'Come up to my room. We can take off our coats there and be comfortable until dinner is served.'

She held his hand as they climbed the stairs and she pulled him into her room, closing the door behind her. She released him to remove her outer garments, tossing them on a nearby chair.

She turned to help him with his top coat. 'I will be your valet. It is only fair, since you were my maid.'

He was frozen in place, wanting only to gather her into his arms and tumble with her on that nearby bed. There could not be a riskier proposition than indulging in his attraction to her. Even if she had rejected Tranville, he had laid a claim upon her and would lash out if he knew she'd chosen Jack instead. Jack would welcome a battle with Tranville, but he was not willing to risk the man retaliating against Ariana or his mother.

Ariana seemed free of any such concern as she lay his top coat on the bed. She also placed his hat and gloves there. Clever girl. The bed would act as a clothes press at the moment, she'd silently informed him, not the place of his imagined pleasure.

There was a knock on the door and a male voice, 'Ariana! We're having refreshment in the drawing room. One of the girls was given a bottle of Madeira.'

'Marvellous!' She turned to Jack. 'Would you like some Madeira before dinner? The other roomers here are a friendly sort.'

Better to dampen his temptation with wine. 'I will do as you wish.'

She searched his face and he fancied she could see the battle raging inside him. 'I wish for many things, Jack.'

His brow wrinkled.

She smiled. 'Madeira, I think.'

Jack wanted her with every muscle and vein in his body, every aching of his soul, even though he knew, with Tranville's involvement, his desire could lead to nothing good. Still, she was fresh and vibrant and full of life, and Jack was so very sick of war and death.

He took in a breath and held it for a moment, before gesturing towards the door.

Arm in arm, they descended the stairs and entered the drawing room. The first person Jack saw was the actor who'd befriended him in the tavern and had taken him to watch *Romeo and Juliet*.

'Why, Jack!' The man came forwards, extending his hand. 'What the devil are you doing here?' He turned to the other man there, another actor who had joined them that night after the play. 'Look, Franklin, it is Jack.'

Their greetings were as friendly as if they'd been long-lost friends accustomed to addressing each other by given names. Jack was quickly introduced to two actresses in the room, Susan, who was about Ariana's age, and Eve, a bit older.

Ariana waved a hand, interrupting. 'Henry. Jack. How do you know each other?'

The man, whose name Jack had not learned until that moment, answered, 'Jack and I are drinking companions. Or at least we were the other night.' Henry turned to Jack.

'You, my dear fellow, did not tell us you were privy to Ariana's bedchamber—the first man invited in there, as a matter of fact. At least to my knowledge.'

He was the first?

Ariana broke in, 'Did Jack not tell you he is painting me? He is the portrait artist who is portraying me as Cleopatra.'

The actor clapped him on the shoulder. 'You sod. You did not say a word of it, not even when we were at the theatre.'

'You were at the theatre?' Ariana blinked.

Henry led him to a side table. 'Come on. I will pour you some of this fine Madeira.'

Both the Madeira and the conversation flowed freely until dinner was announced and they withdrew to the dining parlour. At the dining table more wine filled their glasses and the talk was all about the theatre—who'd won what role and how had they secured it.

Henry turned to Ariana. 'The thing I want to know is how you managed to convince Tranville to give you the part of Cleopatra without going to bed with him.'

Ariana fluttered her eyelashes at him. 'On my merits as an actress, perhaps?'

Henry laughed. 'Your mother cursed like a sailor when she discovered the part was not hers.'

Ariana glanced at Jack. 'My mother has a jealous streak.'

Henry rolled his eyes dramatically. 'You are not jesting. She is a fine actress, though, as fine as Sarah Siddons.' He poured Jack more wine. 'Tranville paid a pretty price to get Kean, too.' He winked at Jack. 'But in hiring a portrait artist, the fool hired his own rival.'

Ariana said, 'Tranville is a lecherous old man, as are most of the gentlemen who come to the Green Room.'

The other actresses loudly agreed with her.

Jack attempted to let the talk of Tranville flow past him and just enjoy the free-speaking of these theatre people, such a contrast to his own family where so much went unspoken.

'Tranville has wealth, though,' the older actress remarked in a wistful tone. 'He is a fish worth catching.'

Ariana nodded. 'More my mother's type, I would say.' She turned to Jack. 'Did you know he financed the play?'

It was not as easy for him to speak freely. He hesitated. 'To benefit the theatre he would say, but it was clear whose benefit concerned him most.'

A dark look came over her face. She waved her hand. 'At least I get my portrait painted.'

Quickly recovering her good spirits, she held her own while the others teased her about Tranville. The good spirits in the room were infectious, and Jack almost relaxed.

After dinner they walked as a troop to the theatre, their laughter condensing into little clouds in the cold air. Again Jack was admitted backstage. Ariana presented him to Mr Arnold, who seemed pleased that he was painting Ariana's portrait and made encouraging noises about using him again if the portrait improved ticket sales. Jack was also introduced to Mr Kean, even more deep in his cups than Jack himself.

Ariana left him to dress for her role, and Jack settled in a chair with a view of the stage. Henry produced a bottle of wine for him and a glass. He sipped the wine, trying to hold the backstage commotion and confusion in his memory for later sketching. Jack imagined drawing the scene in the style of a Rowlandson print, busy with activity, colourful people and great humour.

A beautiful woman dressed in costume approached him.

Daphne Blane.

'You are my daughter's portraitist, are you not?' She neglected the usual civilities of a greeting.

Jack rose. 'I am indeed. Jack Vernon at your service.' He bowed.

She extended her hand to him. 'Daphne Blane.'

'Your fame precedes you, Miss Blane. I knew you immediately.' He clasped her hand, which felt cold and stiff.

Her smile was equally as icy. She looked him up and down. 'Now I begin to understand.' She shook her head. 'Still, my daughter is a fool to choose you over...' She hesitated. 'Over other gentlemen.'

'I am merely the artist who is painting her portrait.'

Her brows rose at this falsehood. 'Well.' She eyed him again. 'You had best do a very splendid portrait.'

'I will try,' he responded. 'It is a great opportunity for me to paint your daughter.'

She tilted her chin in acknowledgement.

He shivered. What had it been like for Ariana to have such a mother?

Soon the play began. Although Jack was watching it for the third time, this was the first performance he felt free to merely enjoy. Ariana became Juliet, but retained some of herself as well. When she was not on stage or changing her costume, she stood with him in the wings, no longer Juliet, but simply Ariana. The other dinner companions kept him company, as well, passing along more titbits of gossip, which seemed to be their preferred conversation.

When the play ended, Henry suggested Jack and Ariana come to the tavern where he and Jack had first met.

Ariana shook her head. 'I cannot. Mr Arnold wants me

to greet some of the patrons in the Green Room.' She turned to Jack. 'Come with me. I will introduce you as my portrait artist.'

Jack finally gained entry to the Green Room, as the guest of the play's leading actress, no less. There had been no Tranville to bar the way. While there, he spoke with as many wealthy men who might be interested in future commissions as he could. Ariana had no shortage of covetous gentlemen wanting to speak to her. Not all of these men were reprobates like Tranville. How long before she would meet one worthy of her?

He shook his head to rid himself of such thoughts.

She rushed up to him. 'I've found a gentleman interested in a history painting.'

Jack was presented to a man about Tranville's age.

'You paint battles, eh? And portraits? I've half a mind to have you paint me in my old Horse Guards uniform.'

'My father was in the Horse Guards,' Jack said.

'Damn me, you don't say?' The man peered at him.

But Jack was distracted. He'd spied Tranville's son, Edwin, in the crowd.

The old rage rumbled inside him.

'Vernon is your name?' the man went on. 'There was a John Vernon in the Horse Guards in my day.'

Jack could barely attend to him. 'My father, sir.'

Finding someone who knew his father would ordinarily have pleased Jack a great deal, but the sight of Edwin, his face scarred now, brought back that night in Badajoz.

Edwin swayed with drink as he leered at a ballet dancer who walked past.

'You do not say.' The former compatriot of his father fell silent for a moment. 'Now I comprehend the connection,' he burst forth suddenly. 'Tranville is paying you to paint this actress, is that not so?'

Jack glanced back to the man. His response was terse. 'That is so.'

Edwin had sidled up to one of the actresses from Ariana's boarding house, Susan, the younger one.

Jack bowed to the former Horse Guard officer. 'I must beg your leave, sir.'

The man looked relieved. He clapped Jack on the arm in farewell.

Jack crossed the room to where Edwin toyed with a long ribbon on the sleeve of Susan's dress.

He rubbed the ribbon against his scar. 'Received this in the siege of Badajoz—' His eyes widened at Jack's approach.

Jack gave him no greeting. 'I would speak to you, Susan.'

She glanced towards Edwin and fluttered her lashes. 'In a moment.'

'Now,' Jack said.

Edwin seemed to recover some composure. 'Didn't expect to find you here, Jack. Hoped they'd sent you to the West Indies or some such place.'

A posting where soldiers died of fevers.

'Not your lucky day, then, is it?' Jack said through gritted teeth.

'Well, well, you've found me out, Jack. Not even m'father knows I'm in London yet. Was in Paris, y'know.' His words were slurred.

'Paris!' Susan's eyes brightened.

Jack turned to her. 'Come with me, Susan.'

She looked from one man to the other, but did not move.

Edwin favoured her with a white-toothed smile. 'The young lady and I were engaged in a very pleasant conversation. I am loath to have you interrupt me telling her all about Paris.'

An intoxicated Edwin was too dangerous to trust.

'I must interrupt.' He took Susan's arm.

'Now see here, Jack!' She tried to pull away.

At that moment Ariana appeared. 'What is this?' Her voice was tense, but cheerful.

Jack gave her an intent look. 'I need to speak to Susan. Now.'

Ariana smiled. 'Of course you do. I shall entertain this gentleman while you talk.'

Edwin tossed a wary glance at Jack, but he happily returned his gaze to Ariana. 'By all means.'

Jack's gut twisted at leaving Ariana with the likes of Edwin, but he knew Ariana would not leave with the man. Susan might.

She was not happy to be led away.

He took the young actress to a corner of the room. 'Stay away from that fellow, Susan. He is no one you would wish to know.'

She shrugged off his grasp. 'He's Tranville's son. He should have money.'

'He is not worth it. Believe me.'

She put her hands on her hips. 'Why should I believe you?'

Jack leaned down to her, his expression brooking no argument. 'Because I know him to be cruel to women.'

Her hands dropped to her side. 'How cruel?'

'Violent.' He could not say more. 'Trust me on this, Susan.'

She chewed on her lip as if calculating her decision. 'Introduce me to some other gentleman, Jack. Then I'll agree to leave that one alone.'

He introduced her to the former Horse Guards officer, who was equally as delighted to meet her.

Jack hurriedly manoeuvred through the crowd to return

to Ariana and whisk her away from Edwin. As he made his way, the rumble of voices around him started to turn into the roaring flames of buildings afire. One man's voice sounded like musket fire. A woman's laughter became a scream. He could not move.

Ariana came to him. 'What is it, Jack? You look unwell.'

The memories of Badajoz were about to engulf him again. 'I must leave.'

She took his arm. 'I will go with you.'

She led him to her dressing room where the maid helped her change into her own clothes again. From behind a screen, she asked him about Edwin. He could only repeat what he had told Susan. The sounds in his head did not abate.

Then they walked outside and headed towards her boarding house, but the noises in his head remained. It had rained and the streets glistened with moisture, making their footsteps echo in the still damp air. The sound reverberated in Jack's head, like ghosts shouting at him. His muscles were taut, ready for flight. Every shadow seemed like a marauding soldier. The air smelled of burning wood.

Ariana glanced behind them. 'Look, Jack, there's a fire!'

He spun around. The scent of smoke had been real. The fire was some distance away, perhaps at a warehouse on the river, but the orange glow was visible in the sky and the smell of smoke had drifted. A crash sounded nearby, a wagon overturning perhaps, spilling its contents.

Suddenly he was completely back in Badajoz.

With a cry he pulled her to the wall of a building, flattening her against its brick surface and shielding her with his body.

She gasped. 'Jack, what is it?'

He pressed against her, the sights and sounds of Badajoz so strong now he could do nothing but act as if they were real.

'Must hide.' His voice cracked.

'What is happening?'

He could not speak, could not explain.

She put her arms around him and held him. He clung to her tightly as Badajoz returned to him once more.

'You are safe,' she murmured. 'You are safe. No need to hide.'

It seemed an endless period of time that he was caught in the living nightmare. She held him until a semblance of reality returned.

He released her and pushed himself away. 'I must be mad.'

'Tell me what happened.' She looked alarmed.

He took off his hat and ran a trembling hand through his hair. 'I was back in Badajoz.'

She touched his arm. 'You had a vision?'

He shook his head. 'I suppose you could call it a vision. You know the paintings of war in my room? It was as if they'd come to life and I was in them.'

She came closer, threading her arm through his and holding him next to her. 'You are not there,' she said soothingly. 'You are in London with me.'

He started to walk—and to try not to run. 'It has happened before. I think I must be mad.'

She did not slow their stride. 'You were certainly frightened. I should think if I had seen war as depicted in your paintings, my memories might sometimes overtake me. It is over now, though.'

They reached a street to cross. He could not even say which street it was. The area looked strange to him, even though they must have walked the same route going to the theatre.

As they crossed, she said, 'We are almost at the house.'

With each step the sounds of Badajoz still rumbled. He thought if he could only make it to her door and say goodnight, he could quickly run to his studio and hope to reach it before the vision engulfed him again.

They reached her door and she pulled a key from her reticule, but she took his hand before opening the door. 'You are coming inside with me.'

'I should not.' The sounds roared louder.

She gripped his hand. 'Until you feel calm again. Just for a minute.'

'Ariana, I should not come in with you.'

'No one will blink an eye about it, believe me.' She opened the door and stepped inside, pulling him in with her.

He followed. The house looked strange, lit only by an oil lamp on a table in the hall. Flashes of the Frenchwoman's house in Badajoz intruded. Again he saw the broken furniture, the papers scattered everywhere, the haunted eyes of the woman's young son.

She led him above stairs to her room, turning a key in the lock after closing the door. 'See? We will be safe here.'

She removed her cloak and gloves and lit a taper from a coal glowing in the fireplace. She used it to light every candle in the room. He was grateful. The more light, the better he felt. She helped him off with his top coat, but this time did not put it or his hat and gloves on the bed but on the chair. That done, she went over to a cabinet in the corner.

She took out a bottle of brandy and two glasses. 'Sometimes I need this to calm down after a performance so I can sleep.'

She poured for him, not giving him a chance to refuse.

With her drink in hand and the bottle in the other she

kicked off her shoes and climbed on the bed, sitting cross-legged. She patted the space next to her. 'Sit with me.'

He removed his shoes and joined her, taking a long sip of the warming brandy.

'Will you tell me of Badajoz?' she asked.

He shook his head, unable to even utter words of refusal.

She did not press him, but merely refilled his glass when he emptied it. The brandy slowly calmed him and he was able to breathe normally again. His heart no longer pounded like the regiment's drums.

'Cannot speak of it,' he mumbled, suddenly exhausted. 'And there are drawings I cannot show. But really I ought to bid you goodnight.'

'In a little while,' she murmured. 'You should rest first. Let us take off your coat and waistcoat so you can lie down for a minute.'

He allowed her to remove his garments and loosened his neckcloth.

'You might as well take off your trousers, too,' she said, unbuttoning them as he lay against the pillows.

The brandy and exhaustion were fogging his mind. He ought not to allow her to remove his trousers. 'I should return to the studio.'

'After a brief rest,' she cajoled. 'I will wake you in ten minutes.'

'Ten minutes.' The bed felt very warm and comfortable. Perhaps it would do no harm to rest for ten minutes.

Ariana smoothed his hair and stared down at his handsome face. As she had anticipated, it had only taken him a minute to fall as soundly asleep as a child.

The vision, or whatever it had been that seized him, had frightened her. He acted as if he'd been in another time and place, as if he saw and heard things she could not. She knew very little about madness, but could not believe him insane. She preferred to think that the fire had triggered a very realistic memory.

Badajoz. She tried to recall what she knew about it. The battle had occurred about three years ago, shortly after she'd left the school to join the theatre company. All she'd been thinking of in those days had been performing on stage. Still, she knew many soldiers had died at Badajoz. Was that the place where the English soldiers rioted and looted the town? She could not remember.

She drew her finger across Jack's forehead and thought of Jack's paintings leaning against his bedroom wall. If the real horror of war was worse than that, she could not imagine what he must have endured. To think she had been consumed by the frivolity of the theatre at the same time he had been living in a nightmare he could not shake even now.

She was pleased he slept peacefully.

She slipped out of her room and hurried up another flight of stairs to the maid's room, waking the poor girl to help her untie her laces and corset.

'Thank you, Betsy,' she whispered to the girl.

Betsy had already lain back down to sleep.

Ariana hurried back to her room, opening the door carefully. Jack's eyes were still closed and his breathing even. She pulled off her dress and slid out of her corset. Sitting at her dressing table, she took the pins from her hair, brushing it smooth before putting it in a plait. Not bothering to change into her nightdress, she put two more coals on the fire, blew out the candles, and climbed into bed next to him clad only in her shift.

She adored being close to him. He rolled over to face her, and she could just make out his features in the dim light that came from the fireplace. Her eyes grew heavy, but she did not wish to sleep. She wanted simply to gaze at him, so peaceful now when a short time ago he had been terror-stricken.

From her first glimpse of him she had suspected he was a complicated man. Tonight she'd seen him in complete control of his emotions one minute, then totally at their mercy at another, lost in a vision that terrified him.

Her last thought as she drifted off to sleep was that she was becoming very attached to this soldier artist of hers.

Ariana woke to a cry.

'Release her!' Jack thrashed in the bed as if he was fighting someone. 'Stop!'

She sat up and reached for him, but he flung his arm so hard he knocked her back down.

Heart pounding in fear that he might end up hurting one of them, she grabbed his arm and held on as he fought her. 'Jack. Wake up. You are dreaming.' Her shift rode up to her waist and her hair came loose of its plait.

'Fire! The building is on fire.'

He'd alarm the house. She managed to climb on top of him, even though she knew her strength was no match for his. She covered his mouth with her hand. 'There's no fire. Wake up.'

He sat up and seized her upper arms.

'Wake up!' She was on her knees, straddling his legs, but there was little she could do when he held her in such a tight grip.

His eyes flew open, wild and confused and terrifying.

'It was a dream, Jack.' She tried to make him see her. 'A dream.'

He blinked and finally focused. 'Ariana?' He suddenly embraced her tightly against his chest.

She stroked his neck. 'Shh. It's over. It was only a dream.' She also needed calming.

'Ariana.' He buried his fingers in her hair and brought his lips to hers.

His kiss was one of desperation, as if she were his very last tether on sanity. She opened her mouth and he deepened the kiss, his tongue thrusting hungrily against hers.

Her one brief affair could not compare to this. Desire swept through her and she kissed him back, tugging her shift up until they broke apart and she pulled it over her head. He removed his shirt and with a swift motion, she was suddenly beneath him. He moved his hands over her, kneading her breasts, rubbing her nipples until she thought she would cry out at the exquisite torture. He slid his hand between her legs, stroking her until she writhed beneath him, slick and ready. She pressed her fingers into his skin, soundlessly begging him to fulfil her need.

He obliged her, thrusting inside her so strongly she gasped, not in pain but in a thrill unlike anything she'd ever anticipated.

She lifted her hips to him, meeting each thrust, the sound of their breathing filling her ears. The attraction that had first drawn them together and the desire that continued to flare exploded between them.

She'd known he possessed this passion, but she'd not known he could unleash the same passion from within her. Their coupling was wild, frenzied, urgent. A part of her understood his lovemaking came from whatever dark place he'd been in his dream, but, if he needed comfort for it, she wanted to comfort him.

They moved as if created for each other, faster, hotter, harder, together.

She needed the end to come, but she wanted this to last

for ever. Just when she thought she could stand no more, her release came and, as attuned as they were, his came at the same moment. She wanted to cry aloud for the joy of it.

He stifled her cry, kissing her in that moment of satiation, that moment they were made one in pleasure.

Collapsing beside her, he lay very still. She nestled against him, pressing her lips to his body, entwining her legs with his.

He put an arm around her, holding her close. 'I should not have done that,' he said, his voice low and rough.

She moved her lips against him. 'Do not say that. I know you liked it as much as I did.'

He lifted her face to his and gave her a long kiss. 'I liked it very much.'

She laughed and slid on top of him. 'It was marvellous!'

He rubbed his hands along the bare skin of her back. 'We should not become lovers, Ariana.'

She put her lips on his forehead, his nose, his chin. 'Why not? Why deprive ourselves of enjoying this while we can? Besides—' she felt his arousal grow again '—it is too late.'

He groaned in reply, and joined with her once again.

Chapter Ten

Jack woke to a chilled room and Ariana's warm naked body next to his. He gazed at her face, so beautiful he wondered if he could ever capture such loveliness in her portrait.

He ought not to be lying next to her, even though this was where he most wanted to be. Waking from that dream, he'd needed her. All resolve to resist her had vanished.

He glanced towards the window. The dim light of dawn peeked through the curtains. He'd spent the whole night with her.

Very slowly he eased himself up. She mumbled something and he froze. She rolled over and he waited until he heard her soft, regular breathing. Carefully he climbed out of the bed. The bare wood floor was even colder beneath his feet than the room itself. He untangled the bed covers and placed them over her, then walked to the fireplace to put more coal on the dying embers. At least she would wake to a warm room.

Jack discovered his clothing neatly folded on a chair, everything but his shirt, which he found beneath her shift on the floor. He dressed as quickly and as quietly as he could, watching her the whole time. Holding his shoes in his hand, he walked towards the door in his stockinged feet.

The bed covers rustled.

'You are leaving?' she murmured, her voice raspy with sleep.

He turned back. 'I tried not to wake you.'

She sat up in bed, her hair a jumble of curls. 'Why must you leave? You are not painting today, and we are not going to the Egyptian Hall until later.'

He glanced at the door. 'The house is still quiet. I will not be seen.'

She grimaced. 'No one here will mind that you stayed the night with me.'

It was not what they thought of him spending the night that concerned him. 'Your friends here all speak so freely. It is one thing for them to talk of me as your guest for dinner, but quite another if it is mentioned that I spent the night. It is best if no one knows.'

She stared at him. 'You are worried that Tranville will hear of it?'

He nodded. 'That is precisely it.' He stepped to the side of the bed and brushed the hair from her face. 'I will see you later when Nancy and I come to collect you.'

She clasped his hand and brought it to her lips. 'Until then, Jack.'

It was all he could do not to taste those lips again, to throw off his clothing and return to the delights of her bed, the delights that banished his demons, at least for that space of time. Jack cared nothing if Tranville became enraged with him, but his choices could hurt people he cared about. His mother. Ariana.

For them Jack must take care with Tranville. He must confine his contact with Ariana to the studio. They must go on as merely artist and subject.

With that resolve, Jack left the bedchamber and walked quietly down the stairs, hearing and seeing no one. Once outside he put on his shoes and started for Adam Street. The city was coming to life with carriages and wagons and workers hurrying on their way. Street vendors carted their wares, crying, 'Fresh pies,' or, 'Dutch biscuits,' when he came close enough to hear.

Jack purchased a spicy gingerbread biscuit, wrapping it in his handkerchief and putting it in his coat pocket to eat with his morning tea. It would save him the trouble of breakfasting at his mother's table and the risk of finding Tranville there again.

The brisk morning air felt good in his lungs, and his ears were free of the whisperings of Badajoz. He could almost feel happy.

When he crossed the Strand to Adam Street, however, Jack's growing good mood fled. Tranville emerged from his mother's door and turned in his direction.

Tranville strode up to him. 'Up early, are you, Jack?'

'As are you, Tranville.' He tried to keep his voice even.

Tranville made the pretence of a smile. 'Your mother's household are all still abed.'

Jack ground his teeth.

Tranville laughed softly, aware, no doubt, that he'd annoyed Jack. He suddenly stepped back, eying Jack as if seeing him for the first time. 'You look as if you slept in your clothes. Where have you been?'

Jack met Tranville's eye. 'If I have slept in my clothes, sir, you may be certain I am too much of a gentleman to discuss it.'

Tranville laughed out loud. 'Been with a woman, eh?'

Jack did not answer.

Tranville glared at him. 'I hope this woman of yours is not keeping you from working on the portrait. I want to see what progress you have made.'

'There is nothing to see.' Jack glared back.

'What?' Tranville's brows rose. 'You've done nothing? Time is of the essence, you know. It is almost March and the play will run in April.'

'I am aware of the timing,' Jack replied stiffly.

Tranville jabbed the air with his finger. 'Well, do not dally. I wish to know the instant it is finished. The instant I may see the final product. And it had better be soon.'

Jack nodded brusquely. 'You will be so informed. Prepare to bring the balance of my fee at that time.'

'Do what I want when I want it and you will be paid.' Tranville started to walk away, but turned back. 'In fact, I want you to make two portraits. One is my gift to Miss Blane; the other will be mine.'

Jack disliked the idea of Tranville owning even an image of Ariana. He shot back, 'The fee is double, then.' Tranville would be a fool to accept such terms.

'Double?' Tranville huffed. 'It will not take you double the time, I dare say.'

He inclined his head in disdain. 'It will delay me from accepting other commissions. Take it or leave it.'

Tranville's eyes had narrowed menacingly.

Jack added, 'I expect half the sum by tomorrow, or I will have to accept another commission.' A commission he did not have, but Tranville could not know that.

Tranville frowned, but finally waved his hand as if swatting at a fly. 'What is money to me? I'll pay your trifling amount.'

He was a fool, Jack thought.

Tranville waved his hand again. 'I have no more time to waste with you.' He hurried off.

Jack watched him turn the corner on to the Strand.

'Go to the devil,' he muttered before proceeding to the studio.

* * *

That afternoon, Ariana checked the window again to see if Jack and his sister had arrived yet. This time she was in luck. She saw them walking up to the door.

She ran into the hallway outside her room and called to the maid, 'Betsy, my guests are coming. Tell them I will be one minute. They can wait in the hall.'

'Yes, miss,' Betsy replied from below.

Ariana hurried back into her room and put on her new deep green sarcenet pelisse that had just come from the mantua maker. A matching green hat and buff gloves completed her costume. She took a quick glance in the mirror, hoping Jack would think she looked well in it.

She returned to the top of the stairs, seeing only Jack gazing up at her. Her senses flared with the memory of his arms stroking her, his body engulfing her. By the time she reached the bottom step, she saw that his sister stood next to him.

'I am all ready.' She smiled at Nancy. 'It is a pleasure to see you again, Miss Vernon.'

Nancy curtsied. 'For me as well.'

Ariana smiled at her. 'Your Michael is not with you?'

'He had to attend his classes.'

'What a pity.' Ariana had wanted Michael and Nancy to have their outing together as well.

She turned to Jack. 'Mr Vernon, thank you for suggesting this outing.'

Nancy looked confused. 'Jack told me it was your idea.'

Ariana grinned impishly at Nancy. 'It was.'

Jack opened the door for them and they stepped outside on to the pavement. 'If you do not mind walking, I suspect it is no more than a mile to Piccadilly.'

'Walking will do,' Nancy replied.

Jack turned to Ariana. 'Miss Blane?'

She took his arm. 'Walking it is.'

Nancy seemed more subdued than she had on their first meeting, but Ariana supposed it was because Michael was not with her. Ariana envied the girl her young love. There was much to be said for being courted by a respectable young man and looking forward to a conventional, predictable life.

She, however, had chosen otherwise and must be content with what her life provided her. The excitement of performing. The freedom to do as she wished. No one expected an actress to be chaste. She could choose to share her bed with Jack, if she so desired. She did, most ardently, desire to share her bed with him again.

Nancy became more cheerful when the Egyptian Hall came into view. 'It looks like the prints we saw of the buildings in Egypt.'

The building's façade was intended to resemble the entrance of an Egyptian temple, its three storeys were made to look as if they were one. Two huge statues of Isis and Osiris stood high above the entrance, which was flanked by two columns as tall as the ground floor. Egyptian symbols, appearing as if carved in stone, embellished the window frames.

'It looks grand,' admitted Jack.

He paid their admission and they entered the building, soon walking into a huge musty room with a display of large wild animals in the centre, birds and smaller mammals in cases lining the walls.

Ariana gazed around in disgust. 'They are all dead.'

These creatures, once running, flying, chasing prey, had been stuffed so that people could gaze upon them. She glanced at Jack, who returned an understanding look that made Ariana flush with pleasure.

'Oh, my!' Nancy immediately hurried over to the elephant. She had to hold on to her hat to look up at it. 'I never imagined elephants to be so huge.' She walked around the centre exhibit, gasping at the hippopotamus and the polar bear and the zebra.

Ariana was left standing alone with Jack.

She put her arm through his. 'She seems in better spirits.'

'Better spirits?' He looked surprised.

She tilted her head. 'You and your sister are very quiet today.'

He put his hand over hers. 'There is much I cannot say in front of Nancy.'

She grew warm at his touch. 'I am very much in sympathy with that statement. What is troubling Nancy, though?'

He glanced over at her. 'I do not know.'

She whispered, 'If I can contrive it, I shall try to find out.'

He slid a look towards a wall covered with dead birds. 'I will leave you to it, then, and will become fascinated by these colourful fowl.'

She resisted a strong urge to kiss him. Their gazes caught and she saw a mirror image of her yearning. The desire between them flared with such heat, it was a surprise the dead birds did not burst into flames.

'I had best examine these birds,' he murmured.

She took a breath. 'Yes. I shall keep your sister company.'

She joined Nancy, whose initial enthusiasm for the big animals seemed to have flagged. The girl was staring blankly at the zebra.

'It certainly looks like a horse, does it not?' Ariana said.

Nancy blinked and darted a glance to her. 'Yes. Yes, it does.'

'You seem unhappy today, Miss Vernon,' she began. 'What is amiss?'

Nancy sighed. 'Nothing, really.'

Ariana made Nancy look at her. 'I am not convinced.'

Nancy gazed down at the polar bear. 'Oh, it is just that Lord Tranville keeps talking of finding me a husband.'

Tranville again.

'Does he?' Ariana said in a harsh tone.

They wandered over to look at display cases of dead reptiles.

'I suppose he thinks he is helping,' Nancy went on. 'But I do not think I want to be married yet.'

'Have you explained to Tranville about your Michael?'

Nancy blushed. 'You keep calling him *my* Michael, but we are mere friends.' She sighed. 'Besides, he has a year of studies to finish and then he must work for someone. And—and he may not want me.'

'Not want you?' It was clear to Ariana that Michael was besotted with her.

'Because of my family, you know.'

Ariana did not understand at first, but it dawned on her that outside the theatre world, liaisons with gentlemen made a respectable woman a social outcast. For Tranville, of course, it merely increased his cachet.

Two young men in dandified clothing began casting them impertinent looks, appearing as if they had just about worked up the courage to approach.

Ariana tilted her head in their direction as a warning to Nancy, but the young woman seemed oblivious that she had attracted such attention. 'We had better join your brother,' Ariana told her.

Jack smiled as they walked over to him. Together they left that room in search of one with Egyptian artifacts.

Jack had a chance to ask, 'Did Nancy say what is troubling her?'

'Apparently Lord Tranville is still talking of finding someone to marry her,' Ariana whispered.

'That damned man,' Jack uttered through clenched teeth.

They found a room displaying South Seas curiosities, including preserved insects and reptiles, as well as more dead birds. Ariana was eager to move on to another display, but Jack seemed intent on minutely examining every shell and piece of coral in the room.

'Let us go on,' she whispered to Nancy, taking her arm. She called back to Jack. 'We will be in the next room.'

This housed the American exhibit dominated by a large statue of a red-skinned Indian dressed for battle. Two gentlemen stood examining it. Ariana saw immediately that one of them was Edwin Tranville; the other was an older man who was on the theatre's national culture committee with Lord Tranville. She glanced at Nancy, who frowned and turned back towards the door, but not before the older gentleman, Lord Ullman, saw them.

He waved his hand and approached. 'Miss Blane!'

Lord Ullman was an average-sized man in his forties with thin hair and a thick waistline.

'Miss Blane, how good to see you.' When he glanced at Nancy his eyes grew large. 'May I be presented to your enchanting friend?' He sounded as if he'd forgotten how to speak.

Ariana pursed her lips. Lord Ullman probably assumed Nancy was also an actress, a ripe fruit ready for his picking. She darted a glance at Edwin, who was looking at them but did not approach. One was a nuisance, but the other could be trouble. Jack certainly would not want his sister near Edwin.

She made the introduction Ullman requested, speaking

quickly. 'Miss Vernon, this is Lord Ullman, who is known to me from the theatre.'

'Charmed, my dear.' Lord Ullman bowed.

Nancy made a polite curtsy.

Ariana turned to Lord Ullman. 'Nancy is not with the theatre, sir. She accompanies her brother, who is the artist painting my portrait. He is in the next room.' She was confident Ullman would lose interest once he knew Nancy was not one of the trinkets on sale. 'I requested that Mr Vernon bring me here to view the Egyptian artifacts. I want to be certain my portrait as Cleopatra has authenticity.'

Lord Ullman continued to gaze at Nancy. 'I see.'

Ariana added, 'We were about to leave.'

Ullman did not heed her. 'Do you assist your brother, Miss Vernon?'

Nancy's forehead creased in confusion and she darted a wary look toward Edwin. 'When he asks me.' She stepped back towards the door.

Ullman smiled at her. 'I am delighted you assist him today. It is my good fortune to meet you.'

Nancy was saved from responding to this unwelcome flattery by Edwin.

He'd sauntered up to them, giving Nancy an unfriendly glance. 'I seem to be knocking into Vernons everywhere I turn.'

'I am equally as pleased to see you,' Nancy retorted sharply.

Lord Ullman scowled at Edwin. 'Dashed unfriendly of you, young man. I will not have it.'

Ariana curtsied. 'We must leave. Good day to you both.'

She and Nancy hurried to find Jack.

Nancy ran up to him and pulled at his sleeve. 'Jack! Edwin is here, of all people.' She turned towards Ariana.

'He is Tranville's son and we've known him since child-hood. He was a hateful boy, always harassing me and picking fights with Jack. He looks terrible with that scar.'

Jack looked out into the hall and saw Edwin in the doorway of the next room. The two men glared at each other.

Jack turned back to Nancy. 'Stay clear of him.'

'You do not need to warn me about Edwin.' Nancy pulled on her brother again. 'I do not want to be here, if he is here. Can we leave now?'

Jack looked to Ariana.

'We have seen enough for me,' she said, although they had not spied even one Egyptian artifact.

They made their way through the building and out of the grand doorway back on to Piccadilly.

'I dislike it that Edwin has seen us together twice now,' Jack whispered to Ariana as they stepped away from the building.

Ariana tried to give him a reassuring look. 'I explained we were doing research for the portrait. I doubt it could be credited as anything more.' Her curiosity burned to know the origins of such extreme reactions to Edwin Tranville. Would Jack ever tell her? she wondered.

'I am just glad to be away from him.' Nancy glanced around at the shops that lined the street. 'Jack, may I visit the perfumer for a moment?' The shop was right there.

Jack checked back at the door of the Egyptian Hall as if to see if Edwin followed them. 'I'll stop in Mr Hewlett's, then.' He pointed to a shop with a sign saying Thomas Hewlett Oil and Colourman. 'And meet you in front of the perfumer's shop.'

Ariana accompanied Nancy into the perfumery, although her mind was not on scent, but on Jack. She cared about him, cared that he was disturbed by Edwin, cared about what happened to him in the past as well as the present. She was surprised at the depth of emotion he aroused in her. She'd not expected to feel so strongly about a man again.

Until she met Jack.

'I should like to buy a throwaway for Mama,' Nancy told her as they walked to the counter.

A throwaway was a small vial of perfume, sold in a small amount so the purchaser could sample many different mixtures of scent. Nancy approached the shop keeper and began discussing fragrances. She pointed to the pretty gilded and enamelled glass bottles that would hold the scent.

Ariana wandered back to the shop's window and gazed out into the street as Nancy's discussion went on and on. After a time, she saw Jack come from the colourman's shop. 'I will wait with your brother right outside,' she told Nancy.

Nancy nodded and lifted one of the slender bottles up to examine it more closely.

'She will be a few minutes,' Ariana explained as she walked out of the shop and Jack approached her. He still looked disturbed.

'I wish Edwin Tranville did not distress you so, Jack.'

He took her hand in his for just a brief moment. 'Forgive me. I am not good company.'

'Being with you,' she murmured, 'is enjoyment enough.' She checked to see if Nancy was still occupied with the clerk. 'I wish you would come to my room tonight, Jack.'

The lines at the corners of his eyes deepened. 'It would not be wise.'

'I do not care who discovers us,' she said valiantly.

His expression was serious. 'We must not be seen together. Tranville can make a great deal of trouble for you. We should not meet, except at the studio.' He blew out a breath. 'Come to the studio in the morning tomorrow. We can work all day.'

She nodded. He spoke of work, but she longed to repeat the pleasures of the previous night. She pointed to the package in his hand, wrapped with brown paper and tied with string. 'What did you purchase?'

'Some brushes and colours that I needed.' He gave a half-smile. 'A great deal of Cremora white.'

For her portrait.

She smiled back at him and gazed into his eyes. It was as if a spark flared between them, a shared passion that would take little to ignite.

Nancy came out of the perfumery carrying her purchase, even more carefully wrapped than Jack's. 'I chose a lovely blend of rose, violet and jasmine.'

'It makes me yearn for spring.' Ariana smiled.

Nancy looked at Jack. 'I hope Mama will like it.'

Jack put his arm around her. 'Of course she will like it.'

They walked back to Henrietta Street. The day had not at all turned out as Ariana had hoped, and she had the rest of the afternoon, the evening and the night to endure before she would see Jack again.

That night, after what seemed an interminable performance of *Romeo and Juliet*, Ariana did her duty in the Green Room. Tranville was there, deep in conversation with Lord Ullman, his expression quite serious. She chewed on her lip and hoped Ullman had not mentioned she'd been with Jack.

To her relief Lord Tranville did not approach her, although his eyes followed her like a cat watching its prey. She shivered and turned away.

Unfortunately, as she turned, Edwin Tranville, glass in hand, stood directly in her path.

She tried to walk past him, but he stepped in her way and smirked. 'I wonder what my father would think if he knew you were out with the Vernons.'

She lifted her chin. 'I cannot fathom why he would care.'

Edwin took a gulp of his drink. 'Ullman told me all about it. My father, pathetic old man that he is, pursues you. Is that not right?'

She sniffed. 'If you are not in your father's confidence, you can hardly expect to be in mine.'

'*Touché*, my dear.' He laughed and drained the contents of his glass. 'But before you brush me off, let me tell you something about Jack. He may fancy himself above his betters, but his mother is nothing but a common whore.'

She almost slapped him, offended to the core on Jack's mother's behalf. But she would leave Jack out of it.

Ariana leaned conspiratorially towards Edwin. 'Someone called my mother that once,' she whispered. 'Her lover shot him.'

Edwin shrank back.

'Be careful with your words, Mr Tranville. You might find yourself challenged to pistols at dawn.' She strode away and joined a group that included Mr Arnold.

As she glanced back, Edwin made his way to where his father and Ullman continued to converse. His complexion remained deathly white.

Chapter Eleven

Jack rose early the next day, so early he begged breakfast from his mother's cook in her kitchen, discovering from her chatter that Tranville had not shared his mother's bed the previous night. Not knowing if that boded well or ill, he returned to his studio to prepare another canvas while waiting for Ariana.

Dressed only in a paint-stained shirt and trousers, Jack undertook the physical work of constructing the frame and stretching the linen. It was a good distraction from the anticipation of seeing her again. Their time together at the Egyptian Hall had been ruined by Edwin's presence, but today, with any luck at all, there would be no Tranvilles to spoil the work.

Because it must be work, not pleasure, that they indulge in today, although the memory of making love to her still fired his blood. He knew he wanted nothing more than to take her in his arms once again and carry her to his bed, to the devil with his painting.

He laughed out loud.

Whom was he attempting to fool? Painting her excited him almost as much as tumbling into bed with her. He wanted the painting to be everything she wished. He wanted the image he created of her to last for ever, her beauty, her essence, preserved for all time

When Jack finished stretching the canvas, he placed it on his easel and walked into his galley to prepare his paints. He needed to mix up a great deal of lead white to use in preparing the canvas. The more expensive Cremora he would save for the painting itself. On a stone slab, he mixed the pigment powder with linseed oil, adding a few drops of turpentine until achieving the exact consistency he desired. With his palette knife, he scooped up most of the mixture and tied it into a small bladder which he'd prick with a tack to extract small amounts of pigment at a time. The rest of the white he scraped on to his wooden palette.

Returning to the easel, he chose a wide brush and began to cover the linen canvas with thin, even layers of white. When the canvas was totally dry it would be ready.

Some artists now purchased canvases already prepared, but Jack liked the methodical nature of this task, engaging enough of his mind to empty it of other thoughts, but lulling in its simplicity.

It also saved him money.

By the time he'd finished and cleaned up the studio, the streets outside were noisy with activity. He could almost feel Ariana near.

He arranged the *chaise-longue* to make the best use of the light and exchanged the canvas he'd just prepared for the one that was dry and ready.

When he glanced out of the window, he was not surprised to see her on the pavement, looking up at him. Before she even knocked he opened the door to her.

'Jack!' she cried, her face aglow with pleasure.

As soon as he closed the door behind her, she rushed

into his arms, raising her face for the kiss he now knew he'd been awaiting since dawn. She kissed him eagerly, laughing beneath his lips, pulling off her gloves and her hat as she did so. Hairpins rained down as her thick hair fell loose. He unfastened the hook of her cloak and it slipped off her shoulders to the floor. Her hands were quickly beneath his shirt, raking the muscles of his back and heating him with urgent desire.

His need for her was intense, not only for physical release but to be joined with her, to feel connected to her, as if they were one.

She pulled off his shirt and placed her moist mouth on his chest. He raised her skirt and pressed her against his aching loins.

As he opened his eyes he realised the windows that flooded the room with light also made it possible to see into the studio. With a groan of frustration for having to delay even a few seconds, he lifted her into his arms and carried her into the bedchamber.

Plunged into relative darkness, Jack blinked until he adjusted to the windowless room. He placed her on the bed, and she swivelled around so her back faced him. 'Undo my dress.'

He put his hand on her shoulder. 'Wait. There may be consequences for what we do.'

She spun around and made a sound of exasperation. 'What consequences if no one else knows of it?'

He took her chin in his fingers. 'I meant…we could create a child.'

Her mouth formed an O. She swept her fingers through his hair. 'I know what to do,' she murmured. 'Do not fear. One cannot be around the theatre and not learn such things.'

He relaxed.

'Will you undo my dress?' she asked again, moving her hair out of the way.

'It will be my delight.' He kissed the nape of her neck before undoing the hooks and untying the laces. He pulled the dress over her head and made short work of the laces of her corset. She pulled off her shift and both items were added to the pile of clothing on the floor. Naked but for stockings and shoes, she was an erotic sight. He scrambled to remove his trousers.

She watched him, her eyes widening in pleasure as he stood before her, naked and aroused. 'Jack, do you know how truly magnificent you are?'

He crouched down to reach her feet, pulling off a shoe. 'It is I who should be saying those words to you.'

She sighed. 'I am too outspoken. I know.'

His hand slid up her leg to reach the garter of her stocking. 'Too beautiful, perhaps. Nothing else.'

She played with his hair while he rolled down first one stocking, then the other. When he stood she touched him, her fingers examining the male part of him, a sweet torture that drove rational thought out of his mind.

He moved on top of her on the bed and began a torture of his own, tasting the elegant length of her neck, the luxury of her breasts, the hair that led him to her most feminine place. He felt a surge of masculine energy as she writhed beneath his touch and he rose above her.

'I want you,' she murmured to him, always speaking aloud thoughts he kept silent.

She was more than ready for him. He slipped into her easily, but forced himself to move slowly, wanting to prolong this delicious sense of oneness, wanting to savour her for as long as he could.

The sensations grew and soon there was no wanting at all, just rushing toward the pleasure. All that existed was

Ariana, moving in perfect unison with him. Joined to him. He seized that feeling, clung to it, begged it to stay.

His climax erupted and all thought, all feeling, was engulfed in the explosion of pleasure. He spilled his seed inside her and she convulsed around him. Stars burst behind his closed eyes and heaven seemed in easy reach. Their dual moment of pleasure lasted longer than he thought possible, longer than with any other woman.

When it ended, he almost collapsed on her, but stopped himself before crushing her under his full weight. Instead he slipped to her side and lay on his back, his eyes still closed. He was trying to create in his mind an image of what they had experienced, trying to put shape and colour to it. It resembled illuminations he'd seen at Vauxhall Gardens last summer, wild and bright and joyful.

He turned and held her close, kissing her long and languidly.

'That was—' she began.

He covered her mouth with his fingers. 'Allow me to be the outspoken one. That was…quite nice.'

'Such hyperbole.' She laughed. 'I have almost no experience in these matters, but I believe *I* would describe it as wonderful.'

'Almost no experience?' His brows knitted. What woman spent years in the theatre without such experiences?

'There was only one man, Jack.' She stroked his face to ease his frown. 'An older actor when I was barely nineteen, and it lasted not even a week.'

The pain from that experience showed on her face. 'He taught me a great deal—but nothing of love.' Her voice sounded clipped. 'Indeed, I feared I could no longer be tempted by a man until I met you.'

She had resisted every gentleman in every Green

Room? Even the one with the fine carriage he'd seen her with that first day at Somerset House?

His disbelief must have shown on his face, because a wounded look flickered in her eyes. 'My mother is known for her liaisons with gentlemen from the Green Room. I am not.'

He touched her arm. 'I do not doubt you. I'm merely astonished you could avoid such gentlemen.' For years? It did seem unbelievable.

She took a breath. 'I manage them. Turn them down without dealing too severe a blow to their vanity. I am quite skilled at it. That is why I do not worry about Tranville.'

Jack moved away and sat up. 'Be wary of him, none the less. And his son. Was he at the theatre last night?'

Her eyes shifted. 'He was, but he did not speak to me.' She pressed herself against his back. 'Do not allow mention of him to ruin our time together.'

The warmth and softness of her naked breasts against his skin threatened to arouse him again, to persuade him to abandon any thought of painting and simply make love all day.

He took a breath and angled his head towards her. 'We should work.'

'One more kiss,' she urged, coming close and pulling his head to her lips.

Her kiss fired his senses again, but he pulled away. 'We really must work. We'll lose the light.'

She sighed. 'I suppose you are right.'

She climbed off the bed and padded across the room, naked and graceful in her bare feet on the wooden floor, all sinuous lines and muted colour. She opened the bandbox and removed the white muslin gown they had decided upon, draping it over her shoulder. 'You know, the prints at the Royal Academy showed the Egyptian women without shoes. I think I should forgo shoes, don't you? Cleopatra's feet would be bare.'

Bare feet. Bare skin. He thought of the Cleopatra of his imagination, the one who wore the sheer costume, naked underneath, but regal and alluring.

'I have another idea,' he said. 'Put on the other muslin gown.'

'The other one?' She looked surprised. 'I thought we decided on this one.'

'We did.' He left the bed and quickly began dressing. He wanted to see if the sheer costume matched the image in his imagination. 'I should like to see you in the sheer one again.'

She regarded him as if he were crazed. 'Very well, but I thought my stays showed through too much.'

He kept his gaze even. 'Do not wear your stays. Just the gown.'

Her eyes widened.

'Indulge me.' He searched for an explanation. 'The dress is transparent. Show me how it looks this way.'

She appeared wary. 'You wish me to pose without my undergarments?'

It was akin to asking her to pose nude, something even prostitutes considered shameful.

'Not pose. I just want to see.'

A sensuous smile came over her face, the sort of smile his imaginary Cleopatra would make. Ariana removed the filmy muslin gown from the box and slipped it over her head. She turned to face him.

He grabbed a fistful of the gold chains she'd brought from the theatre, and took her hand. 'Come into the studio.'

She allowed him to lead her into the other room, so bright with sunlight that they both blinked. He tied one of the gold chains around her waist and draped the others about her neck. Walking around her, he watched how her skin showed through the fabric, how the transparency played with colour and light. The thought of painting her like this was a challenge that fired his blood, even if it was too scandalous to consider.

She arched one brow. 'Do you wish to paint me in this?'

He stared at her a long time, very tempted to say yes. Instead he waved a hand. 'No, change into the other gown. I just had the desire to see this one.'

The next two weeks were glorious ones for Ariana. Her afternoons were often filled with rehearsals for *Antony and Cleopatra*, and the evenings still required she be at the theatre, where she helped out as needed. She did not even mind attending the Green Room after performances, because she always found a way to mention that Jack was painting her portrait. But the mornings were what made life glorious. Each was spent with Jack, making love in his bed, then sitting for the portrait.

Sometimes when Jack was painting, his concentration was so intense they did not speak at all. At other times they shared the stories of their lives.

Jack seemed to select very carefully which bits of his life he shared. He told about the time before his father's death, but little of afterwards. He talked of Spain and Portugal, of the sights, sounds and smells there, but not of the battles in which he had fought.

Ariana found herself chattering on as she remained posed as Cleopatra. She told him of growing up in a girls' school, of her mother and her mother's lovers, of how she ran off to join the theatre company.

One blot on this idyll was the portrait itself. At first it

fascinated her, how her image seemed to float to the surface as the days progressed, but there was something missing in the portrait. She was disappointed in it, and Jack well knew it.

Another distressing element was that the portrait was almost completed. Indeed, she really did not need to sit for him any longer, but neither of them spoke of that.

This day, after she finished the sitting, she stood back and surveyed the painting.

'It is lovely, Jack…' Her voice trailed off.

'But?' He spoke the word more as an accusation than a question.

'You know what I think.' She hated to go over this again. 'It lacks emotion.'

He made a frustrated gesture. 'I am painting what I see.'

His observation was acute. The canvas was mostly white, as if Cleopatra sat in a room of white marble, but the white had subtle shades of colour in the shadows, in the hieroglyphics, in the other details of the room and her clothing. Cleopatra herself blazed with colour. Her skin. Her hair. Her eyes, outlined in black. The gold around her neck sparkled, and, although there was only a peek of red cushions on the piece of Egyptian furniture upon which she lounged, the colour echoed the red of her lips.

She had no doubt this all took great skill, but what made Jack's work special to her was missing. She'd tried and tried to explain.

'You are ignoring the emotion, Jack.' She did not know how else to say it.

He shook his head. 'This is no different from when I painted Nancy.'

'The painting of Nancy made her look alive. You could see all that youthful passion in her face, all her hopes and yearnings for the future.'

He threw up a hand. 'That is nonsense, Ariana. Nancy sat for me and I painted what I saw.'

'Then you see me as flat and lifeless.' Her voice rose. 'You showed how you loved Nancy when you painted her.'

He straightened. 'Do you accuse me of having no feelings for you?'

He had shown her in dozens of ways how he felt about her, but he had never spoken of loving her. It hurt her that he never spoke the word, even now.

'What are your feelings, Jack?' She pointed to the painting. 'You hide them on the canvas.'

He strode towards her and seized her by her shoulders. 'You have to ask me, Ariana?' His eyes showed a depth of emotion that took her breath away. Why was that not in her portrait?

'Why does the painting have to pose the same question, Jack?' she murmured. 'You can do better than this. What do you feel when you are painting me?'

He released her and turned away, raking a hand through his hair. 'That Tranville will possess your portrait and will look upon it every day.'

'Tranville,' she said abruptly.

Would she never rid herself of Tranville? Even though he no longer pursued her, she still felt his eyes upon her when he was in the Green Room and when he sat in his box while she was onstage. Sometimes during rehearsal he sat in the back of the theatre. Watching.

She did not mention that to Jack.

'I will also have a copy of the portrait,' she reminded him. 'I should like it to reflect what has passed between us when I look upon it. I should like other people to see those emotions when they look at engravings of it.'

He averted his gaze.

She turned away and headed towards the bedchamber door. 'I am going to change my clothes. If we are done for the day, I must get to the theatre.' She did not know the target for her anger; Tranville for his intrusion or Jack, who allowed him to be so important.

She pulled off her costume and flung it on to his bed. She'd just started to dress when Jack entered the room.

'Are you able to stay a little longer?' he asked.

She took a weary breath. 'I think I ought to go.'

He walked over to her and put his hands on her shoulders. 'I believe you are right about the portrait. I want to try something.'

His touch melted away her anger. 'What?'

His hands slid down her arms to around her back. 'Pose for me in the transparent gown.' He untied the strings of her corset. 'Without your stays.'

Her brows rose. 'Without wearing anything beneath?'

'Yes.' He was very close to her, his fingers untying her laces. 'From the day you brought the costumes here, it has been the image I yearned to paint. Maybe that is the answer.'

She stared at him.

'I realise you would endure much censure if the final portrait showed your nakedness, but I will paint over it. The final portrait will show you in the other white gown.'

Ariana imagined Jack's eyes, serious and intent, boring into her, perusing every inch of her near nakedness, reaching into the very depths of her soul. The prospect excited her mind and her senses, arousing her as his stroking fingers aroused her in bed. Her heart pounded rapidly.

These were the emotions she'd envisioned in the portrait.

She shrugged out of her corset. 'Let's do it,' she cried. 'Let us start right now!'

Chapter Twelve

Nancy bade Michael farewell at the corner of Adam Street and The Strand. He would have to run to reach his class at Somerset House in time. She insisted he not walk her to the door. They always dawdled when saying goodbye, thinking of one more thing to say before parting.

She watched him rush away, smiling at his limber gait. He turned around and saw her and paused as if he might return and walk her all the way. She moved the bouquet of flowers he had purchased for her to one arm and waved him on.

It would be just like Michael to make himself late because of her.

She sighed. What would she do if it were not for him? Michael was her most faithful friend, a far better friend than her old Bath schoolmates who used to whisper behind her back about her mother and Lord Tranville when they thought she did not know. Michael would never do that.

If it were not for Michael, Nancy would hardly ever set foot out of the London house. Her mother never went out now that Lord Tranville had begun to call. Nancy had begun to dislike Lord Tranville's visits. He always seemed to be assessing her, as if he was trying to decide how he could marry her off.

Nancy lifted Michael's flowers to her nose and walked slowly the rest of the way home. When she reached her door, she heard the clock chime one. She'd told her mother she'd be back by noon.

From the hall she heard Tranville's voice in the drawing room. Hoping to avoid him, Nancy walked quietly to the back of the townhouse, and started down the servants' stairs to the kitchen to put her flowers in water.

Their manservant was on his way up. 'Hello, Wilson,' she said cheerfully. 'Would you mind telling Mama I have returned? I'll be in my bedchamber after I tend to my flowers.'

Wilson looked up at her. 'Your mother asks that you come to her, miss.'

Nancy took one more step down. 'I'll see her later. She has a caller.'

Wilson stood in her way. 'Your mother expressly asked that you come to the drawing room as soon as you returned.'

Nancy sighed. 'Because I am late, I expect.'

He extended his hands. 'I'll take your things and see to your flowers, miss.'

Was her mother that upset with her for being late?

In the narrow space of the stairway, she first handed Wilson her flowers, then her hat and gloves. Finally she took off her cloak and handed that to him as well before turning and stomping up the stairs back to the hall. Realising she was acting in a rather childish manner, she collected herself, smoothed her skirt and hair, and entered the drawing room.

'Nancy, you are home,' her mother said as soon as she stepped through the doorway.

Tranville and another gentleman stood. It was the gentleman from the Egyptian Hall, the one who had looked at her so rudely. Why would he be calling on her mother?

'Ah, Nancy, my dear. How good to see you.' Tranville strode over to her. He took her hand in his. 'Come, say hello. I believe you have met Lord Ullman.'

Lord Ullman's face was flushed. He bowed to her. 'Miss Vernon. It is a delight to see you again.'

She curtsied. 'Good day, sir.'

Her mother patted the chair between her and Lord Ullman. 'Come sit with us. We have been having a nice chat.'

Nancy did not see why her presence was necessary for them to continue their nice chat, but she lowered herself into the chair.

Lord Ullman leaned towards her. 'How are you this fine day, Miss Vernon?'

'Very well, sir,' she murmured.

'Your mother said you were visiting the shops?' he continued.

'The Covent Garden market, sir,' she replied.

'And did you purchase anything?'

'Flowers, sir.' She could not imagine why he was interrogating her so, and why her mother was smiling.

'We have been talking about you,' her mother said.

Nancy quickly turned towards her.

Lord Ullman reached over and patted her hand. 'Nothing but praises, my dear.'

Lord Tranville stood. 'In fact, Lord Ullman has something he wishes to say to you.' He extended his hand to her mother. 'Come, Mary, let us leave the room for a moment.'

Her mother clasped his hand and let him assist her to her feet, which she could do very well on her own. Nancy's heart thumped painfully. She did not wish them to leave her alone with Lord Ullman. 'Mama, wait—'

Her mother merely tossed her a fond look before walking out of the room. Tranville followed and closed the door behind him.

Nancy glanced in alarm at Lord Ullman. She had never before been alone in a room with a gentleman with the door closed. Not even Michael.

Lord Ullman moved his chair closer to her, so that their knees touched, then he took both her hands in his. 'My dear Miss Vernon, I have thought of nothing but you since that moment—that precious moment—of first seeing you in the Egyptian Hall.'

'I cannot imagine—' she began, trying to pull her hands away.

He held fast and brought one hand to his wet lips. 'I have been in a passion for you—'

'Sir!' A passion? This was shocking. He was nearly as old as Tranville.

He kept making her hand wet. 'I cannot rest until you say you will be mine. I want nothing more in this world than to possess you.'

She jumped to her feet. 'Speak no more! I—I am too young for this.' She could not believe her mother had sanctioned this shocking exhibition. 'I have hopes of marriage, sir. I am too young for an affair. I cannot do it.'

He laughed at her and again put her hand against his wet lips. 'You foolish, darling girl. I would never dishonour you with such a request. It is marriage I seek from you.' He fell to his knees. 'Miss Vernon, will you consent to be my bride?'

Her throat seized in panic. 'Your bride?'

She sank back in her chair. He rose from his knees and pushed his chair even closer. 'I have your mother's approval and Lord Tranville's. It is he who has brokered the matter. All that is wanting is your consent.'

Brokered the matter? What did that mean? Had Lord Tranville sold her? Had her mother agreed to it?

'No,' she cried. Her thoughts were racing. She wanted to refuse him, but would her mother be angry with her if she did? 'No. I—I mean, I cannot answer now. Please do not require me to answer. This is too sudden for me.'

He finally released her and gave her room to breathe. 'I quite understand. You know so little of me.' He smiled indulgently. 'Let me assure you, I am a wealthy man. My title is an old one and my finances are as solid as the Bank of England. I am a widower with two delightful children who are in great need of a mother. I am as healthy as a horse.' He patted his chest. 'And, if I do say so myself, lusty enough for a young wife. It shall be my life's endeavour to please you and see you happy.'

Lusty enough? She cringed. He was nothing like the lovers of her fantasies, of the novels she read. He—he was fat. And old. And he had very little hair.

She could not catch her breath. 'Please…'

He stood, but lifted her chin with his hand. 'I will bid you adieu for this day. Your mother and Lord Tranville will, I am confident, ease your maidenly mind.'

He bent down and actually put his lips on hers. It was like being forced to kiss a raw fish.

He straightened. 'One more assurance I will make to you. I naturally forgo any expectation of a dowry. In fact, I agreed with Tranville that, with our marriage, I ought to assume the financial support for your mother as well as for you, and, I further assure you, I am a very generous man.'

Tranville *brokered* the support of her mother as well? Her mind raced. Why would he do that?

Lord Ullman made a deep bow, turned and walked out of the room.

Nancy wiped her lips with the back of her hand and grasped her throat. She bent over, uncertain if she would faint.

Her mother and Tranville bustled in.

Her mother rushed to her side. 'You did not say yes, Nancy dear? I am so surprised.'

Tranville looked stern. 'He makes you a decent offer. More than you have a right to expect.'

Nancy stared into her mother's eyes. 'Do you want me to accept him, Mama?'

Her mother blinked. 'Why, of course. You will be set for life.'

'And so will you—' she snapped.

Tranville interrupted her. 'Now, now. Never mind that. This is about you, not your mother.'

Nancy gaped at him. Perhaps her mother did not know of that part of the bargain. 'But, you—' she began.

'Hush!' He glared at her. 'Do not be a fool and throw this offer away, girl.'

'It is a wonderful match, Nancy. More than I could ever have dreamed for you.'

She shot to her feet. 'I—I need some time. Give me some time.' She pushed by them and headed for the door.

'He will not wait for ever,' Tranville said.

Nancy stumbled into the hall and whirled around, not knowing what to do.

'Nancy?' her mother called from the drawing room.

With a tiny cry, Nancy opened the front door and ran out into the street, without her hat or her gloves or her cloak, not thinking anything but that she needed to find somewhere she could breathe.

A woman's voice sounded from behind her. 'Miss Vernon!'

* * *

Ariana, exhilarated and optimistic about the portrait, had just walked out of Jack's building when his sister rushed by her. If she took time to alert Jack, Nancy might disappear from sight.

Ariana ran after her. 'Nancy!'

The girl showed no sign of even hearing her. She seemed to be rushing straight to the river. Ariana could only think she meant to jump in.

She caught up to Nancy near the water's edge, seizing her arm and pulling her away from where the path led straight into the water.

'What are you doing?' Ariana cried. 'What is wrong?'

It seemed to take the girl a few moments to recognise her. 'It is you, Miss Blane.'

'Were you going to jump in?' Ariana's heart was still thumping.

Nancy shook her head. 'I—I want to go to Somerset House. To find Michael.'

Ariana put an arm around the girl. 'I see.' She spoke in a consoling tone. 'To find Michael. But why do you wish to find him?'

'Oh, Miss Blane!' Nancy flung her arms around Ariana's neck and burst into tears. 'It is so awful. What am I to do?'

Ariana let the fit of weeping die down before asking Nancy to explain. The whole appalling story spilled out. Lord Tranville had arranged for Lord Ullman to propose marriage to her. The poor child! Poor Michael.

'The worst thing is,' Nancy gulped. 'My mother *wants* me to marry him. And he is old enough to be my father. And he is fat!' She burst into another fit of tears.

'There. There.' She patted Nancy's back until she calmed again. 'I am sure there is a way to fix this.'

'Nothing can be done!'

She held the girl longer. 'We must go back and tell Jack.'

Nancy pulled away. 'Jack hates Lord Tranville! He'll fight a duel or something.'

'Jack will help you, I know he will,' she murmured. 'You must tell him about this.'

'No one can help me.' Nancy covered her face with her hands. When she dropped them again, she sighed. 'Oh, very well. We will tell Jack.'

Ariana took off her cloak and wrapped it around the shivering girl. She held on to her as they walked back to Jack's door.

Nancy talked the whole way. 'The thing is, if I marry Lord Ullman, he will be the one to support Mama. Lord Tranville added that to the marriage agreement. If I refuse, then maybe he won't pay Mama any more money and we'll have nothing to live on.'

Ariana almost tripped. 'Lord Tranville provides your mother's support even now? I thought his...connection...to her was in the past.'

'He has always supported us.' Nancy nodded. 'Since my father died. We would be in abject poverty if he had not. It will break Mama's heart when she discovers he doesn't want to pay for her any more.'

It had been clear that Jack's mother had once been Tranville's mistress, but Ariana had not known he'd also provided Jack's family's support. 'Why should it break her heart?'

'Because Mama is so in love with him. Lord Tranville is more important to her than anyone else, even Jack and me.'

Was Jack's mother foolish enough to prefer Tranville over her own children? She thought her own mother was the only one to prefer a man—any man—to her child.

'She gave up everything for him,' Nancy went on. 'But, of course, I believe we would have starved otherwise, even though Jack says not.' The girl looked at her quizzically. 'I thought Jack would have told you all this.'

Ariana would have thought so, too. 'Perhaps he did not think it important.' Not important that his mother was supported by Tranville and in love with him to boot.

Nancy's forehead creased. 'I truly believed Lord Tranville loved Mama, but, if he loved her, he would not want to stop taking care of her. He can afford Mama now better than before he inherited his title. It is as if he wants to be rid of her.'

They reached Jack's building. 'Come, we'll knock on the door.' She sounded the knocker.

Jack was still wearing his paint-spattered shirt. 'Ariana?' He saw Nancy and his eyes grew wide. 'Come in.'

'Oh, Jack!' Nancy rushed inside and flung herself into his arms, her tears flowing again. He looked over her shoulder at Ariana with a question in his eyes.

She made a gesture for him to wait.

'Sit down, Nancy.' He coaxed her over to the *chaise-longue*.

'I'll make tea.' Ariana left them and went into the galley.

She could hear Nancy's halting explanation and her brother's outraged response. Now she had two upset persons on her hands.

She carried in the tea.

Jack was pacing. 'Tranville has interfered enough. It is time I dealt with him.'

Nancy turned white. 'Mama will not like it if you quarrel with him.' Her eyes grew huge. 'You mustn't fight a duel!'

'It would serve the man right,' Jack muttered.

'No!' Nancy wailed.

Ariana hastily placed the tray down and sat beside her. 'Your brother will not fight a duel.' She stared at Jack. 'Will you, Jack?'

He continued to pace. 'Of course not, but I will deal with him.'

She pointed to the tea. 'Let us drink the tea and calm down a little.'

'I want no tea.' Jack glowered. He headed toward his bedchamber. 'I need to change my shirt.'

Nancy blinked away tears. 'Are you certain my brother will not fight a duel?

She clasped Nancy's hand. 'I am very certain.'

'He dislikes Tranville so.'

Ariana disliked Tranville, as well, for causing so much unhappiness to these people she cared about.

Ariana poured her a cup of tea. 'Here, drink this. It will help you feel better.'

She took a sip and sighed. 'I wish I could tell Michael about this. I should so like to talk with him.'

'When will you see him next?' Ariana asked.

'Dinner tonight, if he comes. But I probably won't be able to speak with him alone.'

The mantel clock sounded half past four.

Jack stepped out of his bedchamber, still tying his neck-cloth. He looked at Ariana. 'Are you not late for the theatre?'

Nancy looked alarmed. 'I have made you late!'

Ariana patted her hand. 'Actresses are supposed to be late on occasion.' She made Nancy look at her. 'Would you like to come with me to watch the rehearsal? It will be a nice diversion.' She glanced at Jack. 'You could collect her later or I could send her home in a hackney coach.'

Jack turned to his sister. 'Nancy?'

She nodded, wiping away her tears with her fingers. 'I could come back in a coach in time for dinner.' She looked at Jack. 'Will you tell Mama where I am? I—I'd rather not face her right now. Tell her I will not be late.'

'I will.' Jack buttoned his coat. 'Let us leave immediately. I want to catch Tranville if he is still with Mother.'

Ariana gave Nancy her cloak and wore one of the shawls she had originally brought for the Cleopatra costume. Jack walked them to the Strand to put them in a hack. Luckily one waited nearby.

He helped Nancy into the coach and turned to Ariana.

She placed a hand on his cheek. 'Take care, Jack.'

He covered her hand with his. 'That is usually my warning to you about Tranville.'

Their gazes locked for a moment before he helped her into the carriage. As it drove away, she watched his figure recede in the distance.

Perhaps Nancy's prediction of doom had infected her as well, because Ariana could not help but feel her future with Jack had also undergone a dismal change.

Once the feeling took hold of her, she could not shake it.

Chapter Thirteen

Jack hesitated only until the hackney coach was out of sight before walking with a determined stride to his mother's door.

When he entered, Wilson was dressed to go out.

'Mrs Vernon was just sending me to your studio, Mr Vernon.' The manservant peered behind him. 'Miss Nancy is not with you?'

'She was with me until a moment ago,' Jack explained.

He heard his mother's voice coming from her bedchamber at the end of the hallway. 'I am merely concerned, Lionel.'

'Nonsense. She's run to her brother,' Tranville answered. 'Leave her.'

'I merely wish to know for certain.' His mother emerged from her room and saw him in the hall. She rushed up to him. 'Jack? Jack? Is Nancy with you?'

'No, Mother. She has gone with Miss Blane to watch her rehearse.'

'She's gone with Miss Blane?' Tranville emerged from his mother's room.

Good God. Had Tranville taken her to bed while her

daughter's whereabouts were unknown? And she had gone? The two of them were abominable.

'She wished to see the rehearsal.' Jack looked from one to the other. 'I see you found something to occupy yourselves in her absence.'

'Jack!' His mother blushed.

'See here, boy—' Tranville began.

Jack held up a hand to silence them. He walked to the drawing-room door. 'I would speak with you both now.'

Wilson gave Jack a very fleeting look of approval before turning to his mother. 'Do you have need of me, ma'am?'

'No, no, Wilson. You may go back to whatever you were doing.' She followed Jack into the drawing room.

Tranville walked in after her and closed the door behind him. 'You have no call to talk to your mother or to me in that tone, boy. In front of a servant, as well.'

Jack spun on him. 'Stubble it, Tranville. The servants can hardly be shocked by anything that happens in this house. I came here out of concern for my sister. I demand to know what is going on with this marriage business.'

'It is a wonderful offer,' his mother said in a weak voice.

'When did you learn of it, Mother?' Jack asked her.

She looked as if he'd asked an odd question. 'Lionel told me of it this morning.'

'Was the settlement arranged when he spoke to you?' he continued.

'Of course.' She lifted her chin. 'Lionel saw to everything.'

Jack turned to Tranville. 'You negotiated a marriage settlement for my sister without discussing it with her family first? What gave you that right?'

Tranville's eyes flashed. 'A regard for your family. Is that not sufficient for you?'

'Lord Ullman is a wealthy man,' his mother interjected.

'That may be so,' Jack replied to her. 'And if he is a man of good character and Nancy desires him, I can find no objection. But we know nothing of Ullman. Tranville made these arrangements without a word to you, to Nancy or to me.'

Tranville took a step towards him. 'How dare you question me, sir? Ullman is a gentleman. I made the arrangements because I saw a way to help your sister and I seized upon it.'

'Nancy will want for nothing married to him,' his mother explained. 'She will have security.'

Jack ignored Tranville. 'As I understand it, Mother, *you* will want for nothing if Nancy marries this gentleman. *You* will have security.'

'See here,' barked Tranville. 'I've had enough of this.'

'*I* will have security?' his mother repeated. 'I do not comprehend your meaning.'

Jack inclined his head toward Tranville. 'The marriage settlement included an arrangement for Lord Ullman to assume your financial support. Did Tranville neglect to explain that part to you?'

She turned to Tranville, her eyes wide. 'Is this true, Lionel?'

Tranville gave Jack a murderous look, but he spoke to Jack's mother in a placating tone. 'Mary, I did not wish to trouble you with such details—'

'My mother is Nancy's guardian.' Jack countered. 'She should have been told *all* the details, especially the one that so involved her.'

His mother wrung her hands.

Tranville clasped her fingers. 'I thought only of how you dislike dealing with numbers.'

'But I should like to have known this.' His mother's voice was barely audible.

'You could have included me on the numbers,' Jack countered. 'As Nancy's brother, it would be logical for me to deal with the financial part of her marriage settlement.'

'You?' Tranville laughed. 'What do you know of such matters?'

'I have lived in the world. I know its costs.' He had supported himself on his half-pay and his art commissions for almost two years now. 'And I know my sister.'

His mother blinked rapidly as she looked up at Tranville. 'I did not know you wished to be rid of my support, Lionel.'

He reached for her again, but she stepped back. 'Mary, my dear girl. I would never renege on my promise to you. I made this request by design. It *fulfils* my promise. Otherwise I should not have made it.'

'It saves you a great deal of money,' Jack added in a sarcastic tone.

Tranville turned on him. 'That is of no consequence. It is your mother's reputation I was thinking of.'

'My reputation!' she cried.

'By having Ullman take over your support, I restore your good name.' His tone was mollifying.

She returned a very sceptical look.

He stepped forwards and stroked her arm, speaking soothingly. 'You see, no one could perceive anything untoward about your son-in-law paying for your support. In this manner, I erased any obstacle to your daughter's acceptance in polite society. Or yours. Ullman marrying Nancy and taking over your support removes any taint of impropriety.' He smiled patiently. 'Surely you cannot argue with that.'

Her expression remained wounded. 'You have not expressed concern about impropriety before this.'

'Indeed, it seemed the least of your concerns,' Jack inserted.

Tranville shot him an angry glance, but put an arm around Jack's mother. 'My dearest, surely you understand how the situation has changed. I have an obligation, with my title, to marry again—'

She wrenched free. 'Marry again?'

'Of course I must marry again.' He made himself look regretful.

Jack stepped forwards. 'You damned hypocrite. You are *planning* to marry.'

It seemed clear to Jack now why Tranville had so suddenly dropped his interest in Ariana. He was courting some society miss and keeping his nose clean of mistresses in the meantime. Explaining Jack's mother's support to the young lady's wealthy papa might have created a nasty problem for him. Ullman had come to the rescue.

Jack shook his head. 'You took it upon yourself to negotiate with Ullman so you could rid yourself of any further connection with my mother and marry without impediment.'

Tears welled up in Jack's mother's eyes. 'Is that true?'

Tranville glared at Jack before focusing back on her. 'I must marry, Mary. I must keep the title in my family and that means ensuring the heir will be of my blood. I must sire more sons. Do you not see that the war almost took my only one? Edwin's injury could have cost him his life.'

Only because Jack and two other soldiers had refrained from killing him in Badajoz.

'I need more sons. You must see that, my dear,' Tranville pleaded. 'It is my duty.'

'I'll hear no more about it.' She pulled away from him. 'If—if you will pardon me, I—I must speak with Cook about dinner.'

Jack frowned as his mother rushed out of the room. It

pained him to see her so wounded, but it was long past time she recognised Tranville for the man he was.

As soon as she was gone, Tranville wheeled on him. 'That was not well done of you at all.'

'Not well done of me?' Jack laughed. 'The responsibility rests on your shoulders, Tranville.'

Tranville's eyes bulged. 'I refuse to apologise for arranging a proposal for your sister that is far better than she deserves. Nor for negotiating a marriage settlement that protects her and your mother.'

'Cut line, Tranville. You do not have my mother's interests at heart. You embarked on this plan to rid yourself of any ties to a former mistress so some young lady equally as hapless as my sister will think you promise fidelity.'

'You malign me greatly. Do you not remember who I am?' he shouted in outrage.

'I do indeed know who you are,' Jack's voice turned low. 'You are the man who keeps my mother tied to you, in case you should ever have need of her.'

'You cur!' Tranville's face turned red. 'This is the thanks I get for using my position to help your family. Let me tell you, your sister is damned lucky any man would want to marry her, let alone a peer of the realm.'

Jack leaned into his face. 'My sister would do credit to any man. She is a fine person.'

'She is tainted by her mother.'

Jack's hand curled into a fist. 'And, you, sir, are the man who tainted my mother.'

'You ungrateful wretch,' Tranville shouted. 'I rescued your mother from poverty.'

'Even if that were true, you could have assisted her without requiring she repay you in bed.' Jack's anger filled every pore of his being. He was hard pressed to keep control over his fists. The last time he experienced such anger had been at Badajoz, finding Edwin.

The emotion sparked the rumble of cannon fire in his ears.

Spittle dripped down the corner of Tranville's mouth. 'It was my money that sent you to school and purchased your commission—'

Jack ignored the pounding of the guns in his head. 'Because my mother saved for it—'

'Because I was generous enough that she could afford it.'

Jack turned away, forcing his mind to stay in the present time. The battle he needed to wage at the moment was with Tranville.

'Do not profess generosity.' Jack raised his voice above the din in his head. 'My mother continues to repay you. At your whim.'

Jack's mother had left the door ajar and their voices carried far enough for the servants to hear every word. Jack could not care. He was fighting on two fronts, the war in his mind and the one with Tranville.

Nancy climbed down from the hack and walked up to her door. From the drawing-room window she could hear Jack and Lord Tranville's raised voices, but she could not hear what they were saying. She cringed, hating angry words, but she must involve herself in this shouting match. It was about her.

She'd been a coward to run away from her mother and Lord Tranville. A grown woman would see it as her responsibility to deal with them. It was her marriage they were planning, her future. She must act on her own behalf.

By the time she and Ariana had arrived at Drury Lane Theatre, Nancy had calmed enough to remember that a woman had the right to refuse a proposal. All she need do was say no. She told Ariana she wanted to return home to tell her mother. She knew Jack would support her wishes.

Nancy hurriedly opened the front door and entered quietly. In the hall, the voices sounded even louder. She froze.

'Do not try to tell me, Tranville,' she heard Jack say, 'that Ullman suggested taking over Mother's support. It was you, thinking of your own plans to marry.'

Nancy frowned. Lord Tranville was planning to marry? That's why Lord Ullman would be supporting her mother?

'I have explained enough to you, you insolent puppy!' Tranville responded. 'I did this for your mother and your sister, because of my esteem for them both.'

'Drivel,' Jack shot back. 'And what happens if my sister refuses Ullman? What then? Do you continue to pay my mother's support?'

'Your sister would be a fool to refuse his offer,' Tranville cried, his voice rising to a shrill sound. 'In fact, you can tell her this. I will cut off your mother's funds if your sister refuses Ullman.'

Nancy gasped. Cut off her mother's funds? What would happen to her mother then? She'd have no money. Worse, her heart would be broken.

'This is how you honour your word to my mother?' Jack's voice was scathing.

'As far as I am concerned, I fulfil my promise by making this arrangement with Ullman. I've ensured her support and that is what I promised her.'

Lord Tranville was forcing her to marry Ullman. Nancy started backing towards the outside door.

Jack went on, 'As far as I am concerned, both my mother and sister are well rid of you. I will support them.'

'You?' Tranville laughed. 'We will see about that. I can ruin you with a word—'

Nancy put her hands over her ears and groped for the doorknob, opening the door enough to slip out. Again outside, she covered her head with the hood of Ariana's cloak and walked slowly and mournfully to the Strand. Her legs felt as if they were weighted with rocks and her heart felt even heavier. If only she could curl up in a ball in some alleyway. Perhaps she would freeze to death by the morning.

She lifted her chin. That was ridiculous and childish, and it was time she set aside childish thinking. If nothing else, today was forcing her to grow into a woman and to face the world as it really was.

Lord Tranville was not the man she'd believed he was her whole life. If he loved her mother, he would not leave her without a penny and marry someone else. He just wanted to bed her mother, that was all.

Nancy covered her mouth and breathed rapidly against the sick feeling that idea created.

Tranville used her mother merely for carnal reasons, and Lord Ullman, with all his talk of being lusty, wanted her for the same reason. This was not *Romeo and Juliet.* One meeting with a person could not create love. Ullman could not possibly love her.

Neither her mother nor her brother could protect her from her fate. Lord Tranville held the strings and was playing them all like the puppets she'd seen at the fair.

If she refused Ullman's proposal now her mother's heart would be broken, Jack's career as an artist would be ruined, and they'd all be poor.

For once in her life it was her responsibility to take care of the family. She must accept Lord Ullman.

Tears rolled down her cheeks and she felt terribly alone.

She walked toward Somerset House. At this moment, she was in great need of a friend.

She wanted to see Michael, to tell him how her life had changed since their carefree walk through Covent Garden that morning. Unlike earlier that afternoon, she was not rushing blindly to Michael's side. She merely wished him to know what she must do, for if she did not, what would happen to them all?

She walked solemnly, tears silently falling. When she crossed Southampton Street, a man coming from the direction of Covent Garden brushed against her, then caught her arm, and pulled her so she was facing him.

'Well, if it isn't little Nancy Vernon.' The scarred face of Edwin Tranville looked malevolently down upon her. His breath smelled of whisky. 'And walking the streets all alone.' He laughed. 'A street-walker. My lucky day.'

'Let me go, Edwin,' she snapped.

But he did not let her go. Instead he dragged her against the wall of a building. 'I want a kiss from the street-walker.'

'Stop it, Edwin.' Nancy squirmed.

She lifted her leg and slammed her heel down hard on Edwin's foot. He let go of her and she struck his face. With no gloves on, her nails scraped his scar.

He gave a cry of pain and immediately cupped his cheek. Nancy gave him a hard push and he careened into the brick wall of the building.

She ran, frightened now, because she realised how dangerous it could be to walk on the street alone. She heard Edwin shouting behind her, but she did not look back. She ran all the way to Somerset House and hid in one of the doorways before checking to see if he had pursued her.

It did not surprise her that he was nowhere in sight. Edwin always ran away crying if someone fought back.

Nancy leaned against the wall and tried to catch her breath. She was afraid to emerge from the doorway, but afraid she would miss Michael if she did not.

The sun had dropped low and the shadows had grown to ominous lengths. It should be near time for Michael's instructor to release him. She stepped out of her hiding place.

Students started to pour out of the building. Some of them eyed her as they walked past, making her frightened all over again, but then she saw Michael laughing at something a companion said to him. She could not see his blue eyes from this distance, but she was certain they twinkled with amusement and their corners creased with tiny lines. She knew she was safe.

She waited until he was closer. 'Michael?'

Several eyes turned to her, all very speculative. Some of his companions made catcalls.

'Nancy?' Michael walked over to her. He turned to the others. 'Stubble it, fellows. This is a friend.'

There was more laughter, but Nancy did not care. She'd found Michael.

'What are you doing here?' he asked with a worried frown. 'Is something amiss?'

'Will you walk me home, Michael?' She was eager to get away from these spectators.

'Of course.' He waved to the others. 'I shall see you all tomorrow.'

'Have a good night!' one of them called. The others laughed and hooted.

He led Nancy away, but waited for her to start speaking. She would not tell him about Edwin. She'd pretend that had never happened. Taking a breath she began to explain why she'd braved the dangerous streets alone to see him.

She told him everything, including what she'd heard Lord Tranville say about denying her mother financial support.

'What else can I do, Michael?' she asked him. 'Do you think I am right in saying I'll marry him?'

'I cannot advise you about this.' He answered in a voice she hardly recognised.

His face was stiff and unfriendly. He looked so…different.

'Do you want to marry him?' he asked after another pause.

She shook her head. 'I had not even thought of marriage before this.' Marriage had felt like a *some day* sort of thing, a distant dream, one or two years away, at least. 'I think I must marry him for my mother's sake.'

'He is wealthy,' was his only comment.

They walked on, but Michael watched his feet more than where they were headed. Adam Street was only two roads away. Once inside her house again she would not be able to speak freely with him.

He broke their silence. 'I should beg off dinner tonight.'

'No!' she cried. 'Why?' She could not bear it if he were not with her when she had to face her mother and brother.

'Your family has much to discuss.' He pressed his lips together into a grim line. 'I would intrude on your privacy.'

She was suddenly afraid that if Michael said goodbye to her right now she would never see him again. Her heart beat as fast as when she'd been running. She could no longer breathe. Everything turned black and her legs gave way.

'Nancy!'

She felt his strong arms around her, holding her.

'I need to sit down,' she gasped.

He kept her in his embrace. 'We are near Savoy Chapel. We might sit there.'

He helped her to the chapel, which was dark. The door was unlocked, however. They went inside and sat in a back pew.

She tried to catch her breath. 'Don't leave me alone, Michael. Don't leave me.' Tears poured from her eyes. She tried very hard not to sob aloud.

'I shall not leave you,' he murmured consolingly. 'I will see you safely home.'

'No. That's not what I meant.' She could not speak until she caught her breath. 'If…if I marry, will you still be my friend?'

He wrapped his arms around her and held her very tight. 'If you must marry—' It seemed as if his voice cracked. He took a deep breath. 'You shall always be in my heart.'

His answer calmed her even though she was uncertain what it meant. To be always in Michael's heart seemed a good thing, though, especially as her own heart was breaking.

Jack tried returning to his studio to work. After Ariana had left, he'd made great progress on the new version of her portrait, but he could not continue now, not even if he lit every lamp and candle he possessed. There was too much disquiet inside him.

He decided he would collect Nancy at the theatre. He needed to see Ariana, needed her comfort and optimism. Jack hurried out of the door and strode quickly to the Strand, but there were no hackney coaches in sight. He walked to Charles Street and the Drury Lane Theatre, thrusting away the internal rumblings of Badajoz.

He entered the theatre through the back door and made his way through the labyrinth that was the backstage to the wings. No one questioned his presence.

Ariana was on stage with Edmund Kean, rehearsing a

scene from Act One. '...I'll seem the fool I am not; Antony will be himself.'

Kean responded, 'But stirr'd by Cleopatra. Now, for the love of Love and her soft hours, Let's not confound the time with conference harsh.'

These were not soft hours, Jack thought. He glanced around and did not see Nancy, but he felt in control of himself again.

Ariana saw him as she left the stage. She hurried up to him. 'I did not expect you,' she murmured. 'What transpired with Tranville?'

The pleasure of being with her surged inside him. 'I confronted him and my mother. He did not like it. That is all really. Where is Nancy?'

Her eyes widened in surprise. 'Why, she never came here. She had the hack take her back home.'

He stared at her. 'She did not come home.'

'Oh, Jack!' She looked away. 'I should have stayed with her, but she seemed calm. And she was determined to return home.' She grasped his arm and pulled him towards the door. 'You should go back. Find Michael. I wager she went to him.'

He wrapped his arms around her, not caring at the moment who might see them. 'This has been a hellish day.'

She hugged him back, holding him tightly. 'I cannot help you search for her; I am in tonight's performance.'

'I know,' he murmured. 'Come tomorrow, as early as you like.' He took her face in his hands and kissed her, hungry for her lips.

When he moved his lips away, she caressed his cheek. 'She will be at your mother's home when you return. With Michael at her side, you can bet upon it.'

He nodded, but could not believe it. Today he could only believe in unhappy endings.

Chapter Fourteen

The next morning Ariana rose early and hurried to Jack's studio. She'd been so worried about Nancy and Jack, she'd slept little. It was odd to care so much about other people, to think of them before thinking of herself.

She passed the door to Mrs Vernon's apartment, hoping Nancy was safe in her bed and not in some terrible mischief. Ariana never should have let Nancy go home alone.

She quickened her step to reach Jack's door, letting herself inside with the key he had given her.

He stood at his easel, in stockinged feet, dressed in his painting shirt, brush in hand. She'd almost forgotten about the portrait, so much had happened since she'd sat for him in a costume more scandalous than posing in one's nightdress.

He looked up at her entrance and smiled. 'You did come early.'

She pulled off her pelisse and hung it on a hook. 'I could not sleep.'

She rushed to him and was gathered into his arms, forgetting to care if paint got on her dress. His mere warmth, his scent, was comfort to her. 'Tell me. I have worried so. Did you find Nancy?'

He released her and nodded. 'It was as you predicted. She was at my mother's place by the time I returned there.'

She released a relieved breath. 'What happened to her?'

'Nothing. She took a walk, she said.' He still held her. She examined his face and found only worry there.

'She changed,' he said. 'Somehow between here and my mother's house, she changed. She said she'd decided to marry Lord Ullman after all, giving as her reason a desire to be respectable and to wear pretty gowns.'

Ariana was aghast. 'But what did she say of Michael?'

'She did not mention him, except to say he'd left word he would not be at dinner.' His brow creased. 'I must conclude you are mistaken about Michael and Nancy. He has not declared anything more than friendship to her, ever.'

'Oh, I am not mistaken,' Ariana insisted. 'Nancy and Michael have a grand love for each other, although they may not know it yet.'

'If so, it is a doomed one.' He rubbed his face. 'I must have argued with her for two hours. She would not hear anything I said. She just insisted she wanted to be a countess.'

'I do not believe it,' Ariana said.

Jack frowned. 'My mother dispatched a message to Tranville to bring Ullman to call this afternoon. Nancy will accept his proposal.'

Ariana leaned against him again. 'This is too dreadful.'

Jack's voice rumbled in his chest. 'This is all Tranville's doing and my mother is going along with it. Even after—' He stopped.

'Even after what?'

He released her and picked up a brush. 'Tranville plans to remarry.'

Ariana's jaw dropped. 'Remarry!' She could not be more surprised. There had been no talk at the theatre about him courting anyone.

Jack turned back to the canvas and she looked at it for the first time since the previous day. 'Oh, my!'

He gazed at it as well. 'What do you think?'

The portrait was a long way from being complete, but already it was a vast change from the first one. She was Cleopatra lounging in the same pose as before, but the expression on her face simmered with sensuality, as if this image were indeed casting her gaze upon her lover.

'It promises more than I ever dreamed,' she whispered.

He made a gratified sound. 'There's much more to be done. I need to work more on the transparent effect of the gown.'

Jack had so vividly depicted a blush of skin beneath a thin wash of white pigment Ariana could almost feel the silkiness of the fabric. Because he'd draped it to conceal the dark pink of her nipples and her most feminine parts, the portrait did not look bawdy; it appeared reverent.

'It is remarkable.' She hugged him from behind. 'You have done it!'

He turned to her. 'I need to finish the background, refine the rest. I wish I could use every bit of daylight, but I want to be present when Ullman calls on my sister.'

She touched his cheek. 'Even if Nancy accepts Ullman today, she still can change her mind before marrying him.'

He frowned. 'I cannot see that as likely.'

She gazed at the portrait again. She'd almost despaired of Jack ever transforming the work into a great painting, but he had done it. It seemed a terrible shame to cover over the sheer gown with the other one. It suited this sensual Cleopatra.

She gave Jack a swift hug. 'Let us not waste the day.

Come and help me with my laces. I'll change into the costume, and you can get back to work.'

Never had a painting emerged from Jack's brush more quickly. Exhilarated, he worked until the afternoon advanced, wanting to seize every second of time. The clock chimed the half-hour and he realised it was near the time to go to his mother's. He wiped his brush and dropped it in a jar of turpentine.

'I surmise we are done for the day.' Ariana uncoiled herself from her posed position.

'I wish it were not so.' Jack covered his palette with a cloth. 'But I am expected at my mother's.'

'For Lord Ullman to call,' Ariana finished for him.

He and Ariana had spoken very little the whole day. He'd been so absorbed by the work he'd almost forgotten to give her breaks. Time passed without his being aware of it.

At this pace both the portrait and a copy could be ready to deliver in two or three weeks. If Tranville still wanted them, that is. His marriage plans might have changed matters. If so, Jack would willingly forgo the balance owed him.

Ariana stretched. 'I wish I could speak to Nancy. Maybe I could discover why she has changed her mind so completely.'

Jack covered his palette to keep the paint moist for the next day. 'I wish you could as well.'

Ariana walked over to the canvas. 'I am amazed.'

He pulled off his paint-streaked shirt and put an arm around her. 'It is as if I am transported. Nothing exists but the painting and you.'

She turned and wrapped her arms around his neck. Her kiss drove even the painting from his mind. Beneath the thin fabric of the costume she was warm and soft and he was consumed with desire for her.

Her lips still touched his. 'Do we have time?' she murmured.

'We have time.' He lifted her into his arms and carried her to his bed.

Their lovemaking was swift and sensuous and thrilling in its intensity. They were attuned to each other now, each expert in knowing the most arousing way to touch, the most erotic way to move. Rushing against the clock lent a new intensity to the lovemaking. When their passion was spent, Jack held Ariana in his arms, loath to release her and proceed on his undesired errand.

The clock chimed the quarter-hour.

'You must hurry,' Ariana said. She slid from his arms and the bed and gathered their clothing from the floor.

He groaned and rose to dress for the meeting with Ullman. They'd become as expert dressing each other as in making love. Ariana pulled fresh linens for Jack from the chest of drawers. He assisted her with her corset and the laces of her dress. While he donned his clean shirt and his good trousers, waistcoat and coat, she folded his painting trousers and her costume, putting it away neatly into the bandbox.

He tied his neckcloth. 'Will you be late to the theatre?'

She shook her head. 'Not at all. I have plenty of time.' She pinned up her hair. 'I would wish you good luck this afternoon, but I have no idea what good luck will mean in this situation.'

They hurried out into the studio where a sudden cloud darkened the room. He closed the curtains. 'Perhaps we will all be struck with lightning and our worries will be over.'

She shook him. 'Do not say that! Not even as a jest. I want nothing to happen to you or your family.'

Jack felt a surge of tenderness for her. 'Forgive me. It was not a good jest.'

She squeezed his arm. 'You must tell yourself that somehow things will work out well.'

He gave her a sceptical look.

'Do say it,' she insisted.

He kissed her again. 'Somehow things will work out well.'

She smiled approvingly and put on her hat.

When they stepped outside, Jack said, 'I'll walk with you to get a hack.'

She shook her head. 'Go to your mother's. I shall be fine.'

When they reached Jack's mother's house, Tranville and Ullman approached in the opposite direction.

'I'll not leave you now,' Jack said under his breath.

Lord Ullman broke into a smile and quickened his pace. 'Miss Blane! How delightful to see you.' He glanced at Jack with a quizzical look.

Ariana stepped forwards. 'Lord Ullman, allow me to present Mr Jack Vernon.'

Jack inclined his head to acknowledge the introduction.

Lord Ullman broke into a smile and thrust out his hand for Jack to shake. 'Of course. The portrait. I could not put together the connection. Delighted to make your acquaintance and I am delighted to be calling upon your lovely sister. Delighted.'

Tranville's expression was less than friendly. 'You promised the portrait soon, Jack. When will it be done?'

'Two weeks,' Jack responded. So much for Tranville forgetting about it. 'If you pay, that is.'

'I'll pay.' Tranville glared at him.

Jack nodded to Ullman. 'I will be at my mother's directly. As soon as I've seen Miss Blane to a hackney coach.'

Tranville stepped to her side. 'I will escort Miss Blane, Jack. You go with Lord Ullman.'

Jack turned toward Ariana. 'I think not.'

'Do not cross me, Jack,' Tranville snapped.

Jack's hand formed a fist. He was ready to do battle.

Ariana stepped between them. 'Go with Lord Ullman, Jack. See to your sister. Her needs take precedence this day.'

Tranville smirked.

Jack could not disagree with Ariana.

Ullman lifted his hat. 'Good day to you, Miss Blane.'

As Tranville walked away with Ariana, she turned and gave Jack an approving smile.

Jack gestured towards his mother's door. 'Come inside,' he said to Ullman.

Wilson took their things, and Jack ushered Ullman into the drawing room. The man looked eager and nervous, more like a fifteen-year-old at his first ball than an earl of mature years.

Ullman was a portly man whose face was the sort that would sport jowls in ten years. Jack imagined he would shrink with age until Nancy towered over him. It sickened Jack to think of Nancy with such a man.

Ullman glanced at Nancy's portrait, which hung on the drawing-room wall. 'So lovely.' A thought seemed to occur to him. 'Did you paint that?' He sounded surprised.

Jack felt the insult even though Ullman seemed oblivious of having made it. 'Yes. An early work of mine.'

Ullman walked over to the portrait and examined it closer. 'Upon my word. It is good.'

This was not making Jack like him any better.

'Please sit, sir.' Jack did not know how much time he had before Nancy and his mother walked in. 'And tell me of this interest in my sister.'

A beatific expression appeared on Ullman's face. 'I cannot explain it. That day in the Egyptian Hall when I saw her it was as if I had seen an angel. I could not get her out of my mind. I confess I dared not hope to see her again until I remembered the—the—the connection between your family and Lord Tranville, so I began discussing with him how to proceed.'

Jack looked him in the eye. 'I wonder that you did not seek me out for that discussion.'

Ullman turned red. 'I—I—I—Tranville acted in your stead, he told me.'

Jack merely nodded. There was no use to travel that road one more time, not when Nancy intended to accept the man.

He did, however, skewer the man with a pointed gaze. 'Tranville vouches for your character, but bear in mind if you mistreat my sister in any manner, you will answer to me.'

Ullman's eyes grew fearful.

Jack added, 'I spent ten years in the army. I am able to defend my sister in countless ways.'

Ullman nodded vigorously.

At that moment Jack's mother entered the room, and the two men stood.

'Lord Ullman, how nice to see you again.' She glanced around the room. 'Lionel did not come with you?'

'He will be here shortly, Mother.' Jack said, his tone clipped.

'I have asked Wilson to bring tea,' Jack's mother told Ullman.

Wilson served the tea, and while Jack's mother poured, the three of them engaged in a conversation that thoroughly covered the weather, past, present and to come. Jack was almost grateful when Tranville finally did walk in.

Jack's mother greeted him with cool politeness, a contrast to his spirits, which seemed inordinately high.

Into the already tense atmosphere walked Nancy, pale as paste, dark circles smudging her eyes. Jack wanted to whisk her out of the room.

'I am so sorry to keep everyone waiting.' Her voice was no more than a whisper.

Jack glanced over at her portrait. The contrast was so striking it might not be the same person. Gone was the innocence, the eager hopefulness, the sheer excitement of being alive, the essence of Nancy that Ariana insisted he had captured in the image, the very qualities of the painting that had led Ariana to speak to him that first day.

Ullman stepped over to her, taking her hand and leading her to a chair. 'Miss Vernon, the wait was a trifle when the reward is seeing you.'

Nancy indeed looked as if she needed assistance to cross the room.

'Well, well.' Tranville clasped his hands together. 'I believe we should leave Nancy and Lord Ullman alone for a time. They have matters to discuss.'

Jack forgot to care that Tranville was managing things. His concern was for his sister.

'Nancy—'

Her gaze met Jack's and she shook her head very slightly.

Tranville and his mother were almost to the door. Tranville turned. 'Come, Jack.'

Jack leaned down under the pretence of kissing his sister. He whispered in her ear, 'You do not have to do this.'

But her eyes were filled with resignation.

He tried again. 'I can take care of you and Mother—'

She shook her head and waved him away.

'Listen to me—'

'No, Jack,' she whispered angrily.

'Jack?' his mother called.

He reluctantly left the room.

In the hall, his mother said, 'We can wait in my sitting room.'

The room was off her bedchamber. Tranville walked in and went directly to a cabinet, producing a bottle of port and a glass.

'Would you like a glass, my dear?' he asked her.

She shook her head and turned away from him.

'Jack?' Tranville lifted the bottle.

Jack would welcome some drink, but not his mother's port at Tranville's invitation. 'I think not.'

Jack's mother sat and picked up some sewing.

Tranville pulled some papers from the inside pocket of his coat. 'Do you wish to read the settlement, Mary?'

She shook her head. 'Jack, will you read it and let me know if it is adequate?'

He read it through. Twice.

The document appeared thorough and detailed, every possibility addressed, all to the advantage of his sister.

'It appears to be in order.' He folded it up again and placed it on the table.

Tranville gave him a smug look.

'She will be secure for life?' his mother asked.

'She will,' Jack was forced to agree. Ullman could give Nancy more than Jack could ever dream of doing.

'Should I sign it, then?' she asked.

'Wait.' Perhaps Nancy would not go through with it.

They waited in silence, except for Tranville's tuneless humming, which nearly drove Jack mad.

Finally a mournful-looking Wilson came to the door. 'Miss Nancy says you may return to the drawing room.'

Tranville snatched up the settlement papers and they all headed for the drawing room.

When they walked in, Nancy turned to them, her eyes glistening with tears. 'Mama,' she said in a weak voice, 'you may wish me happy.'

Chapter Fifteen

That evening Tranville patted the pocket of his coat, feeling the velvet box inside. He smiled to himself. He'd intended this event to take place later, but seeing Ariana that afternoon had persuaded him that there was no need to delay.

He'd waited long enough. Playing it cool with her had not worked at all. Ariana had seemed perfectly content without his attentions.

His plan had been to wait until her portrait was complete, at which time he would formally make it his gift to her, but Jack was dawdling. Tranville decided not to wait even two more weeks. The time was now.

Tranville crossed the foyer of the theatre. He was early and only a few people had arrived for the evening's performance. Ullman was supposed to meet him here.

Ullman was a good sort, well-humoured and harmless. At least Ullman had been the spur for Tranville's renewed campaign. He felt like clapping his hands in delight.

Tranville made his way to his box. He would not show himself backstage. Better he approach Ariana later, in the Green Room. All he required was to be private with her.

He glanced around the theatre, at the lavish gilt, the rich red curtains, tier after tier of boxes. He imagined the theatre filled with three thousand people, all applauding Ariana in her role as Cleopatra. He imagined being congratulated in the Green Room afterwards, complimented on his foresight regarding London's newest sensation. He even imagined Kean approaching him to thank him for the opportunity to perform with her.

Everyone would know she belonged to him.

Ullman entered the box with a furrowed brow. 'Good evening, Tranville.'

Tranville blinked. 'I expected you to be in raptures this evening. Do not tell me something has gone wrong with your engagement.'

Ullman shook his head. 'Not at all. It is just that I met Lord Darnley outside. Apparently there are considerable rumblings about the Corn Bill. He is exceedingly worried about riots.'

Tranville waved a dismissive hand. 'Fiddle. He is being alarmist. The people would not dare raise a commotion.'

Ullman looked unconvinced. 'I wonder if I ought to send Miss Vernon—I mean, my dear Nancy—to the country. She and her mother could stay at the country house. Get acquainted with the children.'

Ullman was making this molehill of unrest into a mountain peak, Tranville thought, but it might work to his advantage to have Mary out of town.

She was the one person who depressed his spirits with her refusal to face facts. Surely she could comprehend how his life had changed, how a vigorous man such as himself needed a young wife to beget more children. His departed wife had banned him from her bed when she'd still been capable of bearing sons. What a great disappointment his wife had been, so lacking in sensitivity.

Mary had once perfectly understood his masculine needs, never complaining of other women in his life. She used to accept that a man of his nature needed variety. He had no idea what had turned her so sour.

He waved the thought of Mary away and imagined Ariana dressing for the performance tonight. His loins ached.

Soon, he promised himself. Soon he would seat himself on a chair in her dressing room and watch the tantalising process of her donning a gown.

He clapped Ullman on the shoulder. 'I am certain Mrs Vernon and Nancy would enjoy a visit to the country.'

'Thing is,' Ullman went on, 'I must stay here. These matters before the Lords are too vitally important.'

Tranville nodded in agreement, although he could not see a man like Ullman affecting the decisions that needed to be made on the Corn Bill. 'You could send the ladies without you if it makes you feel easier.'

Ullman rubbed his chin. 'I am considering a special licence and marrying her right away. It would be so much better for her to go to the country as my wife.'

At that moment Edwin entered the box. 'Did I hear you talk of a wife? Are you marrying, Ullman?' He sat next to his father and leaned a foot against the box's railing. 'Who is the lady?'

Ullman beamed. 'You were present when I first laid eyes upon her. I am marrying Miss Vernon.'

'Nancy Vernon!' Edwin sat up straight. 'Good God.'

Tranville grabbed his arm and leaned into his ear. 'You will keep your mouth shut or I'll cut off your quarterly portion.'

Edwin blinked. 'Lovely girl,' he muttered to Ullman.

'I am considering a special licence and marrying without delay.'

Edwin gave him a lascivious look. 'You have reason to rush?'

Ullman began to prose on about the Corn Laws and the threats of unrest in the city. Edwin looked alarmed.

While those two fools fretted over unrest that would never come to pass, Tranville consulted the programme in his hand, looking for Ariana's name. The play was a comedy, *The Country Girl*, and Ariana had a minor part.

He threw down the programme in disgust. She was not listed. That sort of treatment would soon change when she, not her mother, played the leading role.

Three hours later Mr Arnold stuck his head in the dressing room. 'Ladies, time to make your appearances in the Green Room. Some haste, if you please.'

The performance had gone well, and Ariana and three of the other actresses who had walk-on parts lounged in their dressing room. The other three roused themselves at Mr Arnold's directive, and now hurried to clean their faces of stage make-up and dress in their prettiest gowns. Ariana remained in her chair, feeling no compunction to move.

Mr Arnold gave her a severe look. 'Ariana, enough dallying. I expect you in the Green Room in five minutes. The gentlemen are waiting.'

'Yes, sir,' she replied.

After he left the other girls laughed. 'You care nothing of the waiting gentlemen, do you?' one said to her.

Her housemate Susan said, 'She's too moon-eyed over her artist.'

Ariana smiled. 'Can you blame me?'

'He's handsome enough, but he'll never have as much money as Lord Tranville,' Susan admitted. 'I saw Tranville in his box tonight. His son was with him. I do not see why your artist dislikes the son so.'

'I would heed his warnings, none the less,' Ariana said.

Susan nodded. 'I will, but only because the fellow drinks too much. Are you still resolved to break the father's heart?'

Ariana sighed dramatically. 'He has transferred his interest to another, I have heard.'

'Well, she's a lucky one,' another of the actresses said. 'I wish I could persuade him to look my way.'

Susan laughed. 'You have been trying that all season.'

She was welcome to him, Ariana thought. All she wanted was to go home and crawl into her bed. The sooner she slept, the sooner morning would come and she could go to Jack and find out what had happened with Nancy.

She dallied longer than five minutes and wound up walking to the Green Room alone.

As soon as she entered, Tranville approached her. 'May I speak to you, Miss Vernon?'

She had no wish to converse with him, but Mr Arnold had taken notice of her late entrance and would not like it if she cut such an important gentleman.

'Of course, sir.' She stepped away from the doorway.

'Speak with me in private,' he said. 'I beg you, allow me a few minutes.'

He intended to tell her he was to be married, she thought. Foolish of him to think it would matter to her. All that mattered was his marriage would free her to be openly seen with Jack.

'Very well,' she responded.

She thought they would speak directly outside the room but he brought her back into the theatre, leading her into his box. There were still some candles burning there, but the light was dim.

He bade her sit down.

To her surprise, he dropped to his knees and pulled something from beneath his coat.

A velvet box.

'This is a gift for you.' He placed it in her hands.

She felt a surge of anxiety. 'You must not—'

He put his hand over hers, his face inches away. 'Open it,' he demanded. He felt dangerous at that moment. As Jack had warned her he could be.

She opened the box.

Inside was a bracelet, sparkling with diamonds and emeralds.

She gasped. 'This is not for me.' He was merely showing it to her, for her opinion perhaps.

'It most certainly is for you.' He lifted it out of the box. 'See? It matches your eyes.'

She pushed his hand away. 'I do not accept gifts.' He *knew* that. 'My position is unchanged on the matter.' She stood.

He seized her wrist and made her sit again. 'You misunderstand me. This is a mere sample of what I am able to give to you.'

'I want nothing from you.'

He tossed the bracelet aside and grasped her other hand. 'Let me explain.' He paused as if searching for words. 'Ullman made me think of it.'

Ullman?

He peered directly into her eyes. 'I am not asking you to be my mistress. I am proposing marriage.'

'Marriage!' she cried.

'Marriage.' He nodded. 'Do me the honour of being my wife, becoming my baroness.'

Her stomach turned. *She* was the woman he planned to marry, the woman for whom he would cut off Jack's mother's allowance.

She grasped at straws. 'You cannot marry an actress.'

He laughed and patted her hand. 'Why not? Did not Elizabeth Farren marry Lord Derby?'

Ariana remembered being told that the actress-turned-countess, Elizabeth Farren, had bounced her on her knee when she'd been three years old. 'No matter. I cannot.'

His voice dropped and his eyes grew flinty. 'Has Jack spoken against me?'

'Jack?' His manner alarmed her.

He held her hand so tightly it hurt. 'He turned you against me, did he? I swear I'll ruin him.'

He must not blame Jack. Her mind raced. She had to remedy this.

She put on an indignant expression. 'This does not involve my portrait artist, sir. It involves *me*. My acting career.'

He loosened his grip. 'Do not fear. You shall have your chance on stage. You will be a sensation in *Antony and Cleopatra*. I would not deprive you of that moment of glory.'

'And afterwards?' She already knew the answer. A baroness did not appear on stage.

He laughed. 'As my baroness, you will be far too busy with important matters to think about the theatre. We shall become a powerful force in London. You for your beauty, and me for my influence. You will hold grand balls and be hostess at important political dinners. We can travel. To Paris. To Naples. To Vienna.'

It sounded like death to her. One whole night with Jack would be worth more than a lifetime with this man, and Jack was the only man she knew for whom she would consider giving up the stage.

She took a deep breath. 'Lord Tranville, you, indeed, do me an honour. I must consider your proposal very carefully.'

'You cannot say yes?' His brows rose.

She needed to tread carefully. 'Not an immediate yes.'

He released her. 'I will take that as a yes.'

'Please do not. But I shall consider your offer in all seriousness.'

'I do not see any reason for delay.' He spread out his hands. 'I can give you the world.'

She moved away. 'You would not wish me to say an impulsive no, would you? Giving up the stage is no trifling matter to me.' She must consider a way out of this, a way to make him not want her. 'I must be certain.'

'You will not miss being an actress. How can I convince you?' He grabbed her in his arms and kissed her.

If he thought his kiss would convince her, he was mistaken. It almost made her gag.

She pushed him away and spoke sharply, 'If you take liberties with me, sir, I shall not believe your intent is honourable. I will not be tricked into a liaison.'

'It is no trick.' He responded with a hungry look. 'I want you for my wife and nothing will stop me.'

She stood. 'I wish to leave now, sir. If you will pardon me.'

He stood as well and thrust the velvet box with its valuable bracelet into her hands. 'You must accept my gift.'

She handed it back to him. 'If I accept your offer, I will accept your gift. Now please escort me back to the Green Room or move out of my way so I may return there alone.'

He pressed himself against her. 'I will escort you, my dearest love.'

Somehow she bore his company back to the Green Room. He would not leave her side, and to her dismay, he whispered his intention into her mother's ear. Her mother's immediate reaction was displeased shock, but later she took Ariana aside when Tranville was distracted by Mr Arnold.

'You fool,' whispered her mother. 'You did not accept him right away? We could be set for life.'

We?

Of course. Her mother would relish such a close relationship to a baron, especially one with deep pockets.

'I have no wish to give up the theatre,' Ariana explained.

Her mother laughed, and some people turned their heads at the sound. She came even closer to Ariana's ear. 'The theatre is nothing. Say yes and marry as quickly as you can before he comes to his senses.' Her mother flounced away.

Ariana interrupted Tranville's conversation with Mr Arnold. 'If you gentlemen will pardon me, I bid you goodnight.'

She moved quickly and had almost got away when Tranville caught up with her. 'My carriage awaits you, my dear.'

She was forced to ride with him and when it pulled up to her residence, he manoeuvred her into another kiss. Ariana finally escaped and hurried inside.

From a gap in the curtain of the drawing room, she watched for his carriage to pull away.

She walked slowly upstairs without any idea of what to do and wishing it was not the middle of the night. She would have to wait until morning to tell Jack.

Jack entered the Seven Stars near Lincoln's Inn Fields, the latest tavern on a search through at least a dozen dark and noisy taverns starting near Somerset House. He'd been searching for Michael all night, through the dark London streets in a widening circumference. The rumblings of Badajoz pursued him each step of the way, but he ignored them.

Nancy's happiness depended upon it.

Michael had not attended his classes that day, Jack had discovered. He'd not been in his rooms. One of his fellow architectural students told Jack that Michael had been with a young woman the day before, the same day he'd failed to come to dinner, the day Nancy had made her decision to marry Ullman. It did not take much to surmise that Nancy, when missing, had gone to Michael and had told him of her plans.

Jack made his way through the narrow tavern, searching each table, suspecting it would be to no avail. He seriously considered giving up his search, but was not eager to brave the dark, shadowed streets again and the memories that assaulted him there.

In the very farthest corner of the room, he saw Michael, sitting alone at a small table, a tankard of ale in his hands. He did not even notice Jack's approach.

'I have been searching for you.' Jack lowered himself in the seat across from the elusive man.

Only then did Michael look up. 'Jack.' He lifted his tankard. 'Have some ale.'

Jack gave his order to the tavern girl and turned back to Michael. 'No one has seen you all day.'

Michael shrugged. 'I took a very long walk. Through Mayfair, actually. A personal study of the architecture there.' He took another sip of ale. 'Mount Street has some interesting townhouses. I wished to examine the style and construction of them.'

Mount Street was where Ullman's townhouse was located.

Jack's ale was set down before him. 'Your conclusion?'

'I could assess the residences as being quite fine.'

Michael's expression was pained. 'But I cannot aspire to live in one of them.' He drained his tankard and asked for another.

Jack peered at him. 'Are you foxed?'

Michael gave him a wan smile. 'I wish. Unfortunately, I have been doing more walking than drinking.'

At least Jack would be able to reason with him. 'I came to talk to you about my sister.'

Michael looked away.

Jack persisted. 'I know Nancy sought you out the other day, so I surmise she told you of Ullman.'

A muscle in Michael's cheek flexed. 'I wish her happy.'

Jack leaned forwards. 'She is not happy. She cannot be. She is miserable, but I cannot talk her out of this folly.'

'It is not folly to marry a man who is able to give her every luxury in life,' Michael countered in a mournful tone.

Jack dismissed his words. 'Would you marry a woman for whom you have no regard, simply for her money?'

Michael looked defiant. 'I might.'

'You would not, and neither should Nancy marry Ullman.' Jack levelled a direct gaze at him. 'You know my sister's character. You know her romantic nature. This engagement to Ullman fulfils none of those romantic notions of hers. It is wrong for her, and I want to know what you intend to do about it.'

'I?' Michael's brows rose. 'I can do nothing. I have nothing to offer any woman. I must complete one more year of study and even after that it will take time for me to earn a creditable income.'

So he had been thinking about it. Jack was encouraged. 'You know wealth means nothing to Nancy. She is doing this to please my mother.'

'More than to please her mother.' Michael drank again.

'Do you not know that Tranville will cut off your mother's funds and ruin your chances as an artist if she does not marry? She is in a desperate position, Jack.'

Nancy knew of Tranville's threat?

He waited until Michael looked back at him. 'Listen to me. We must not allow Tranville to blackmail us into sacrificing Nancy's happiness. I will take care of my mother, Michael. You must take care of Nancy.'

'I cannot—'

Jack would not hear it. 'I will help you as much as I can. I suspect your father will as well. Nancy would not mind if all she had was one miserable room as long as she shared it with you. Indeed, she would find such a situation romantic.'

Michael shook his head. 'She has never indicated anything of the sort towards me. No romantic feelings—'

'She ran to you first, did she not? She told you more about her reasons for marrying than she told her family. Why else would she do that unless she felt a romantic attachment to you?'

'It is friendship she feels.' He lifted his tankard to his lips.

'Fustian.' Jack pushed Michael's hand down. The ale splashed on the wooden table top. 'Listen, Michael. You, me, Nancy, my mother—we will all muddle through somehow no matter what Tranville threatens. I am persuaded we will have food enough to eat, clothes on our backs and roofs over our heads. Life will improve as time progresses.'

Michael averted his gaze.

Jack was losing patience. 'Michael, look me in the eye and tell me you do not love Nancy, and I will walk out of here and never trouble you again.'

Michael looked him in the eye. His words were clear and deliberate. 'I love your sister more than I love my life.'

The intensity of emotion in Michael's words stunned Jack and echoed inside him. He could not help but glance away.

Michael's father had once told Jack to look for a revelation in his art, that moment when he knew what separated his work from that of other artists, that piece of truth that was uniquely his. He'd thought Sir Cecil was merely spouting nonsense until Ariana had shown him the truth in his art.

Jack felt his whole body go warm, as if he'd been suddenly bundled in a blanket. He knew the truth in Michael's words was the truth in his heart.

He loved Ariana more than he loved life.

He wanted to be with her always, could not imagine a day without seeing her smile, without basking in her energy and optimism, her belief that everything would turn out right.

He almost jumped off his chair. He wanted to dance on the table to tell the world he loved Ariana and would happily live with her in one miserable room as long as they were together.

He looked back at Michael and it was all he could do to contain his excitement.

Michael gripped his tankard as if he were gripping a life line. 'I will say it again, if you did not hear. I love Nancy more than life itself. I love her enough to do what is best for her. I love her enough to respect her wishes, even if it puts a dagger through my heart, even if it means I must let her go.'

These words dampened Jack's enthusiasm.

Jack looked him in the eye again. 'Do not confuse desire with duty, Michael. My sister thinks she must martyr herself for our mother and for me, but do not delude yourself into thinking she desires being Ullman's wife. Look beyond what she has said to you into what is in her heart. She has this romantic notion that she is the only one who can save her mother and brother, but you, Michael, are the only one who can save her. The question is, are you man enough to try?'

Michael looked miserable. 'I cannot answer you now, Jack.'

Jack knew his own answer. He would allow nothing to end his time with Ariana. He intended to ask her to share all her tomorrows with him. He intended to ask her to marry him.

If he could only convince Michael to do the same. 'You do not have much time. Nancy seems determined to rush into this marriage. You must act swiftly.'

Chapter Sixteen

Ariana let herself into Jack's studio early the next morning. To her surprise, he was not standing at his easel. The curtains were still drawn and the room was empty. She hung her pelisse on the hook by the door.

The sounds of loud breathing came from the bedchamber.

She smiled and tiptoed across the studio. Quietly she stood at the side of his bed and gazed down at him. He lay on his back, one arm flung above his head, the covers twisted between his legs. As when they made love, he wore nothing. Her eyes lit on the scars here and there on his chest, reminders that he had not always stood behind an easel.

She sat on the bed and gently traced each mark of some Frenchman's sword with her finger, glad, at least, that he need never face the horror of war again.

He turned his head and mumbled something unintelligible. His eyelids twitched and opened. It took him a moment to focus on her.

Then he smiled and reached for her.

She fell into his arms willingly. 'Good morning, Jack.'

She'd intended to walk into the studio and immediately tell him of Tranville, but she could not bear to speak of it upon his awakening.

'You are a welcome sight.' His voice was raspy with sleep.

He pulled her down into a long deep kiss and she vowed that she would somehow make everything right for them. Rid them of Tranville's interference in their lives.

She wanted to love Jack for a long time, so long that she refused to think of their ever parting. He might never speak the words of love to her, but he showed the emotion whenever he looked at her, touched her. In his painting of her.

Between kisses, he undressed her, tossing her clothing off the side of the bed. His lips against her breasts were as familiar to her as breathing and his hand caressing her flesh was now a recognisable thrill. He knew exactly how to give her the greatest pleasure possible. She could only hope she gave him the same in return.

Today's lovemaking took on a special poignancy for her. Their relationship, already so complicated it had to be kept secret, was bound to become even more difficult now that Tranville had proposed to her.

Jack's skill at arousing her drove those worries from her mind. When he groaned in pleasure at her touch, she felt triumphant and powerful. It was like a dance between them, first her move, then his, then they moved together.

Some unspoken communication between them set a leisurely pace, unhurried, but as intense and sensuous as it had been the day before when they'd rushed through lovemaking.

Ariana gasped when he entered her. She pressed her hands against the firm muscles of his buttocks, holding him fast lest the connection between them be broken. As their passion grew, she stopped thinking and merely lost herself in the dance, which became faster, wilder as he drove into her and the intensity of sensation grew and grew. She heard her own voice making urgent sounds, begging him to move faster.

When she thought she could bear it no more, the pleasure reached its crescendo and she cried out. A second later he spilled his seed inside her, his convulsing also as endearingly familiar as a dance's final bow.

Ariana seemed to float back to the bed, again feeling the texture of the bed linens against her back, the cool air on her skin. He made a partially successful attempt to cover her with a blanket and nestled her in his arms.

'I could get used to this way of waking up.' His voice sounded full of emotion.

An emotion she shared.

She kissed his bare skin. 'I am surprised you were still asleep. I expected you to be at the easel.'

He nestled her closer but paused before speaking. 'I was out very late last night.'

'You were?' He'd been avoiding the streets after dark. 'Did you have a repeat of your visions?'

'Almost.' He held her close. 'I heard the sounds. I could almost feel the visions pressing against my brain.'

She hugged him. 'But it was not like before?'

'No.'

They lay entwined in each other's arms for a few more precious moments. She thought she felt a tension build in him.

Finally he said, 'We must get up. Get to work.'

He rose from the bed and walked to the pitcher and basin on the bureau to wash. Ariana pulled out the sheer muslin dress.

'Why were you out so late?' she asked, putting the dress on over her head.

He watched her, his eyes warm. 'I was looking for Michael.'

'Did you find him?' She fixed the gold chains around her waist.

'I did and I tried to convince him to talk Nancy out of this marriage, but I am not at all certain he will do it.' He put on his painting shirt and trousers. 'He admitted being in love with her.'

She smiled at that, a sad smile because love seemed so complicated for all of them.

He went on. 'When Nancy left you the other day, she went to Michael.'

Ariana was not surprised. 'She was running to Michael when I first found her.'

When they were both dressed, they walked out to the studio. Jack opened the curtains and set up his easel. Ariana made tea in the galley. She discovered some biscuits in a tin for Jack's breakfast. He ate quickly and began readying his paints, poking the small bladders with a tack and squeezing paint from them onto his palette.

She put the tea things away and leaned against the galley doorway. 'I have to tell you something.'

He smiled over at her. 'I have to tell you something as well, but you must go first.'

'I discovered who Tranville intends to marry,' she began.

His expression turned sour. 'Who is it?'

She inhaled a very deep breath. 'It is me.'

Jack stared at her in stunned silence, not believing his ears. 'You?'

She nodded. 'He proposed last night.'

He could barely make himself speak. 'What reply did you give him?'

Her posture went rigid and her eyes grew wide. 'I told him I needed time to consider his offer.'

He could only stare at her.

He'd just begun to hope for a future between them. He had been about to agree they could declare their attachment openly. He intended to propose marriage to her himself. Now it all seemed impossible.

She stared back at him. 'Jack. I am not going to accept him.'

He turned away, but said, 'He is wealthy. You would become a baroness.'

Her voice was tense. 'If you do not think those things should matter to your sister, why should they matter to me?'

He had no counter to that.

Suddenly his hopes for a future with Ariana seemed dashed. What would Tranville do to Ariana if she refused him? What would he do to Jack's mother if she chose Jack?

He faced her again. 'What does Tranville threaten if you do not marry him?'

'Threaten?' Her voice rose very high. She cleared her throat. 'His only threat is to end my career on the stage if I do marry him.'

Jack would never have asked her to give up the theatre.

He turned back to the easel. 'We should work.'

She walked over to the *chaise-longue* and assumed the pose she'd used for both portraits. Her expression, however, was troubled.

Jack dipped his brush in some of the white and dabbed at the canvas. His brush seemed to move at random.

'I will make him change his mind,' she said. 'I will make him think it is his idea, not mine, and then he will have reason to feel guilty instead of vindictive.'

Jack could not see a way back to her. If she married Tranville, she was gone, but even if she did not, Tranville would never sit still for Jack being the man who stole her from him. He would find a means of taking away everything that meant something to her.

'Do not be too upset, Jack.' Her voice was low. 'Please.'

He tried to focus on the painting. 'This is not good news, no matter what you decide.'

'No matter what I decide!' Her voice was indignant. 'There is only one choice.'

Somehow they got through the morning but it had been a quiet, mournful time. When the mantel clock struck one, Jack declared their session over. Ariana said she had a rehearsal to attend.

Helping her dress into her street clothes was a difficult intimacy to endure. He was tempted to thumb his nose at Tranville, his family, the theatre, even art itself, and jump back into bed with her.

Instead, he did not even kiss her. 'I will not need you tomorrow,' he told her. 'I can finish this in a day or two.'

She responded with a questioning look. 'You told Tranville two weeks.'

Because he wanted as much time with her as possible.

'To put on the finishing touches and to make the copy, I will need two weeks. It is not crucial for you to pose for me.'

She looked wounded and confused.

He tried to mollify her. 'I am engaged most of the day tomorrow with Lord Ullman,' he explained. 'Ullman apparently wishes to show us his townhouse and God knows what else.'

'Very well,' she murmured.

A few minutes later as Jack watched her walk up the street towards the Strand, he had a notion he understood how Michael had felt after parting with Nancy.

* * *

Nancy was seated in her room, wrapped in a woollen shawl because the fire was merely one measly dying coal, the coal bucket was empty, and she did not want to rouse herself to get more. She just sat, staring into the flame of one candle on the table beside her. All she wanted was to sit alone and be miserable.

There was a knock on the door and Wilson's voice. 'Mr Harper has called, miss.'

Michael! She bounded out of the chair.

'I will be there directly, Wilson,' she called through the door. 'Tell him to wait. One minute.'

She turned around, looking down at her gown, wondering if it was good enough, but changing it would only delay seeing him.

It would have to do.

She brought her candle to her dressing table and hurriedly tidied her hair. To think she'd almost refused to have the maid pin up her hair this morning. She peered at her face in the mirror and rubbed at the dark smudges under her eyes and pinched her cheeks to put some colour in her face. She looked terrible. She should not even show her face to Michael, she looked so awful.

Once when she had almost refused the chance to walk to the shops with Michael because she looked a fright, he told her it was foolish to think she could be anything but pretty.

The memory made her smile.

She hurried downstairs, but slowed as she approached the drawing room. It would be so painful to see him, painful to part from him again.

She peeked into the drawing room. He stood with his head bowed, so very still. It frightened her a little. He looked like the man who had come that day to tell Mama that Papa was dead. She'd been very little, but she remembered.

'Michael?'

He lifted his head and smiled a bittersweet smile. 'I had no classes. I came to see if you would like to take some air.'

Just like before, when they'd been carefree friends.

'I would like that very much,' she replied.

Wilson must have been hovering because he appeared with her cloak, hat and gloves. They were soon on the street.

'Where would you like to walk? To the shops?' He sounded almost like the Michael who used to take her on walks.

She sighed. 'Do you know what I would wish? I wish there was somewhere to walk like the park in Bath by the Royal Crescent, somewhere with lots of trees and greenery. I want to smell spring in the air.' *One last time*, she almost added.

It felt as if life would end when she married Ullman.

Michael did not answer right away. 'I suppose we could walk to St James's Park. There is much greenery there.'

'Oh, let us go there, then!' She took hold of his arm.

Michael frowned. 'I am not certain your mother would approve, though. The park has a reputation.'

She blinked up at him. 'A reputation?'

He tilted his head. 'Well, let me say that two people might be very private there.'

She stared into his eyes. 'My mother need not be told of it.'

They walked in silence for a while until Michael spoke. 'I saw Jack last night.'

'Did you?' She did not wish to talk to him about Jack.

'He said you are to marry very soon.'

She did not wish to talk of that either, *especially* not that. 'We are to be married by licence. It is faster.' The banns would not have to be read in each of their home parishes for three consecutive Sundays and no Certificates of Banns would be required as proof.

'You could marry in two weeks, then,' he murmured.

That is exactly what she had been fearing, but she and Michael often had the same thoughts at the same time.

They fell quiet again until reaching Charing Cross.

'This is such a romantic place,' Nancy said.

'Romantic?' Michael sounded sceptical. 'It marks the spot where the coffin of Queen Eleanor last rested before she was entombed in Westminster Cathedral.'

She pushed him a little. 'It was romantic for King Edward to mark all those places with crosses. This was the last.'

He laughed. 'That is romantic? I must take your word for it.'

She shot him a vexed glance. 'Oh, you are teasing me.'

He touched her hand. 'I have missed teasing you.'

Nancy's eyes stung with tears. She blinked them away. 'Let us hurry to the park.'

Hand in hand they ran the short distance to the park and were out of breath when they reached its wide path. Some others were taking advantage of the fine day, but the park was by no means crowded.

Nancy looked up at the trees, holding on to her hat as she did so. The trees were tall and showed spring buds. The lake was dotted with geese gliding in its shimmering blue water. It took Nancy's breath away.

'We must find a bench so that you can rest,' Michael said.

She did not at all feel fatigued, but she let Michael lead her to a bench facing the lake. Fragrant green shrubbery surrounded them. When they sat Nancy could no longer see the other people on the path. It felt to her like no one else existed in the world except her and Michael.

'I am glad you brought me here, Michael,' she whispered to him. This would be a memory to cherish for a lifetime.

'I wanted to be private with you,' he murmured, his voice both enticing and sad. 'To talk to you.'

She did not want to talk. What could she say to him? She just wanted to be with him, to pretend that this moment would never pass.

He gazed into her eyes. 'I need to make certain you are happy.'

'Happy?' Her voice rose and her tears could no longer be blinked away.

He gazed at her with such anguish, she thought she could not bear it. It seemed as if time had slowed down, as if he moved very slowly, putting his arm around her back, enfolding her against his strong chest. He held her like that for the longest time.

While her ear rested against his heart, he spoke, 'If— if I had anything to offer you I would not let you marry Ullman. I would marry you myself, but I have no money at all while I am finishing my studies and no prospects for the future if I do not finish.'

She felt the timbre of his words through his body, words she longed to hear, but words that could change nothing.

'I love you too much to cause you the sort of suffering you would endure if I claimed you for my own,' he went on. 'But it is killing me to think of you with any other man.'

She slid her arms around his neck and looked into his face. 'You do love me, Michael?'

'With all my heart.'

He took her chin in his fingers and seemed to consume her with his eyes. She felt such a rush of feeling, feelings she had never felt before. That morning she'd thought she'd been dying, but now, this touch, this gaze from Michael made her feel more alive than ever before.

She took a breath and inhaled his so-familiar scent. He smelled wonderful. 'I—I thought you were my friend, Michael. Now I know I was wrong. You are my love. My only love.'

His eyes sparked with pain but, still holding her chin, he leaned down and placed his lips on hers.

Her first kiss, she thought, dismissing Lord Ulmann's slobbering attempt. Michael's was the kiss of which romances were created.

He kissed her again and again, doing lovely things with his tongue. Who would have guessed a man's tongue in one's mouth would be so thrilling? The kisses made her feel all achy inside, but in a wonderful way.

Abruptly he pulled away and set her at an arm's length from him. It felt as if he'd suddenly travelled as far as the West Indies.

'I cannot trust myself, Nancy. We must take care.' He was breathing harder than when they'd been running.

She suddenly understood something. These were the sorts of feelings men and women experienced before they tumbled into bed with each other. She understood as a woman what the pleasures of lovemaking could be.

With the right man.

Her tears erupted once more. 'I do not want to stop, Michael,' she cried. 'I do not want to ever part from you, but what am I to do?'

His lip trembled and his eyes turned red. 'I cannot offer you anything but my love. I have no money. No position. No prospects until my studies are done.'

'And then you will go back to Bath, to the position that awaits you?' He had told her many times that an architect in Bath, a great friend of his father's, was willing to take him into his firm.

He seemed to brace himself. 'Yes.'

In the short space of a year Michael would be ready to marry.

She tried not to sob. 'If only I were not trapped.'

He looked into her eyes. 'Jack says you are not trapped, that he can support you and your mother.'

'I know he thinks that.' She pressed her hand against her forehead. 'But Tranville vows to ruin him and he has cut Mama off without a care.' For all she knew, Tranville could ruin Michael as well. 'Can I take such a chance with their futures? I should never forgive myself if I caused them suffering.'

Michael glanced away. 'If only I could help all of you. If I had even one year, I swear I could support you and your mother. My father could help Jack find work, as well.'

'You are so dear.' She dared to take his hand in hers. 'How I wish all this would disappear and we could be back in Bath.'

He made a crooked smile and squeezed her hand. 'Nancy, we never knew each other in Bath.'

She fluttered her lashes. 'But we should know each other now.'

'Where is Lord Ullman's estate?' he asked, his voice cracking.

'Lincolnshire.' Far away from Bath. She would never see Michael. If only she could live near him, see him sometimes, speak to him, she could fight off despair, but he would never come to Lincolnshire.

Tears flowed again and Michael held her once more. 'I am so sorry, Nancy. So very sorry.'

Chapter Seventeen

Ariana spent a miserable afternoon. Luckily Mr Kean pleaded illness and ended the rehearsal even before it began, so no one discovered she could not remember her lines, her marks, or anything, really, except that Jack had avoided looking at her when she'd left the studio.

She wished she could be rid of Tranville once and for all. He blanketed everything and everyone with misery.

That evening she avoided the Green Room and instead asked Henry to walk her home. Swearing him to secrecy, she confided in him about Tranville's proposal. She did not tell him of falling in love with Jack.

'The best *on dit* of the century, and I must not speak of it.' He rolled his eyes and sighed.

She laughed. 'It is not quite that important.'

Loud voices came from inside a nearby tavern. There was an atmosphere of tension in the streets that had been absent when she and Jack had walked this same route. It was all about the Corn Bill. The House of Lords was debating a bill to prevent the price of grain dropping. Now that the war had ended, grain from Europe was driving down the prices and landowners' ability to sustain their estates was threatened. Unfortunately the bill being debated would increase the cost of bread.

Ariana heard 'We need bread!' coming from the tavern. She felt a shiver of fear, reminding her of when Jack had been overcome by his memory of Badajoz.

Henry strolled along as if oblivious to the disquiet of the streets. 'You should have kept the bracelet, you know,' he mused.

She gave him an exasperated look. 'You know I do not accept such gifts.'

He shook a finger at her. 'You should. Selling that bracelet would yield enough to support yourself for a year or two.'

She laughed. 'Believe me, it would have cost me much more to keep it. Tranville attaches himself like a leech. Even if you do not give him an inch, he takes an ell.'

As they passed by another tavern a man burst from the door, practically colliding with them. He was full of drink. 'We'll send those lords to the devil, you mark my words.'

Ariana jumped away in fright.

Henry manoeuvred them away from the man and continued as if nothing had happened. 'You must do something scandalous if you wish to be rid of Tranville. Something that would make him look buffoonish. Gentlemen despise looking buffoonish.'

She tried to compose herself. 'What would make him look buffoonish?' She added sarcastically, 'He is an important man.'

He grinned. 'You could have a wild, public affair with someone totally his inferior, such as—' he paused '—an artist or some such person.'

He and their other housemates often teased her about Jack, although she admitted nothing to them.

'How could I be certain Tranville would not take out his wrath against the artist?' Her question was rhetorical.

Henry threw up his hands. 'Then do something outrageous. Dance naked in a fountain or something!'

She gave him a playful punch. 'The weather is still too chilly for that.'

They dropped the subject, but the word *naked* hung in her mind.

The next day Ariana had a message delivered to Tranville asking him to meet her at Jack's studio to view the portrait. Jack would be away with his mother and sister at Ullman's townhouse.

She let herself in to Jack's studio, as she had done so many times before. The curtains were drawn and this time no sounds of sleep could be heard. She peeked into the bedchamber and her heart lurched at the site of the tangled bed linen. She walked over, running her fingers over the blanket, resisting the temptation to make up the bed. She lifted the pillow to her nose and inhaled the scent of him.

She wanted him. Was desolate without him.

Wrenching herself away, she hurried out to the studio and opened the curtains to bring in the light. Carefully she took the cloth off the canvas and gazed at her image. Cleopatra, nearly naked.

The clock chimed three, the time she'd asked Tranville to appear. He kept her waiting fifteen more minutes. Finally she saw his carriage draw up to the entrance.

When she let him inside, his face was flushed with excitement. 'I am eager to see the portrait at last. There is no time to waste to get it to the engraver.'

She helped him off with his top coat, hating touching even the cloth of his clothes.

'Where is Jack?' He clapped his hands together and looked around.

'He is attending to a family matter,' she replied.

'Ah, yes.' He nodded. 'Calling on Ullman.'

'Should we have waited for him?' she asked.

He gave her a mooning look. 'Not at all. I relish the chance to be alone with you.'

She cringed.

He followed her over to the easel, breathing audibly in his apparent excitement.

She stopped him before he reached it. 'I warn you, it is unlike any portrait you have ever seen.'

He smiled knowingly. 'How can it not be when it is of you?'

She made herself laugh gaily. 'Not of me, recall. It is Cleopatra.'

She stepped out of his way so he could view the canvas.

He stared, unmoving, not speaking.

'Is it not grand?' She exaggerated the excitement in her voice.

He still did not speak. His complexion grew even redder, and she felt triumphant. He was reacting in the way she had desired.

'I cannot wait to see it on playbills and magazines and print shops,' she went on, rubbing it in as vigorously as she could. 'Will it not bring hordes of people to the play? Will not everyone talk of it?'

He still stared.

The painting looked even more wonderful than the last time she had seen it. Cleopatra lounged on the chaise, facing the artist, her expression showing precisely how Ariana felt when Jack was about to make love to her. Her hair was loose about her shoulders as if ready for bedding, and her lips were red and slightly pursed for kissing. The pink of her skin showed through the transparent gown, leaving little to the imagination. There was no doubt at all that Cleopatra was naked under the sheer fabric.

Tranville finally spoke. 'What is the meaning of this?' His voice sounded like a growl.

She pretended to misinterpret him. 'See? It shows Cleopatra, the seductress. Most artists show Cleopatra dying with the asp, but I thought that would be too dreary. This portrait depicts the queen's power over men and her own ambition. Do you not like all the nuances of white Jack painted? It is such a contrast to her earthiness, is it not? Was that not brilliant?'

His fingers flexed. 'You are naked.'

She laughed, acting as if he'd made a joke. 'I am hardly naked. Except for my feet.'

Her feet were bare but for a gold ring Jack had painted on one of her toes.

'You undressed for Jack.' He suddenly sounded dangerous.

She made herself smile patiently. 'I dressed as Cleopatra.'

'Whose idea was this? To—to pose naked,' he sputtered. 'Was it Jack's?'

Inside her anxiety grew, but she made herself sound gay. 'It was my idea, of course. What would Jack know about Cleopatra?'

Tranville swung away from the portrait to face her. 'What has been going on here while you forbade me to visit? I did not pay Jack to bed you.'

She took a step back. 'Bed me? Do not be ridiculous, sir. You commissioned a portrait, which you promised was to be *my* possession. I told Jack what to paint, and I like what he did.'

'Do not lie to me, Ariana. I do not take well to lies.' His eyes bulged with anger.

She had to pretend not to be affected. 'Now you are being ridiculous. You are the one who decided to attach yourself to me. I am an actress and I shall always behave like an actress. This painting is perfect for me. It will interest people in coming to see my performances. They will talk of me and write about me, as they did my mother in her grandest days. That is what I want.'

'Are you trying to flummox me?' He advanced closer. 'Because if you are, I will not be pleased.'

She put her acting skill into play. 'I am not flummoxing you, Lord Tranville. This is the portrait of Cleopatra that will catapult me into fame. I shall be London's latest sensation—'

'This is Jack's doing,' he muttered. He pointed to the portrait. 'He convinced you to pose for this. He told you that nonsense about success.'

She stared him down. 'Of course he did not. It was solely my idea—'

He peered into her face. 'I have no doubt Jack made you think so. He wants to make me look like a fool.'

'How can *my* portrait make *you* look like a fool?' She made her voice incredulous, even though she wanted the portrait to do precisely that.

'Because it is no secret that I am determined to make you my wife,' he shot back. 'And no wife of mine will pose in the nude.'

Ariana lifted her chin. 'I have not accepted you, Lord Tranville.'

He glared at her. 'But you will. Because I will see you never work on the London stage again if you do not marry me.'

She put her hands on her hips. 'You cannot scare me,

sir! There are other theatres. If I am a sensation elsewhere, you can hardly stop me from returning to London.'

'Consider this, then.' His voice was deceptively mild. 'If you do not agree to marry me, I will ruin Jack. I will make certain he never paints again. Do not doubt I can do that.'

She did not let her gaze waver, but inside she wanted to scream in protest.

He straightened. 'Furthermore, I will prevent his sister from marrying Ullman. I arranged that betrothal and I can undo it—'

That was no threat.

Droplets of spittle spewed out from his mouth. 'Jack's mother has been dependent upon my generosity since her husband died. I will withdraw my financial support from her. Jack will be forced back into the army, and I'll have him sent to the West Indies where he will likely die of the fever. His mother and sister will wind up in the poor house—'

Ariana wanted to weep, but, none the less, she held up her hand in defiance. 'I do not see how this affects me.'

He leaned into her face with a dangerous look. 'Mark my words, I will do it! Unless you get rid of that painting and marry me, I will exact my revenge upon Jack and his family as well as on you.'

She made herself give him a sarcastic expression. 'You will cause those people unspeakable suffering unless I agree to marry you and destroy the portrait?' She threw her head back and laughed, covering her growing despair. 'How very lover-like of you, my lord.'

The door suddenly opened. Ariana looked up to see Jack staring at her in angry surprise. His sister stood behind him.

'What are you doing in my studio?' he asked.

What could get worse? 'Why, hello, Jack.' She forced a cheerful voice. 'I am showing Tranville my portrait.'

He removed his coat and hat and walked towards her, looking precisely like a stalking cat. 'You did not have my permission to be here or to show my work.'

She waved a dismissive hand. 'Oh, but it is my portrait. I used my key to enter.'

'I gave you the key for my convenience, not yours.' His eyes shot daggers at her.

Tranville bustled over. 'See here, Jack. You ought to be flogged for painting this portrait of Ariana. I'll not have it. I'll have none of it.'

'Why, what is wrong with it?' He walked around to the other side of the easel and gave Tranville a defiant glare. 'It is my best work.'

Nancy walked over, darting a quick glance to Ariana. 'Let me see.'

Her eyes widened.

Ariana's misery grew. All she'd strived for was falling into tatters at her feet. She was desperate to mend things. She walked over to the canvas against the wall and turned it around. 'This is the portrait Jack wanted. I insisted on the other one.'

Her pose was the same, but no pink skin showed beneath the gown. Gone was the seduction in her expression, replaced by a blank face.

'That is more like it.' Tranville nodded in approval.

Ariana wanted to protest. This portrait was leached of all life and emotion. All love.

Tranville looked relieved. 'Well, well, I am very pleased with this one. Very pleased, indeed.' He levelled a stern look at Jack. 'But you must answer to taking liberties in creating the other portrait. You led this young lady into a scandalous position.'

Jack pointed to the portrait on the easel. 'This is the better painting.'

Ariana felt a pang inside as he defended his work.

Tranville raised his chin. 'You allowed Miss Blane to pose for you like this.'

Jack's jaw flexed. 'She did not.' He pointed to the other portrait. 'She posed like that. The other is my contrivance.'

Ariana felt tears sting her eyes. She was trying to protect Jack, and Jack was trying to protect her.

Tranville glanced towards Ariana. 'Why did you tell me it was your idea?'

'It is the portrait I want to show the world,' she said.

'Nonsense,' Tranville barked. 'It will be destroyed. See to it, Jack. The one against the wall goes to the engraver. When will it be ready?'

'A few days,' Jack replied.

'Send word and I'll have it picked up,' Tranville made a signal with his fingers, the sort gentlemen make when ordering servants about.

Jack looked him in the eye. 'You owe me for two paintings. Pay my money or you will get nothing.'

Tranville made a wheezing laugh. 'You will be paid, but I want a new copy made.' He started to walk to the door, but stopped halfway and barked at Nancy, 'Did you accept Ullman's invitation to the theatre?'

'Yes,' she replied.

'And your mother and brother will also attend?'

'Yes. He invited all of us.' She looked puzzled.

Tranville smiled. 'Excellent! Miss Blane and I will be sharing the box. She does not perform tonight.' He gave her a significant look. 'Come, my dear.'

His voice alone made her skin crawl.

She cast a glance at Jack, who returned one of anger and injury. She could not blame him. If she stayed to explain to him why she'd brought Tranville here, she would make matters even worse. Her only choice to preserve the illusion that Jack was merely an artist doing her bidding was to leave with Tranville. She believed Tranville's threat and intended to do everything in her power to keep Jack and his family safe from his wrath. If she only knew what to do.

Before she walked out of the door with Tranville she sent Jack one more look, pleading for understanding and begging his forgiveness. He simply turned away.

On the street, Tranville said, 'My coachman was told to circle round. He should be here soon.'

She started off. 'I will walk.'

He seized her arm. 'We have more to discuss.'

Once in the carriage, he reached into his coat pocket and took out the velvet box containing the bracelet. 'I expect you to wear this tonight.'

She pushed it away. 'I've not accepted your invitation to the theatre or your proposal of marriage, sir.'

He handed it back to her. 'Take it. You will go tonight or I will carry out the ruin of your friends. I have no doubt that will influence your decision.' If this were a play she would have said he paused for dramatic effect. 'And you will accept my proposal of marriage.'

Dear God. What was she to do? She accepted the bracelet. 'I will take it as long as it does not obligate me.'

He laughed, a diabolical sound. 'It is not the bracelet that obligates you.'

Jack sat with his head in his hands. He'd considered the portrait a private matter between him and Ariana, not to be shared with anyone, least of all Tranville. Showing Tranville the painting had been like inviting him into their bedchamber.

Jack burned inside. She had betrayed him in the deepest way, using his art to achieve her ends. She wanted the scandal that painting would create. She wanted people to talk about her and to come to the theatre to see her. Had she really thought that Tranville would go along with her plan?

All Jack had wanted was for the people he loved to be happy. He shook his head. That was not true. He wanted to paint and he wanted people to admire his paintings as Ariana had done that first day he'd met her. She was not the only one with ambition. His ambition had led to the portrait as well as hers.

He heard Nancy walk back to the easel. 'Jack, you never even hinted about this painting. Why did you keep it such a secret?'

He rose and joined her. 'Is it not obvious?'

She took a step back and regarded the painting again. 'It is obvious she posed for this.'

He nodded. 'I thought it best not to admit that to Tranville. I never meant it as the final portrait.'

'But it is marvellous.' Her voice was awed. She transferred her gaze to the other one. 'This is not as good.'

He rubbed his face. 'Nancy, you ought to be scandalised.'

She returned a world-weary look. 'You forget that we grew up in scandal.'

He'd once hoped he could keep the scandal from touching her, his dear little sister. Now look what hand life had dealt her.

He ached for her. 'Nancy, one more scandal will not kill us. You can still refuse Ullman—'

She turned her head away. 'Speak no more of it. My mind is made up.'

'But—'

She swung back at him, eyes flashing. 'Do not tease me more! I am going to marry Ullman and there is nothing more to say on it.' She turned back to the portrait, as if doing so shut the door on the topic. 'Do you know why I like this one better?'

He shook his head.

'You—' Her voice cracked. 'You poured your love for her in it.'

His heart broke for her. 'Nancy—'

She shook her head, but smiled sadly. 'We are talking of you now, Jack. You cannot deny that you love her, not with this evidence before me.'

He also could not admit it, not without putting even more unhappiness on Nancy's shoulders. 'It is a painting, Nancy.'

She walked over and sat beside him, holding both his hands, and looking into his eyes. 'Do something for me, dear brother. Do not deny that you love Ariana, and if you have pretended not to love her, you must tell her of your true feelings.' She shook his hands. 'You *must*.'

'It is complicated,' he protested.

She laughed, but it was a depressing sound. 'I am beginning to think all love is complicated.'

Chapter Eighteen

Ariana sat unhappily in the theatre box, Tranville triumphantly at her side, his son with him. She despised them both.

'This is a cruelty, sir,' she whispered to him. 'I was given to believe you had a fondness for Mrs Vernon.'

He looked surprised. 'I am fond of her. Exceedingly fond. That is why I included them in this invitation.'

She had difficulty believing her ears. 'Do you not think it painful for her to be forced into my company?'

He continued to look baffled. 'I do not see why it should. Mary understands that I must marry.' He waved a hand. 'Mary is a good sort. She has always understood me.'

She shook her head. 'And you would repay her good nature by cutting off her money and sending her to the poor house?'

His expression lost all affability. 'That would be at your hands, my dear. Yours and Jack's. The two of you decide that matter.'

'I do not understand why we must sit with any of the Vernons,' Edwin complained.

She turned her head away.

The door to the box opened. Nancy was the first to enter, followed by a very handsome woman Ariana guessed at once was her mother.

'Lawd, here they come,' Edwin Tranville muttered.

Lord Ullman entered after the ladies. 'This will be a delightful evening!' he exclaimed. 'A theatre party.'

Nancy brought her mother over to Ariana, just as Ariana glimpsed Jack entering the box and remaining inside the door.

'Mama,' Nancy began. 'May I present to you—'

Tranville took Ariana's arm and pulled her closer to him. 'My dear Ariana, allow *me* to present to *you* Mrs Vernon, who I understand you have not met.' He turned to Jack's mother. 'Mary, this is Ariana Blane, my intended bride.'

Ariana felt her cheeks burn with anger on Jack's mother's behalf. She curtsied. 'Mrs Vernon, it is I who should be presented to you.' She glared at Tranville. 'And Lord Tranville misleads you. I have not accepted his suit.'

'She will accept me, Mary. I have every confidence,' Tranville said smoothly.

Poor Mary Vernon looked ashen. 'It is good to meet you.'

It struck Ariana too late that she had inflicted additional injury on Mrs Vernon. How much worse it must feel to be thrown over for a woman who refused Tranville than for one who'd accepted him.

Tranville took no notice of Mrs Vernon's distress. He gestured to a table at the back of the box. 'Jack, pour us all some champagne. We shall make this evening a celebration.'

Jack glowered at him. Ariana could see that every muscle in his body protested against doing something Tranville requested of him.

Mrs Vernon started to sit in one of the back seats.

'Please sit in front, ma'am,' Ariana said to her. 'You

will have a much better view of the performance, which, I assure you, I do not require.' If Tranville had not had her pulled from her very minor part in the play, Ariana would have been on stage. Besides, the very least she could do for this poor woman was prevent her from having to witness Tranville fawning over his intended bride.

Ullman ushered Nancy to another chair in front. 'You may sit between your mother and me, my dear. Would you like that?'

'Thank you,' Nancy said in a flat voice.

Jack silently handed glasses of champagne all around.

Tranville lifted his in the air. 'I propose a toast to our betrothed couple. May you always have wedded bliss.' He turned to Jack. 'To the beautiful portrait of Ariana.' Next he raised his glass to Ariana. 'To the portrait's subject, as well, and to the future I am certain she will embrace.'

Edwin gave a dry laugh. 'We all need to drink after that toast.' He downed the entire contents of his glass in one gulp.

Ariana took the smallest sip. Never had a drink tasted so sour, although it was fine French champagne. She glanced at Jack, who never put the glass to his lips.

It was a relief when the play began, although Jack sat behind her she was acutely aware of every shift in his posture, every nuance of his breathing. He'd said nothing to any of them, yet he was the only one she wished to speak to. With Tranville at her side there was little chance of that.

Nancy sat stiff and unmoving in her seat. She reminded Ariana of a porcelain doll with blank eyes and an expressionless face. She imagined Ullman having to move her arms and legs to change her position. It was a heartbreaking contrast to the girl who laughed with her Michael. That Nancy had been the young beauty Jack had painted in the portrait at the Royal Exhibition, the portrait that first gave Ariana the excuse to speak to Jack.

It seemed so long ago. She fingered the diamond-and-emerald bracelet Tranville insisted she wear. It felt as cold and lifeless as poor Nancy.

Watching Mrs Vernon was also painful. If Nancy were a doll made of porcelain, her mother was one made of rags. It seemed remarkable that the poor woman could remain upright.

To make matters worse, Ariana's mother, playing the lead part, had seen her in the box with Tranville and had given her a look that was both approving and somehow vexed. Undoubtedly Ariana's mother would have something to say to her when next they met.

On the pretext of adjusting her shawl, Ariana glanced back at Jack and found him staring, not at the stage, but at her. If she could say only one word to him she would feel more at ease, but her best means of protecting all of them was to treat Jack as if he did not matter in the least.

Somehow they all endured the first half of the play, ironically a comedy. When intermission came, Ullman took Nancy out to display to his acquaintances. Edwin drank the contents of one whole bottle of champagne. Jack sat next to his mother, and Tranville forced them all to listen to him pontificate on the theatre, a subject on which he fancied himself an expert.

During this soliloquy of Tranville's Jack took his mother's hand and held it. The tenderness of the gesture made Ariana want to weep.

There was a knock on the door and servants delivered a plate of cheese and fruit and pretty pastries. Ullman and Nancy returned and Tranville urged them all to eat.

Ullman pulled Tranville aside. 'I have heard news of unrest—'

Ariana took the opportunity to approach Nancy.

'Use this to make yourself happy,' she whispered.

Ariana unclasped the bracelet and put it in Nancy's palm. 'Do not make a foolish mistake, Nancy, I beg you.'

Nancy glanced down at her palm and up again at Ariana. At least there was some expression in her face, even though it was shock. Nancy hurriedly stuffed the bracelet into her reticule.

Ariana took a plate of food for herself as if that had been why she had risen from her chair. She'd given Nancy the means to be with her Michael. Two years, Henry had said the bracelet could support someone. That should be all the time they'd need.

Jack was suddenly behind her. She sensed him even before she turned to him.

'Pardon me,' he said in a stiff voice.

'Jack.' She could not disguise the yearning in her voice.

He avoided her gaze. 'I am here on my mother's behalf. I would not have her or my sister endure this alone. Please step aside so I might serve my mother.'

She glanced over to see Tranville still involved with a gesticulating Ullman.

'Jack, please forgive me—'

His expression hardened even more and she stepped aside.

Tranville was suddenly making his way towards her. 'Get me a plate, would you, my dear? Ullman has invited us to his townhouse after the performance for a nice supper, but I am famished now.'

She felt like shouting in frustration. She wanted to talk to Jack, to explain. Tranville prevented it and also contrived to extend the night's agony even longer. How much more did he intend for them to endure?

On the way to Ullman's townhouse, Jack glanced out of the window of the carriage, immediately sensing something different in the air, an odd energy in the streets. The hairs rose on the back of his neck and the sounds of Badajoz echoed in his ears.

'We must be watchful this night,' Ullman remarked. 'I heard rumours of gangs angry about the Corn Bill. Tranville assured me it will come to nothing, but I am not so certain.'

Tranville's carriage had pulled out ahead of them with Ariana inside.

They crossed Princes Street, moving toward Piccadilly. Jack kept a vigil at the window, watching men gathering in groups here and there. He sat up straighter. 'There's trouble afoot.'

Ullman's hands flew to his chest. 'Good God!'

The carriage continued into Mayfair where throngs of men grew thicker.

Inside Jack's head the screams and gunfire of Badajoz mixed with the rumblings of these men on the street.

'Are we safe, Jack?' Nancy asked nervously.

He turned around to her. 'I will keep you safe.'

The coachman suddenly stopped the carriage. Jack opened the slot to speak to him. 'What is it?'

'They are attacking the carriage up ahead,' the coachman cried. 'I dare not go on.'

Jack opened the carriage door and leaned out. Several men swarmed around Tranville's carriage.

He ripped off his top coat and hat. 'You take them home now,' he ordered to Ullman.

Jack jumped down.

'Jack, come back!' his mother cried.

Jack called to the coachman, 'Drive to Adam Street and do not stop for anything.'

'Yes, sir!' The coachman signalled the horses to move and turned the carriage on to a side street that would lead them back to Piccadilly, away from the marauders.

Jack ran toward Tranville's carriage where about a dozen men had encircled it and were rocking it back and forth. The coachman was attempting to fend them off with his whip and keep control of the horses at the same time.

Jack heard shouts of 'Down with the Corn Bill!' and 'We need bread', but the words suddenly muffled in his ears. As if someone had taken him by the collar and thrust him aside, Jack slammed against a wrought-iron fence in front of a townhouse. He was no longer in Mayfair, but in the fortress town of Badajoz and the men shouting in the street were red-coated soldiers.

'It is not Badajoz,' he said aloud, pressing his hands over his ears.

'Stop!' he heard Ariana cry. 'Leave us!'

At the sound of her voice Jack pushed himself away from the fence and advanced on the attackers, shouting a Celtic war cry that had once sent Frenchmen fleeing.

Some of the attackers ran off, but one of them spun around and swung his club at Jack's head. He ducked and the club struck the carriage with a loud thud. Then he seized the man's wrist, bending it until the weapon fell to the ground. Another man caught him from behind, restraining him so the first man could pummel him with his fists. Jack twisted, trying to get loose. He knocked the man's hat off, but could do little but try to block the man's punches.

'Jack!' Ariana appeared at the window.

'Get back!' he shouted.

She did not heed him. She leaned out of the window and grabbed the man's hair. The man tried to wrench away and almost pulled her out of the carriage completely.

Jack shouted again. 'Tranville! Hold on to her.' He could just glimpse Tranville trying to beat off the attackers on the other side of the carriage.

Ariana still gripped the man's hair when Tranville pulled her back inside. The man lost his balance and let go of Jack.

Jack lunged towards the other man, landing an uppercut to the man's jaw and sending him into a spin. A third man came at him, and the man Ariana had grabbed reached for his club. Jack seized it first.

'Get rid of him, boys!' the man shouted.

The few men left came after Jack.

Jack called to the coachman, 'Go. Now.'

'No!' Ariana cried as the horses began to move.

Jack wielded the club as he'd once used his sword, striking out with such ferocity, his attackers backed away. As soon as they did, he turned and ran for the moving carriage.

'He's getting away.' Jack felt them at his heels, the sounds of their laboured breathing loud in his ears. One man tried to grasp his coat. More hands groped at him, but he jumped towards the open window of the carriage and hung on.

'Off! Off!' A new attack. Tranville struck Jack's arms with his walking stick.

Ariana snatched the stick from Tranville's hands. 'It is Jack, you fool!' She climbed over Tranville and took hold of Jack. 'Do not let go.'

The carriage rocked and swayed as Jack searched for a foothold. He managed to wedge his toes into the gap between the folded step and the body of the carriage.

The carriage did not slow until they reached the gas-lit street of Pall Mall. 'Where should I go?' the coachman asked Jack.

'Henrietta Street,' Jack told him. 'Take Miss Blane home.'

Jack climbed inside the carriage, where Ariana threw

her arms around him. 'I thought they were going to kill you.'

'I am not so easy to kill,' he told her.

Jack tripped over Edwin, who was cowering on the carriage floor, protecting his head with his hands.

'You bloody coward!' Tranville shouted at his son. He hit Edwin with his stick. 'You shame me!'

Tranville took no notice of Jack and Ariana. Jack collapsed in the seat facing her. She sat next to Tranville.

'Sit up, you gutless recreant.' Tranville pulled Edwin up by the scruff of his neck.

Edwin took the seat next to Jack. 'Leave me alone,' he wailed.

Edwin's father, however, directed a string of invectives at him, until he fully realised Jack's presence. He straightened his clothes and merely glared at his son.

'Where are we going?' Tranville asked.

'To take Miss Blane home,' Jack answered.

The carriage clattered more sedately over the cobbles and Jack's breathing slowed to normal. Ariana fished a lace-edged handkerchief out of her reticule and reached over to dab above his eye. 'You are bleeding.'

Tranville seized Ariana's wrist. 'Where is your bracelet?'

It took her a few seconds to answer him. 'I do not know.'

'Those cursed ruffians must have pulled it off you.' Tranville huffed. He turned back to his son. 'See? While you were snivelling and weeping like a girl, those ruffians stole the bracelet. Cost a fortune, I'll have you know.'

Ariana stared at her empty wrist. 'I hope they put it to good use.' She relaxed against the cushions, and Jack thought he saw her smile.

The carriage stopped in front of her building and Jack

jumped out to fold down the steps. He gave Ariana his hand to help her down.

Tranville yelled at Edwin, 'Move out of my way. I must see Miss Blane safely inside.'

Jack closed the carriage door. 'I'll do it.' He turned to the coachman. 'Make haste. I hear more ruffians approach.'

'No!' Edwin cried, 'Let's get out of here!'

The coachman grinned. 'Yes, sir!' He cracked the whip above the horses' heads and they started off before Tranville could protest.

Ariana did not wait for the carriage to be out of sight. She threw her arms around Jack. 'Thank God you are safe.'

He held her tightly against him. 'I've been through worse.' He took her face in his hands. 'But you were foolish to put yourself in such peril.'

She gazed up at him. 'I could not sit by and do nothing.'

He laughed. 'Apparently Edwin had no such qualms.'

He enfolded her against him.

Shouts and the sound of breaking glass still rang out in the distance.

He released her. 'You should not remain on the street.'

She grasped his hand. 'Then you must come inside with me. Don't walk these dark streets alone tonight.'

He'd banished the ghosts of Badajoz. 'I am no longer afraid.'

She pulled at his coat. 'Come in anyway.'

He followed her inside and up the stairs to her room. Once in her bedchamber she tossed away her shawl and lit some candles from a taper.

She helped him off with his coat. 'They have torn it.' She poked her fingers through a seam to show him.

'It is of no consequence.' He cared nothing about his

coat, not when he was consumed with the desire to hold her in his arms.

She took his hand and led him to the bed. Unbuttoning his waistcoat, she said, 'Let me see what they have done to you.'

He felt a pang of pain as he shrugged out of his waistcoat.

She lifted his shirt over his head and gasped. 'Oh, Jack!'

He looked down at his chest and could see multiple marks of angry red. By tomorrow, he knew from experience, they would turn blue and purple. She touched one of them and he winced.

'They seem a bit tender,' he said, though in truth they ached like the devil. 'I do not believe any ribs are broken, however.'

'What can I do for you?' Her voice was filled with helpless concern as she touched one mark after the other.

He grasped her hand and brought it to his lips. Still holding it, he asked, 'Do you have brandy?'

She moved away from the bed. 'An excellent idea.'

It took her less than a minute to retrieve a bottle and two glasses. She climbed on to the bed with them and poured a full glass for him.

The warming liquid felt very welcome, indeed. Jack let his gaze rest on her as they sipped the brandy. When she looked up their gazes caught and held. He drained his glass.

'Jack, I am so very sorry.'

He blinked in surprise. 'For what?'

She wiped a hand across her forehead. 'For all the pain I have caused you and your family. At every turn, I have only made matters worse.'

He put aside his glass and reached for her. She came

willingly into his arms. 'Tranville is to blame. We can even blame him for putting you in danger tonight. He ignored the warnings of unrest.'

She sighed against his chest. 'I despise him. I shall never marry him, but how I shall prevent him from impoverishing all of you and sending you to the West Indies, I do not know.'

'Is that what he held over your head?' His muscles tensed.

She nodded.

Jack had to hold his mother culpable for some of this. He would have dispatched Tranville long before had she not extracted that promise from him.

It was time to break his promise.

He removed the pins from Ariana's hair and combed it loose with his fingers. She sighed with contentment as he did so.

'I will discover a way out of this, Jack. I swear I will,' she murmured. 'I have been waiting for some opportunity. As with your sister—' She clamped her mouth shut.

He moved so he could look into her face. 'What about my sister?'

'Nothing,' she said, but her eyes were wide, as if she was forcing herself to keep them steady.

'Tell me.' He used a firm voice and a firmer expression.

She leaned against him again. 'I found a way to help her, if she chooses it, that is.' She lifted her wrist.

He stared at it. 'You gave her your bracelet.'

She kept her eyes wide. 'Tranville said the ruffians snatched it.'

He laughed and hugged her against him once more. She twisted around and straddled him, burying her fingers into his hair and kissing his lips, his neck, his ears.

A moment before he'd been weary and sore, but now

there was nothing but the erotic feel of her lips against his skin, her eager body demanding to join with his. He swiftly rid them both of the rest of their clothing and soon they were naked in each other's arms once more.

Their lovemaking was a wild feast, as if they'd both been without food for days and days and suddenly were given a banquet.

He needed to touch her all over, to taste her, to cherish the feel of her, the scent of her, the sounds she made as their passions heated higher and higher. All the while his mind flashed with images of her. As the seductress Cleopatra in his painting. The innocent but passionate Juliet on stage. The smiling joyful girl who turned a walk to the Royal Academy into a lark. The courageous fighter who had come to his aid tonight. The beautiful, confident, intelligent young woman who stood next to him gazing at a portrait in the Royal Exhibition and dared to speak to him about it.

He wanted to paint all these images of her, and discover more to paint in the future. He wanted some day to paint her holding his child in her arms.

That was his last coherent thought before sensation overtook him and they devoured the last ounce of pleasure together. Moving in unison, their passion built until it exploded inside them, a sparkling dessert of joyous intensity that suspended itself in time.

He knew they would experience such loving again and again. He'd vanquish their enemies, embrace family and friends, and live a happy life.

With Ariana.

He kissed her, his seal of resolve, although he spoke none of it aloud to her. Only four words did he speak as the candles burned to nubs.

'I love you, Ariana.'

Her eyes filled with tears and she clung to him. 'I love you, too, Jack,' she cried, her voice cracking. 'I will love you for ever.'

He squeezed her tightly against him.

Her breathing slowed to the even cadence of sleep, but for Jack a flood of pain remained, the physical pain left from multiple strikes of clubs and fists.

Jack lay awake, aching all over, making use of his sleepless time by considering how to bring their troubles to an end. All plans he conceived led down the same final path.

He must deal with Tranville, once and for all.

Chapter Nineteen

The next morning Jack struggled to get into his waistcoat, trying not to make sounds that would show Ariana every move was an agony. He was not successful.

She hurried over. 'You are still in pain. Let me help you.' She guided his arms through the armholes and slid the waistcoat on to his shoulders. He started to button it, but she stopped him. 'I will do that.'

'I am not so debilitated I cannot button my waistcoat,' he protested, but he liked having her close and fussing over him.

'I do not mind helping you.' She reached for his neckcloth.

He remained still while she wrapped it around his neck and tied it with a neat Mathematical that almost disguised its having been worn in a fist fight the night before.

She patted his chest when done. 'There. Now give me a moment and I will finish mending your coat.'

He carefully lowered himself into a chair near hers and enjoyed the domestic image of her pushing the needle and thread through the ripped seam of his coat.

Another Ariana he wished to paint, he thought.

When she finished she helped him on with his coat. 'I do wish you would allow me to come with you.'

He put his arms around her and leaned his forehead against hers. 'It is best I see Tranville alone.'

He must fight it out with him.

She frowned. 'I know I have made things worse. It is no wonder you do not wish me there.'

He lifted her chin and looked into her eyes. 'If no one is with me, he will not have to fear losing face. It will be just him and me.'

She sighed. 'Very well.'

'I will come to you afterwards, I promise.' He touched his lips to hers.

She threw her arms around his neck and kissed him back, a kiss that almost made him forget his errand with Tranville and the soreness of his muscles.

When the kiss ended she continued, 'I could at least come to the studio with you and help you change your clothes.'

He shook his head. 'I need to stop by my mother's and assure her I am in one piece. I'll manage.'

He knew she would not wish to inflict her presence on his mother.

Jack supposed any happiness came at some cost. In order to make things right for Ariana, for himself, for Nancy and his mother, he needed to break his promise and have it out with Tranville, once and for all. He must also inform his mother that he was in love with Ariana.

She put her arms around him and held him.

'Time for me to leave,' he murmured.

The descent down the stairs brought new aches, which Jack attempted to ignore. Ariana walked him to the door and gave him a final kiss.

As he opened the door and was about to walk outside, she pulled him back. 'Jack, I have a bad feeling about this.'

He kissed her again and held her close for a moment. 'Say somehow things will work out well.'

She smiled, recognising her words to him. 'Somehow things will work out well.'

He left her, glancing back once to see her watching him from the doorway. He waved and hurried on his way, the exertion of the brisk walk actually easing his stiffness and making the aches more bearable.

Wilson let him in his mother's door. 'Master Jack, you are unhurt.'

Jack smiled at Wilson's reversion to the name he'd called him in childhood. 'You heard of my adventure, I see. I came to reassure Mother, as well. Is she up?'

'In the dining room,' the manservant replied, lines of worry returning to his face.

Jack hurried into the dining room.

At the table with his mother sat Tranville.

Jack was stunned. 'What the devil—?'

His mother rose from her seat to embrace him. 'I was so worried about you.'

'Yes, I knew you would be.' He kissed her on the cheek and whispered in her ear, 'What is he doing here?'

She led Jack to a chair. 'Lionel came here last night.'

Jack stared at him. 'You spent the night here?'

Tranville gave him an incredulous look. 'Of course I did. I could not go back to Mayfair after all that rioting business.'

'What about Edwin?'

Tranville frowned. 'I sent him off with the coachman.'

Jack turned to his mother. 'You allowed him to stay, after all that has transpired?'

Her cheeks turned red, but it was Tranville who responded, 'Your mother is an excellent woman.'

A foolish one, thought Jack, appalled at his mother's behaviour.

'Come, have breakfast,' his mother said.

He shook his head. 'I merely came to assuage any worries you might have had over my welfare.'

His mother glanced toward Tranville. 'Lionel told me you were not seriously hurt.'

'I am glad you were spared distress.' Jack said stiffly. He turned back to Tranville. 'I want to speak with you. Not here. Name the hour and I will call upon you.'

Tranville wiped his mouth with a napkin. 'No need. I will call upon you when I am finished eating.'

Jack nodded his agreement. 'I will expect you soon, then.' His mother did not look at him as he left the room.

Wilson met him in the hall, an anxious look upon his face. 'Tell me what to do. Your sister is missing.'

'Missing?'

'The maid thought she was abed when she came to tend the fire earlier, but, when she peeked in a moment ago, she realised the bed was filled with pillows.' He handed Jack a folded piece of paper. 'She left your mother this note.'

Jack peered at him. 'You read a note addressed to my mother?'

Wilson lowered his head. 'It was not sealed. I thought only to protect your mother. And your sister.'

Jack opened it and read:

Dearest Mama,
I have run away. Do not try to find me and do not worry. I shall be kept very safe. Forgive me, but I cannot marry Lord Ullman. You will not be poor,

though, for you will always have a home with me. I
will write to you very soon.
Your affectionate daughter,
Nancy

Nancy had wasted no time, he thought. He folded the
note again.

Wilson asked, 'Do I show it to your mother—?'

'Show it to her after Lord Tranville has left,' Jack told
him. 'And tell her I will come back and talk to her about
it.' He clapped Wilson on the shoulder. 'Do not worry, this
is good news.'

Wilson looked relieved. 'If I may be so bold, I did not
think Miss Nancy was happy in her betrothal.'

Jack smiled at him. 'I heartily agree.' He pointed to the
note. 'She will be happy now, though.'

Wilson turned to a chair in the hall. 'I have your hat and
top coat.' He helped Jack on with his coat.

Jack walked back to his studio and opened the
curtains to let in the light. He went over to his easel
where Ariana's portrait still remained. He aimed it into
the light and gazed upon it as he waited for Lord
Tranville to arrive.

Ariana paced her room, looking out of the window at
every round to see if Jack was coming back. She very
much disliked not knowing what was happening.

There was a knock on her bedchamber door. The maid
Betsy called through the door, 'Someone is here to see you,
miss.'

Ariana gasped. How could she have missed seeing
him arrive?

She flung open the door and rushed past the maid.

'Thank you, Betsy,' she cried as she ran down the stairs.

The hall was empty so she hurried into the drawing room, ready to fling herself into Jack's arms.

Instead she came to an abrupt halt.

Nancy and Michael, fingers entwined, turned at her entrance.

Nancy immediately rushed over to her. 'I know it is unforgivable for us to call at such an early hour, but we do not have much time before our coach departs.'

Michael came to her side and grasped Ariana's hand. 'I do not know how to thank you—'

Ariana looked at them both in bewilderment. 'But why are you here?'

'To thank you,' Michael began.

'And to convince you not to make the same mistake that I almost made.' She gazed adoringly at Michael. 'I might have given up on happiness if not for your gift.'

Ariana smiled. 'The bracelet?'

It was a good revenge on Tranville to give Nancy the bracelet and a much better gesture than seeing her in the poor house.

'I suggest you not sell it in London, though,' she told them. 'Tranville discovered it missing and thinks the ruffians last night took it from my arm. He will be looking for it to be sold here, I suspect.'

'We shall heed your advice and sell it later,' Michael assured her. He cast a worshipful glance at Nancy. 'I have funds enough to see us to Gretna Green.'

Ariana surmised that was where their coach was headed.

'But you must promise me something,' Nancy said, a pleading look on her face. 'You must promise not to marry Lord Tranville.'

Ariana laughed. 'That I most certainly will promise.'

Nancy continued, 'You must marry Jack.'

Ariana sobered and looked down at the carpet. 'I—I cannot promise that, but I do assure you I love Jack with all my heart.'

'Then you must marry him!' Nancy insisted.

Michael put his arm around Nancy. 'Let it be enough that she will not marry Tranville. She and Jack must work out the rest.'

Nancy blinked up at him. 'You are so wise, Michael.'

Ariana thought them quite endearing. And quite young. 'Whatever happens,' she said, 'do not worry. Just be happy.'

'We will!' cried Nancy. She bit her lip. 'Perhaps you had better not tell Jack where we have gone.'

She hugged the girl. 'Do not fear. He will not stop you. He loves you both.'

Nancy sniffled. 'I should be desolated if my brother was angry at me for this.'

'He will not be,' Ariana assured her.

Michael glanced at the clock on the mantel. 'We had better make haste.'

Ariana hugged them both and wished them well once more, and watched them depart with tears in her eyes.

When Tranville's knock sounded on the door, Jack was seated on a wooden chair, his hands steepled against his lips.

He was ready.

He rose and walked slowly to the door and opened it.

Tranville entered hurriedly, already removing his hat and top coat. 'See here, Jack. I must speak to you—' Jack walked away from him '—about Edwin.'

'Edwin?' He was taken aback.

Tranville gave him a pleading look. 'No one must know of his cowardice. It is a terrible shame upon our family.'

Jack turned away. Could it be Tranville was giving him the means to rid them all of Tranville, once and for all?

'Do you want more money for the portraits?' Tranville sounded desperate. 'I will pay you more money.'

'I do not want money.' Jack was calculating. How far could he go?

Tranville lowered himself into a chair and put his face in his hands. When he looked up it was with a resentful expression. 'You always were the one to show off and make Edwin look cowardly. Even when you were boys.'

'I did not make Edwin a coward.' Jack pointed to Tranville. 'You reared him, not I. But you will not speak to me in this manner ever again. I am finished with your abuse and Edwin's. Do you wish the world to know the extent of Edwin's cowardice? I will be delighted to oblige.'

'No!' Tranville looked aghast. 'I will be a laughing-stock. Me, a *general*. A peer of the realm. To have such a son—' He shook his fist. 'It was his mother's doing! She turned him into a namby-pamby.'

And who was responsible for that poor lady's unhappiness? Jack wondered.

'Very well. I will keep silent.' Jack glared at him. 'In exchange I want you out of my family's lives. I want you to settle a sum on my mother that will pay in interest what you dole out to her quarterly. I want you to resign from your damned theatre committee and make no further effort to see Miss Blane. You will not involve yourself in my life, my mother's life, my sister's nor Miss Blane's. Do you understand me, Tranville?'

Tranville's face turned red. 'You overstep your bounds.' He rose. 'No inferior tells me who I see and what I do. Go ahead and tell the world my son is a snivelling coward. Who would believe you?' He started for the door.

'Wait,' Jack cried.

Tranville stopped.

'I have proof.'

Tranville's expression was scornful. 'Proof of what?'

'Of Edwin's cowardice.' He paused. 'Of more than his cowardice.'

Tranville looked concerned.

'Wait a moment and I will show you.' Jack left him and went to gather a packet from his trunk. He'd broken his promise to his mother and now he would break his word. He returned to Tranville.

'What is this nonsense?' Tranville barked.

'Badajoz,' Jack said.

He opened the packet and lay the pages in a row on the floor. Strung together they told the story of Badajoz.

Tranville stared at them. 'That looks like—'

'Edwin.' Jack continued to lay them down.

Jack had drawn his memory of the incident, from his first glimpse of Edwin trying to rape the woman, to him choking the boy, to Edwin's being slashed in the face by the boy's mother.

Tranville took a step back. 'You made this up.'

Jack kept his gaze level. 'It happened. Edwin was too drunk to know I was there.' He lay down the last pages, showing the two officers who'd also witnessed part of the scene. He'd not drawn their faces or shown their uniforms. 'As you can see, I was not the only one there.'

Tranville kicked at them, scattering them. 'Fabrication.'

Jack picked up one of the papers and showed Tranville the back, correspondence in French with a date a month before the siege.

Tranville threw it aside. 'Edwin's face was cut storming the wall of the fortress.'

Jack spoke quietly. 'You and I both know Edwin hid at the bottom. I saw him, cowering among the dead.'

'You are lying!' Tranville lunged at Jack, knocking him to the floor, scattering the sketches.

Tranville put his hands around Jack's neck and tried to squeeze the life from him. Jack dug his fingers into Tranville's eyes and he let go. Jack sprang to his feet, but Tranville grabbed his ankles and knocked him down again. The two men rolled on the floor, hitting with their fists. They smashed into the canvas and Ariana's portrait fell on top of them. Jack pushed it aside, and got to his feet again, seizing Tranville by his coat and slamming him against the wall.

'Stop this, Tranville,' Jack shouted. 'You cannot win. It is time to give up.'

But Tranville's eyes burned red and he tried to lunge at Jack again. Jack stepped aside and Tranville fell against a table, smashing it to pieces.

He got back on his feet. 'I'll kill you!'

There was some pleasure for Jack in feeling his fist connect with Tranville's jaw, but the fight would solve nothing.

Tranville grabbed a leg of the table and swung it at Jack, who ducked and managed to put his hands around the weapon. The two men strained for control. Jack's muscles trembled with the effort and he won the contest. The chair leg was in his hands.

Tranville backed away.

At that moment someone pounded at the door.

Jack glared at the older man, who was clutching his sides, trying to catch his breath.

'Enough!' Jack threw away the chair leg. 'Let it be over.'

Jack walked to the door and opened it.

An army officer, wearing the red coat and white lace of the Royal Scots, stood there. 'General Lord Tranville?' he said with surprise.

Jack gestured to where Tranville leaned against the wall, wiping blood from the corner of his mouth. 'What do you want?'

The man still looked mystified. 'Sir. I inquired at your townhouse and was sent to the lodging of Mrs Vernon, who sent me here.'

Tranville waved a hand. 'Yes. Yes. For what?'

The officer stood ramrod stiff. 'I have been sent to inform you that your services for your country are again requested. It is my duty to inform you that the Emperor Napoleon has escaped from Elba and is now in France raising an army.'

Tranville managed to stand upright. 'Napoleon escaped?'

The officer clicked his heels. 'Your presence is requested immediately at the Adjutant General's Office.'

Tranville tried to straighten his clothing. 'I will come with you at once.' When he passed Jack, he growled, 'It is not over, Jack.'

He followed the soldier out to the street and into a waiting carriage.

Jack leaned against the door jamb. Only one thing was decided as a result of their altercation.

Jack was about to go back to war.

Chapter Twenty

Quatre Bras—16 June 1815

Jack rode into the protection of the centre of the square. The East Essex regiment quickly assumed the formation as the French lancers began their attack. The regiment had already endured artillery fire, now the terrifying aspect of charging horses and men with tall plumed helmets and long pointed lancers filled their vision.

'Make ready,' Lieutenant Colonel Hamerton shouted as the lancers' horses pounded through the tall rye grass, racing towards them.

The infantrymen's fingers twitched on the muskets' triggers.

'Wait for it,' Jack cautioned.

Napoleon had marched from Paris faster and sooner than anyone predicted. Blücher's forces were still some distance away in a battle of their own. If the French army was victorious here at Quatre Bras, there might be no stopping Napoleon.

The sight of the soldiers in the square, the smell of men

who'd marched since midnight, the pounding of guns and advancing horses' hooves seemed more real to him than his life as an artist. Maybe he'd dreamed Sir Cecil's instruction, the exhibition at Somerset House, Ariana's portrait.

Her lovemaking.

He'd said goodbye to her and refused to encumber her with promises. If *Antony and Cleopatra* was a sensation, who knew where success might lead her? Even Tranville could not stop her then.

'Present!' Hamerton shouted. The lancers were so close Jack could see the hairs of their moustaches.

The men took aim.

'Fire!'

The muskets exploded in the summer air.

'Reload,' Jack called through the smoke, but the men near him didn't need reminding. After reloading, the front line fired and dropped down so that the back line could fire. The men moved in a steady, methodical rhythm, one line firing, the other reloading, while the lancers came at them, shouting, firing, impaling. When the first wave passed, more cavalry came, a never-ending onslaught.

Some of their lances hit their mark and men fell. They were quickly pulled into the centre of the square and others immediately closed ranks. Their firing never ceased. Jack kept moving, encouraging the men, watching for weak points, firing his pistol.

It all seemed so automatic, so familiar.

For one second time froze in Jack's mind and he saw the scene before him as if it were a painting. Blue sky and clouds like cotton wool, tall rye, still green and waving in the wind, verdant, thick woods in the distance. The violence, death and destruction marring its beauty.

A man screamed and blood gushed from his eye. He staggered backwards to join the growing number of dead and wounded. One brazen French lancer took advantage and broke through the square, riding straight for Jack. Jack raised his pistol and fired. The Frenchmen fell and his dazed horse galloped away. They threw his body outside the square.

The cavalry still came, slowed only by the piles of their own dead, until the East Essex were strained to fatigue. The square, becoming smaller and smaller as the numbers of killed and injured grew, could not hold for ever. Despair showed on the tired soldiers' faces.

Hamerton shouted, 'Look, men! The Scots!'

The Royal Scots regiment appeared, quickly forming a square and joining the fight. Jack glimpsed Tranville among them and all his rage at the man came rushing back.

After Tranville had left Jack that day of their altercation he'd sent a missive informing Jack that he had not abandoned his plan to ruin him, his family and Ariana. Their destruction would merely be delayed until he and Jack returned from Belgium.

If they returned.

A pistol shot zinged past Jack's ear, and he raised his hand as if he could ward off another one. He'd be damned if he would allow death to catch up to him now. His family depended upon him to come through.

And he wanted to at least glimpse Ariana one more time.

Ariana feared she had entered a nightmare.

Four days earlier Ariana, Jack's mother, her maid and her manservant, Wilson, boarded a packet at Ramsgate and travelled, first by sea, now by land, bound for Brussels.

Ariana had come in order to see Jack, to spend with him whatever time they might have before the battle.

She was too late. The battle with Napoleon had begun.

The sound of cannon fire had reached them early that afternoon and it boomed louder and louder the closer they came to Brussels.

Ariana had begged to accompany Jack to Belgium, so she could see to his needs or tend his wounds or whatever women do who follow the drum. If the unthinkable happened, she wanted to hold him in her arms one last time.

Jack had refused her.

He insisted she stay to perform in *Antony and Cleopatra*, to become the sensation on stage she had once so desired. Her success was her best protection against Tranville, he'd said. Worse, he refused to bind her to him. When he had said goodbye, he'd freed her.

But Ariana did not wish to be free. In her mind she was already bound to him.

Ariana performed the play and used the second Cleopatra portrait, the near-naked one, to advertise her role in it. The painting was displayed in the foyer of the theatre and its engravings appeared on handbills, in print shops and in magazines. The scandal it created filled the theatre seats.

It was soon forgotten. Napoleon's return drove all else from everyone's minds.

As soon as *Antony and Cleopatra* closed, Ariana turned down all future roles and instead made plans to travel to Brussels. Half of London was travelling there, why not she? At least in Brussels she'd have a chance to spend more time with Jack again, even if only an hour, a day, a week.

Or so she had thought.

Jack's mother had insisted upon coming with her, and Ariana had been unable to refuse her after causing the woman so much misery. The two ladies sat opposite each other now in the crowded carriage bound for Brussels. Above the din of the creaking springs and clopping hooves could be heard the sounds of cannon fire.

The battle had begun and Jack was very likely in it. He'd be enduring the sort of horror Ariana had seen in the battle paintings against his bedchamber wall.

Boom. Boom. Boom.

Mrs Vernon flinched and covered her mouth with her hand.

Major Wylie, an aide-de-camp of Wellington's who was travelling in the carriage with them, patted her arm. 'Do not fear, ma'am. The guns are at least ten to twenty miles distant.'

Ariana glanced out of the carriage window. All day long they had seen throngs of people travelling in the opposite direction, away from Brussels. Now the crowd of travellers was even thicker.

'Major, if there is nothing to fear, why are all these people leaving Brussels?' she asked.

'I questioned some of them at the last posting inn.' He smiled reassuringly. 'They are merely being cautious. There are many who have remained in the city. Why, the Duchess of Richmond was said to have given a ball last night. Wellington attended it. He does not sound worried, does he?'

Ariana was not convinced.

The quaint hamlets and farmland receded and soon they entered the city streets of Brussels.

'No turning back now,' she murmured.

The carriage made its way up a long, winding hill, past large ornamented houses, shops sporting signs written in

French, and a majestic cathedral. The summit of the hill was the finest area of the city, where the Parc of Brussels was surrounded by the Palace of the Prince of Orange and extraordinary public buildings.

Major Wylie offered to help them procure rooms at the Hôtel de Flandres adjacent to the Parc. When the coachman stopped at the hotel's entrance and Major Wylie jumped down, more cannon fire sounded. His faced creased in worry, but he escorted them into the hotel and easily arranged rooms for them. The hotel had been full, the clerk explained, but many of their guests had left that morning. Several good rooms were available.

Wylie left them as he was to report to the Place Royale, and Wilson accompanied him, hoping to bring the ladies back some reliable news. Ariana felt too restless to sit and wait for his return.

'Come, Mrs Vernon,' she said. 'Let us take a walk, explore the Parc.'

Mrs Vernon nodded.

The Parc was even more beautiful than Ariana had expected, so huge the squares of London paled in comparison. Its wide expanse of grass was criss-crossed with gravel walkways and dotted with shade trees, fountains and statues. Magnificent ornate buildings surrounded it like a decorative frame. Few people were strolling there, although Ariana could easily picture how it might have looked filled with soldiers and their ladies, walking and lounging in the warm summer weather.

As she and Jack might have done.

'They said that the battle would not happen for weeks,' Mrs Vernon said, more to herself than to Ariana.

Mrs Vernon had proved to be a sad and silent travelling companion, only speaking to Ariana when absolutely necessary. She could not blame the older woman for not wishing to be companionable. Ariana had caused Mrs Vernon's sadness, after all.

'Indeed,' she responded, more to herself than to Jack's mother.

A sudden burst of cannon fire startled them, and Mrs Vernon lost her footing. Ariana steadied her.

She drew away. 'How clumsy of me.'

'You are fatigued.' Ariana withdrew her hands. 'Shall we turn back? See if our rooms are ready? You can rest a little. We can dine and retire early.'

'As you wish,' the older woman said.

Ariana gave an inward sigh.

They retraced their steps, and Ariana distracted herself by trying to see the sight as Jack might have seen it, as he might have painted it.

It was too painful.

She attended instead to the style of architecture. 'Michael would like to see all these buildings, would he not?' she commented to Mrs Vernon.

'I suppose,' the woman answered.

Michael and Nancy had rushed back from Gretna Green when the news of Napoleon's escape reached them. Husband and wife now, they were presently staying in Mrs Vernon's rooms on Adam Street.

'It is lovely here.' Ariana glanced towards Mrs Vernon.

She had tears in her eyes.

Ariana touched her hand. 'Do not be distressed. Jack will come through this.'

'Jack—' Mrs Vernon's voice was almost as soft as the breeze. 'We cannot know what will happen.'

Ariana put an arm around her. 'We shall pray for him.'

The cannons fired again and Ariana whipped her head around as if expecting to see French soldiers charging down the scenic paths.

Instead Wilson approached.

They hurried to meet him. 'What news, Wilson?' Mrs Vernon asked. 'What did you discover?'

'There is a battle not too far distant.' The manservant took a moment to catch his breath. 'Fifteen or twenty miles from here at a place called Quatre Bras.'

'Is Jack in it?' Ariana asked.

Wilson swallowed. 'We must assume he is. His regiment, the East Essex, is in it.'

'And Lord Tranville?' Mrs Vernon's voice rose.

'Lord Tranville!' Ariana could not believe her ears.

Wilson looked at Mrs Vernon with great sympathy. 'He should be in the battle as well. He is assisting General Pack with the 9th Brigade.'

The older woman turned ashen. 'I would like to return to the hotel.' She walked briskly away.

Ariana turned to Wilson. 'I cannot believe this.'

Mrs Vernon had made this journey because of Tranville.

Wilson looked grim. 'The East Essex is in the 9th Brigade, miss. They may encounter each other.'

Adriana nodded.

An encounter with Tranville could not be good for Jack.

Early the next morning Ariana discovered the city was in a panic. Belgian soldiers galloping through had proclaimed the French were on their heels, but other reports declared that was not true. Ariana walked toward the Place Royale in search of someone who could give her reliable information. She ran into Major Wylie, who told her that the previous day's battle had been a draw, at best. The English forces had held their own, but Wellington was readying for another even bigger battle.

While people continued to flee the city in any sort of

vehicle they could find, other wagons rolled in full of wounded men, their eyes fatigued with pain, their uniforms stained with blood. Ariana grieved at the sight of them.

'Are they from yesterday's battle?' she asked a man who also watched the grim parade.

'From Quatre Bras,' he said.

Wagon after wagon passed, with more and more soldiers. Ariana was riveted to the sight, fearing the next wagon might carry Jack. Finally one of the wagons was full of soldiers whose uniforms looked like Jack's.

She ran along side. 'Are you from the East Essex?'

'We are,' one man answered wearily.

'Do you know Lieutenant Vernon? Do you know how he fared?' she asked.

'Last I saw he was in one piece,' the man told her.

In one piece. Her heart leapt with joy.

'Do you know about General Lord Tranville?'

They did not know.

She asked every wagon after that one if they were from the 9th Brigade, if they knew anything about Tranville.

She must have asked twelve wagons before a soldier answered. 'I am Royal Scots. We were with the 9th Brigade.'

'Do you know the fate of General Tranville?' she asked.

The man laughed derisively. 'Oh, he is as he ever was.'

She did not know what that meant. 'He is unhurt, then?'

'Unhurt, miss,' the man said. 'And a damned shame it is.'

Ariana hurried back to the hotel to give Mrs Vernon the news. Mrs Vernon, her maid and Wilson were waiting for her in a sitting room.

She approached Mrs Vernon's chair and lowered herself to look directly in the lady's eyes. 'I've learned that Jack and Lord Tranville are unhurt.'

Mrs Vernon closed her eyes. 'Thank God.'

Wilson touched her shoulder. 'I have secured space for us in a carriage, but we must leave now.'

'You three must go.' Ariana stood. 'I am staying.'

'Staying? Why?' Mrs Vernon leaned forwards in her chair.

Ariana gave her a resolute look. 'There is to be another battle. If Jack is hurt in it, he will probably be brought here.' Her throat tightened with emotion. 'And I will be here to take care of him.'

'Then I will stay, too.' Mrs Vernon leaned back.

Wilson bowed to her. 'I must remain with you, ma'am.'

The maid's eyes darted from one to the other. 'Well, I am not going off alone.'

The hotel soon filled with wounded men and they all assisted in their care, waiting for the next battle and what news it would bring.

That evening it rained as if the heavens had opened up. Tranville glanced around the peasant's hut and sniffed in disgust. His billet for the night was no more than one room with a straw mattress for a bed and a table and chairs of rustic wood worn smooth by generations of use. He glanced heavenwards. It was dry, at least, and its fireplace was well stocked with wood.

He had plenty of orders for the officers, most of whom had done well the previous day, he had to admit.

He fixed the men with a glare. 'I'll have no laggardly behaviour, do you hear? You tell your men they are to hop to or they'll answer to me.'

'Yes, sir!' chirped a young lieutenant.

Captain Deane merely assumed a bland expression. Tranville detested that. Never could tell what the man was thinking. Captain Landon merely nodded.

'Landon, I want you to find Picton tonight. See if he has any message for me.'

Landon glanced over to the small window, its wooden shutters clattering from the wind and rain. 'Yes, sir.'

'And stay available to me tomorrow. I may need you during the battle.'

'Yes, sir.'

Landon was a good sort. Knew his duty. Got messages through posthaste. The result of good breeding, no doubt. Landon came from a good family, not a middle-class upstart like Deane, who'd risen to Captain through the ranks. That was a high enough rank in Tranville's mind and he'd seen to it that Deane rose no further. Pity Landon chose to befriend Deane.

It would have been better if Landon had made friends with Edwin. Landon and Edwin deserved their promotions to Captain. Tranville had only wished he could have advanced Edwin even higher in rank, but it had not been all up to him.

He glanced over at his son, who was sitting on a stool near the door sipping some brandy from a flask he'd packed with him. Yes, indeed, Landon would be a good influence on Edwin.

There was a knock on the door, and Tranville signalled for Edwin to open it. With a desultory expression, Edwin complied.

'Oh, Good God,' Edwin drawled, stepping aside.

Jack Vernon stood in the doorway, half a head taller than Tranville's own son.

'Mind your boots, Vernon,' Tranville said. 'This dirt floor is bad enough without you tracking in mud.

Jack kicked the cakes of mud off his boots on the doorjamb.

'Hurry up,' Tranville ordered. 'You are letting in the rain.'

Jack removed his shako and shook off its moisture before he finally stepped through the doorway, his top coat dripping on the floor. Tranville might have rung a peal over Jack's head for it, but he'd been distracted by Captain Deane, who poked Landon and inclined his head towards Jack. What the devil was that was about?

Jack exchanged a glance with the two men before turning back to Tranville, but not quite looking him in the face. He stood at attention. 'A message from Lieutenant Colonel Hamerton, sir.'

Tranville snatched the message from Jack's outstretched hand. Favouring Jack with the nastiest glare he could muster, he took his time opening the folded paper and reading it. He folded it back again. 'You will wait for my reply.'

If the others wondered why he did not order Jack at ease, let them. Jack well knew why. This was a good opportunity to remind Jack that there was unfinished business between them. The ruin of Jack, his family, and his...*actress*.

No one would believe those fool pictures of Jack's. He'd invented them. Edwin might be a coward, but no Tranville would assault a woman and child, even if they were Spanish papists.

Besides, Edwin had proved he was not a coward. At Quatres Bras he'd remained just where he was supposed to remain. At his father's side. It was not quite being in the throes of combat, as Jack had been, but they were inside a square, somewhat exposed to artillery fire and musket balls.

Tranville stretched his arm and wrote as slowly as he could, making a show of pausing between each word, as if he were considering what to write. When he finished he folded the note and gestured for Jack to come closer. 'A word with you, Vernon.'

Jack was forced to lean down to him. Tranville expelled a breath on purpose, directly on his ear. 'You had better hope some Frenchman runs you through, Jack. Otherwise, when we return to England, you and your family will wish you were dead.'

Jack straightened, a muscle flexing in his jaw.

'Leave now.' He pretended to re-read Hamerton's letter.

'With your permission, I'll leave now as well,' Landon said.

'Go.' He waved him away.

Jack executed an about-face and walked out of the door, Landon right behind him.

'Do you have further need of me?' asked Deane.

'Of course not,' snapped Tranville. 'All of you go.'

Deane and the others filed out, the last man not quite latching the door. Edwin was forced to get off his stool to close it.

Tranville pointed a finger at him. 'You had better do yourself credit in battle tomorrow. Show some gumption for a change.'

Edwin's face turned pale and he took a long draught from his flask.

Once outside of Tranville's billet, Landon and Deane pulled Jack aside. 'Do you have time for some tea?'

Jack nodded gratefully. The rain, still falling in sheets, had soaked him through and left a chill.

They led him to a small storage building, which was their shelter for the night. At its entrance they'd made a small fire from bits of wood. A kettle rested in its coals. As they stepped inside, Jack saw another officer wrapped in a blanket and snoring in a corner.

Over tin mugs of tea, Jack told the two men how and why he'd broken his word to them.

'You are safe,' Jack assured them. 'I did not show enough to identify you, not even your uniforms.'

Deane rubbed his face. 'I hope some Frenchman puts a ball through his head.'

'Watch your tongue, Gabe,' Landon cautioned.

Jack rose. 'I had better deliver my message.'

He shook their hands and hoped they both made it through the following day.

Before he walked out he turned to Deane. 'Did you find safety for the woman and her son?'

'I did,' Deane answered. 'In fact, I saw her in Brussels. She lives here.'

Landon sat up straight. 'You did not tell me that.'

Deane shrugged.

'And the boy?' Jack asked.

Deane looked from one to the other. 'In the army.'

Jack shook his head. The boy could be no more than sixteen, too young for battle. Some of the Belgian forces had cut and run from Quatre Bras. Perhaps the boy had been with them and would be safe from combat tomorrow.

Would that they all could be safe.

The next day it was almost noon before the cannonade began again, louder and closer.

Ariana and Mrs Vernon continued to help to tend the wounded men, bringing water and clean bandages, trying to comfort them as best they could. A few of the soldiers had come from Jack's regiment and she'd asked each of them if they knew how he fared. Last they'd seen he was still standing.

All the while, the distant sounds of battle continued. Ariana thought of Jack with each boom of artillery fire. She went out as often as she could, in search of news of the battle.

More wounded men rolled into the city, some reporting that all was lost, others saying, 'Boney is licked.' No one really knew which it was.

It was late that night when word finally reached them that the French were in retreat. The Allies had won the battle, but at great cost. It was said the battlefield was littered with the dead and dying. Ariana prayed Jack was not among them. Surely she would know if he were wounded. She would feel it in her own heart.

By morning the wounded were still arriving in droves. Hospitals, homes and hotels were full and the wounded poured out into the street.

Mrs Vernon insisted upon going to the Place Royale personally to find word of Lord Tranville. Because he was a general, she was convinced someone would know if he was alive, wounded or dead. Ariana only hoped they also would have word of Jack.

The officials at the Place Royale were too busy to spare them even a word. As they were ushered out, a young officer approached the building.

Edwin Tranville.

'It is Edwin!' Mrs Vernon ran up to him.

'Good God,' he said, his voice dripping with disdain. 'It is you.'

She ignored his rudeness. 'Your father. Do you know of him? Is…is he—?'

Edwin rubbed the scar on his face. 'He was struck down!' he wailed. 'Struck down in the battle. In the hedges near the sunken lane. Our men saw him fall. I—I could not be in the battle, you must understand. My horse went lame. I was forced to stay behind.' He dropped his hands and gazed heavenwards. 'If only I had been there.'

Mrs Vernon turned white. 'Edwin. Do not say he was killed. Do not say it.'

He lifted a shoulder in a casual gesture. 'He did not come back from the battlefield. That means he is dead or will be shortly.'

She rushed at him, clutching the front of his coat. 'He might still be alive and you left him there?'

He pried her fingers away. 'Madam. The battlefield after the battle is a very dangerous place. Looters do not care who they kill.'

She seized his coat again. 'You tell me exactly where the men saw him fall. Exactly where.'

He gave her the direction, although his description meant little to Ariana. Mrs Vernon released him, and Edwin brushed himself off and started to walk away.

Ariana stopped him, fear of his answer nearly keeping her from speaking. 'What of Jack?'

He snorted in disgust. 'Last I saw he was standing, but one can always hope.'

She struck him across the face.

He raised his arm and she expected him to hit her back but a general hurried by and he gave it up, leaving her only with a scathing look.

Mrs Vernon came to Ariana's side. 'I am going to go and find Lionel, Ariana.' Her chin was set in resolve.

'You will do no such thing!' Ariana exclaimed. 'It is ten miles away.'

'I do not care.' She started for the hotel. 'I will never forgive myself if I do not try.' After the rigours of travel and exhaustive work helping care for the wounded, Mrs Vernon already looked ready to drop.

'You cannot do this,' Ariana cried.

'I must. I cannot bear to think he will die in some field.' Her whole body trembled.

Ariana held her by the shoulders and took a deep breath.

'I will go. I will find him.' And as she searched for Tranville, she would look for Jack and hope not to find him among the dead.

Chapter Twenty-One

Jack shifted the burden on his shoulder and told himself to take one more step, then another, and another. The sun was hot and he was thirsty, but he dared not stop. Furrows from wagons that had travelled the road after the rains made walking even more difficult.

His burden groaned.

'Stay still, Tranville.' Jack almost lost his footing.

'Ought to walk.' Tranville's voice cracked with pain.

'Faster this way,' Jack managed.

Tranville couldn't walk. His leg was broken and the wound in his side would start bleeding again if he tried to hobble on one foot. There was nothing for it but for Jack to carry him.

During the fierce fighting of the first infantry attack, Jack had glimpsed Tranville fall. After the battle, he heard that Tranville had been left on the field. No one could verify he'd been killed, and because it was getting dark, no one was inclined to go and search for him.

The end of Tranville and his threats. Jack ought to have felt…something. Triumph? Relief? He did not know.

All he could feel was hunger and thirst. Jack ate and drank and his mind cleared.

What he felt was grief—on his mother's behalf. Tranville's death would break her heart.

No matter how Jack felt about the man, his mother had loved him for more than twenty years. How could Jack look her in the eye if he did not at least try to find him?

Covering his mouth and nose with a cloth, Jack had returned to the battlefield and picked his way back through the dead to where he'd seen Tranville struck down. He found him.

Alive.

After a hellish night listening to the wails of the dying and fending off looters who were combing the fields and stripping the dead, Jack carried Tranville out and joined throngs of wounded soldiers walking on the Brussels road.

He shifted Tranville on his shoulder and staggered on, wishing they'd not missed the wagons carrying the most seriously wounded. He tried to keep his mind blank, but the sights, sounds and smells of the battle forced their way back in. He again saw flashes of the artillery canister that had struck down his horse, and the shock on the Imperial Guard's faces when the British squares refused to break. He again saw his men cut down, heard their screams and smelled blood, excrement, gunpowder and sweat.

Jack shook his head. His back ached and he faltered under Tranville's weight. Pausing to balance himself again, he was relieved when Tranville lost consciousness. It made it easier to pretend he carried a sack of potatoes instead of the man he'd detested almost his whole life.

Jack pretended he would see Ariana again if he only kept moving. One step, then another. The ploy worked; his pace picked up. He wished he'd painted a miniature of her. The days of battle had blurred her image in his mind.

After Quatres Bras he tried to draw her, but the rains soaked his paper and her image washed away.

It might take months or a year before he'd be able to leave his regiment, and by then who knew what changes might have occurred in her life.

In the distance, coming in the opposite direction, Jack caught sight of a horse led by a man and woman. His mind immediately became riveted to that horse. He'd give anything for it…

He kept his eyes on the animal as best he could, but it was often out of view in the thick crowd on the road. He wondered if Tranville had enough money in his pockets to buy the horse.

Suddenly it seemed as if the men in front of him parted like the waters of the Red Sea, giving him a clear view of the horse and the woman who led it. He could not see her face, but something about her made it hard for him to breathe. She stopped and seemed to stare at him.

He did not dare believe.

'Jack!' She ran towards him.

His voice came out no more than a whisper. 'Ariana.'

She reached him and gaped at the burden he carried. 'Oh, my,' she cried. 'Oh, my.' She reached for him tentatively. Because he was so laden, she merely touched his face.

Her hands felt too gentle, too real.

The men surrounding them called out in approval, and her companion led the horse over to where they stood. Jack had to blink. His mother's manservant, Wilson, held the horse.

'Master Jack.' The man's voice cracked. 'I'll help you.'

Ariana quickly took hold of the horse's head while Wilson relieved Jack of Tranville, who groaned with the shift in position and roused momentarily while Wilson lay him over the horse's back.

Ariana wrapped her arms around Jack. They stood still, simply holding each other. He inhaled the scent of her hair, savoured her familiar curves, felt as if he were where he most belonged. Holding Ariana. His throat was so tight with emotion he could not speak.

'I told you I would not say goodbye to you,' she rasped.

'I never will.' She clung to him, then suddenly moved out of his embrace, putting her hands on his face, his arms, his chest. 'Are you injured?'

He shook his head, but, truly, he could not remember.

'Come.' She draped his arm around her shoulder to bear some of his weight. 'I will tell you of Brussels.'

She asked nothing of him, instead filled the long walk with details of their journey, descriptions of their time in Brussels. When they finally reached the hotel, she took him straight to her room. Jack collapsed on her bed and fell into a deep, dreamless sleep.

Jack woke to bright sunlight pouring into the room and to the scent of hot tea and porridge.

Ariana stood nearby with folded clothing in her hands. 'You are awake at last.'

He sat up. 'How long did I sleep?'

She smiled. 'About fifteen or sixteen hours. It is Tuesday morning.'

He looked around for his clothes. 'I must report to my regiment.'

She handed them to him. 'Wilson has performed some magic and found you a fresh laundered shirt and stockings. He has cleaned and mended your uniform so it looks almost new, and he polished your boots.'

Jack grasped her hand and pulled her down next to him, placing his lips upon hers. 'I fear this is all a vision. I fear that you, the food, those clothes will disappear—' He stopped himself and shook the thought from his mind. 'How is Tranville?'

'He is much better. Wilson found a surgeon to set his leg. Your mother is taking care of him.' She melted against him and kissed him in return. 'You need not worry about reporting to your regiment,' she murmured. 'Wilson got word to someone that you saved Lord Tranville. You do not have to hurry back.'

He released a deep breath, too grateful for words. 'Wilson has been a busy man.'

She stood. 'Eat your breakfast and get dressed. All the hotel could provide today was porridge.'

Porridge smelled like ambrosia.

She moved a table near to the bed and placed the breakfast tray on top of it. 'I will be right back.'

He looked at her in alarm. 'Do not leave.'

She smiled. 'I will not be long.'

He hated to have her out of his sight, even for a second, but hunger took over and he devoured the porridge and drank all the tea. By the time he was buttoning his coat, she had returned as promised, carrying something else wrapped in brown paper and tied with string.

'This is for you.' She placed it on the table and took away the breakfast dishes.

He untied the string and removed the brown paper.

And gazed in wonder at the contents.

She had brought him a box of charcoal and one of pastels, as well as a stack of fine drawing paper protected between two thick sheets of pasteboard.

He glanced up at her, unable to believe his eyes. 'How? Where?'

Her expression turned so loving it was almost painful for him to look on her. 'A shop in Brussels. I knew you must draw.'

He felt as if he'd been imprisoned in a dark dungeon and someone had given him a key back into the light. He could not speak. He only knew one thing for certain—he would never say goodbye to her again.

She started for the door. 'You need time to draw. I will return later.'

'No! Wait.' He lifted his head. 'Stay for a moment. I first must draw you.'

She returned to him and brushed her fingers through his hair. 'Very well, but there is no hurry, Jack. You will have many chances to draw me.' Again her face wore the loving expression his fingers itched to capture on paper. 'Because I intend to love you for ever.'

'As my wife?' he asked.

'As your wife,' she replied in a breathless voice.

He laughed with joy, catching her in a quick embrace that made them tumble on to the bed. 'No hurry, wife? Then there is something I must do before filling this paper with drawing.'

She laughed along with him. 'You place loving me before drawing?'

He looked deeply into her eyes. 'I place loving you before everything.'

Epilogue

London— June 1817

The walls of the exhibition room at Somerset House were again filled with paintings of every sort covering every inch of wall space, but this year, with Canova's visit and the excitement around Elgin's marbles, sculpture was all the rage.

Jack, virtually alone in the room, gazed up at his painting. It hung in a slightly more advantageous position than his paintings of three years before.

'Progress,' he chuckled to himself.

He'd become successful since returning from the army. His painting of Cleopatra, unbeknownst to him at the time, had made his reputation. He'd come a long way from the artist who had stood in this very room, fighting for his sanity.

He stared at his painting and remembered that day.

'Which painting pleases you so?' a low, musical—and amused—voice asked.

He turned and beheld a breathtakingly lovely woman,

looking precisely as if she had emerged from one of the canvases.

She had: *his* canvas.

He greeted her with a kiss upon her alluring pink lips, a liberty the nearly empty room afforded him.

She smiled. 'Do say it is the portrait of the mother and child.' She pointed to his painting.

'Do you like that one?' he asked.

'I do, indeed.' She stood on tiptoe and repaid his kiss with one of her own. 'It is most lovingly painted.'

'Lovingly painted?' Jack tore his gaze away from her face and back to the painting. 'I agree. Most lovingly painted.'

'Yes,' she murmured.

The painting showed Ariana seated in a garden, smiling down at an infant with curly auburn hair and green eyes. Their daughter, Juliet, the very image of her mother.

Members of the Royal Academy hailed the painting as a modern Madonna. It brimmed with emotion, the members said, perfectly capturing maternal love.

He and his wife remained arm in arm, gazing up at it.

It was a long time before Jack spoke. 'Where are my mother and Nancy?'

'They are all with everyone else looking at the sculptures. Nancy said to bid you adieu, though. She was feeling a little fatigued. That happens, you know, in those first months. Michael took her home.'

Nancy was expecting her second child. Her first had been born over a year ago, a boy who delighted in stacking blocks. You'd have thought the sun rose and set with him the way Nancy and Michael doted on him.

Jack understood perfectly. All little Juliet had to do was break into a smile and his insides melted like candle wax.

'And Mother? Is she fatigued as well?' he asked.

'She very well may be, but you know she will not say a word about leaving if she thinks Tranville wishes to stay.'

Tranville.

Jack had certainly failed to separate them from Tranville. Jack's mother had married him. Tranville proposed after Jack's mother had nursed him through the fevers that came after his injuries. He recovered eventually and his broken leg healed, thanks to her care. During those months Tranville became rather dependent upon her. She, predictably, forgave him everything.

Jack had hired solicitors to make certain she had an excellent marriage settlement and generous pin money, both of which Tranville could not alter under any conditions.

Tranville acted as if the whole episode with Jack's family and Ariana, even his rescue, had never happened. Jack was not quite so forgetful. He tolerated Tranville out of love for his mother. As it had always been.

Jack and Ariana did not see them often. The *ton* apparently had forgiven Jack's mother her fall from grace as soon as she became Lady Tranville and their lives ran in a different social circle.

At least Jack did not have to endure Edwin's company. Edwin was unwelcome at his father's house and there was nowhere else Jack might encounter him. Tranville paid Edwin's allowance, but rarely spoke of him. It seemed Tranville could forget a son as easily as forgetting the havoc he'd created in so many lives.

'You are looking serious,' Ariana told him.

He smiled at her. 'Well, you mentioned Tranville.'

She made an annoyed face. 'Do not let him spoil our enjoyment of your success.' She gazed back at the portrait and sighed. 'Is our daughter really so perfect?'

'She is like her mother.'

She held him tighter. 'More talk like that and I might allow you to paint me as Katharine.'

Ariana was rehearsing for an August production of David Garrick's *Katharine and Petruchio*.

'I would be delighted.' Jack glanced around the exhibition hall and saw they were alone. 'This room will always signify a moment when my life was altered for ever.'

'When your first paintings were selected for the exhibition?' She smiled.

He shook his head. 'When I first saw you.' Jack placed one hand against her cheek and gazed into her eyes. 'There is something I wanted to do then, but could not.'

'What?' Her voice was breathless.

'This.' He took her in his arms and placed a kiss upon her lips more scandalous than the portrait of Cleopatra.

* * * * *

Author Note

My apologies to Miss O'Neill, the actress who really did play Juliet to Edmund Kean's Romeo at Drury Lane Theatre, January 1815, and Katharine in *Katharine and Petruchio*, August 1817. There was no performance of *Antony and Cleopatra* at Drury Lane Theatre in April of 1815, but Kean, who played many Shakespearean roles, might have performed the play. My story is peppered with other real people and places. Mr Arnold, the theatre manager, was hired when Sheridan's newly rebuilt Drury Lane Theatre almost fell into financial ruin. A committee similar to the one to which Lord Tranville is appointed really did exist and included Lord Byron for a brief time. The places my characters visit in London were all real, the Egyptian Hall, Somerset House and its Royal Exhibition, the perfume and colourist shops.

The Royal Scots and East Essex regiments were part of the same brigade and fought together at Quatre Bras and Waterloo. Lieutenant-Colonel Hamerton, Major-General Pack, and Lieutenant-General Sir Thomas Picton really were in the battles of Quatre Bras and Waterloo. The depiction of those battles is as accurate as I could make it.

The glimpse of Brussels in June 1815 is from a memoir, *Waterloo Days; The Narrative of an Englishwoman Resident at Brussels in June 1815,* written by Charlotte A. Eaton, who travelled to Brussels with her brother and sister, arriving on 15 June one day before Ariana, the day of the Duchess of Richmond's ball. Accompanying Miss Eaton was Aide-de-Camp, Major Wylie, although I made him travel with Ariana one day later. It is Miss Eaton's account of Brussels that showed me what Ariana witnessed there.

Miss Eaton visited the Waterloo battlefield after all the dead had been buried. She wrote:

> …but it was impossible to stand on the field where thousands of my gallant countrymen had fought and conquered, and bled and died—and where their heroic valour had won for England her latest, proudest wreath of glory—without mingled feelings of triumph, pity, enthusiasm, and admiration, which language is utterly unable to express.